NIKKI OWEN

THE KILLING FILES

Harlequin MIRA is a registered trademark of Harlequin Enterprises Limited, used under licence.

First Published in Great Britain 2016
By Harlequin Mira, an imprint of HarperCollins*Publishers*
1 London Bridge Street, London, SE1 9GF

© 2016 Nikki Owen

ISBN 978-1-848-45441-5

58-0616

Our policy is to use papers that are natural, renewable and recyclable products and made from wood grown in sustainable forests. The logging and manufacturing processes conform to the legal environmental regulations of the country of origin.

Printed and bound by
CPI Group (UK) Ltd, Croydon, CR0 4YY

To Brian — this one's for you, Mr Blue Sky.

Chapter 1

Undisclosed confinement location—present day

The room is dark, damp. I cannot see properly. I have been caught, that much I know, but I am unsure by whom. The Project? MI5? Someone else? I don't know how I got here. I don't know how I am going to escape.

I lift my head but it feels heavy, a loaded sack filled with potatoes. I inch it back. My breathing is hot, the air a woollen blanket on my face, thick and scratchy, and, as my sight begins to adjust to the dark, slowly, like a curtain being lifted on a stage, I start to see small slivers of solid items. Where am I?

A room. I think that is what this is, but I am unsure. Then what? A cell? Prison confinement again? But I was found innocent. I am free, I tell myself. I am not guilty, have not killed anyone, yet even when I say the words to myself, for some reason, they don't seem right, instead feel out of place, a code reassembled in the middle.

One breath, two. My eyes begin to adjust to the gloom and my sight registers small globules of shapes. The corner of a wall, the shard of a window—snapshots only of a whole picture. There is a seat of some sort, a table perhaps, but beyond that, nothing. The air is too black for me to take an inventory, the atmosphere sticky tar turning all the soft daylight into hot, putrid night as adrenaline starts to spurt out into my blood creating short, sharp alerts. I am not safe here.

It is then I hear it: the rustle of movement.

'Who is there?' My voice clicks with a cotton bud dryness, and I wonder how long it is since I last drank water as my brain rapidly attempts to calculate timings and bearings and any scrap of geolocation memory it can cling on to.

'Who is there?' I repeat, yet there is no answer, only darkness. A worry rises inside me, but I press it back, not wanting to panic, not wanting to melt down here and now.

Focus. Breathing. I can hear someone breathing, there, on the whisper of the air. I inch my eyes left, sensing what exists but almost not wanting to acknowledge it. Have I put them there, whoever it is? Is that what this is—a hit? Did I try to kill them? I didn't murder the priest, but I doubted myself then, in court, at the trial. And then a horrific thought strikes. What if I have been on an operation for the Project and this is the result? A body on the floor beside me, injured by me and waiting to die. A killing I may later have no memory of.

My torso remains as rigid as possible, not daring to move. How did I get here? I think hard, connect my cognitive thoughts, but no matter how much I try, nothing shakes, as if my memory has been erased.

As if who I am doesn't really exist.

The person's breathing is shallow now, gravelled and raspy. I know what bleeding out sounds like—the sharp, slicing quality of oxygen intake—but this is not it. And yet, there is an urgency to the breath, a desperation that I cannot place, but it makes no sense why. I am a doctor so should know the signs, but still I cannot place them. What is wrong with me?

I blink three times and try hard to concentrate, to return my brain to function mode, focusing again on the room for clues. The edges. They are shrouded in black, but the window above affords a slip of light that plops in a puddle to my left.

It is then I see it—an arm—and a gasp slips from my mouth.

I track the limb, milky-white skin on a long, limp wrist, different to my own arms, my muscled, tanned ones, with bitten nails and dirt in the creases. Even in this murky room, I can tell that this arm is clean, scrubbed.

I keep all my attention on the body part and attempt again asking who they are, instinctively counting the time as I wait. The numbers sooth me as seconds rack up in twos, the action slowing, at least for the moment, the anxiety that is building inside, but when I ask again who is there and no one answers, a moan slips from my lips. The urine-coloured light has all but disappeared, yet somehow I start to see something slithering into view. A long, T-shirted torso. An elegant, white neck. A skull.

A face.

A scream pierces the air and I am shocked to realise it is mine. I catch my breath, frantically slap my hands up and down, straining to thrash my body forward from the seat, but still my pulse flies. Because there is a face, a face staring back at me, a face I know. Shaven hair, sharp cheekbones, gapped teeth and pool-blue eyes, eyes that even in this tar-black air, shine. My hearts races, my chest tightens. How can she be here? How have I let this happen? We are all in danger now, all of us.

'Doc.' The voice comes from the head on the floor.

I slam my eyes shut, not wanting to believe what is here, reciting an algorithm in a vain attempt to calm myself.

'Doc, it's okay.' The voice is a cotton sheet flapping in the breeze, a rustle of green grass. 'Doc, I'm okay.'

My eyes open. One millimetre then two, gradually allowing my sight to do the work my brain does not want to understand. My friend is here. My only friend in the world is lying crumpled on the floor beside me.

'Patricia?' I say, testing out the word. 'You are out of Goldmouth prison.'

'Yes, I got out on parole, remember? Two months after you.'

Confusion, worry. They spin round my head fast. 'You are here. Why are you here?'

'Because they have us,' she says, the Irish lilt to her voice still there as I remember, but scratched now, torn. 'The Project have caught up with us. You can't hide from them any more.'

The Project have found me—that's why I have woken up here in this room. They have entrapped us and there is only one way it will end: someone will die.

'We have to get out. Tell me your status—are you injured?'

I listen for her reply, but there is only silence.

'Patricia?' Yet there is no answer, no words back to me as I continue to repeat her name over and over again in the gloom. When I finally stop calling for her, I flop back, flooded with fear, fear of myself, of who I am. Because it's me—I have done this. I have caused this to happen. I slam my head back and back again, crying out, yelling into the thick, black air. Why can't I recall how I got here? Why don't I recognise where I am? Why?

Why?

One solitary, fat tear slides down my cheek. 'Do not die.' The words slip out, silent, unbidden. 'Please, do not die.'

My eyes search for Patricia's body, for an arm or a head, anything that can reassure me she is okay, that my friend is okay.

'I am sorry,' I say. 'I am sorry. I am sorry. I am sorry.'

I stop, haul in oxygen, listen for signs of life, but in the ten long seconds that next pass, the only sound audible in the thick, foul air is the rasp of my own breath.

Salamancan Mountains, Spain,
34 hours and 59 minutes to confinement

The sun is blinding me. I kick off my running shoes, prop my hand on my forehead and, squinting towards the distance, listen to the morning as the mountains wake up. Clicking cicadas, dry summer grass rustling in the breeze, pregnant lemon and orange trees groaning under the weight of fat fruit spritzing citrus into the air, the distant bleat of a mountain goat—all the sounds that are now familiar to me, part of my daily routine. The security camera lights surrounding my hidden villa glow green, six lenses in total covering every angle of the property. The Salamancan earth is slowly rising.

I pick up my coffee cup, drain it then pad inside, counting my steps where the terracotta tiles are cold on my soles.

One, two, three, my feet move forward until twenty-four arrives and I halt at the sink, my eyes watching everything. I set down my cup, pick up a white cloth and dry last night's dishes: one plate, one knife and fork and one small wine glass. Opening a metal cupboard, I slot the crockery away, all of it easily fitting in, the only occupants in the large, spotless space.

I scan the rest of the kitchen, returning everything to its place. One pan, one white jug with a scratch seven millimetres long on the inside of the handle, one metal pot, small, for milk to warm at night when the sun rests and the night blanket covers the sky where the stars switch on and glow until morning. I count them all and document them in my head and, satisfied all is correct and present, I close all the cupboards and, stretching up my arms high into the air, recite the words I have spoken now every day since I came here to hide from the Project and MI5.

'I am Dr Maria Martinez. I am thirty-three years old.' My fingers ripple in the warm air, a gentle wisp of a breeze drifting in through the small open window, its wooden frame cracked yet solid. 'I am innocent of murder. I am free.'

I stretch my hands further into the void, my muscles elongating into the empty space around me as I go through my routine to remind myself who I am, because if I did not tell myself, I fear I would be lost entirely. My hands fan out and my muscles are taut and strong, and, when I twist towards the glass door of the oven, my reflection stares back, green contact lenses patched over brown eyes, black hair dyed platinum and sawn in clumps to my small skull, the flesh on my face and limbs deep and sun-brown, lines thick and grooved and ingrained into my worn skin and elbows and ankles and knees.

'I am Dr Maria Martinez. I am thirty-three years old,' I repeat, inhaling, my back arching downwards and my arms reaching forwards so my palms flatten on the floor, the tiles cold on my skin, tiny sharp jolts reminding me I'm alive. 'I am innocent of murder. I am free.'

The yellow morning rays shine warm on my face. I close my eyes and I breathe it all in, moving, exhaling, saluting the sun, feeling my body work as one with my mind as I repeat my chant over and over, losing my thoughts to the repetitive medicine of it, allowing my brain to soften itself of the millions of cognitive connections automatically made every second of the day and night. I bend my knees now, toughened skin touching down on the terracotta as I crease my spine upwards towards the ceiling, eyes still closed as I battle in my head with the pictures that sway before it, pictures of the loud, excrement-filled prison I was kept in, of the court trial and the beatings and the discovery of the Project entire, the shredded sordid secrecy. I breathe, try to let the thoughts pass by me as my spinal cord folds inwards now, rippling the muscles of my torso up and down, feeling them creak and stretch after the running outside, shorts riding up and itching my skin, vest top stuck to me with sweat, and even though the irritation of it is sharp, I continue focusing, letting my brain be even a little bit at ease with who I am, all the while chanting, reminding, never ever forgetting, because without conscious thought, what would we be?

Ten minutes pass in the early morning sun of my movements across the tiles and in the empty air, and, when I am ready and complete, I stand, exhale and open my eyes. The sun shines into them and I blink as my sight adjusts to the hazy film of the day that yawns out ahead of me, my mind registering with a glow of satisfaction that there are no people to attempt to converse with, no social games for me to decipher how to play. I turn to the sink. I extract one small glass from the cupboard to my left and, filling it with water, drain the contents, and mouth refreshed, rinse out the glass, and return it to its home.

When I am certain all is in its place, I wipe dry my palms on the back of my running shorts and pad towards the lounge, grateful for my daily routine, for each phase of it I have created. Every day since I left prison and came here to hide from the Project and MI5, after my morning run and yoga, I spend three hours tracking and documenting the latest news stories on the US National Security Agency prism scandal and any terrorist crimes or cyber security threats that I think the Project may be involved in.

I am just entering the lounge past the wooden crates on the floor when, today, it happens. I don't know if it's the thought of analysing the latest news on the NSA that has triggered it off or if it is because I slept badly last night, nightmares of prison waking me up in sweat-filled fits, but the memory arrives, fast and bright, not the hazy part of clouds that normally occurs when such recollections float to the surface, but this time quick, a taser prod, switching my mind from what is in front of me to what is inside, to a distant drug-hazed memory.

'No!' The sound of my solitary voice rings loud in the silence, sending the birds in the orange trees outside scattering in random directions.

I grip the kitchen sink. This process, this feeling, it is now familiar, so many times over the years has it passed, but still there is a fear as my brain is thrown into recalling something locked deep within my subconscious.

Something from my past.

Chapter 2

Salamancan Mountains, Spain.
34 hours and 56 minutes to confinement

Suddenly I am not standing in my Salamanca kitchen, but instead am in a white clinical room, a room that now, from my dreams, from my nightmares, I know well.

I am fifteen years old, limbs long and thin, jutting out at awkward Bambi angles. I am sitting robot-straight in a metal bed and my long matted rope of thick black hair is uncut and wild and resting on a white hospital gown where freckles puncture plump sun-kissed skin, cashmere soft, no lines yet of a longer life lived. ECG probes sit glued to my small rib cage and concave abdomen, and in the background the pit-put of a heart rate monitor hums.

I turn my head and see him. The man. I intake a sharp breath, but there is no surprise in it, no immediate concern, as if I have been expecting him, as if this, here, is a routine that offers me some strange, warped comfort.

'Your vital signs are good,' the man says. His voice has a Scottish lilt, each word a slice of a knife, a slow turn of a screw. 'Can you tell me who I am?'

'Dr Carr.' My voice is a feather, a butterfly wing. I shiver.

He smiles and when he does, his lips slice thin and it makes me think of a cut on my arm. 'And you have a special name for me, don't you, Maria—what is it?'

'Black Eyes.'

I can feel my nerves rise and so I scan the room as a distraction. The walls are white and by them stand three stainless steel seats and two cream Formica tables. There are no pictures or soft materials, just brown plastic blinds and two officers guarding the doors with handguns hanging by their sides. I don't like it and so start to jig my leg.

'Maria, look at me. Can you look at me?'

'No.' Jig, jig. 'I want to go home.'

His smile slips and, without warning, his arm whips out and slaps my leg still. 'Stop stimming and look at me.'

A sting like one hundred needle points pricks my skin. My leg drops still. I want to scream at him, jolted by the feel of his touch, but am too scared because I know he could shout and the noise would bother me too much, and so instead I attempt to do as he says so he won't touch me again.

He rolls his fingers into his palm and withdraws his hand to his lap. 'I'm sorry for that,' he says. 'We are on a tight deadline today.'

I strain my eyelids, force my sight to stare straight at him, but it is hard, hurts, almost in an uncomfortable way, as if opening my eyes to his, to anyone's, would allow them to see into me, see into my thoughts. In the end, I only manage to make contact for two seconds then have to look away, exhausted.

He inhales. 'For the next few hours, I want you to practise making eye contact for half a conversation. This will help you slip more seamlessly into a regular situation if you ever go operational. Make you appear more…normal. Yes?' He smiles and I think I see tiny eye creases crinkle out on the corners of his face, but I am unsure. 'Yes, Maria?'

'Yes,' I respond on autopilot.

'Good. Look at me.' I do. 'One second longer, that's it. Two, three, four… Good. You can lower your eyes now.'

I drop my gaze, shattered, as he takes notes in green ink on a yellow page. Behind him, a woman walks over, petite, a tattoo of a cross on her brown neck, hair so closely cropped to her scalp, it appears to shine. The woman stops and whispers in Black Eyes' ear. I cannot hear them so I bend forward a little, yet, when I look down at my thin, gowned body, the probes sticking out, it is merely crumpled, having barely moved at all. Beside me the heart rate monitor beeps faster.

My body shifts on the bed. Black Eyes is nodding now to the woman who has appeared in the room and at first, the words they whisper fade into the squashed air, but after two then three seconds, their sentences filter through as, slowly, my ears switch fully on.

'The programme is showing her skills are improving, Dr Carr,' the woman whispers. 'Her handler at the church is communicating very positive results.'

'Such as?'

'He gave her a complex code to crack and she did it within thirteen seconds.'

'Good. Good. What else?'

She consults her notes. 'The subject's IQ is exceptionally high, photographic memory sharp—she is obsessed with classical composers, tracks all their family details, their names, all their pieces—'

'Has she learnt to play the piano yet?'

'Yes. Self-taught, Trinity College London, Grade Eight standard within three weeks. Further information: the way in which she can sense acute sounds and scents is exceptional—I know you were concerned about that.'

'Hmmm.'

'And her dexterous skills, her technical assimilation—it's getting faster. She can take apart and reassemble a radio clock, for example, within three minutes now, last time it was five. Her handler at the school recorded that.'

There is a nod from Black Eyes as he turns and provides me with a narrow stare. 'We have been operating for twenty years now and this is our breakthrough. She's the only one the conditioning appears to be working on.'

'Yes.'

He looks to her. 'MI5 will want to hear about this.'

The woman hands him a slip of white paper. 'Done. Here are the results we sent over to our contact there.'

Black Eyes scans the data, his fingers pinching the page, each a spindled vine of pale flesh. 'All these people we have conditioned and tested, and none of them are quite like this test child, this Maria Martinez. What is her confirmed subject number?'

'375.'

'Subject 375. Yes.' He taps the paper. 'We have some scenarios I would like to use her for, see what she can do. MI5 are pressing us to assist them with unusual security threats—cyber elements, computers etcetera. Let's see how she can help us.'

His head dips and, without warning, his skeletal fingers creep forward so that they skim my calf. I instantly flinch, but he doesn't appear to notice, instead seems in some kind of trance. 'It's okay,' he says to me. 'It's okay.' Then he turns to the woman. 'She is strong, but not yet old enough to fight, but soon…' He lifts his hand, knuckles and flesh hovering in the air, and the thought occurs to me that he may hit me. 'While she is here, we will ask her what she knows.'

The woman frowns. 'But won't that stay in her memory, the covert details are just that—covert. What if she recites them when she is back in her normal environment?'

He shakes his head. 'We will give her Versed as we always have, administered before she is dispatched home to Spain. It has worked well so far.' He looks to me. 'It will wipe her immediate mind so no secrets are divulged—she will simply believe she has visited the specialist clinic with her mother because of her Asperger's.' He hands the woman the paper. 'The Versed drug means she will be unable to recall fully what she has or has not done, but enough remains in the subconscious for her to be useful until she reaches an age where she can be fully operational. It is important that you learn this.' He folds his arms. 'The subject may recall things, facts, but they will be hazy—like dreams. But we need that. We need this data, this training we give her, to remain stored in her brain somewhere so we can use it when the time is right.'

'Maria?' He is talking straight to me now. A rush of heat prickles my entire body and I don't know what to do. My eyes search for a way out but there are no exits, here, anywhere. 'Maria,' he says, voice unusually soft, low, 'where are we?'

But nerves rack me, and instead of speaking, I press my back into the bed, the cold cotton of the gown skimming my knees, goosebumps popping out.

'I want to go home.'

'You will. But first—that's it, look at me, good—answer me: where are we?'

I look between the woman and Black Eyes. When I open my mouth, my voice trembles. 'I am in a Project facility.'

'And who are the Project?'

'It is a covert group linked to MI5.'

'And what do we do?'

Despite myself, despite my resistance, the words trip from my mouth, as if they are preset, robotic. 'The Project is a covert programme formed in response to a global threat of terrorism and, specifically, cyber terrorism. It trains people with Asperger's to use their unique, high IQ skills to combat security alerts. Only MI5 knows the organisation exists.'

'And the UK government?' he asks. 'What of them—do they know who we are?'

'Negative. They have no knowledge of the Project's existence.'

'Good.' His chest puffs then deflates as his head bobs up and down, a smile snaking in to his face. 'Good.'

The woman nods once to Black Eyes then leaves via a door that has no handles or hinges. Black Eyes waits for her to exit then turns to me, perching himself on the end of the bed. I grip the sheets tight. At first he does not speak, but then, after two seconds, he opens his mouth and a precise, metallic voice strides out.

'You will not remember being here, Maria. You won't recall this conversation, you won't recollect the details of the tests we carry out on you. But know that we are always watching you, are always…here for you. We are everywhere.' He leans to the side and, from a metal trolley, picks up a loaded syringe. My heart rate rockets.

'You are at school now, yes?'

I swallow, confused. 'No. I am not at school now. Now I am here.'

He pauses, one second, two, three, his teeth appearing to clench. 'Your teacher next year,' he says finally, exhaling, 'he will be working for us, helping us to watch you. These people you see nearly every day—they are your handlers. Even your family priest. But of course, you won't—' a strange mewed laugh emits from his mouth—'you won't remember.' He sighs. 'I cannot believe I am telling you this now—you'll only forget. But Father Reznick, your friendly Catholic priest—he's one of us.' My eyes go wide. The priest? But I saw him kissing Mama. 'Oh, the big brown eyes! Maria, I am growing to know you well now. You do remind me of my own daughter...' He drifts off, momentarily looking downwards, the needle resting in his fingers, and I glance to the door and wish I could run. 'Anyway,' he says after a moment, 'do not worry. When you go on to university and work, we will have our people there, too, Project people like me and you, people who will watch over what you do, even though you won't, at the time, know they are with us.' He flicks the needle with a finger. Sweat beads pop out all over my face. 'Oh, there's no need to fret,' he says now, leaning in, studying the sheen on my forehead. 'We are friends, aren't we?'

I recoil. 'I do not have any friends.'

He halts, tilting his skull. 'No. No I don't suppose you do.' He drifts off again for a second, then, checking the needle, he handcuffs my wrist with his fingers and pulls my arm towards him. 'Your mother, Ines—lovely woman, isn't she?'

I say nothing, instead watch his eyes narrow as they inspect the vial for air bubbles. Vomit wells in the base of my throat.

'Shame she is on her own now after your father, Alarico, died. Loneliness is a terrible thing. Car crash, wasn't it?'

Alarico, my papa. Hearing his name makes my head spin a little, my heart ache. The vomit rumbles.

'Still,' Black Eyes says now, his Scottish lilt dancing on the cold air, 'she's a strong woman, your mother, a lawyer like your father, but, well, more forthright. She'll make a good politician when she hits the Spanish parliament after she's got over her little…illness. Your brother, too—Ramon, isn't it? Seems like he's following in their legal footsteps what with his fondness for debate club. Quite the family. And family, Maria, it's important, keeps us together…'

Black Eyes is leaning in to me so close now, I can see the faint shadow of stubble on his chin, feel the hot garlic and tobacco of his breath on my neck. I want to scream. I want to run a million miles away, but no matter how hard I try, I cannot bring myself to move, and even if I did run, where would I go? Where would I ever go?

'You though, Maria—my…our test child,' Black Eyes says now, 'for you we have plans. We would like you to become…a doctor. Try and press that into your subconscious, hmmm? Even though this will make all of today fade away. A plastic surgeon, specifically. We need to test your dexterous skills, hone them so they can one day be of use to us. Study in Madrid at the University Hospital there—that's where one of our handlers resides.' He smiles, a flash of crooked, tombstone teeth. 'Do you understand?'

I nod.

'With words.'

'I understand.'

'Good. Because you are the one our conditioning is working on and we wouldn't want all these trips your mother takes you on to be wasted now, would we?'

'Mama believes she is taking me to an autism clinic,' I say, an unexpected flash of defiance streaking through me. 'She does not know what you really do. You are lying to her.'

He stares at me. He levels his black, bottomless eyes at me and delivers a look so chilling that, even with my emotionally challenged brain, I get a shiver of fright.

'We have a bit of terrorism to fight out there,' he continues now as if I had never spoken. 'Pesky little terrorists trying to break into our computer networks, into our global infra structures. But now—' Black Eyes taps my arm, lowers the needle to my skin '—now, my dear, sweet Maria—now you will forget...'

Chapter 3

Salamancan Mountains, Spain.
34 hours and 53 minutes to confinement

I come to. I tumble into the present day, gasping in a sharp gulp of oxygen, falling against the kitchen table in my Salamancan villa, sweat pouring from my brow and arms and bare, wobbly legs. I go to haul myself up, blinking furiously, desperate for water, but almost instantly another subconscious recollection arrives, dragging me back into a deeper, stronger dream. More lucid and glaring.

This time I see myself sitting at a desk in a Project tech lab. The walls are regulation white, and around the bottom are long strips of brushed steel, all bases for junction boxes that contain red and green bulbs that flash on and off by a control panel to the left. Computers sit in pre-allocated slots, controlled acoustics used to minimise background sounds for the subjects, subjects like me who inhabit the zone. There is spatial sequencing and lights and levels that are all compartmentalised to define their use, everything routine, expected.

My fingers tap a keyboard and I notice they are older now, not fifteen this time, but tanned, longer, the fingers of my stronger twenty-year-old self. I am writing detailed notes from memory into an online file, classified Top Secret, scores of data and times and geolocations going directly from my brain to the computer. There is a photograph on the screen of a woman with caramel skin wearing a hijab draped under pink-rose cheeks. She has a prominent, aquiline nose and her eyes are so brown they look as if they are constructed of pure liquid. Her picture is superimposed on the file and as I type, I record details of her, of this woman who I have known for two years but who has now caused problems for the Project. My informant, my asset in the field, code named by me as Raven, a bird symbolising good omens, yet the keeper of deception, of tragedy.

A beep sounds and I stand, quick, lithe, the colt now a thoroughbred as, turning to the right, I march out of the door and to the main corridor warren of the covert Project facility. Scanning the area, I proceed straight to Room Six, where I enter through the thick metal door, shut it and turn.

Raven lies on the floor. She is splattered in blood and on her head, her black veil lies splayed out, torn down to her neck, exposing cut, charred skin and deep, gaunt eyes. Gone is the rose of her cheeks, replaced now by two worn-out hollows, and when I look at her I know she is the enemy, yet for some reason, a lump forms in the base of my throat and I have to swallow it away.

A Project officer, younger, files over to me. He wears a grey shirt made with soft cotton fabric and beneath the front of the right hand shoulder is the letter H followed by a three-digit number.

'I was called here,' I say. 'What do you require?'

He turns to me but makes no eye contact. 'You need to guard the detainee. I have been asked to go to the control centre. I will be back in three minutes and thirty seconds.'

He turns, exits, and I do not move. My eyes stay ahead, my body now defined, muscles strong, hands skilled and slim from the medical school training.

'M-Maria?'

The woman lifts her head from her slump on the floor. Her gaze is raised to me but I do not look at her. The lump in my throat tightens.

'Detainees are not permitted to talk,' I say, eyes front.

'It is you, isn't it? Maria? You…you cut your hair.' She coughs. Blood speckles the white tiles, and her eyes dart left and right then settle back on me. 'I know you think I am the enemy, but I am not. That's just what they made you believe.' She heaves in oxygen. 'They set me up, Maria—you have to believe me. They'll do it to you, too, if they have to. I'm not a terrorist…' She coughs again, wipes her mouth. 'They'll be back soon, so you must listen. There…there is a file. It's encrypted.' She licks her cracked lips. 'It's on a file within a computer that's not…that's not attached to anything, a standalone device. No server is linked to it, but it contains a file that you created, a hidden file, away from the Project. Do you understand? Do you understand what that means?'

'Detainees are not permitted to talk.' I strain not to look at her. She is the enemy, and yet her words, her injured presence—they bother me.

'It has details, the file,' she continues, 'ones they cannot track. It will give you what you need—confidential data, who the Project has tested on, the files and names of who they've killed. What they're doing is wrong, Maria. They can't treat people like this, they can't act like gods of the world, and yet that's what they do. Give man power and I give you an eternity of pain.' She spits out some blood and I fight the urge to wipe it away because, for some reason, I feel connected to this woman but I don't know why.

'Maria?'

'Detainees are not permitted to…' I trail off, confused, unsure which side she is really on.

'You are struggling, I know,' she says now, low, laboured, 'struggling with who I am…but we were in the field together. Maria, I helped you and you helped me. They'll mess with your memory after they've done with me, like they always do. The file will give you what you need, tell you what you've done—the truth! Find out who you really are, Maria! I know you, I do. We were…we were friends.'

My eyes briefly flicker to her then, snapping back into position, I look away. 'I have no friends.'

The door bolts open and the officer with the H on his shirt returns accompanied by two other, higher ranking officers. They stride to Raven, haul her up, but as they pull her away, she digs in her feet. 'The file,' she whispers. 'Find it!'

They yank her forwards and as they do she shouts, 'They will make you complete it, Maria! Prepare, they told us. Wait. Engage! Eliminate the threat. They will make you kill me! You know this, Maria, I know you do. Fight it,' she says, her feet leaving trails of blood in their wake, 'fight the Project! Help!'

But I do nothing, instead watch her go and as she does, as she is dragged screaming away past the cold, pale doors of the

Project walkways, what bothers me about her so much comes to me, slapping me hard on the face.

'I never knew your name,' I say aloud to the now empty room, the words echoing in a void that can never be filled. 'I never knew your name.'

The image begins to swirl away, soft at first then faster downwards as a noise vibrates in my ears and I realise it's the radio alarm clock clicking on, blasting a newscaster's voice into the kitchen.

I intake a sharp breath and my eyes fly open taking in a woozy, hazy view of my warm, sun-drenched kitchen. I touch my head with a shaking hand then, falling forward, grab a glass, fill it from the tap and drain the water until it is sliding down my chin, fangs of liquid on my shocked skin. I slap the glass down, slam back into the wall, smear my lips with the back of my hand and try to steady my breath. The memory, the subconscious dream still fresh in my mind—these have happened before, but not this strong, not with her so vividly in them. I throw my hand to the side, feel my way forward, the image of the hijab throwing me off centre. What she said about the files—was that true? Did she store a data file at the Project? Did that actually happen? I spin round, brain firing left and right. My notebook. I need my notebook, need to write it all down, record it so I can track it and try to make sense of what is hidden in my head.

The news piece on the radio is talking about the American national security agency, how Edward Snowden has revealed more information and is in hiding now. I try to pay attention. I try to press it all to my mind so I can lose myself and record it all on my wall, but the words are too much, the noise all too loud and I can't think straight, the dream of the woman and her screams still lingering in my mind even in the bright glare of the summer sun. A dull moan slips from my mouth and I slap my hand down on the radio, silencing it as I count the steps that I now stumble into the lounge.

My eyes automatically scan the solitary armchair, the old brown piano with its back against the wall, the towers of books that sky-scrape their way across the room, the thousands of newspaper articles plastered to the wall, covered in scrawled notes of black pen and pin tacks and sketches of blank faces of people I don't remember. I look at it all, my sight hazy, struggling to focus until, finally, I spot my notebook on the cabinet island by the far wall.

I immediately go to it, flip past the pages of algorithms and codes and sketches of Project facility buildings, all vague memories of events and details, and scratch out what I have just seen. Done, I slam the book shut. I stare at the cracked brown leather cover that curls at the corners. My memories, my nightmares are in there, the ones I don't know about, the details and facts I cannot even recall occurring and yet, somehow they are in my head. Somehow, despite the drugs, I recall them. But why?

I think of Raven. What if there is a file? What if I have just recalled something that happened a decade ago despite the drugs Black Eyes gave me? If the file the woman stowed away is at the Project, does that mean it is still there, now, after all these years? I hold out my hands, look at my fingers, long slim trained doctor hands, a plastic surgeon's, helping to reconstruct faces and injuries and a mix of disgust and sadness hits me. The Project made me become a doctor. It was not my choice or conscious will, instead it was a foregone conclusion, a *fait accompli*. But what are we when we are not in control of our own choices and life? What does that eventually do to us? And what do we eventually do as a result?

I stare again at my fingers and skin and cut-to-the-quick nails. I am Dr Maria Martinez. Raven said they would make me kill her.

Did I?

They have made me believe I have killed before, they got me convicted of the murder of a priest because they—MI5— wanted me hidden and out of the way when the NSA prism scandal broke out, just so the Project would not be uncovered. They framed me, despite my innocence, to suit their own ends, but even then I doubted myself, because if who I am and what I do in life has been decided and directed by the Project, if they have drugged me all along, how will I know with any certainty what really happened?

And who it has happened to?

I reopen my notebook. Perhaps if I scan the pages again, if I link my thoughts here to the wall and the research and the faces and facts, I can make some connections between what I know and what I have just seen. I can lose myself in my thoughts and record everything that swims to the surface of my memory, linking it, if I can, to the NSA, to MI5 and the Project, find some comfort purely in the challenge and routine and order of it all, safe in the knowledge that I won't take it any further, that I don't ever want to leave here and the sanctuary it provides, and if they don't find me, I can remain hidden in my villa forever.

I look up at my wall. I study the multiple news articles

and anonymous faces and facts and arrowed figures, and just as I am about to reach forward and readjust a pinned article so that it sits neat and straight and in order next to the others, the emergency cell phone shrills into the calm morning silence.

And everything stops.

Chapter 4

Salamancan Mountains, Spain.
34 hours and 46 minutes to confinement

I pick up the cell, slamming down the button so the shrill will stop hammering into my head. 'Who is this?'

'Maria, it's Balthus.'

'You are speaking on the emergency cell,' I say, fast. 'Is there an urgent situation?'

'What? No.'

'Then why are you calling me?'

'You haven't contacted me for three days and I was worried.'

The ring of the cell still bangs in my head. I shake it. 'Four days.'

'What?'

'I have not called you for four days.' My eyes catch the sunshine dancing a waltz along the curves of the glass panes. I focus on it and, gradually, my head calms down. 'You said three.'

There's a pause. 'Maria, we agreed when we spilt up in

London—you'd stay in touch, contact me every day. I got worried when you didn't call.'

'Why?'

'Because I care for you. Because I promised your father before he died I'd look out for you.'

'Oh. Okay.' The glass panes twinkle in the daylight. 'I had another memory today.'

'What? When?'

'At 0612 hours this morning.'

I pick up my notebook and proceed to tell him what happened. He listens. This is what he does, Balthus Ochoa—I talk and he listens. When he was the governor at Goldmouth prison in London where I was incarcerated; him listening led me to find an encrypted file that uncovered the Project and my subsequent involvement in it. He has always told me how he promised my papa that he would be there for me, tells me he cares for me, and I catch myself feeling what must be gratitude towards him, but I never know how to express it, do not understand how people say what they feel inside.

'That's odd,' Balthus says now, his voice a layer of gravel, a boulder on a mountain.

'What is odd?'

'Well… Okay, so it may be nothing, but there's something bugging me about the standalone computer the woman in your flash mentioned, but I can't figure out why it bothers me. Maria—the memory with the woman, with Raven—do you remember which Project facility that was at?'

'No. I only recall the facility with Black Eyes when I was younger. That was in Scotland. That is the facility Kurt brought me to. Do you not remember this?'

'Jesus, how could I forget? I bloody well suggested you see that therapist after you were acquitted—and he turned out to be working for MI5.'

'He was working for the Project.'

'That's what I said.'

'No. You said MI5. Kurt—although his real name is Daniel, a Hebrew name meaning *God is my judge*—when he was meeting with me he was only working for the Project. By then—'

'By then the NSA prism scandal had been exposed and MI5 wanted to ditch the whole Project because they were scared of a similar blow-up.'

My eyes rest on the wall, on my drawings and newspaper articles and lines of connections and notes.

Balthus sighs. 'I don't know, I just... What they did. I still can't believe the Project framed you for the murder of that priest just to get you in prison and out of the way, so they could then get rid of you.'

'So they could kill me to eradicate any connection to the Project.'

'Yes.' He pauses. 'Yes.'

The window in the lounge is open, and in the breeze the muslin curtain drifts in and out, the white cotton veil of it brushing the tiled floor as it passes quietly through the room.

'Anyway, look, Maria,' Balthus says after a while, clearing his throat, 'the other reason I wanted to call was just to let you know that there's been no sighting or word from the MI5 officer who posed as our prison psychiatrist—Dr Andersson. You were asking about her.'

Dr Andersson. Her face instantly springs into my mind.

Swedish blonde hair, ice-blue eyes, freckled pale skin. A vision
of her making me take apart laptops, timing me to complete
a Rubik's cube—all the tasks she was doing to monitor me
without my knowledge. I shiver. 'She has not approached you
or any of Harry's family?'

'No. No, I don't think so. But Maria, listen—how are you
about Harry now, since his death? It's been six months since
Dr Andersson shot him on the court steps when she was aiming
to kill you. Harry wasn't just your barrister or even simply
your papa's old friend—I know you had a soft spot for him.'
He pauses, three silent seconds passing. 'I just worry about
you. It's a lot for any of us to process, never mind for you.'

I am momentarily stuck for words as a strange tightness
presses against my chest. 'The Kubler-Ross grief model says
I should be at acceptance stage now.'

'And are you at that stage, Maria? Do you accept Harry's
death? He cared for you a lot.' I can hear him swallow. 'We
both did—do.'

I swallow and clench my jaw as conflicting feelings of
anger and sadness wash through me. A tear escapes. I reach
up, smear my cheek dry.

'Dr Andersson killed Harry. MI5 killed Harry.'

'Yes.'

Over on the window ledge, a small bird with golden-brown
feathers lands on the white wood. It dips its head once, then
going very still, it looks up, free, and flies away. For a few
seconds, I watch the now empty, open space where the bird
stood then, inhaling, I look back to the cell phone.

'Did Patricia get parole?'

'Yes,' Balthus replies. There is a rustle of paper on the

line. 'I told her you were okay, in hiding from the Project, let her know what you did—sending the texts to MI5 and the Project on Kurt's phone in London so they both thought you were dead. She understands you're hiding, that you can't contact her.'

'And Dr Andersson has not been trailing her?'

'No. I'm in touch with Patricia—all seems well. You two struck up a good friendship in Goldmouth. I'm glad, I'm…' He stops. 'You need friends, Maria. I hate the thought of you being on your own.'

My eyes catch the room. The solitary chair, the bare, white-washed walls, the cell phone lying on the upturned crate with Balthus's voice trapped inside.

'Look, Maria,' Balthus says after two seconds, 'I don't know why, but something about this Raven memory of yours… Well, I know I mentioned it just before, but it…well, there's something about it that rings a bell, but I don't know what.'

'Is it a recent recollection?'

'I don't know. I…' He trails off. 'It's just, well, something Ines told me when she called me when you were in prison. I don't know if it even means anything, but it was weird.'

'The word 'weird' means a suggestion of something super-natural.'

'What? No, no, I didn't…'

'Weird can also mean connected to fate, to a person's destiny.'

'Okay. Well, anyway, she was specific, Ines, about talking to me, about calling me and telling me what she did.'

'When exactly was this?'

'It was before the retrial.'

'What date?'

'I don't know.'

'Why not?'

'Maria, my memory's not as accurate as yours. But, look, it was strange. We hadn't spoken for years—since Alarico's death, in fact—and then, after her visit to you in Goldmouth, she calls out of the blue talking about… God, what was it…? Something about secrets… Damn it. I can't remember. I just know she was acting odd.' He breathes out. 'It's probably irrelevant anyway.'

'How did you know she was acting odd?'

'What? Oh, I don't know, her tone of voice, perhaps? It was like she was under pressure or something, as if there was someone there, maybe. In danger? I really couldn't say for sure.'

I go quiet, not understanding how a simple tone in a voice can lead to so many unconfirmed conclusions.

I pick up a book, one of many on computer coding and language, a routine, orderly subject, and place it on a tower of other research, and turn to my board. The faces containing different expressions, different photographs of people who I know, sketches of those I vaguely recall from hazy, drug-filled dreams. Ines, my mama, sits there, a photo taken from her Spanish parliament file, her face sculptured and clean, coiffured black hair, gold jewellery, shoulder pads and rouge. Next to her my brother, Ramon, thirty-five now, tanned, lean, a slick of tar-black hair on top of defined cheekbones, the black suit he wears to his legal firm tailored in place. And then my papa, an aged, more lined photograph, yet still I can see very visibly his eye creases, his lined skin, his crisp white linen shirt, and by his side is me, my hair long and dark, and Papa's arm is over my shoulder, holding me, the only person, back then, I would allow to touch me without instantly jumping or yelling. I close my eyes. I can still smell him—the spice cologne, the ink from his quill where he used to write in his study. I open my eyes and look at an image pinned to the right—a fading picture of Balthus, Harry and me taken just after we won the retrial, after I was acquitted. My fingers trace Harry's face. His skin is plump and black, and when he smiles, he too, like my papa, has eye creases that crinkle outwards, his tortoiseshell-rimmed spectacles perched on the tip of his rounded, shiny nose. Next to him is Balthus. Balthazar Ochoa. Name meaning lone wolf. In his picture he is tall, athletic even for his fifty-plus years, his skin washed with the Mediterranean sun, his black hair silver at the tips, his face consumed by two brown pools of eyes. But while Harry and Balthus's bodies are relaxed and smiling, mine, in contrast, is rigid and tight, flinching at close group contact, my olive skin pale from months of incarceration, hair dark and sawn into a jagged cut that grazes my temple and neck, eyes sunken into razor cheeks. I touch my neck. The Salamancan sun has drenched my skin now into a deep golden hue, my dark pixie cut is bleached blonde and my once-brown eyes are replaced by green contacts. A fake look for a fake world.

'Maria? Are you still there? Look—I was thinking. The flashback you had, the one with that woman—I think you need to understand where that facility is and get to it—I can help you. If there is information there, it could mean we could put a stop to it all, to all this madness. Maria, it could end the Project.'

Heat rushes to my head accompanied by a clear, frosted image of Black Eyes and his tombstone smile. My eyes go to my villa, safe and hidden. 'No.'

'What?'

'I said no. I do not want to understand where the facility is.'

'But Maria, why track all the NSA stuff in connection to MI5, the explosion of it all, if not to get at the Project?' He pauses. 'Look, you're not on your own. I know you think you are, but you're not. You have me. You have Patricia. Jesus, you even have your mother and brother. Maybe they can even help? Ines knows a lot of people high up in the Spanish government—she's Minister for Justice now.'

Black Eyes. Raven. My tortured, sweat-drenched nightmares that keep me awake in the middle of the night when there is no one to soothe me. I glance to their scratched sketches on the wall. 'No.'

He sighs. 'Please. Just consider it. Say if you could connect what I can hopefully remember from a conversation with Ines to what you have told me about this woman—Raven? It may help you know where the memory is coming from. If you know the facility, it will lead you to the file.'

I open my mouth to tell him no then hesitate, but I do not understand why.

'This woman,' Balthus says now, pressing on, 'she said the file she loaded up will give you what you need to know, tells you what you've done, that it will help you know who you really are. Why note down all the dreams you recall, Maria, want to know how it's all connected, if you don't want to find out how to put an end to it all?'

I look down, confused. I thought the answer was obvious.

'I have my notebook. I like to record information. That is why I require the details. I just record the data, all of it.' I glance to my coding books, to the structure and the formality of them.

'But this woman said the files could help you. Don't you want to know who she is, find the file? Don't—' there is a pause and when he speaks again, his voice is oddly lower, more quiet '—don't you want to know who you really are?'

I look at Balthus's photo on the board, stare at all the unframed images and notes and encryptions and news articles, and, after a second, they all start to blur into one solid image of colour. I switch, glance to the turrets of books in neat, multiple piles, to the solitary seat, the makeshift wooden crates for tables, to the single toothbrush that lies on the shelf. I walk three steps to the worn piano by the wall, gently press my finger down on a key, the smooth ivory cold beneath my skin. F sharp tolls out.

'I know who I am,' I say after a moment. 'I am Dr Maria Martinez, a plastic surgeon, born in Salamanca, Spain. I want to remain hidden. I do not want to go back to the Project or to their files or to anyone from there. It is too chaotic. I will record what memories appear, but no more. I do not want to endanger my family.' I glance to the image of Harry. 'I do not want to endanger you and Patricia.'

'I understand that, I do. I really do,' he says. 'But they'll find you, Maria. You know that, I know you do. I worry about you there on your own with no one. You need answers. I can help you. I have a contact. I sent you an email about him. He's called Chris. He's a hacker, used to be in Goldmouth. He can—'

An alarm sounds, high, war-siren sharp. My head jerks up.

'Maria? Maria, what's wrong?'

I sprint to the laptop, head dipped at the noise, but my feet are so sweaty, I slip on the tiles, toppling into the crate, knocking the computer clean off the upturned box.

'Maria?'

I shake myself off, wincing at the scream of the siren, dragging the laptop over to me, scanning it fast.

'Maria? Shit. Can you hear me? Maria? What's happening?'

Leaning forward, keeping my fingers strong, steady, I click the icon flashing on the screen.

'Someone is on my property.'

Chapter 5

Undisclosed confinement location—present day

I don't know how much time has passed. I blacked out, only coming to now as somewhere in the room a noise clicks high in the air, one, two, three, four.

My body instinctively bends forward, brain attempts to gauge the level of danger and then I remember: Patricia.

I call her name, yell into the abyss of black. There is a click, another trip of light mixed with darkness and then, finally, a voice, singular, pure.

'Doc? Doc? Are you there?'

She's okay! 'Patricia?'

'Doc!'

'What is your status? Are you injured?'

'No. No, I don't think so, but…my leg—it hurts. Help me, Doc.'

I open my mouth to ask her specific diagnostics, but the air is so black and hot, so suddenly suffocating that it feels as if a palm is being pressed into my nose and mouth, an acrid taste of metal poisoning my lips. I struggle hard against it. I have to know where we are, and yet nothing here seems to make sense, but I do it. My conditioning, my training, despite my horror at it, kicks in and I begin to function on cognitive thought.

'Doc! Doc, where are we?'

Click. The sound, there again on the surface of the room—it makes me halt.

'Doc—what was that?'

Tap, tap, tap. My heart rate rockets. 'Patricia, stay still.'

I listen. It's like the beak of a robin on a window pane.

'Who is there?' I ask to the thick stench of the room. Click, tap. Click, tap. My breathing becomes fast, shallow. 'Who is there?'

But no answer comes back. I slap away the fear and strain my neck, try to catch sight of something, anything, but just as my eyes clear, just as they begin to see through the haze, the click sounds again and something happens inside me.

A heat, a surge of liquid in my veins burns its way through me, scalding one second then freezing the next, and an ice-blade of pain stabs me. I cry out.

'Doc! Doc, what is it?'

My mouth opens to yell, but I am mute, a primal fear taking over, a tsunami of fight or flight, the words, *'You are in danger! You are in danger!'* screaming over and over in my head, and I must be moaning, groaning, because I can hear Patricia shouting at me to stay awake.

My eyelids vibrate, brain attempts to calibrate a connection, find an answer to what is happening to me, but the codes, numbers, solutions that instinctively inhabit my head are all jumbled up, as if I have been shaken like some unwanted toy then discarded on the ground and kicked under a bed to gather dust and wither.

'Patricia,' I gasp, my chest ready to explode. 'Escape. I need you to escape.'

'I don't… My leg aches, Doc, but I think I can…' A grunt, a scrape. 'My hand—it's free.'

'Does that mean…' The searing pain is so hot in my chest now, it burns and I have to force myself to concentrate once more on my eyes. 'Does that mean, if your hand is free you can be mobile?' And then I spot something: a lick of light. There! In the corner…

'Doc, it won't…I don't know. Oh, God. My leg feels numb.'

The single sliver of light disappears and I try to reach out, grab where it was but nothing moves. A hazy, grey film is slowly bleeding over my lenses.

'Something is happening to me…' I swallow. 'Drugged,' I slur. 'I must be drugged.'

'Are we…' Patricia's words waver. 'Does that mean we're at the Project? At their facility?' There is a shake in her voice, a tremble.

And then I hear it: water. A trickle of water, a rush of liquid. I shake as a terrifying thought tears into me: we are drowning. We are not actually in a room or a cell or in a locked-away facility, but we are drowning, almost dead already and this haze, this grey film, this distant cry of Patricia's Irish voice that I can only just detect is the last twisted haemorrhage of my lie of a life. The Project have found me, are to kill me and now this is it, here: death.

'Can you feel any water around you?'

'What? I… Wait.' A scream, a gurgled cry. 'Doc, I'm hurt!'

Panic swells. 'Drag yourself free. Quick!'

'I don't want to die!'

'Stay awake!'

'I…I can't breathe.'

I struggle to cough, try anything—a lick of my lips, a last gulp of oxygen—anything to dismantle the rolling tide as, to my side, Patricia groans.

'Pull your arms up!' I shout. 'See if there is anything you can grip on to.'

'There's nothing! Only a… Oh, Jesus, help! It hurts! Doc, help, please…'

Her voice stops, abrupt, a TV being switched off. 'Patricia?'

Nothing.

'Patricia! Patricia, shout to me that you are…'

I stop breathing.

My hands form two fists, knuckles white, chest bursting, ribs ready to crack, as my mind prepares, because this is it. The final seconds of me, of my life. Dr Maria Martinez.

Gone.

Salamancan Mountains, Spain.
34 hours and 32 minutes to confinement

I shut down the alarm and haul in a breath.

'What's going on, Maria?'

'Wait.' My eyes remain locked on the computer screen, but my vest has become sweaty and it itches my skin. I scratch my stomach, up down, unable to stop as the nerves seep out.

'Maria, for God's sake, what's happening?'

'The red icon is flashing.'

My skin flushes, feels as if it's burning, nerve endings so sensitive to the change in the fabric. It is too much to bear.

I rip off my vest, throw it to the floor. The relief is almost overwhelming.

'Anyone on the cameras?' Balthus says now.

I flip open the surveillance programme then pause. The reality of what could happen slams me in the face and I recount Abel's binomial theorem to focus my mind.

No matter how many times I scan the CCTV film, it comes back blank, eight square, grey, live pictures of the fields and walls around the villa. No trespassers, no intelligence officers, just everything as it was before I stepped inside the house.

'The cameras are displaying no signs of intruders.'

My body leans back as my mind attempts to get a handle on what is happening, already planning ahead on what I may need to do. As I think, a whip of wind lashes at a funnel of cypress trees outside, sending a swarm of starlings scurrying into the sky, and it is so sudden, so fast and loud that I jump, slapping my hand to my chest.

'Maria, is everything all right? Talk to me.'

The starlings rush away, their swarm temporarily blackening the sky.

'Birds,' I say.

'What?

The last remaining starling flies into a candy floss cloud. 'I was frightened by a murmuration of birds.'

'A mumur-what…?'

I stare at the now empty branches outside, wiping the sweat from my face. The air is static. For a moment, I swear a shadow glides over the sand-coloured earth, its hazy contours rippling over the deep green cypress tree giants that guard the perimeter of the villa, but when I blink and rub my eyes it is instead the tall, scorched grass reeds I see, their long, stretched shadows swaying innocently in the morning air, but each movement of the reeds vibrates in my eardrums. I take the heels of my palms, bang them to the sides of my head to try and dislodge the sound.

'Maria?'

One more hit and the reed rush will be gone…

'Maria? Maria, answer me.'

Bang. Done. 'What?'

'Did you install the tripwire system I told you about?'

'Yes.'

'And it's not flagging anything up?'

'Negative.'

'Then what could have triggered the surveillance? Could there have been a system error?'

I consider this but am unconvinced. The CCTV shows no trespass entry, so why the alarm? My mind scans through every tiny detail, yet still concludes that all is as before—the fields are empty for several kilometres, the long gravel drive is free of foreign vehicles and the only car is an old black truck I use on the rare occasions I need to drive into the village in the fading evening sunlight for supplies. So why did the alarm sound? A colony of nerves collects in the depths of my stomach and my thumb taps my forefinger.

'Maria, do you think you are in danger?'

My eyes flicker to the window then return to the red icon that still flashes on the laptop. 'I cannot say with certainty until I run a complete check. But…'

Another shadow creeps across the cypresses again, this time more distinct, more clear.

More human.

A bolt of electricity shoots down my spine. 'Someone is here.'

'What?'

I grab my notebook, hide it behind a stack of books and run to the window, adrenaline immediately spiking as I slam my back against the wall and count to three.

'Maria, have you seen someone?' Balthus calls out, but I ignore him because if I shout now, if I utter one single word, whoever is out there will know my location.

Another shadow passes by. I track it. Breath heavy, heart rate way beyond acceptable, I count my steps as I drop to the ground, crawling to the opposite side of the window then standing again, acutely aware that I am unarmed, and yet instinctively knowing what to do. It scares me, always has. It scares me that if someone came in now, I am trained to not even need a gun to kill them.

Slowly, I inch my head up to the window ledge, one millimetre, two, three, until I reach the edge where the citrus scent from the groves beyond drifts in. If someone is standing by the outside of the wall, then, if I move one centimetre further, they will detect my presence. My cortisol peaks. Taking one bare foot forward, I raise my hands and step to the left, manoeuvring my body so it slips almost invisibly to the side, my brain instructing me, from some hidden training tactics manual, what to do. *Prepare, wait, engage.* For some reason, the phrase flicks into my mind. *Prepare, wait, engage*, and I realise, with revulsion, that I am recalling something the Project must have trained me on.

But, despite my disgust, I do it. I track the area, I pause, listen to every minute sound, to each tweet, rustle, bleat, creak, creating a full itinerary, a complete map of the exact scene before me until I am ready. Ready to engage.

I exhale, long, deep into my diaphragm as the sunlight dances across my eyelids, cheeks, onto my forehead, my neck, onto my bare sweat-drenched shoulders as, gradually, one millimetre after the other, I peer over the edge to the glazed window.

There is a face staring right back at me.

Chapter 6

Salamanca, Spain.
34 hours and 28 minutes to confinement

Dr Andersson stares straight back at me.

I yell out her name, alerting Balthus, still on the cell, as Dr Andersson ducks out of sight, running towards the far entrance where the kitchen yawns wide open, exposed to the fields and beyond.

'Maria,' Balthus whispers, 'where is she?'

Panic. Sheer panic and chaos rise now as I look to the cell phone. I need it, cannot have any noise give away my location. Checking left and right, I count to three then, fast, drop down and crawl on all fours, scurrying forward, snatch the cell then scamper back, slamming my body into a corner, hidden by a tower of books and by the lost, cracked crates that scatter the room.

I catch my breath, try to think.

'Maria? Talk to me.'

I gulp down saliva. 'She is here,' I whisper. 'Dr Andersson.'

'Oh shit. Oh shit. She's with MI5 and MI5 want the Project gone. That can mean only one thing, right?'

'She is here to kill me.' The words hang in the air, a foul

stench jarring against the fresh, fragrant green grass burst from the fields beyond. For a moment, I freeze, not wanting to acknowledge that my peaceful retreat, my quiet hideaway has been shattered.

'MI5 want all connections to the Project to disappear,' Balthus says. 'Kurt—Daniel—he said that to you, right? That's why he wanted you to stay with him. The Project did not want to disappear, they broke away and wanted you with them; MI5 wanted you gone. Maria, you're right. Oh Jesus. She'll kill you—she's a trained officer.'

I scan the kitchen door—nothing. Yet. 'I am trained also.'

'Yes, but she, well, she's not like you. She won't hesitate to do what she's been told.'

I open my mouth to respond to Balthus when I stop. The image of Raven floats to my mind. *They will make you kill me.* I have no recollection of what I actually did to her, no tangible evidence of whether I ever hurt the woman or not—no real idea of who I am, of what I am, in truth, capable of.

I glance to the window. It is open. Another bird sits there now on the wooden ledge, head jerking right and left. I can see its feathers soft and shining even from here, a brown and black sheen shimmering in the morning sun.

'There is no sign of her,' I say, turning to the phone. 'She may have a map of the dwelling.'

'How did they find you?'

'What?'

'MI5,' Balthus whispers. 'How the hell did they find you? You've been off radar.'

I think for a moment, uncomfortable. Have I made a mistake in my encrypted file tracking? In my proxy ISP emails? 'It is possible they may have infiltrated some files if they have the right technical people to carry out the hack.' My eyes glance to the laptop open on the crate. 'I need to hide my notebook.'

'What? Maria, get out of there!'

A clatter of crates rings from outside, followed by a shatter of glass. Every single part of me drops still.

'What was that?' Balthus whispers.

My eyes dart to the side, unable to answer Balthus as I focus, every part of me on fire, desperately pressing back the guttural fear that surges upwards. I need to move now, get to the laptop then leave, but if I go to the right, I'll have to open the door to the bedroom where my bag is stored, yet if I turn to the left and head past the kitchen where Dr Andersson may be, then I have no chance of grabbing the laptop and notebook.

My instinct is to go into meltdown, to curl up into a ball and slam shut my eyes and plead for this all to go away, so hard is it for me to cope. Yet even as my brain shouts at me to run, gradually, like a rainbow appearing on a stormy day, something happens—a change, a simmering, butter-coloured difference: I become calm. A coolness crackles over me as, in my head, an instinctive knowledge takes control, and over and over in my mind one phrase shoots across the shadows of my thoughts: *prepare, wait, engage.*

Up ahead, the kitchen door, before closed, is now swinging open.

My hairs stand on end. 'She's here.'

'What? Get…you…she…' The phone crackles, Balthus's voice dipping in and out of audio.

I grip the cell tight, telling myself that if I do so, maybe, somehow, I won't be on my own.

Every muscle in me becomes rigid, ready, suddenly not caring about the illegal means in which I was trained by the Project, because, right now, I want to know it all, want desperately to remember every tiny detail of what I was taught, because it could save me. My eyes land on the lone toothbrush on the shelf by the wall.

The phone flickers again.

'Maria? Maria, are you okay? Are you there?'

Balthus. The sound of his voice, the familiar curve of it floods me, for some reason, with relief.

'I am here.' I keep my volume low—there are sounds creaking from the kitchen.

Prepare.

I do a rapid assessment. I am wearing my running gear. I am fast, fit, but even when I calculate the time and trajectory at which I can sprint, I know that if Dr Andersson has a gun and surveillance of her own, I will never escape unless I can get to the bedroom.

'Can you get out?' Balthus says.

'The bedroom door opens onto the shed where the truck is parked—it is my only safe route out.'

'Good! Can you get to the door?'

I look to the kitchen, calculate the angles and trajectory. 'I cannot determine if I can be seen.'

'Well, is there another way?'

I think fast when my eyes, scanning the area for Dr Andersson's face, see something, something long, thick, rusty—solid.

An iron bar by the cabinet, one I use for the fire pit outside, now sits discarded, tossed to one side after I got distracted from obsessing over tracking every tiny detail about the NSA scandal.

The kitchen door suddenly sways, a waltz, one, two, three, one, two, three, dancing in and out of the room. Is she here? I look to the iron bar then back to the door, and even though it screeches when it swings, too loud for my ears, for my senses, I slap the aggravation it causes aside because it offers me something, that unbearable noise: it offers me cover.

I drop like a stone. Flat to the floor, I scurry along the tiles so fast, so quick that by the time the second creak sounds, my fingers are handcuffed to the iron bar and, on the third creak, I am hauling it up and crawling back to where the window sits.

The cell phone crinkles and Balthus's voice trickles in. 'Where are you?'

'Home.'

'No, I mean… Oh, it doesn't matter. Have you got the laptop and book?'

'No.'

'But you can get them?'

'Yes.' I glance to where they still sit. Right now, it is all a matter of timing.

Wait…

I rest my back for a moment against the cool wash of the wall and listen. My hands squeeze the iron bar as I assess where the danger source is, scanning my memory, determining what I should do next. For some reason, after two, three seconds pass, I find myself slowly coming to a stand. It surprises me, the move, makes my pulse rocket, but still I do it, slipping the cell phone into the band pocket of my shorts, watching as my feet, ghost-like, become taut, engaged, and before I can stop myself, before I can order my body to halt its course, I am holding the iron bar aloft and preparing to stride straight through the kitchen door.

Eliminate the threat.

'Maria,' Balthus says, 'have you left yet?'

'No.'

'Why?'

'I can eliminate the threat.'

'What? No. Just get the laptop and notebook and run.'

'Negative. The best course of action is to—' I see her. There, in the solitary cabinet, a waterfall of blonde hair reflecting in the glass panes in the wood. My chest tightens as panic shoots up. 'She is here.'

'What? Christ, Maria. Move!'

I go to run, to dart out of the way, but before I do, before my feet flip fast enough, the window behind me shatters, a clap of thunder in the silence. Shards of glass rain down onto my bare neck, shoulders, arms and legs, scissor splinters tearing apart the warm, suede air of the summer sun.

A bag is thrust over my head, plunging me into a sudden frightening, claustrophobic darkness. I thrash about, frantic to get out, and, as I lift my arms to try to rip the bag off my head, the iron bar slips from my grip and clatters to the tiles.

'Maria? Maria?!'

The bag becomes tighter and tighter, and Balthus's voice echoes from the phone, the sound of him reduced to just lost, helpless words drifting alone into the ripped, fractured room.

Chapter 7

I wake up once more to find myself still alive.

Woozy, weary, my eyelids flicker as my sight takes in a panoramic view of the room, of the black, the stench. My muscles ache and throb, and in my head is a searing pain that shoots down my neck to the base of my back and stays there, pulsating, a globe of pins pricking my skin and bones. I curl my fingers into fists. The hallucination, the memory of it all floods back, the water, the feeling of drowning all fresh in my mind as if the shore were still at my feet.

'Patricia?' I croak. 'Can you hear me?'

There is a cough. 'D…Doc?'

'Patricia?' Hearing her voice makes me happy for one solitary, exquisite second and I let out a small whoop. 'What is your status?'

A laugh ripples out, weak, vanilla, but there. 'I love how—' she halts, hacks up something from her throat— 'I love how even in a shithole like this, you're still so formal.' She gags then hauls in a shoal of breath. 'My leg's killing me.'

'Your leg is killing you?' I panic, confused. 'How can your leg kill you?'

'No, no it's not…' She laughs again, but it does not sound like her, as if were altered somehow, down an octave. 'Doc, it's a phrase. Remember those? I taught you about them in prison. My leg's not *actually* killing me—it just means it really hurts.'

'Oh.'

Some time passes, but I don't know how much. I drift in and out of consciousness, the blackness of the room throwing a blanket over everything, rendering each line of vision I try to establish useless. Slowly, though, after a while, an element of lucidity begins to return. It is small, the tide of it, the clarity that trickles back towards the shore, towards the solid certainty of the land in my mind, but nonetheless it is there and, for the first time since I awoke in this room, there is a grip of strength inside me.

'Doc, where are we?'

I let out a breath, one controlled exhalation, then think. Location, logistics. How did we get here? If there are drugs in my system, then how were they administered and why? To transport me? But from where? And if so, does that mean Patricia has been drugged too?

For the next few moments, we remain silent. Patricia, lying on the floor at whichever side she is, sings some type of Irish lullaby, a song about the sea, and for ten seconds, I become calm, listen only to her melody, all whipped vanilla cream and light chocolate soufflé. I know it is wrong. I know that for her to be here means danger, being in this room trapped with me, yet still, as she sings, as her voice dances through the air, gliding through the gloom, I feel a slice of gratitude, of selfish thankfulness that my friend is near to me.

'Hey, Doc,' Patricia says after a while, after the serene song has faded into the dark air, 'do you remember when we first met?'

'Oh. Yes. It was a Tuesday.'

'Was it?'

'Yes.'

'Cool. And do you remember what you said to me?'

The image of the scene flashes in my mind. Patricia, tattoos of the Virgin Mary and a blackbird on her arm, me bending forward to analyse them without saying anything at all to Patricia until she spoke again to me, telling me I was 'getting a little close.'

'The first words I spoke to you were about your name,' I say. '"Patricia. It is the female form of Patrick. Patrick means—"'

'Means nobleman.' She laughs, joining in the end of my sentence. There is a sigh, small, mewed, and I find myself breathing more easy at the sound. 'Your face was all bruised, Doc, do you remember?'

'Yes.' A flash comes to me, an image of a fist to the face. I swallow.

'Doc, I'm so sorry I brought it up. Are you…are you okay?'

'Why do people think I am a freak?'

'Huh?'

'Why do they call me weird?'

She wheezes into the air. 'I don't know, Doc. People are idiots. They don't always see that it's okay just to be who we are. Last time I looked, we were all, by, well, our very human nature, I guess, different to each other. At what point does different turn into weird? Who the hell knows? My answer? It doesn't. We just are who we are, and the quicker the world accepts that, the better a place it will be.'

I sit and think about what my friend's words mean and how, when I am confused, she seems to cut through the bewilderment, and the clouds in my head part a little quicker and the cage that surrounds makes me feel just a little less isolated.

After a few moments Patricia coughs. 'She worked for MI5, right, that Michaela?'

'Yes. She did.'

'Jesus, it's fucked up shit.' She pauses, the blackness of the room pressing down on us. 'I'm glad I met you, Doc, even though we're locked up now in God knows where—I'm glad I met you. Without you, I…I wouldn't have got out on parole so fast—that Harry lawyer of yours helped me, before he… well, you know.' She inhales. 'I still think about my mum, how she was in pain. It was the right thing to do to, you know…to end her life. I'd do the prison sentence all over again if I had to, just so she wouldn't have to suffer.'

'Euthanasia. That is what you did.'

'Yep.' A sniff. 'Yep.'

'I am sorry you are sad,' I say after a moment.

'Thanks, Doc. Thanks.'

We sit, the two of us, in silence and thoughts where the blackness of the room covers us almost totally. My muscles ache. I try to roll my shoulders to move the blood in them, but when I do, each bone creaks and my neck at the back goes rigid.

'Er, Doc, you there?'

'Yes. Of course.'

'I can see something.'

I forget my sore neck and jerk forwards. 'What?'

'On your hand, there—some light.'

I look down. She's right. I can see my hand for the first time, illuminated by a globule of buttered light. Adrenaline shoots through my bloodstream as inch by inch, a rash of light spreads from my hand, to my wrist, shining on the rope tying me down, then it continues up my arm to the well on my inside elbow, until it shows me something that I did not at all register until now.

'Doc, what is it?'

I blink, check once more, but there is no denying it, because I am a doctor—I have seen thousands of them.

'Doc! What?'

I start to shake. 'The drugs are in my cubital vein.'

'The cubital… Wait, what?'

'The cubital vein resides in the ante cubital area.'

'What? Doc, you'll have to explain in words I can understand, because you—'

The light shines bright. My panic hits a high. 'There is a needle in my arm!'

Salamancan Mountains, Spain.
34 hours and 20 minutes to confinement

The bag on my head has blacked everything out and all I can see through the pin-prick gaps of fabric are shards of sunlight and shadows of shapes. I try to get a handle on where Dr Andersson is, but the bag is so scratchy on my face that it is becoming distracting, and the urge to yank it off, claw at my face over and over until the heat subsides, is almost overwhelming, but when I reach up one free hand to pull, it is snapped back.

'Move.'

I gulp in buckets of breath, sucking on the bag as she pushes me forward, my bare feet flopping over the tiles. Then, we stop. For a moment, there is complete quiet. I jerk left and right, disorientated as I try to pinpoint where Dr Andersson is, willing her to utter one more clipped accent of a word, but all I can hear is the sound of my own breath rushing in my ears as if a sea shell were being held to my head. I don't move. My muscles scream out at me, itching in agony where Dr Andersson pinches my wrists and shoulders. And all the while my cell phone sits hidden in the band of my shorts.

There is a click of a phone, but it is not mine.

'It's me,' Dr Andersson says now, her voice a punnet of plums, a rich slate board of cured meats.

Another voice speaks from what must be her cell. 'Is it her?' A male, speaking in pebbled English. Who is he?

'Yes. It's her.' There is a tug on my wrist. 'Stay still!' I wince. 'Her hair's blonde now, she's skinnier, but it's still Martinez.'

'Good. Good. Well, you know what to do. We have to put an end to the Project. And she's it.'

My mind races. *She's it. She's it.* Nerves rise in me, immediate, urgent, but the will to survive, to forge something that will get me out of this situation is stronger than even my urge to curl up in a ball, moan and hide.

'You cannot kill me,' I say, spitting out fluff and fibres.

She slides a plastic tie around my wrists, pulls it tight then walks away, her boots slapping the tiles. 'I'm sorry,' she says, and then there is utter silence as she seems to go into another room. Where? The kitchen? I slam my head left and right to determine where Dr Andersson is, stagger back a little and count in my head, the numbers not only soothing me, but allowing me to analyse the time frame and give me a slice of clarity. I reach thirty, listen. Nothing. Just the starlings on the cypress trees in the fields and the light tidal rush of grass in the wind. My body relaxes a little, shoulders softening—and then I remember: my cell.

'Balthus,' I whisper.

There is a scratch of static and then one word. 'Maria?'

His voice is low, quiet, but hearing it, knowing he is there makes the heat of the bag, the confusing disorientation of it all more easy to bear.

'Maria, are you okay? My God, she's going to kill you, you have to get out. Can you?'

'I do not know.' I blink, try to gauge any shapes from behind the fabric. I sniff the air. 'Chanel No. 5.'

'What?'

'It is Dr Andersson's scent and I can smell it. The scent was strong before, but now is less so. Judging by the distance now of the perfume, it means she is not in the room, yet she still remains on the property.'

'Well get to another room then! Move out of there.'

He is right. It is a risk, but if I can get to the bedroom, I can run.

I begin to raise my arms, slow at first, the plastic ties digging in, then fast, projecting the direction in the dark my body will need to crawl when the scent of perfume suddenly becomes so strong it feels as if my head will explode at the sensory assault.

'Where do you think you're going?'

She's here! I go to grab the bag with my tied hands, desperate to run, but Dr Andersson hauls me back, slams my arms down.

'No!' I yell.

'Just stop fighting. God, Maria.'

I kick out, but Dr Andersson's grip on me is tight and she jerks her elbow into my ribs. My torso folds in like a pack of cards, my eyes watering, lungs burning as I heave the bag so hard into my mouth to claw some oxygen that I begin to suffocate. There is a fierce kick to my shin. It catches me on the bone, ripping a fire up my leg, expelling the fabric momentarily from my mouth allowing air to slip in. I lash out my tied fists, but she knocks my head, pinning me against the wall.

'How long have you been tracking the NSA?'

'Let me go.'

She exhales hard and shakes her head. 'I'm tired,' she says. 'I've come a long way and my family are at home and I'm missing my daughter's third birthday for you, for this, so just do—' she shoves me hard against the wall then loosens her grip '—as I say, Maria. Jesus.'

I hear her stride away, and I catch short sprints of breath, listening, a wild animal caught in a trap. There is a rustling of paper, tearing.

'What are you doing?'

'Finishing what I was supposed to do when you were in Goldmouth.'

The tearing restarts and I realise: she is at my wall where my news articles and images sit, tearing them off from the plaster, tracking the data I have traced. I toss my head left and right, shout out, but another kick hits my shin, harder this time, felling me, knocking me clean to the floor where a punch reaches my stomach, a balled fist sinking into my abdomen. I yell, curl up as a stab of heat shoots through my whole body and amidst it all the cell phone slips further down and all I can think about is not the pain that roars through me but the cell phone, Balthus, and whether Dr Andersson has seen it.

I have to do something quick. Taking in a fractured breath, I roll what I think is to the left then hit something. What? The wall? A crate? I go rigid, adrenaline mixing into a lethal cocktail inside me.

'She has everything here—news articles, the lot.'

She's talking somewhere on her cell again. My eyes blink at lightning rate as I listen out for a clue, for anything. Is Balthus listening, too?

'There is CCTV all over the place,' Dr Andersson continues.

'You'll have to destroy all evidence,' the man replies, voice breaking up, 'erase any trace of her presence. We are at the agreed rendezvous point. Surveillance is pulled back so no ops can be tracked. It's down to you now.'

A rendezvous point—does that mean her team are near? I try to think it through, but my brain is so overloaded by the bag and the adrenaline that it is almost impossible to be coherent, and if I—

There is a crash. The breaking of items, the pulling of drawers, throwing of books to the tiles—she is tearing apart my villa. I try to think fast and what to do and then I remember: my notebook.

Some time passes. I try to count the seconds, track the minutes, but pain from the kicks comes in waves, swelling then rolling back. After a while, crashing over, I hear her stride into what I think again is the kitchen and I take my chance.

'Balthus?'

A second, two then: 'Oh, thank God. What's happening?'

I tell him fast then blink, try to see.

'Maria, have you slipped the ties from your wrists?'

'What? No. I have tried but it is secured with some type of—' A smash. I wait, swallow, '—with some type of hard plastic that I am unfamiliar with.'

'Hang on. Can you feel it, the plastic?'

I touch the tether with my fingertips. 'Yes. Why?'

'How small are the groves on the tether?'

I feel. 'One millimetre depth.'

'I think I know which type it is. If it's just one millimetre, sounds like it's the new restraints we sometimes used at the prison.'

A flicker of hope begins to burn. 'Do you know how I can untie it?'

'Yes…I think so.'

There is another smash from the kitchen. 'Then tell me. Fast.'

After three, perhaps four minutes, Dr Andersson returns. Her boots sound lighter now on the tiles as if she has changed shoes and when she walks, the drift of her perfume is softer, more weak. She marches up to me and halts. The bag, cemented still to my head, scratches at my face but I try hard to ignore it, bite my lip, keep my back steady and wait.

For a moment, there is no movement. She is crouching in front of me, I think—I can just make out the outline of her body in front of me. But more than that, more than simply her presence, is the heat of her, of another person that catches me off guard and, oddly, the thought strikes me that this, now, is the first time in six months that I have encountered, with such geographical closeness, another human being.

'Right,' she says finally, 'let's do this, shall we? The day is getting on and so is time.'

The bag is whipped from my head and my skin, slapped by sunlight, stings as, for the first time, my eyes blinking over and over, I get a complete look at Dr Andersson as she looms now in front of me. Her blonde hair is tied up into a ponytail that slides down her back and rests down her spine all the way to her hip bones. Her forehead is high and sharp and peppered with freckles, and on either side of her straight nose sit two rose crescents for cheeks, each propped up by defined, prominent bone structure. I choke, spitting out the fibres of fabric from my mouth and throat.

'What do you want?'

She offers me a smile, the one I remember from Goldmouth, with white teeth and scarlet, plumped lips. 'I want to do my job and get home. I understand you're on the harsh end of this, I really do, but MI5 wants the Project to end, which means I have to deal with you, end you.' She takes out a gun. 'I'm really very sorry, Maria. I always rather liked you.'

And then, with one bullet, she shoots me in the leg.

Chapter 8

Undisclosed confinement location—present day

'Doc, are you sure there's a needle? Can you see it?'

'Yes. But the light is fading again.'

The blackness has reclaimed the air, but, now I know the needle is there, I will my arm to move as much as it can, wriggling my fingers in an attempt to feel the point of the metal inserted into my veins. At first, nothing shifts and I feel so thirsty, am so desperately weak and tired that my mind begins to think it has imagined the entire thing.

And then it moves, there, the needle, in the crease of my elbow. Just one pull at my skin and veins.

'Can you see it now?' Patricia says.

'No. I can feel it.'

'Doc, you know what this means, right?'

I go to speak the words *they are drugging me again* but instead clam up, an instinct to yell out, to cry as loud and deep as possible welling up inside of me. This was not supposed to happen again. No, no, no, no.

'Doc, are you still there?'

'I ran away from them,' I say after a moment, catching my

short, shallow breath. 'I hid. The Project and MI5 thought I was dead after prison. I thought I had escaped it all.'

'Oh, Doc. Doc, I'm so sorry.'

For a moment, in the blackness, it feels as if everything has stopped, as if, here, now, all I have is collapsing on me, folding inwards never to push out again. It feels hopeless. I sit there, silent, scared, until, on the murky moisture of the air there is a rush of something.

'Doc? Doc, you're groaning. What's the matter?'

I squint as hard as I can, frantically forcing my eyes to see something, anything in the dank, suffocating space as to my direct side, the rush sounds again, distinct now, a click licking the air as what must be a liquid begins its gentle whoosh. It is only when I hear again that my groggy brain engages in the intricacies of the noises around me and I realise with a stabbing clarity what is actually happening and what it means to me—what it means to us both.

'What if they are drugging me, so they can transport me to another facility somewhere? If they do that, what will happen to you?'

'I'll be okay, Doc.'

'What if they are intending to kill you? That is what the Project does—it kills those I love.' My breathing begins to speed up in short, rapid intakes of oxygen as the worry inside me escalates.

'Doc, Doc I can't get to you, so look, it's going to happen either way, so try to breathe through it. There, that's it...'

I try so hard to focus on her voice, slam my arms against the rope on my wrists, desperate to escape, to run, hide, because what is charging forward now like a pack of hungry wolves makes my heart stop, makes every sweat gland on my skin scream out in fear. A hallucination.

'Breathe, Doc. Keep breathing. Keep listening to me…'

A body with multiple heads, each one of them spinning 360 degrees, hurtles towards me. I scream. My nails scratch into the wood of the chair, legs kick out, but it does no good, and I know it must be the drug, be the liquid shooting inside my veins, but there is nothing I can do. I am trapped.

The monster is on me now, here in this room. I yell out my friend's name, hear the distant scream of her voice, but I can't reach her. The heads in the image sway, thorns in the breeze, and I hear a voice screech and realise it's mine, because the heads, the faces on them—they are Mama and Ramon. My mother and brother.

'Patricia, where are you?' I yell.

'I'm here, Doc. It'll be over soon. Keep calm, okay? Keep breathing…'

I try to scramble back, tell myself that none of this is real, but still they come, the heads grotesque, twisted out of shape, all images in a fairground mirror, their mouths and eyes huge, each of them laughing over and over like two sick clowns. '*Freak! She doesn't understand,*' they sing. '*She doesn't understand, the freak.*' The children run beside them, children I recall from my school days, and they skip and they chant, *Weirdo, weirdo, stinky nerdy weirdo*. And I ask them what they mean, scream at them to tell me what is happening, but the heads, all of them, family, children, they simply look at me, at each other, and then, just as I think they're going to disappear, they let out one roar of a laugh and, merging together, morph into a gun as tall as a car and shoot me, point blank, in the head.

My eyes fly open. I choke, claw for air, chest ripping, struggling as I look down at myself, at the black room, shaky, scared at what just happened.

'Patricia, the drugs…'

'Sssh. Sssh.'

I stutter, voice cracked and it takes a full minute for my body to settle, for the nightmare of the image of my mama and brother to slowly subside.

'Doc, I'm here. It's okay. It's over. It's over.'

I hear my friend, cling onto her voice as if I was sinking and she were my life raft in the sea. My brain recalibrates itself, but it is taking time and each movement of my eyes and hands and limbs makes the room sway and soar and whip up a pile of nausea in my stomach.

After a moment, after the heat has subsided, Patricia checks on me then asks me a question.

'Doc, you know these hallucinations, right?'

'Y-yes.'

'Well, why's it only happened now?'

My head throbs, throat runs red raw. Everything in the room still fades into black. 'What do you mean?'

'Well, if this needle, yeah, this drug is permanently in your vein, why's it not causing you to trip all the time?'

I begin to think. What she is saying, what she talks about— my brain finally starts to shrug off the drug effects and engage, calculate.

'Doc, I guess what I mean is,' she says now, 'what's making the drug only come out in doses?'

And in the dark, in the foul mouldy odour, I sit and I think and I try to understand what is happening.

And how to make it all stop.

Salamancan Mountains, Spain.
34 hours and 11 minutes to confinement

A searing heat instantly explodes in my thigh.

The room begins to sway, the white sun from the window blinding me, mixing with the pain to create a lethal cocktail, slow at first then faster, and when I look at Dr Andersson her smile appears distorted, as if someone has taken an axe to her head and sliced it clean down the middle. Nausea balloons as blood begins to spew from the wound.

I force myself to keep my hands were they are, fixed in the position behind my back, despite the instinctive compulsion to throw my arms forward and tend to the wound.

As the pain rips into me, I focus on the cell phone, still hidden behind me, knowing that Balthus has listened to everything that has happened. Sweat drains down my face. Ahead Dr Andersson proceeds to tear apart my laptop, pocketing my USB sticks, disabling every part of my surveillance system, all that I have been unable to hide now being destroyed, and it hurts me, every smash, every rip and pilfer—what she is doing feels as if it is physically hurting me, the way in which she is creating pure chaos out of my routine and order.

If she is destroying evidence, it will soon come to the point where she will find my notebook.

I have to stall for time. 'I need to stem the blood flow from my leg,' I say. 'I need to press my hands into it. Untie me.'

She throws me a glance, hesitating for a moment, her eyes on my wound, and I think she may come to assist me, but then she checks her watch, shakes her head and returns to pulling apart my data.

My body is getting weaker. The blood from the wound is slowing a little, but still oozing and if I don't get pressure on it soon, I may bleed out entirely and lose consciousness. My eyes spot the iron bar—it is still on the floor where it fell.

Dr Andersson comes over and crouches by me. 'Maria? Can you hear me? I need you to tell me something—is the Project still functioning?'

'You are MI5,' I say, winching at a stab of pain, 'you should have the intelligence for that answer.'

She sighs. 'I'm looking for a file.'

My ears prick up. 'What file?'

She glances around at the mess. My teeth clench at the chaotic sight. 'There is a file hidden by a woman, a woman you knew, an asset in the field some time ago when the Project was more…useful. Do you know where the file is?'

Sweat trickles past my eyes. Raven, the dream. Does she know? 'What is the woman's name?'

'Ah, now wouldn't that be easy, if I had a name?' She wipes her cheek dry of sweat. 'I'm afraid that's what I was rather hoping you could provide.' I shift, careful not to dislodge the cell phone. 'Do you know where the file is, Maria?'

'No.'

She stands. 'Then I'm sorry, but…' She administers one swift kick to my injured leg. I cry out in agony.

'B…B…' My speech slurs. I must be losing more blood than I thought.

'Where's the file, Maria? Please, just tell me.' She sticks on a quick smile. 'Let's just get this done as fast as we can, okay? I really don't want to hurt you any more than I have to before, well… Just help me out here.'

My eyes narrow as I muster every inch of energy that is left in me, every shard of anger and fear and pain and loss, straight at her. 'Bitch.'

Her smile and shoulders drop. She reaches into her pocket and withdraws a knife, black handle, solid. My brain fires into red alert mode, desperate to move as she slides off a leather sheath to reveal one small, sharp blade, seven centimetres long, the sleek silver of it shining in the summer sun, a gentle light dancing warm and carefree on the glide of the metal.

'I'm sorry I have to do this, but you were supposed to die months ago.' She kicks a piece of computer casing away. 'You evaded our officers then, even dodged my bullet for you outside the court, but not now. I'm afraid we can't risk the service being exposed. You understand—it's this NSA scandal. MI5 don't want the Project blowing up like NSA's prism programme did. The Project was good while it lasted, but it has to end. The file I need—we'll find it. I hear there's been a run of break-ins and knife crime in this remote area.' She glances to the upturned room. 'I'm afraid this will have to look like a burglary that's ended in a murder.'

I look at my leg, panting in air now. The limb is damaged, but the blood loss is finally halting. I can move my toes, but I don't know if I can mobilise my body at all, but my hands are still behind my back and, for now, I need to keep them there…

I start to count.

One.

Dr Andersson takes a step forward.

Two.

She grips the knife tight in her fist, her eyes downturned.

Three.

I glance to the iron bar near on the floor.

Four.

Dr Andersson lunges forward. 'I'm so sorry…'

Five.

I unleash my hands, tethers gone, Balthus having talked me through how to untie them, and, despite the blood loss, despite the odds stacked against me, and the chaos and the fear and the sheer sensory onslaught of the entire situation, I charge forward at Dr Andersson with every single drop of effort I've got.

Chapter 9

Salamancan Mountains, Spain.
34 hours and 7 minutes to confinement

I ram my body hard straight into Dr Andersson.

She yells out, her torso toppling to the left, the knife slipping from her grip, clattering to the tiles. 'Maria, stop! Please, don't...'

She steadies and I think she is going to recover, her hand reaching to a gun behind her jacket, and so fast, without thinking, I haul my whole body up and head butt her in the face.

She reels back, a sharp crack indicating her nose breaking, blood spurting, the fall dislodging her gun and causing it to slide under a table.

I move quick, drag my body up, the bullet wound in my leg throbbing.

'Maria,' Balthus calls from the cell. 'What's happening?'

I survey the damage fast, the slump of Dr Andersson's slight body, her twisted limbs.

'She is alive,' I say. 'Injured.'

'I don't give a damn about her—just get the hell out of there. Get your notebook and bag and run!'

But my eyes catch sight of my ordered articles and photographs and sketches ripped on the floor pressed under Dr Andersson's mashed up body, blood seeping from her ear. For a moment there is a quiet, macabre eeriness to it all as the summer sun glows through the windows, warm and serene over the utter devastation in my villa. I slap a hand to the wall, steady myself, everything spinning a little as I will my brain not to melt down at the chaos. One, two, three. One, two, three. I play out a waltz of numbers in my head, draw in a long breath then, looking up, acknowledge where my notebook is and, glancing at Dr Andersson's splayed limbs, stagger towards the fallen gun.

Balthus crackles on the line. 'Are you on the move?'

'Yes.'

I step over a broken laptop, and stop. There is a torn photograph of my papa lying discarded amidst the mess. It is the one of him with his arm around me, except the picture now only shows me with Papa's arm on my shoulder, and does not show his face or the rest of him, his body ripped off and in two. The sight of the photograph instantly bothers me.

'Papa.' I scan the floor, frantic. 'Where is the other half?'

'What?'

'The photograph of Papa,' I say to Balthus, twisting left and right, crouching down despite the searing pain in my leg, and clawing through the tattered paper that litters the floor. 'She tore it in two. Papa is missing.'

'Maria, you've no time for this.'

But I keep looking, ignoring Balthus, ignoring the sting in my leg, led on instead by the urge to stay connected to my father in any way I can. I lift up a heap of shredded newspaper then drop it, confetti pieces floating in the sun. 'He taught me not to flinch,' I say to myself. 'Papa.'

'Maria? Maria, I know this is hard for you, but you don't have time for this. If MI5 don't hear from Dr Andersson, they'll come to the villa. And if they know where you live, chances are the Project do too.'

Yet it's as if his words have no meaning. All I can obsess on is Papa's picture.

'Maria!'

I lift up files. I throw torn shreds of NSA articles and images around until the air becomes thick with paper and no matter how hard I try, no matter how much I tell myself to leave, I can't, not without Papa, not without seeing his arm around me, safe, secure, knowing I'm not on my own, because I don't want to be on my own, not really, not like this for the rest of my life. And then, as I turn, there, among the broken pieces of laptop plastic, I see him, Papa, his eyes shining bright as if he were still alive, warm, breathing next to me.

'Maria, have you got it?'

'Yes!'

I grab the picture, thrust it to my chest and standing, happy, so happy I have him close to me, even if it's only like this.

'Good. Okay, Maria. Now you need to run. Run now, yes?'

'Yes. Yes.'

I turn, checking the room, glancing to Dr Andersson's body on the floor, then, grabbing my notebook fast from where it lies half-hidden by a stack of half-toppled books, I go to hobble to my bedroom, to the hidden floor compartment containing my emergency bag. But, as I reach the door, there is an almighty scream that fills the room, piercing my ears.

Dr Andersson flies at me. 'No!'

Her hand grabs me as she smacks me against the wall, the picture of Papa floating from my fingertips, notebook flying to the left. She slams me against the wall again, blood instantly spurting from my wound. Flipping me over, she digs her knee into my chest, pinning me down, but my right arm slips free and, crunching my fingers into a fist, I turn, punch her hard in the nose. There is a loud crack. Her head spins back, hand slaps to her face as blood spurts, a crimson slit sliced into her skin.

I shift faster now, heart racing, counting the entire time to focus, my body rolling away, quicker now, Balthus from the cell shouting at me over and over again to get to the door, to get out, but before I do, there is a scraping on my leg where the bullet wound throbs.

I look down. Dr Andersson has dug her nails into my skin, clawing at the injury and she is trying to reach my cell phone. 'Just… Maria, don't do this…'

Heat rockets up my leg and I scream out, stumbling forward, attempting to get to a stand, but my knees wobble and I tumble, my torso toppling forward, body a felled tree, slicing my scalp on the corner of a chair.

Blood splatters in my eyes, disabling my sight, the heat of it, the ooze cloaking my face. My hands flap in front of me as I frantically try to see, attempt to stagger to safety, but Dr Andersson gets to me before I can run. The blood clears and my sight kicks in, but now she has an arm locked around my neck, her hands grasping for my cell phone.

'Who are you speaking to?' she yells. 'Who?'

I smack her hands away and then, spinning round, see it: her gun—under the table where it landed.

And now both our eyes are on it.

Quick, slick, she throws me to the side, lurching for the weapon, my shoulder slamming into the stone floor. She kicks me hard in the stomach and I reel back, the agony of it engulfing me, spiking into my consciousness.

'Jesus Christ, Maria, why? Stay fucking still.' She spits out some blood, looking round for the gun. 'I didn't want to fucking do it like this.'

But I can't let her get the gun, can't let her get to my cell and to Balthus. And then I spot my torn Papa photograph, lying lost next to ripped pictures of Mama, Ramon, Patricia and Harry, and a sudden rage courses through me, one phrase slamming into my mind—*prepare, wait, engage.*

I glance once more to the photographs and I fly. I fly at Dr Andersson and punch her throat, straight on the windpipe, and her whole body instantly folds, collapsing in with a strange gurgle as her hand clutches her skin. I scramble up, eyes scanning the floor. The gun. Where is the gun?

'Stop!' Slam. Dr Andersson's whole body lands on me. I stagger backwards at the weight of her, smothering me almost, impossible to breath, horrified that she is on me, touching me, and I hit out, my legs kicking at her shins, but it does no good. She topples me, my cell phone almost slipping away.

'Maria!' Balthus yells.

My face smacks the tiles, bones crunching as she knees me in the chest. Air shoots out and it feels as if I am drowning, as if every atom of oxygen is wheezing from my thorax as now Dr Andersson's knees pin my torso down, her legs wedged into my skin.

'So it's the governor you're in touch with,' she says, spitting to the floor. 'I know his voice. Maria, it's over. Don't drag everyone into this.'

She shifts to the right, blowing air on her face where her ponytail now hangs in strings of sweat on her face, and as I try and jerk my head out of her way, I see a glint. The bar. The iron bar.

I move fast, automatic. I whip my hand forward and with one swift movement, stretch my arm, grab the bar and, using all the force I can find, smash it over Dr Andersson's head.

Her grip immediately loosens, her fingers go slack. She slips to the side, a slow groan sliding from her mouth and I waste no time. Pushing her off me, I scramble back, crawling on all fours, my eyes darting left and right until they finally land on the gun, wedged now into the wall. I grab it, chest heaving, and, staggering to a stand, point it at her.

'My baby—' she says, eyes rolling in her head. 'It's her… birthday…' Blood loops round her ear now, pooling in the well inside it, and she drifts in and out of consciousness.

I pause at the sight of her, my brain stuck, torn between helping and running.

'Maria?' Balthus. 'Are you okay?'

'She is injured. I should help her.'

'What? No. No! Is she down?'

'Yes.'

'Then go. Go!'

Swallowing, unsure what to do, but knowing Balthus is right, I secure the cell phone, turn, then, throwing one last glance at Dr Andersson's broken body, I hobble away as fast as I can. But as I drag myself across the room somehow, Dr Andersson crawls up, fast and unexpected, catching me slap at the ankle.

'Give me…the gun,' she yells.

She fells me, topples me to the ground, clambering to my chest, fingers finding my throat where they squeeze hard. I choke, gasp for air. My arms stretch out as far as they can, the gun still in my fingers, but it is slipping now, teetering on the tips. My legs flap, nails scratch at her as I try to wrench her off me, but she presses harder, her hands nearly at my fingers now where the gun seesaws, teetering between life and death.

Tears roll down her cheeks. 'I'm so sorry. I hate doing this.'

I feel myself begin to asphyxiate and it is hard to retain a grip on anything at all, the room swaying, my eyes bulging, about to explode. I look round at the torn articles on the floor, at the images of the friends and family that, without ever telling them, I do love. I thrash, yell, but Dr Andersson just digs in harder, strength coming from somewhere, her blue eyes fixed on mine, the sun shining on us and I feel it, there, its heat, and my mind goes to Papa, to his face and eye creases and his complete and utter acceptance of me for who I am.

I have almost no oxygen reserves left.

'Ssssh,' Dr Andersson says to me now. 'It will all be over soon. Sssh.'

A warmth spreads over me, trickling at first then rushing in as, one after the other, faces swim before me—Balthus, Patricia, Harry, Ramon, Mama. And seeing them, watching the contours on their expressions, the grooves and lines, I start to believe that when I die, I will no longer be lonely and awkward and hunted down, but happy and free and regarded as normal.

'Maria? Maria, fight her!'

Balthus? His voice swims into my head.

'Maria,' he shouts, 'don't let them win! Don't let them win!'

His voice, hearing it—it sparks something within me, something that takes hold of the last flicker of a flame inside me. My fingers wriggle. Slow then picking up speed, I find, from somewhere, a fight, a strength and, instead of letting it slip from my hand, I begin to clutch the gun until my knuckles turn white and my breath grows strong. '*Prepare. Wait,*' words whisper in my head. '*Engage.*'

I force myself to look straight at Dr Andersson and, gripping the gun as hard as I can, I make myself focus, make myself do what I am alarmed I've been trained to do, what I must do to survive.

I twist my torso.

'No!' Dr Andersson yells, eyes wide at the sight of the gun. 'No. No… Her…her name is Briony. She's three today. Three. I…I can't let you get away. I can't let you stop me.' And then she goes to press down harder on my mouth, squeezing out the air.

And so I grip the gun hard.

And I shoot.

Chapter 10

Patricia is singing again. The song drifts in and out of my head as if in a dream, the melody and lyrics soothing, rocking me into a state of peace and calm as I think about the drug in my arm, the hallucinations.

The heat in the room appears to have increased. Sweat now drips from my body and while I know I am clothed, for the first time I begin to think about what I am wearing. Can I rip any of it off to cool me down?

'Can you see me?' I ask Patricia. 'I want you to tell me what I am wearing.'

She stops singing and sighs. 'Doc, you know I can't see you. You know, really, that that's impossible.'

'It is not impossible.'

'Yep. It is.'

Unsure what she means, I look to my arm and to the needle, to my body, my clothes. I can see nothing. The weak light that was there before has now gone, leaving a dark, dripping heat in its place, and every movement of my muscles is heavy, thick with fatigue.

We remain for a while as we are. Now and then Patricia will talk about how we may have arrived here, where the Project are, if they are watching us, but each time one of us attempts to conjure any significant recollection of our journey here, our minds come up blank.

Four, perhaps five minutes of silence pass when there is a sudden sound, the first we have heard at higher volume since we awoke in this dank, foul place.

'Hey, Doc, can you hear that?'

'Yes.'

It is there in the air—a ticking, a soft *put, put.*

'That sounds like the stand thing, you know, the drip they had me hooked up to when I was in the hospital ward at Goldmouth.'

I listen to her words. The drip. The one she was hooked up to after she tried to commit suicide in prison. *Put, put. Put, put.* She is right. My brain begins to tick, firing now at the possibility of the hope of some kind of answer.

'How close do you calculate you are to the sound?' I ask, sitting up, alert.

'Dunno. I'm not as hot on this maths stuff as you are. Say a metre away, something like that?'

'No. That cannot be correct. That would mean that you are closer to the sound than I am.'

'Well, yeah. Of course.'

'That does not make sense.'

'Doc, nothing makes sense in here.'

Put, put.

'There!' Patricia says. 'I hear it again.'

The clicking sound hovers in the air now, hanging near us.

'Doc, do you think, like, it's got something to do with your arm, that sound?'

'No. It is not…' I stop, think. She is right—of course she is right. The needle. A drip. I whip my head to the side. 'Have you got your bracelet on?'

'Huh? Yeah, my mam's one. Why?'

'Twist your wrist.'

'Uh, okay.'

'Are you doing it?'

'Yes. Hold your horses.'

'Horses?'

Patricia moves her wrist, and at first nothing happens but then, slowly, a tiny shaft of light appears.

'There must be some small bit of light. It is now reflecting on your bracelet. Keep moving your wrist.'

The bracelet reflection affords a shred of brightness across my body and I begin to look. At first, nothing appears, only a snapshot of my limbs, my knees, legs, but then, as Patricia's arm moves some more, it happens. Inch by inch, upwards, light slithering towards my arm.

'Can you see anything yet, Doc?'

There is a glint where the needle pierces my vein then it fades. 'Move your arm again.'

'This is hurting now, Doc.'

As the weak light returns, the glint comes again, stronger this time and, gradually, like clouds parting in the sky, what lies underneath is revealed.

I gasp.

'What, Doc? What is it?'

I shut my eyes, open them, but it is still there.

'Huh? What? What can you see?'

Sweat slices my head, confusion, deep-rooted fear. 'There is a drip.' I narrow my eyes, desperate to see anything I can. 'It is... It is hooked up to a metal medical stand.'

'I told you.'

'There is a tube and it is...it is linked to the drip bag.'

'That must contain the drugs.'

'Yes, and...' I stop, every muscle in my body freezing rigid. 'Doc?'

Suddenly, everything makes sense. The *put, put* sound. Why the hallucinations only come in phases. Why I cannot move my arms.

'There is a timer,' I say after a moment.

'What?'

I look back to the device, to the stand and the drug bag. 'The drugs are being administered through a controlled, pre-set timer.'

Salamancan Mountains, Spain.
33 hours and 54 minutes to confinement

Dr Andersson's body drops sideways, falling on top of me.

I push her off and choke, her body thudding to the floor, arms slapping to the tiles, and for some reason I notice for the first time that her fingernails are painted crimson, hanging now in long, sleek shapes.

I stare at them, cannot pull my eyes away, my hands rubbing at my throat over and over, skin red, sore, every atom in me screaming for oxygen. A moan escapes my lips.

'Maria?' Balthus yells. 'What's happening?'

I stare at Dr Andersson and her fingernails, and I moan again and again, rocking gently now, back and forth. There is a small round circle one centimetre in diameter in her forehead, a single line of blood trickling from it, same colour as the lacquer.

'She is dead,' I say to Balthus.

'Oh, Jesus.'

A damp circle the size of a dinner plate spreads on Dr Andersson's jacket. It drips to the tiles, painting them red, and at first, paralysed by the sight, I cannot understand why there is a hole in her head while it is her shirt that oozes. Finally, I drag my eyes away from the growing pool on her chest as, slowly, the reality of what I have done begins to sink in.

'I shot her twice.'

'Maria, it's okay. Maria?'

I drop the gun, crawl over, quick, and without thinking, roll the body over. There is a deep red stain shrouding the dark T-shirt on her chest where the bullet entered, shattering her rib cage.

'No,' I say, a whisper at first then louder. 'No, no, no!' I shout as my hands grope Dr Andersson's torso, desperate to stem the blood loss, to close up the gaping hole that has ripped open her skin, bones, heart and head.

'Maria? Maria, talk to me.'

'I killed her.'

'Okay. Okay, I know, I know, but it's okay.'

I look at her breathless body, at my hands soaked in her blood. 'No. It is not. Killing is not okay. It was her daughter's birthday today. Oh my God. Oh my God, oh my God.'

Then, barely realising what or why I am doing it, I find

myself slapping Dr Andersson's face, rattling her shoulders, frantic for her to open her eyes, wake up.

'Who else has the Project trained?' I yell at her. 'Who was Raven? Who was she? Why did you just not refuse to come here? Then you would still be alive! You would still see your daughter! Daughters need their mothers.' Fat tears fall down my face. 'They need their mothers.'

'Maria!' Balthus yells. 'Stop!'

But I shake Dr Andersson's dead body again and again, an anger I don't understand surging inside me, gripping me tight at the chest, making me pant, making my eyes blur and my head drop. I give her body another shake, her skull flopping to the side, when something falls out of the inside of her jacket.

I halt, pick it up. It is a piece of paper, pink, confidential, A4 in size. Slumping back, I wipe snot from my face and peel open the paper. What I see shocks me to the core.

'It…it is my family.'

'What?

I slap the paper to the floor, smoothing it out as what I see sinks in. 'There is a file containing pictures of you, Mama, Ramon and Patricia.'

'What? Where was it? With Dr Andersson?'

'Yes.' My hands shake.

'What does it say?'

My eyes scan it all, not believing what I can see, that they would do this, say this—believe this is right. 'There is one word next to your name and to Patricia's name,' I say after a moment.

'What?'

My eyes swim, head struggles to accept it. But finally, I say it aloud. 'Locate.'

I drop the paper to the floor as my limbs, back, legs begin to shake uncontrollably. 'They are looking for you. They know you are both my friends. They realise you know about the Project.'

'And MI5 want all connections to the Project eliminated.' He exhales hard and heavy, and when he next speaks, his words are low and slow. 'Look... Look, Maria,' Balthus says. 'I know this is...this is not a good situation. But...but right now, you have to focus. You heard what Dr Andersson said before—she was looking for a file. It could be the same file you remembered in your flashback.'

Slowly, I pick up the paper again, eyes glancing to the blood, to the crimson nail-polished fingers. I open it up, the paper. I open it up and force myself to look at it again. 'They want to monitor you all.'

'Okay. Hang on a second. Let's look at this one step at a time. First off, we have to get you out of there. The Project will trace you any time soon. And if you go now you could find the file, figure out where it is. Maria, that file, its contents, it could stop it all.'

He halts now, his breathing only drifting on the phone line. I think about his words, look again at the images of the people I love. My jaw clenches. 'You are all in danger because of me.'

'No,' Balthus says, immediately. 'No. This is because of the Project, because of MI5. But you can help. You can do something.' He pauses. 'Maria, you can stop it. You find the file, you end the Project, you end MI5's involvement in it—you end it all.'

I rub my eyes. Is he right? Can I really end it all? Should I? *Eliminate.* The word swirls around my head, mixing with the image of Raven, with her voice, with her caramel skin and her cries for help. Why can I not remember everything? Where is that file? Papa has died. Harry has died. The thought of it, the agony and confusion and inability through all my life to talk about what has happened to me, to express deep in the pit of my soul how it makes me feel—it drags me in, creates something inside me that I do not fully understand, but will not go. An anger. A deep-rooted belief that what is happening—what has happened—is wrong. *Wrong. Wrong. Wrong.*

I whip forward, and, almost disregarding the blood now, disregarding the limp body of a woman that I myself have killed and the horror that creates, the lives beyond hers that I have just changed forever, I tap down Dr Andersson's chest and arms and legs with my palms until I find what I am looking for: her cell phone.

I stand. I grab the pink confidential paper and, flipping Dr Andersson's blood-smeared cell phone in my fingers, I rip open the back, unclip the SIM then locate a tiny black device, yank it out and, dropping it to the floor, grab the iron bar from the floor and bring it down hard on the black mechanical piece. Noise splinters the air and the device shatters into tiny pieces.

'Maria? What's going on?'

My feet still bare, I kick the shards away. 'There was a GPS tracker in Dr Andersson's phone—I just destroyed it.'

'Won't that alert MI5?'

'Yes. I estimate I have approximately eight minutes to vacate the villa. I have her SIM card.'

'Shit. Shit, shit shit.'

Next I turn, drag myself to the crate, find a box of matches among the mess and, lighting one, put the flame to the pink confidential paper until nothing is left but charred black flakes.

'Maria, what are you doing? Where are you going now?'

I pick up the two halves of the photograph of Papa and, hobbling across to the only two sets of stacked books that remain upright in the corner, I extract my hidden notebook, relieved it has been untouched and unfound, and shuffle towards the bedroom door. 'I am going to take the bullet out of my leg.'

Chapter 11

Salamancan Mountains, Spain.
33 hours and 48 minutes to confinement

Pushing open the door, my wound screaming, I jam my hip into the bed, slamming the old wooden frame across the room, and fall to the floor. There, in the centre, is a trap door. I scramble over to it. A wire, transparent, thin and barely visible to the naked eye stretches across the space and, gulping in oxygen, I track it as slowly and carefully as I can. To my relief, the wire is in its place meaning the latch has not been tampered with.

'How much time's remaining before MI5 get there?' Balthus asks.

'Seven minutes and forty seconds,' I say immediately, consulting only the clock that now ticks in my head. I scour my bedroom. The walls in the room are white and bare, there is only one glass by the bed, one pillow, one small set of drawers and one book by Jean-Paul Sartre entitled *Nausea*.

Moving the book aside, I pull out a rucksack from the trap door under my bed. It is a small, pre-packed, ready to go bag, and, unzipping it, I check the contents. One loaded USB stick with all the encrypted Project data I have found so far, food, water, pay as you go cell phones. I pause, look at it all then, lowering it down carefully, I add in my notebook and the torn picture of Papa and me. The sun peeking in between the muslin curtains that hang from the small window to the left of the bed, I look at the image for two seconds then, shoving it away, haul myself up and stagger to the bathroom.

Scorching heat sears my thigh, walking having worsened the wound. Bending down, I study it. There is blood oozing out, the bullet hole shallow, perhaps five, maybe six millimetres in diameter. I deliberate what to do. If I leave the wound, if I ignore it entirely, then no matter how far I want to run, I will not make it. My eyes glance at the injury one more time. There is only one answer. My original thought was the right one: the bullet has to come out.

'Maria,' Balthus says. 'Time left?'

'Seven minutes and three seconds.'

Staggering across to the en suite, I slap open the door. My sight is a little blurred, the lower blood pressure from the gunshot wound taking its toll, but I manage to sway into the small, windowless room, scraping against the white enamel bath, a brush of blood painting the edges as I pass. My eyes take in the mirrored cupboard and in it my reflection. The sight shocks me. There are small, sharp lacerations to my neck, and where Dr Andersson attempted to suffocate me, deep purple bruises now sprout in the shape of her small fingers. My blonde spiked hair is matted with sweat, eyes dark and heavy, and when I stare in closer, my cheeks that only one year ago were rounded now look sunken and drained, the muscles clutching onto my bones.

Blinking, almost drunk now with pain, I set down the cell phone and the SIM card, and shuffle to the small set of metal drawers to the right of the bath and lower myself down to the edge. Pain swells. I pull out some bandages, surgical scissors, a suture kit then, biting down on my lip, I recheck the wound. The oozing has eased and the blood flow slowed, but it needs attention, fast, and so I slot my finger into the wound. A sharp stab tears through me.

'Maria? Are you okay?'

The cell phone. I had almost forgotten Balthus was still on the line. 'I am in pain.'

'Oh. I... Is there anything I can do?'

I wince. The wound stings. 'No. You are 1,246 kilometres away.'

Sweating, I search for a flannel. Locating one hanging its batwings over the sink, I roll it up and stuff it into my mouth, and, ignoring my burning nerves, rip open a bottle of surgical alcohol. I blink, knowing it will hurt, knowing I have no choice, so I take one large bite down onto the flannel and, counting to four, tip the alcohol onto the wound.

I scream into the flannel, agony searing down my calf, through my thigh. Five long seconds pass before I can look down again, check the area, hands trembling as they hover over my leg, my breathing soft, shallow, brain not wanting to do what it has to do next. Even though I am a doctor, have tended many injuries, my head twitches and I realise I have never before treated myself; at least, I don't think I have.

Swallowing hard, I take out the suture kit and, fingers shaking, lay out what I need, counting and recounting everything in front of me. This is it now. I have to do it.

'How much time left?'

I glance to the cell. 'Six minutes, three seconds.'

Reaching out, I pick up the medical tweezers and grip them tight. Routine, I tell myself. To complete this task, I simply need to follow routine, and so I bite down hard on the flannel and, lowering the tweezers to the wound, I begin to extract the bullet from my leg.

After one minute and twenty seconds have passed, the suture kit is soaked in blood and the procedure is complete.

I drop my head. Pain pulsates through my leg, the bullet now sitting in the soap well on the sink, splashes of red streaking the white enamel bowl where stained medical strips and scrunched up antiseptic pads lie discarded like roadside rubbish. I look at it all and feel a sudden stab of nausea and worry. The mess. The disorder. It takes every slice of willpower in me to grab the cell and the SIM card, and stagger away from it and back into the bedroom.

'How's the leg?' Balthus asks.

I grunt a reply.

The time on the clock by the crate next to the bed reads 07:01. I stop, check for any sounds, for any signs of entry. When all appears clear, gasping at the pain, I grab some clothes from the beat-up drawers, pausing to grit my teeth as a wave of heat from the wound charges through me then ripples away. I wait then change. Black jeans, fresh grey tank top, a checked shirt and a black cotton bomber jacket, shoving them on, counting the items methodically, wincing when the denim skims my injury. I scream then bite my lip. Blood oozes out.

'Maria, I'm worried about you,' Balthus says, but I don't know why. 'How much time left now?'

A slice, a sting shoots through me. 'Five minutes and thirty-seven seconds remaining.'

I wrench on a pair of biker boots, a baseball cap and slip on some clear, no-prescription glasses with a thick, black frame then, grabbing my cell and Dr Andersson's SIM card, turn. This may be the last time I see my villa, I realise. I take a picture of it all in my mind and stand still for three seconds. The silence of the sunshine on my face, the gentle flutter of the morning birds outside, the slow sway of the orange trees in the groves. The air, when I smell it, is warm and fragrant, a fresh, light wisp of heated earth that wanders in through open windows, through unfilled crooks and corner crevices, catching me by surprise. It's then a wave of sadness hits me. I have been happy here. No social rules to follow, no chit-chat to make, no confusing body signals to be unable to read.

I put the cell phone to my ear and speak to Balthus. 'You said you had a contact, a hacker I can go to.'

'Yes,' Balthus says. 'His name is Chris. American, but he used to be an inmate here.'

'Can you trust him?' I step back into the living area, shuffle past the torn newspapers, the splinters of computers and crates, biting down hard on my lip, pressing back the urge to shout out loud that I can't cope with the chaos. The bandage pulls tight at my leg.

'Yes, I trust him. One hundred per cent,' Balthus says now. 'I got to know him well—he's a good sort, good soul. He lives near Barcelona in a village up by Montserrat. I'll text you his address.'

'No, do not text me. It may not be safe. Tell me now. I will remember it.'

'Okay. Okay.'

I hold Dr Andersson's SIM card in my hand and, reaching into my rucksack, open my notebook.

'How much time left now?' Balthus asks.

'Three minutes and fifty-two seconds.'

'You'd better go.'

I hold out the SIM card at arm's length in the sunshine. 'I have one more thing to do first.'

Wiping a bead of sweat from my forehead, I take out an extra cell from my bag and slip the SIM card into it, tapping the keypad fast to check for data.

'You still there?'

I keep my eyes on the phone. 'Yes.'

'What are you doing?'

'Checking Dr Andersson's SIM for data.'

'Jesus,' he mutters. 'Hurry.'

My eyes scan for numbers, codes, anything that may help. At first, there appears to be nothing. The card is clear, the data apparently corrupt, but something niggles. Unsure, I turn to my notebook. Flicking the pages, my brain registers every word, every sketch and algorithm I have ever recorded from my dreams and flashbacks, until I arrive at a series of numbers that looks familiar. I think. Where are they from? Who gave them to me? The configuration is short, complicated, yet, somehow I know that it could be of use, could hold an answer, and I begin to work through it, methodically, efficiently. After seven seconds, I crack it.

'It is a SIM code over-rider,' I say aloud, amazed. How did I know this? Who taught me to use this code?

'What?'

I ignore Balthus, locked on to my task, a missile to target as, one by one, my fingers tap in the decoded key.

'Maria, what's going on?'

Data. Data flashes up, one followed by two lines of it, short, sharp, but then something scrolls up, something new. Something significant. I look again to be sure. Can it be…? My pulse starts to rise.

'It is a subject number.'

'What?'

I analyse the information again in front of me, knowing what it is, but not wanting to say aloud what is true.

'Maria, what can you see?'

'I see a subject number similar to the one on the MI5 report I hacked into from your office.' I track the number, say it in my head, trying to make it true. Sweat steams beneath my cap, escaping past the rim and to my brow as I look at what I see. 'This one is number 115.'

'What? But you are subject number—'

'375.'

We both go silent. The lemon trees in the distance rustle and within them sit small starlings, their heads bobbing up and down in the sunshine.

'It means there are others,' Balthus says after a few seconds. 'If that's a different subject number, it means somewhere else, others like you might still be alive. Jesus…'

Balthus's words pinball in my skull. Others. Like me.

'Could it be connected to the file, to the woman you remembered?'

'Raven.'

'Yes.'

The thought arrests me. The flap of her veil in the breeze, the memory of her invisible face, the smell of the heat and the sand, the secrecy, the hush of some deep, dark void, and her long, loud pleas. I glance again to the subject number—could this be, as Balthus says, connected to her?

I shake my head and look again at the phone, scrolling down then stop. 'There is something else next to the number.'

'What?'

I check again. 'It is a grid reference number.'

'You sure?'

'Yes.'

'Do you think they are related?'

My mind instantly begins to attempt to determine the location of the map point, trying to forge any connection that may be there.

'Maria,' Balthus says. 'How much time's left now?'

'Two minutes, two seconds.'

'Damn it, you have to go. You can't wait any longer. I'm on my way to the airport now. Can you keep the SIM card data safe? Take it with you?'

I drag my brain away from fact tracking and take one more look at the information on the screen. A subject number. A grid reference. Data. How do they connect? If there are others like me out there then is there a chance I can end all this, stop the danger? I want to know who I am. I don't want to be pressing my nose up to the window of life any more.

'I am going to find the file,' I say after a moment.

'Really?'

'I do not want MI5 or the Project to harm you or Patricia or Mama or Ramon. If the file can provide information on the Project that will put a stop to the entire programme, information on others like me, then I have to find it. Dr Andersson came for me today. It will be someone else the next day. It will never stop. And you—and my family—will always be in danger. Therefore, I am going attempt to find the file by locating the facility my flashback was based in.'

Balthus lets out a breath. 'Okay, good, good, but look, let me help you. I know you can handle yourself, but still. Get to Chris's place and I'll fly over there now. We can figure out together what to do next.'

'They will be watching you if you come to me.'

'Then I'll be careful. I have contacts who can help me slip out.'

I look at the ripped images and faces that lie on my villa floor. 'What about Patricia?'

'I'll get her, too. Okay? She'll be safe.'

'Okay.'

'Good. Then go. Please, please, go.'

I ram everything into the rucksack—the SIM card, the extra cell, all of it—I turn to drag myself away then pause. Dr Andersson's body lies lifeless and broken on the floor, her blood already drying in cemented cracks over the shine of the tiles, my eyes on her stomach where a tiny baby girl once was, pale, stretch-marked skin glistening in the morning sun. I look at her one more time then biting down hard on my lip, fighting back an emotion I do not want to feel, I turn and, securing my rucksack to my shoulder, bandaged leg throbbing, walk away.

I wrench open the back door of the villa and am greeted by a blast of warmth and sun. For a second, I let it sink into my skin as I blink at the images of the distant Salamancan mountains, the birds and olive trees and groves upon groves of fragrant citrus fruits. I breathe it all in as, directly in front of me, a Carbonell's wall lizard, rare, endangered, slides onto the fire pit. His skin is yellow, broken by curved edges of black, and, when his tail moves, it whips round, long, thin and fast, his hind legs two stabilisers on the bricks. It hovers there for three seconds, tongue flicking out, then one second gone, it scurries away.

'Time?' Balthus says.

His voice from the phone makes me jump. 'Two minutes.'

'Christ.'

I throw my rucksack into the truck, turn on the ignition, look to the cell. 'I am switching off now.' I go to hit the red button.

'Wait!'

I pause.

'You mean a lot to me, Maria. Just remember that, yes? No matter what happens.'

I sit, unsure what he means or what I am required to say.

'You still there?'

'Yes. The time remaining is one minute and fifty-two seconds.'

'Oh, Jesus. Right, yes, yes, go. Go. Oh and Maria? Please look after your—'

I switch off the cell—there's no time left. I put the vehicle into gear, check all around me for anyone arriving then pull away.

As the truck speeds off, dust billowing in the air, I slip one last glance in the rear-view mirror.

My villa fades away until nothing of it is left.

Chapter 12

Straining my neck, I get a glint of the timer again. Patricia has been quiet, falling asleep at the exertion of moving her arm, so I use the silence to see whatever I can.

It is difficult at first, the room swathed in darkness, a stench of dirty water saturating the air, pricking my nostrils, but it is there, the timer, I know it is, and, despite my head pulsing a pain that shoots like steel through to my shoulder blades, I force my neck backwards, as, slowly, a sliver of light appears.

'Patricia? Can you see the timer?'

But she remains quiet and while worry bubbles, I calm myself. She is okay. She's just sleeping.

My eyes scan the area before the light slips away. The timer is on a clock rotation device. It is small, compact like a shiny penny and is connected directly to a tube that leads to a drug bag hung into a spiked metal medical stand, long and thin. While I have seen devices similar to it before, this one is unlike any other. Its size is unusual, being so small—the timers I am familiar with are more substantial, as big as the base of a coffee mug, but this…? I squint, strain my whole torso—this device is so condensed that it appears unreal, made up, somehow, by a child, not actually functional, rather decorative, for play. As if this is some sort of game.

'Patricia,' I whisper, 'I think I can see the details of it now.'

I track the circumference of the timer, trace the outskirts of its mechanism so I can gauge when it's set to go off next, but what little light illuminates from the window is fading now and it is becoming impossible to see. My body slumps back, exhausted. My neck unable to sustain the twisted position any longer, I am forced back into a front-facing position.

'Patricia, you must now wake up.' When there is no reply, I get concerned. 'I need to check your status. You are injured. Wake up.'

There is a sudden, sharp clunk. I freeze. My fingers grip the chair and my feet curl into the dirt floor beneath.

'Patricia?'

Clunk. It sounds again, once, then twice. My whole body becomes rigid. 'Who is there?'

My voices echoes in the blackness, but no reply comes back.

The rope digging into my skin, heartbeat banging against my rib cage, my eyes track the room straining to see something, anything that will give me a clue as to what is happening.

'Patricia, is that you? Can you move now?'

Steps ring out, there on the air, soles of shoes on stone. My fingers form instinctive fists.

There are more steps, louder now, nearer and I count them. One, two. Closer. I swallow. Three, four. They sound like shoes, smooth sole, not boots. Five, six. I sniff the air and smell aftershave, spiced, heavy. A man?

Two more steps echo, advancing now, sweat streaking past my cheeks and mouth. I try to spit it away.

Seven, eight, nine.

The steps are near now and I can hear breathing, low and gruff, and the spiced aftershave scent now is so strong, it makes me feel sick.

Ten.

The steps halt.

'Hello, Maria.'

My breathing stops, chest ceases, hands grip still. Because someone stands there now, in this room, in this room-size coffin, and even though it is dark, even though the drugs have distorted my lucidity, I know them. I know their voice, the Spanish lilt. I know their face.

The person looking at me right now.

I know who they are.

It is my brother. Ramon.

Montserrat mountain valley, nr. Barcelona.
26 hours and 54 minutes to confinement

By the time I reach the town at the foot of Montserrat mountain the sun is beginning to fade. I swing the truck to a halt and pull the handbrake in place, flopping to the steering wheel as sweat drips past my eyes despite the window being open.

I pull out my cell phone then pause. The seven-hour journey around the cities Valladolid and Zaragoza was hot, dusty, taking longer than normal, sticking only to dirt roads, back routes to stay off grid and out of sight. A breeze brushes my face, and I lean against the window frame now for a moment, let my head rest, my brain recalibrate. I have not stopped. Not to eat, not to drink. Too scared, too worried that, at any point, MI5 would discover what I have done, catch up with me. Kill me. Kill my family and friends. The image of Dr Andersson's limp, lifeless body flashes across my mind mixing with Raven's face, but instead of sadness or upset, a flame of anger whips up inside me and my brain lands on one thought: the file.

I look up now and get my first view of Montserrat mountain ahead. What strikes me most is the colour of the serrated, misty mass rising up on the horizon. It is deep pink. It has a dusky hue to its sharp, unforgiving surface that pierces a clear blue sky tinged with the orange glow of the afternoon sun. The mountain is majestic against the canopies of white pines, of sweet maples and scented lime trees, of hollies and oaks and yews that thrive in its dense undergrowth, and the rocks, when I track them, jut in jagged blades that stick up tall into the air like broken glass bottles glued together in clusters of red clay boulders, thousands upon thousands of years in the making. I track the saw-toothed edges, counting every single one. They would slice a falling body in half like a sharp knife through an onion.

I look now to the area where I am parked. The street is empty for afternoon siesta time. Each house that rests in the town is sand in colour, their windows now closed with white wooden shutters that sometimes swing a little in the breeze, rippling small echoed creaks through the empty, narrow roads. There is a small moped to the right of me, rusty and blue, and when I turn my head, I see an old barrel on its side with a thin black cat curled up asleep on top of it.

Running my hands through hot, sweaty hair, I catch sight of

myself in the truck mirror and lean in. Minute blonde curls lick my brow, black roots are painted along my parting and when I check my cheeks and chin I see that they are dusted with a grey and brown film of dirt and sun. The bruises around my mouth and cheeks are deeper now, crops of small blackcurrant buds smeared on, tiny thorns of cuts welded into my bone and skin. I look beat and tired.

I reach to the passenger seat for a water bottle, drain a litre then, grabbing my cell, dial Balthus, winding down the window, a wall of heat blasting in. I fan my face, prop a hand above my eyes until, finally, the dialing tone clicks.

'I have arrived,' I say when Balthus picks up.

'Nice of you to say hello.'

'I didn't. What is your location?'

'I'm in Spain.'

I check my watch. He is on time. My leg from the wound throbs. I scratch it.

'Are you close to Chris's house yet?' he asks.

I glance down the street. 'I am approximately 1.76 kilometres from my final destination.'

'Okay. I'll be with you soon. Get to Chris. And, Maria?'

'What?'

'Be friendly.'

'Friendly,' I say. 'Friendly is an adjective that means to be kind and pleasant, or in British terms, can be a noun used to describe a match or game that does not constitute part of a point scoring competition. Which one do you require of me?'

'Oh, Jesus.'

We say our goodbyes and I switch off the cell and begin my walk to my final destination. I get one metre and fifty-five centimetres in when ahead an old woman, hair crowned on her head and deep grooves etched into her cheeks, shuffles into the dusty alleyway and halts. She stares at me, stooping, eyes squinting, two cloth bags swinging from her fingers, her body shawled in a tent of black lace. She stays there, one second, two, her eyes locked on mine. My skin prickles. Why is she gazing at me? Is she with them? With the Project? Her eyes appear glazed over, cloudy, and, at first, I don't connect what it is—the unusual appearance, the arresting fear stopping me from concluding the answer. I hold my breath, when her head suddenly turns, slowly, millimetre by millimetre then stops, and I finally understand what I am looking at.

Her eyeballs. They are completely white.

No black pupil, no iris, just the milky, white sclera. She shuffles away and I stand for a moment, shiver despite the heat, then, head down, not wanting to glance at her again, I move on as fast as I can.

When I arrive at the villa of Balthus's contact, I count to thirteen and stop. My heart is racing. My shirt is damp with sweat and when I sniff my arms I smell of body odour. I don't feel comfortable here. Friendly, Balthus said. Be friendly. Does that require making social conversation?

I force my eyes upwards and observe the villa door. It is small, square, two metres in height and creaking. Blue paint peels from the edges like cracked skin on the soles of ageing feet, torn, ripped, and when I scan the inner ridge, splinters protrude. I listen. There is a hiss somewhere, a grass snake sliding unbidden, free among the long rushes that sway drunk to the left. I watch, on alert, yet see nothing among the grass but an old stone fountain stooping, cracked and forgotten.

My nerves rising, I recite a mathematical theory then look again to the door. There is no bell, no buzzer, just an iron ring to bang on the wood, and when I sniff the air, I smell beetroot and jam and old, damp wood. I scan the area once then twice and tell myself that I have to do this. I have to speak to a stranger. And so, counting to three, I knock on the door and wait until eventually the door creaks open and a man stands there before me.

'Are you Maria?'

The first thing that strikes me about him is that he is tall. His shoulders are broad and his frame appears to fill the entire entrance area and when I open my mouth to speak, I find that I am uncertain what to do. Remember, I tell myself, Balthus said *friendly*.

'I am Dr Maria Martinez,' I say. 'Balthus sent me—you know him.' I track the man's frame. 'You are 187.96 centimetres in height. Your muscles are defined, which signifies that you must lift weights regularly.'

'Rrrright.' His accent is American, a low, vibrating twang.

Unsure what else to do, I thrust out my hand as I have seen others do.

He shakes my hand. 'I'm Chris.'

I expect his skin to be rough as the stubble that shadows his cheeks and chin, but instead his palms are soft and warm, reminding me of the freshly baked bread Papa used to buy from the local bakery when I was young. A broad smile now spreads across this man's face and the effect of it takes me by surprise: it is like the white foam of a wave trickling onto a beach, gently soaking into fine sand. I swallow. There is a strange flip inside my stomach.

'Balthus told me a bit about you,' he says. 'It's okay. You can trust me.' A slick of hair flops into his face and when he flicks it away, I notice his eyes are sunken, so much so that it is almost impossible, at first, to see the blue waters of his retinas. He scans the area behind me. 'You'd best come in.'

Yet, instead, I wait, uncertain, my leg beginning to jig. If I go in, it is harder to protect myself if he is not who he says he is, if he is someone I cannot trust.

'Your name is Chris,' I say, 'short for Christopher, yes?'

'Er, yeah.'

I stare past him into the hallway and see mustard-coloured walls and dark, mahogany scraps of furniture leading to a rusty old kitchen with one hob and a scratched enamel sink.

'Chris is short for Christopher,' I say, looking to him. 'Christopher derives from the late Greek name, Christophoros which means *to bear or carry Christ*. It is ranked the twenty-sixth most popular boy's name in the United States of America and has been used as a first name since the early tenth century.'

He laughs: it is light, a ripple of water glistening in sunlight. 'You're funny.'

I don't know what he means, but right then I make a decision.

'I am hungry,' I say, counting up in fives and walking straight in. 'Do you have food?'

Chris presses his lips together and shakes his head, then, closing the door, gestures to the hallway. 'Well, please—come on in.'

Chapter 13

'Ramon?' I croak.

My brother leans forward and moves his arm, but instead of touching me, he reaches out and flicks a switch, sending straw-coloured light seesawing into the room. I blink, the sudden brightness burning my eyes that have been used only to darkness. A corn on the cob bulb swings in the air above.

I immediately panic. 'They have got you! Ramon, are you hurt? Have they hurt you?' I look round, fast, worried. 'Where are we?'

As my eyes adjust to the light, I realise we are in a room, a brick-built room. The walls are dirt brown and smeared with a tar-like paint onto flaky masonry, and when I look closer I see that some of the bricks are not flat or solid but raised and soft, padded with some kind of fabric or filler. I crane my head to the side and see the timer and the medical stand and the bag of drugs, and a lump sticks in my throat, a feeling of dread growing in my stomach.

'Where is Patricia?' My eyes start to roam the soot-covered floor, but there is no sign of her.

'Who are you talking about?'

My brother's voice is rippled like bark. Confusion spills over as I examine him, his tall frame, broad shoulders, lean, taut limbs, a glow that even here shines from a face that has never looked three years older than me. He appears, Ramon, as he always has, his silk tan, his almost plastic features, hair a perfect round mass of slick black. To my relief, he seems okay, uninjured, and yet still something bothers me, something I cannot yet pinpoint.

'Are you...safe?'

He nods. 'Yes. Of course I am.'

I look around. The door is shut, but at least Ramon is with me, and even though I am tied up, there may still be some chance that I can keep him safe. But where is Patricia?

'Does the Project have you too?' I say, words tumbling out as I try to assess the level of danger. 'What did they say to you before they sent you in here?'

He tilts his head the way he used to when we were young. 'M, who is "they"?'

'Do they have Mama, too?'

'Mama is safe.'

'Is she still ill?

'Yes, but stable. The cancer's not spread.'

Air billows from my lungs, yet my chest immediately tightens as I try and think it all through. We must be at a Project facility—that has to be the answer—and somehow, they have captured my brother and put him in here now with me. The Project at least don't have Mama, and her health is steady and yet why does that information not calm me?

My brother reaches forward and flicks another switch, and

the room is bathed in more light, another, smaller bulb this time, casting a tepid, sepia sheen in front of me, illuminating now my wrists. I blink at them and see plastic blue rope that ties not just my arms to the chair, but, as I scan further down, my ankles to the base, too.

I strain forward. 'Where is Patricia?'

'Your friend from prison?' Ramon drops his head, shaking it. 'M, she's not here. Did you think she was?'

I look round, agitated now, the light scratching my eyes and brain. 'Yes. She is in here somewhere,' I say, searching the room. 'She is very ill. You have to help her.' Then I stop, feeling confused, suddenly not aware of what I am saying or why. 'Why are you here? Where is Patricia?'

'M, I don't know what you are taking about.' He raises his hand, slicks back a strand of fallen hair then adjusts the collar on a white linen shirt that has tiny thread lines of blue cotton sewn into the fabric.

'Patricia was in this room,' I say, scanning the room again for any sight of her, worry rising fast. 'You must be able to see her. Or she may have been moved. Did you see her when you came in? Did the Project take her out? Is she safe?'

I raise my head, searching the illuminated ground, but there is nothing there, no sign of Patricia's long frame slumped on the floor or her soft, shaved head, only dirt and bits of maggot-sized white cotton string and the fallen dust from the brickwork on the wall. 'She was talking to me not...' I try to calculate the time, but find I can't... 'not long ago.'

My brother looks at me for three seconds and for some reason I shiver, goose pimples popping out all over my skin. He walks to the dark corner on the far right and returns with a wooden crate. He sets it flat in front of me and takes out a white handkerchief from his pocket, brushes off some dust and sits, crossing his legs, lacing his fingers on his knees.

'M, I'm sorry this has had to happen.'

I barely move, because even though he is my brother, I find that I am suddenly scared. 'What has had to happen, Ramon?'

He glances to the timer. 'Who you think you've seen—it's all just a hallucination. It's…it's all just a side-effect of the drugs. She…she was never really here.' He points now to the medical stand behind me, to the timer that still ticks like a hammer in my ear.

I look back to my brother and a deep, raw fear rears up now, juggernauting forward, reaching my throat, until finally I make myself ask the question I dread the answer to.

'Who was never really here?

He sighs. 'Your ex-cell mate. Patricia.'

Montserrat mountain valley, nr. Barcelona.
26 hours and 44 minutes to confinement

Chris has led me to a room on the right side of the house. He said he would be back in a minute with food. That was thirty-seven seconds ago.

I wring my hands together, squint my eyes in the sun and wait. To keep myself calm, I scan the room for details, automatically searching for a source of focus. Dimensions, corners, curves, grooves. Late afternoon light streams in through a closed, locked window decorated with grey, ripped netting, and because there is no fresh oxygen, the air feels thick and pungent on my face, a faint smell of feet in the air.

The room is small, six metres square. There are seven pieces of furniture slotted against four fading walls decorated with pale green paint, and inside broken wooden picture frames are three old photographs. I step forward and examine them. Three faces, old and grained, stare back. The eldest is a man with white hair. He is stooped and wearing a chewed straw hat, and by his side is a woman of similar old age, an apron squeezed around a balloon waist, eyes dark and wrinkled, mouth downturned. Next to her is one small boy, eleven, maybe, head bowed, but light eyes that light up. In his hand there is a tennis racket and by his foot lies a small, yellow ball, white shorts on his legs, a grey long-sleeved jumper on his torso. Who are they? Why are they here? Do they mean something? Or are they simply pictures of people forgotten in time, never to be recalled or recounted, slipping by silently, invisibly as we do from present to past.

Agitated, I turn my attention to the corner of the room where a computer sits, and walk towards it. Sliding my rucksack from my back, I dig out my USB stick and Dr Andersson's SIM card and, listening out for any signs of this man Chris returning, I switch on the computer.

I call Balthus. 'I am here.' I settle into a small, splintered seat and fix my clothes so the fabric does not itch me.

'Maria? Oh thank goodness. You're at Chris's?'

'Yes.'

I peer at the computer. I need it to find out some information, but, when I turn it on, the connection is slow and no matter how much I tap my finger, it will not speed up.

'Is Chris okay?' Balthus says. 'Is he there now?'

'He is fetching food.'

'Oh, right. What are you doing?'

I get out the SIM card and my USB stick and place them on the dark wooden table where the computer sits. 'I am switching on Chris's computer to see if I can access any information that will tell me which Project facility the flashback was from.'

'Oh, right. Okay. So soon? How are you going to do that? Use the grid reference you found?'

'Yes.'

I do not need to check the reference number from Dr Andersson's phone as it is already in my head, but it is frustrating. I am ready to search, but the computer is still loading.

'Will Chris be back soon?'

'He said he would be one minute.' I check the time, tap my foot. 'He is late.'

When Chris does finally enter the room two minutes and thirteen seconds later, he is carrying a tray containing bread cut into rough chunks, a block of sliced Manchego cheese on a white plate with blue swirls and two steaming mugs of coffee in black cups.

He sets the tray down on the table to the right and puts his fists to his hips. 'Er, like, what the hell are you doing?'

'I am using your computer,' I say. 'Balthus is on the cell.'

'Oh,' Chris says. 'Hi, Balthus.'

'Chris! Good to hear you. Thanks for this.'

Chris picks up the cell and puts it to his ear, and I desperately want to grab it from him, not wanting anyone else's scent on it, but I see the bread Chris has brought and realise it has been several hours since I have eaten and my stomach is rumbling. Reaching across, I grab a chunk of bread, take a slice of Manchego and shove it all in at once. The food all instantly expands in my mouth like soaked cotton wool balls.

'You have been three minutes and thirty-seven seconds,' I say to Chris. Crumbs spit out.

Chris lowers the phone and just stares at me. 'What?'

I swallow the food. 'You said you would be one minute. You were not. You were three minutes and thirty-seven seconds.' Taking the cup, I swig a gulp of coffee. It tastes good—hot, bitter. I start to thaw out, a little less tired, a little less worn. 'What are you discussing with Balthus?'

Chris's eyes follow me. 'Do you have *any* manners?'

'I did not hear you.'

'I said do you have any manners?'

'Oh.' I pause, think. 'No.' I look at my phone at his ear, think of his skin touching it, his smell all over it. I can't stand it any longer. Standing, I unhook the cell from his hand, put it back onto speaker mode and place it on the table.

'What the—?'

'Did she just take the phone from you?' Balthus says to Chris.

'Uh, like, yeah.'

'Don't take it personally. She does that kind of thing to everyone.'

Chris shakes his head, stares at me a little again then eventually picks up a cup and taking a small sip, nods to the computer. 'Why do you need to use my stuff?'

'Stuff?' I frown. Is he referring to the computer? I conclude he must be. 'I have some confidential files to access. Your computer takes a long time to boot,' I say. 'What modem are you using?' I drink more coffee.

'What?'

'You say *what* with reasonable frequency.'

Balthus laughs.

Chris's mouth hangs open, and it seems I should speak some more, but I don't know what to say. The uncertainty of the social situation makes me want to hum, but I know that may seem strange, so instead I divert my anxiety by counting the pixels on the screen while the modem loads to the connection.

'I have to go,' Balthus says. 'Just about to go through customs. Chris, you have the rendezvous location, right? It's not far from you.'

'Yep. Got it.'

'Good.' He pauses. 'Look after each other.'

Chris throws me a glance. 'I think it might be me that'll need looking after.'

Balthus laughs again and I lower my head, listening, unsure what could be funny. 'Okay,' he says. 'See you soon. Stay low.'

'Will do.'

I switch off the cell and Chris blows out a breath then pulls up a stool and sits. 'So,' he says after a moment, 'you know Balthus from prison, right?'

'Yes.' I have counted one hundred and twenty-three pixels, and that's in just the far right corner. I grab my cell, pull it close, sniff it and scrunch my nose, unhappy: it smells of this Chris now, of spiced cologne and baked bread.

'How long were you inside for?' he asks now.

'What is this *inside*?'

'You know, prison.'

I pause my counting. What do I say to his question? The truth?

'It's okay,' Chris says, 'I know your deal.'

'Did we have a deal?'

'What?'

'You said *what* again.'

'What?' He slaps his forehead. 'Jesus. No. I mean I know about your conviction, you being in jail. I don't mind.'

Four hundred and three pixels. 'If you know about my conviction, why did you ask what I was in prison for?'

'Um, I was just…making conversation.'

'Oh.' I don't know what to say. 'Okay.'

He taps his coffee cup now, watches the screen as the modem fires. 'So, whereabouts in Spain are you from?'

I swivel my head so I can see him. 'Salamanca,' I say, unsure whether to tell him or not, and yet finding my lips automatically wanting to speak, as if they have a mind of their own. I look at him in more detail. There is a small rip on the sleeve of his marble grey T-shirt, which is half tucked into dirty light blue jeans, baggy on the leg. I lean in and sniff the air. This close he smells slightly different—raw cake mix spritzed with musk cologne.

I sit back. 'You smell good.'

A laugh spurts out. 'What?'

'I said you smell good. Why are you laughing?'

'I know what you said, it's just that…' He stifles a cough, moves back a little, rubbing his chin, and I find myself becoming concerned at how I may have acted.

'Balthus told me to be friendly,' I say after a second, looking down. 'But sometimes I…say things that people…

that people do not like.' My cheeks flush. I spin back to the safety of pixel counting on the computer, feeling exhausted at the short exchange. Five hundred and two pixels...

For a small while, Chris does not speak, but after a small while, he leans in, not too much, just a little and says, 'You smell good, too, by the way.'

Finally, after a while, the computer splutters into life and the screen I was awaiting pops up. I whip round immediately, ready to search for the map reference.

Chris points to the screen. 'You're going to use a proxy, right?'

My fingers suspend themselves above the keyboard. 'You are a criminal hacker. I thought this would be a secure line.'

He shakes his head. 'No. Well, yes, it is, but I like to make sure everything's like, well, super secure, you know?'

He looks at me, waiting. For what? 'Oh. Yes.' I say, though not sure why.

He smiles. 'Cool. So, you need to use a proxy. I can't have anyone finding me. Finding you.' He tuts. 'Us. Sorry—I promised Balthus.'

'How do I know if I can trust you?'

He shrugs. 'You don't. You just have to, I don't know, take my word for it, I guess.'

A shot of adrenaline charges through me. I look at this man, the black hairs on his arms, his nut-brown skin chalked with tiny scars. The body can tell a thousand stories, Papa used to say to me. You just have to figure out the plot.

Over by the window, the shutter outside swings forward then back silently in the breeze. I look back to Chris. I trust Balthus and Balthus trusts Chris.

'I need to perform a search,' I say, finally.

'No problem. Want me to sort the proxy and stuff?'

I hesitate. 'Yes.'

He delivers me a wide grin. 'Cool.' Then he takes the keyboard and, tapping in a code, sets up what I need to begin.

To calm my nerves, I start in my head reciting all the famous people in the world with Chris as a forename.

Chapter 14

Undisclosed confinement location—present day

I try to understand what Ramon is saying, but it does not make sense.

'But Patricia was here,' I say, searching the floor, the light weaker now, a single shaft of it projecting forward as in my head doubt begins to mushroom.

'No, M, she wasn't.'

'She was there,' I say, nodding forward to the spot I assumed my friend was, but all my sight catches now is an empty space of black dirt floor, dust rising in the shaft of light that beams in the room. 'I heard her,' I find myself saying, 'I did.' My breath is short, sharp and I struggle to understand what is happening.

Ramon shifts on the crate and delivers me a long stare. He clasps his hands together, folds one knee on top of the other and juts out his chin. 'M, it was the drugs. What you saw, heard—it wasn't real.'

His voice is cotton-soft and I try to focus on it, cling to the lifebuoy of the sound, but all I can think of is Patricia, and, when I blink in the gloom, my eyes sting and a wetness prickles out onto the red hot flush of my cheeks. I close my eyes.

'Is she safe?' I say after a moment. 'Does the Project have her?'

'I don't know.'

'Why do you not know?' I open my eyes. I can feel my chest tighten as my sight becomes singular and funnelled.

'M, I don't know anything about Patricia, but what I do know is that it was the drugs you're being given that made you see your friend.' He pauses. 'I'm sorry.'

'Then you have to help me,' I say, an anger, a hint of fire burning up inside me at the confusion, at the fear. 'You have to help me escape.'

His head drops. 'No.'

A shiver from somewhere runs over me. 'Yes. You must.'

He lifts his head now and when he directs his eyes to me, I see they are tinted with light pools of wetness.

I don't speak. I am confused. Nothing here makes sense and even though my brother is with me now, he is not helping me escape.

'M, you have to talk to me.'

I force myself to look at him. He is pristine. The crate upturned, he is sitting one leg swung over the other as if he were posing for a catalogue shoot on the deck of a boat. His hair, when the light catches it, is wet with gel, not a strand out of place and when he opens his mouth, I see his teeth are straight and glowing, and his clothes when he moves are starched and pressed where his muscles flex long and lean from years of early-morning swimming.

'M? M, are you okay?'

'You have not called me M since I was twenty-one,' I say.

'We grew up.'

'Why are you here?'

He hesitates. He opens his mouth then closes it and scratches his chin with his index finger and thumb. I glance around the room. The place still does not look familiar.

'I am here,' Ramon says after a few seconds, 'because I want to help you.'

'Did they send you?'

'Did who send me, M?'

'The Project.'

He stares at me. He says nothing in reply and keeps his gaze on me, on my torso and limbs, and when I turn my head away, unable to bare the intensity of the attention, he scrapes forward the crate and moves closer to me. My breath quickens. I can smell him now, my brother. I can smell his washed skin scrubbed with soap, lemon colgne, and when I raise my nose I get mould and damp from the black of the room, and all the scents mix together to create a bucket of aromas that smack a punch in my nose. I gag.

'M,' Ramon says, moving in nearer, 'what's the matter?'

'The smells,' I say, pressing back my head as far as it will go against the damp wood of the chair I presume I am sitting on.

'Oh, sorry.' He moves back, fixing the crate to its original position and running a hand along his slacks. I breathe out and allow myself a glance left and right then straight ahead towards Ramon. I shake off the scents, try not to let them engulf me.

'Tell me…' I stop, shake my head away from the smell of

mould that remains in my nose. 'Tell me why you are here. They have not hurt you, so what have they asked you to do?'

'I…I cannot answer that.'

'Why?'

But he does not respond.

'I asked you why?'

His eyes rise, but they are not sparkling as usual, are instead dulled and washed out, as if the person behind them is not really there, and for the first time I start to wonder whether he will hurt me.

'Ramon, who tied me up?' My voice rises with my fear. 'Who connected me to the timer and the drug?'

Ramon's eyes flicker upwards towards where the timer now begins to click a little louder, a little more pit pat put into the room.

My eyes dart to the drugs and back. 'The timer is set to go off at intervals,' I say, words tripping out. 'The Project have either forced you to be here or convinced you that they are good. They are not. Untie me and we can escape together.'

He hesitates. 'I can't. I…I can't help you escape.'

'You can. It is simple.' I jerk to the timer. The fluid is rushing faster now. 'You need to untether me—I can take out the needle.'

He fleetingly closes his eyes, inhales a long breath. 'Maria, what do you think is happening?'

The needle starts to dig further into my skin, the liquid building pressure in the vial. Fear flies up. Why isn't Ramon helping me? Why? And then I stop, suddenly understanding the situation. 'They are watching us.'

'What? Who?'

I scan the room for any recording devices, hair matting to my head, sweat dripping. 'They have used fake spiders before to covertly record me, so what are they using now?'

'M, you sound crazy. You're worrying me.'

My eyes land on a hole in the wall, tiny, black, barely visible in the murkiness, but there, real. 'The hole one metre to your left. That could be a recording device.'

He spends two seconds staring at it, then, shaking his head, he returns his attention to me. 'M, do you know what is happening?'

A thought slaps me right on the cheek bone, cold and stark. 'Are you a hallucination?'

At first, he does not utter a word, and then he does something, something odd and unusual. And frightening.

He shoots up to his feet and screams, unexpected, unprompted.

The noise ricochets around the walls. It bangs around my ears and against my skull, and even though the padding on the brickwork smothers some of the sound, my brain feels as if it will explode, the force of it is that much. I cower. Ramon kicks the crate and I can't move, cannot get out of his way because my hands are still tied and the timer still ticks.

After two, perhaps three seconds pass, he finally comes to a stop and heaves in three gulps of breath. The corn on the cob bulb above swings above us. I say and do nothing, too confused to try. Ramon takes one look at me and, withdrawing a handkerchief from his pocket, wipes spit from his mouth, dabs his lips at the corners then, sliding the white cotton cloth back to its home, he clears his throat.

'I apologise for my outburst.'

I don't know what to do. I stay as still as I can and try to assess the situation. What is happening? What have the Project told him? How have they brainwashed him? My pulse is charging through my wrist as I think to myself what I can do, think through the next steps and tell myself that, no matter what happens, it will be okay. Because, no matter what the Project have said to him, Ramon is my brother and he wouldn't hurt me.

Would he?

Montserrat mountain valley, nr. Barcelona.
26 hours and 40 minutes to confinement

Chris taps the screen and sets up the proxy. He creates the information he needs to ensure a secure line and while he waits for the next stage, he stretches his arms high above his head and yawns.

'So,' he says, yawn over, 'how was prison?'

'It was a large, brick-built place constructed in the British Victorian era.'

He drops his arms and looks to me. I face the computer.

'The proxy is ready,' I say.

'Oh. Right.' He leans in to the screen and taps the keyboard in the next required part of the process. His fingers work fast and carefully and I find myself enjoying watching the movement of them as they work, lost in the rhythm of their dance.

'Hey, you know, your conviction was bigger than mine,' he says after a moment, still working the keyboard. 'I don't know if I can trust you.' He turns, grins.

'Why are you smiling?'

'Huh? I was just—'

'I was acquitted of murder in a retrial. You were in prison for hacking government websites. You were not acquitted.'

A laugh spurts from his mouth.

I watch him, curious. 'That was funny?'

He leans back in his chair and lengthens his arms outwards, this time towards each wall and when he does, I see the dark shadow of the hair under the pit of his shoulders.

He looks at me and smiles. 'I like you,' he says.

'How can you make that assessment? You do not know me. I do not know you.'

He nods. 'Okay. Okay, sure, sure.' His arms drop and he turns his torso to me. 'You seem like an oddball, but that's kind of cool with me—and you know Balthus—so I'm going to tell you who I really am.'

I glance to the door. I can be out of it in two seconds and through the main house door in under eight.

'I'm a hacker,' he says. 'I'm from Idaho. I'm thirty-one years old and when I was twenty-three I got my first hacking conviction for smashing open some shit firewall of a defence behind a government military facility.' He exhales. 'Anyway, by the time I reached the prison Balthus was at, the one he was at before Goldmouth, I'd been inside twice more. I was supposed to be extradited to the US from the UK, but it didn't happen. Balthus—he was good to me, helped me with my case.'

Chris folds his arms across his chest and his T-shirt tightens over his rib cage and abdomen, making each muscle and bone jut out, and I watch him, finding myself uncertain, not sure what to think.

'So,' he says, grinning. 'Now you know me at least a little more.' He moves aside, points to the computer. 'It's all ready. What do you want to search?'

Hesitating, I pull my chair towards the computer and, calling up a search engine, I tap in the grid reference number from Dr Andersson's phone. After three seconds, the answer flashes up.

'Switzerland?'

I ignore Chris and look to the screen. Lake Geneva, Switzerland blinks in front of me in straight, formed letters, round and clear. I scan my memory for any connection, but I cannot find one that lights anything up, and even though I have been fed and am not now as tired as before, still my mind runs blank. Is it a place I have been to before with the Project and cannot recall? Is it the location of the Project facility where Raven was held?

'Hey,' Chris says, 'this yours?'

Chris is holding the SIM card from Dr Andersson's phone. I snatch it back.

'Whoa, okay, okay. I was just looking because it's odd.'

I am sliding away the card then stop. 'What is odd?'

He leans in a little. I lean back. 'It's just that, well, it's not a standard SIM card.'

My curiosity, despite my best efforts, is peaked. 'Tell me why.'

'Um, well, do you mind?'

'What?'

He points to the card. 'Can I... If I could have it, I can show you.'

I hesitate as the issue of trust flags again in my brain. But then I think of Balthus, and I find myself slowly handing over the SIM.

'Thanks. Okay so, this groove here, see?'

I bend in, squint. 'Yes. I see.'

'Well, it's computer-linked.'

'What do you mean?'

'It's like, compatible with a computer. But,' he shakes his head, 'not in an ordinary way. See, the groove is specially made, customised, really.'

Neurons fire in my head now, back and forth. 'Is it compatible with this computer?'

He shrugs. 'I guess so. Want me to try?'

'Yes.' I then pause, remember what Balthus told me. 'Please.'

He smiles. 'Okay, then.'

He slots in the SIM card to a slit no more than 1.5 centimetres long on the side of the computer. He takes the keyboard towards him and, tapping in a series of numbers and figures, leans into the screen and waits. His leg is jigging and on his face, his cheeks flush as the late afternoon heat beats in the window where the shutter outside has come loose.

'Ah. Fuck.'

'What?'

He rubs his chin. 'Well, this bit's encrypted.'

I look. He is right. The access to whatever data is on the card is locked, enshrined in a code that is so long, my brain plays catch-up with following it.

'I can access this code,' I start to say, 'however—'

'Oh, I can do it.'

'What?'

'The code. I can hack it. Seen this kind of thing before.'

I suddenly become concerned. 'How?'

'Er, duh? Hello? I'm a hacker. I hacked the US government. They have the highest level of security. Which means, actually, this is high-level stuff, too.' He pauses, looks at me.

I look away, uncomfortable, unsure how to respond. 'Can you access the SIM?'

'Huh? Oh, yeah. Sure. I don't know what all this is about, but if Balthus is part of it, I trust you.'

Chris starts the process at speed. I take out my notebook and write down what he does, the sensation strange—I do not recall learning from someone else like this before, learning coding and decryptions in such a way. Yes, the Project has taught me a lot, but that I have no real recollection of. Watching Chris, gaining knowledge from him it makes me feel… happy, like I'm not on my own, not the only one living in a head like mine.

'Okay so,' Chris says after less than thirty seconds have passed, 'I've brought up the next phase…I'm gonna try moving the cursor over everything.'

On the screen there is a ticker tape of numbers that snake in a line across the glass where a file of black and white sits. 'Look out for an icon structure,' he says.

'What type of structure specifically?'

'Black. Square.'

I stop. A black square structure. Heat rises to my head as I connect two elements. 'When I was in Balthus's office,' I say, fast, 'I hacked into a confidential website through a black square.'

'Cool, well, let's see what we can find.'

At first, when we search, there is nothing, but then, after one, two seconds, everything changes. The screen flickers once, twice and the numbers switch to flat, green lines that crackle across the glass and peak into mountain tops then dip to the bottom of the file. Neither of us moves.

Chris wipes his mouth. 'What the fuck...?'

'What is happening? Is it a loose connection or a faulty wire?'

'No...' He stops. The screen has begun to pixellate fast, out of control as, slowly, something flashes across the glass.

'Holy shit!' Chris says. 'What was that?'

My chest goes tight and my fists scrunch to two tight, nervous balls. 'I do not know.'

The screen goes black. Chris drags his chair towards the computer. 'This isn't right...'

I go to speak, begin to open my mouth to attempt to explain something, anything of what is occurring, when I stop.

Because there, on the screen, is an eye.

Yet it is not static, not an image or a photograph, but real, moving, blinking.

A silent scream slips from my mouth as the eye stares straight back at me. Someone has accessed this computer. Someone knows where I am.

Someone is watching me.

The eye blinks then, as quick as it appeared, it vanishes from the screen without a trace.

Chapter 15

'Holy shit! Holy shit! What was that? What was that?' Chris jumps up from his seat, hands scouring through his hair. 'What the fuck was that?'

'Black Eyes.' I say the words. I say his name and expect to feel fear, yet instead experience a strange stillness, my emotions landing like sediment at the bottom of a glass.

'Black Eyes? What…' He shakes his head. 'What's that? I mean what is…'

His voice fades and he is pointing to the screen now. I look. The eye is gone and has been replaced with a series of words and numbers. I grab my notebook and lean in.

Chris quits pacing and looks. 'That says Black September. Why does that say Black September?' His voice is higher than normal.

I analyse what Chris is staring at, an urgency building up fast. He is right. Black September and the year 1973 are listed. And something else.

Subject number 115.

It is the number from my flashback in the villa. The same subject number that was on Dr Andersson's cell.

Chris stares at it all. 'Holy shit. It's got your name on this. And your age. And…what the…? Is that a clock?'

I look down. There on the bottom of the file is my subject number—375—and my name, plus my age, thirty-three, and by it is a yellow flagged box that clicks each second, minute, hour, day, month and year away.

'Is that…' Chris whistles. 'Is that thing counting down your age?'

I try to think. How is it all connected?

I look up. 'It says September is Black. What does that mean?'

'Seriously? You don't know? Who are you involved with? Shit.' He paces. 'Black September—they were the gang responsible for terrorist attacks in the seventies.' He points to the screen. '1973—that's when it all kicked off. But look—that age thing.'

'It must be tracking me.'

'But how? Why?' He rakes a hand through his hair. 'Whoever this data belongs to, how old you are is a big deal.'

'It is?' I turn back to the screen and scroll down and feel a wave of pain in my stomach. How can all this be linked? How can the woman, Raven, be part of whatever information is on Dr Andersson's SIM, be part of how old I am?

I look to Chris. 'You say this Black September organisation were terrorists.'

'Yeah. Big time serous shit.' He shakes his head. 'You know, it all went underground, the response to it. There was a load of us hackers way back who got wind of some unit that was set up in response to that kind of terrorism, to a shift in approach, but… Hey, you don't think that's connected to whatever you're involved in, do you?'

I hesitate, think about what he has said. Balthus trusts this man. I decide to take a risk and tell him. 'The group who is tracking me… It is called the Project. They are unknown to the government. They are, as you say, underground.'

He blows out a breath. 'Jesus.'

I look back to the screen, back to the data and the facts. If it is linked, then why? And what is the significance?

'We need to get out of here,' Chris says. 'Like, now.'

I turn. He is right. If Black Eyes is watching, they could track our location. I reach for my USB stick, start to download the files.

'What are you doing?'

'Saving the file.'

Chris shakes his head. 'It's protected. I set up a shield. Let me do it.'

'Oh.' I thrust the USB stick to Chris. He takes it.

'You have heard of the word please, right?'

'Of course.' I hold the USB stick out further. 'I need you to download it all.'

'Christ.' He takes the stick and, fingers flying fast, starts to secure the documents to my files.

'Can you retrieve the last section, where it says critical next to my age?'

'Yeah, hang on.' He taps the keys, but the screen suddenly starts to fade fast. 'Shit. This isn't right.'

'What is the problem?'

'I don't know. It's just all disappearing.'

Chris sets up the download, but still the data pixellates until all that is left is a pin-prick dot, minute, black. Then: nothing.

'Shit, is that big eye coming back?'

I stare at the empty screen, an urgency surging forward, expecting to see Black Eyes reappear. 'Did you secure the download?'

'I don't know, maybe, but I do know that if I don't pull this now, we're screwed.'

Dropping to his knees, Chris wrenches the table away and starts ripping out the wires, dragging away lines of cables and as he does, they all spill out onto the floor, rolls of intestines gathering on the tiles. Done, he crawls back out, catching his breath. My USB stick is still in his hand.

'I have been here—' he swallows, hair dropping forwards '—for six months now and not once, not once has anyone found me. And then you show up and a fucking Cyclops springs onto the screen and a bomb flashes up with a whole heap of intelligence data.'

I try to focus on what he says, but my mind races, thoughts screeching round my brain, adding, subtracting. What does Switzerland and Geneva refer to? Why would the Project be connected to Black September?

'Well?' Chris says now.

I snatch the USB and turn. 'I am sorry. I may have put you in danger.'

He stares at me and, at first, I think he is going to leave, going to walk away from me and the chaos I have brought upon him. But then slowly, he does something that surprises me: he smiles and sighs.

'D'you think this is the first time I've been in trouble?'

'Oh.' I think. 'No.'

'Correct.' He turns, pulls one last cable from the wall then, snapping back the pictures of the old people from the wall, he clicks a button behind and a small metal safe door swings out to show a bunch of passports, money, keys and cell phones. 'Handy how the past,' he says tapping the photographs hanging mid-air, 'can mask the present.'

He wrenches a duffel bag from a cupboard, fills it with the safe belongings then turns and checks his watch.

'Look, I don't know what you're mixed up in, but I like you, I like Balthus, and he'll be on his way now and I promised him I'd get you to him. You ready to go before whoever you're involved with finds us?'

I glance round the room, at the ripped computer, at the screen where Black Eyes was. 'Yes.'

'Good. Then let's go.'

I gather the SIM card, my USB stick and my notebook and go to walk, but find that I don't move. For a moment I can't, as all the information I've just seen, all the events of the last ten hours swamp my mind. I don't know who I am. I suddenly want to scream. I want to run back to my villa and hide away forever and never deal with anything or anyone again.

Chris stops, looks to me. 'You okay?' He dips his head, smiling again, creases crinkling at his eyes. 'You ready?'

I look at him, at his eye crinkles. Balthus knows him, I tell myself, he trusts him and his smile is good. I know it is good.

'I am ready to go,' I say after a moment, gripping the strap of my rucksack.

'Great.'

We walk through the back of the house past a broken blue

door and two rusty metal tubs of water to a small black car
with splashy tyres parked in the shaded alleyway, hidden from
the sun. We both get in, Chris driving, and pull away fast.

The dust on the road flies up as the car speeds along a
warren of clay-coloured roads that wind up towards the first
stage of the huge, jagged mountain range beyond. My mind,
as we drive, turns to facts and data and to the people I know. If
the Project are flashing up on a screen in a house in Montserrat,
then they could be anywhere. They could be with anyone.

Glancing to Chris and watching the route we are taking,
I pull out my cell and text my brother and check that he and
Mama are safe.

Undisclosed confinement location—present day

The timer ticks in the room and my panic rises. I look to my
brother. His face is bathed in one streak of light and when the
bulb above his head swings, his cheeks sink in and out of a
blackness.

'Turn off the timer,' I say, but my brother does not move.
'The Project are not who they say they are. They lied to Mama
when I was young and they are lying to you now. Whatever
they are making you do, stop.'

Ramon remains solid and does not shift, not even one inch
as, drop by drop, the liquid in the drip begins to work its way
towards the needle in my arm.

Panic floods me. It will trip soon. 'Ramon—take it out.
Now.'

'They voted you Worst Girl in School. Do you remember
that?'

'What?' Drop, drop. 'Why are you saying this?' The timer is ticking faster now. I count the seconds as they speed by and know that at any moment the drug will enter my veins. 'Take out the needle. I know they will be watching us, you, but you need to do it.'

'You cried,' he says now, as if I had never spoken. 'I know you remember. You cried all night in your room after they voted you worst girl. I slept on the floor because you didn't want to be alone. Five years after Papa died and you still struggled without him.'

His words make me hold my breath. School. It was like a living nightmare. I never understood the rules and, as I got older, the teenage games everyone seemed to be play-ing, especially the girls, baffled me, especially the way they would be with boys. Why couldn't you say someone looked awful if they did, in fact, look awful? Especially if they asked you?

I feel suddenly tired, weak and when I speak, my voice is cracked. 'The boys used to laugh at me. You used to laugh, too.'

He stays silent. For a moment, his chest remains so still that it appears as if he is not breathing at all, even though the air around us is damp and loaded. When he does eventually talk, his voice is chalky, ripped. 'I didn't know what to do.'

I say nothing. The timer ticks.

'You have no idea what it was like.' He sucks in a breath. 'Everyone thought you were odd. The girls laughed at me when you did your odd things and I couldn't even get a girl-friend because of it.'

'That does not make logical sense.'

'That's what I mean!' He tuts. 'You were my sister, but oh my God, it was a pain having you trailing after me.'

He briefly shuts his eyes and confusion swamps me. I don't understand what my brother is talking about or why it exhausts me; trying to figure it out, trying to decipher the social connections, it wears me out. I lick my lips. They are dry. A heat is rising in the room and it feels as if it is closing in on us, as if the walls are surging forward almost, the only space there is the immediate air around our faces. When Ramon finally opens his eyes and speaks, it is about a different subject.

'We are in a city, do you know that?'

I look round. Is he lying? I try to detect clues. There is a window, but it is thick and heavy with a type of black soot and when I track the frame, I cannot see any latch or distinct opening, as if the entire thing has been fused shut some time ago.

'The Project does not have any facilities based in cities.' But then I stop, because, in truth, I cannot be completely certain of this statement. I cannot be completely certain of anything.

My eyes land on the brickwork ahead. 'The walls are padded, Ramon,' I say. 'Why?'

'For your own safety.'

A fear, right then, deep, shakes within me. What have they told him to make him believe this is all acceptable, that this is the right thing to do?

'Okay,' he says, 'so it's time for you to have your medicine now.' He goes to leave.

'No!' Panic hits and I thrust forward but am slammed to a halt by the ropes. 'Wait!'

He stops, turns and as I catch the side of his face unshadowed by the weak light, for a fleeting second I see the face of the brother I knew when I went to school: skin soft and unmarked, no stubble or sharp bones, just plump red cheeks, wide eyes and a deep summer outdoor tan. A small lump swells in my throat.

'Why are you keeping me here?' I say. 'Why are you not freeing me from them? Freeing us?' My voice is quiet, broken.

Ramon hangs his head and when he raises it again, when he lifts his face to mine, his eyes are wet and his mouth is downturned.

'Because I love you.'

The timer clicks and with one, loud rush, the drug enters my blood.

Chapter 16

The woman code named Raven floats into view beneath the sunlight. I observe her face. Her eyes are brown, wide like saucers, and when she flickers her lids her lashes are as fine and as exquisite as threads of silk. The Middle-Eastern sun beats down and bakes our skin covered in cloth and gauze.

She ushers me to move. The woman's hand, now, beckons me, fingers thin, nails round and smooth at the edges, long, elegant bones on the end of her palms gliding towards me, and, as they do, something happens: I begin to float along, an apparition, a ghost.

We move together, simultaneously, the woman and I. She is talking to me fast in Arabic and to my surprise I understand her, even talk back to her, as if it was a language I was born with, have always spoken. We are discussing an operation, a target. She has stopped, the woman, now, here, the desert hot, sticky, sweet honey drops of heat sliding down our skin, and as I look around, there is only a sprinkle of uninhabited sand-coloured buildings nearby. Taking out a computer tablet, the woman shows me something and I peer in. It is a series of algorithms, of equations and numbers, and I understand it all, every single part of it, yet there is a connection missing, a link, but I cannot place what.

The woman slips her hand into a pocket and unfolds a piece of paper. She points to it, holds it near me and I see a code, a complex code on how to hack a social network website. She speaks now again, fast, and mentions the CIA. She talks about how difficult their system is to penetrate but not impossible, that who I am, my age, is vital, and I listen, yet not because I want to join in her hacking, but for another reason, a reason that somewhere inside me feels infected, wrong. I watch myself as I reach into my pocket and switch something on. What? A phone? A tracker? It is unclear, but what I am certain of is that this woman knows me, trusts me, yet I know in my head that I will betray her. The feeling is so strong, so powerful, that a pain radiates across my chest, and, while I try to fight it, an unfamiliar part of my brain tells me that it is the right action to take, the only action—that it is for the greater good. For the Project, I am going to betray her. I am going to hurt her.

I am going to kill her.

Static appears and the mirage of the woman escapes to the sky. She hovers, a bright firefly, beautiful, mesmerising, impossible to catch, and I try to grab the mirage, attempt to keep it locked in my consciousness, stowed away, but it flutters off, flapping left and right until its wings rotate and it disappears from my view entirely.

I wake up and intake a sharp breath.

'Hey. Hey. Are you okay?'

I jump. Chris is to my left, driving. I had forgotten he was here at all. The sky has become darker, sudden deep grey swirls of clouds threatening to open.

'Where are we?' I rub my eyes. The memory of Raven lingers, a warm fug of freshly tumble-dried linen.

'We're on the road way of Montserrat now. You've been out of it a while. You okay?'

'I...' I shake my head and pull myself up straight. 'How long have we been driving for?'

He shrugs. 'Dunno. Twenty-five, maybe thirty minutes?'

I rub my shoulders where they have cemented stiff from a lolling head. I fell asleep. I must have been more tired than I realised. I smooth my hands through my hair, think about the woman I have just seen. Was it just a dream? Was what I felt real, something that has actually happened? I reach for my rucksack on the back seat, scrambling for my notepad—I have to write it all down.

I scratch pen to paper and record everything I have just recollected and glance over to Chris. 'Has anyone followed us?'

'Huh? Oh. No.' His eyes remain on the road. 'It's hot. There's some water in there if you want it.'

I look to where he's pointing where a plastic bottle in a shelf under the dashboard peeks out. I set down my pen, unscrew the cap and gulp down all the liquid, Chris throwing me sideways glances the entire time.

'It's all right. I didn't want any.'

I drain the bottle, wipe my chin with the back of my hand. 'Okay.'

We drive. The clouds have swallowed the sun now,

transforming the sky to a thundering wash of orange and grey that gathers in a soup of broken marble in the air, thick and looming, and when I breathe in I smell a faint aroma of peat and vegetation and burnt tarmac. I wind down the window a little and the outside ushers in through the gap. Rosemary, now, saturates the air, pungent and fragrant, its delicate fragrance mixed with the heavier, muggy odour of rich, rocky moss. I feel a warm breeze on my face and when I look up, the turrets of the mountain bear down, raised and rigid at the summit of the gods. A world ruled by a nature we will never truly understand. I give the turrets one more look then, tuning back to my notebook, finish writing what I recall about my dream.

'What music do you like?'

I look up. 'Why are you asking me that?' I close my notebook and slip it into my rucksack.

'Just thought it'd be nice to talk, you know.' He shrugs. 'Break up the journey.'

I stare at him. 'Oh. Okay.'

'Well?'

'Well what?'

'What sort of music do you like?'

I hesitate. Is this a trick question? There was no intonation in his voice that I traced, but I am never entirely certain. 'Classical,' I finally say. 'I like classical music.'

'Oh yeah? Cool. You like Mozart?'

'Mozart died on 5th December, 1791. I never knew Mozart, therefore I cannot say whether I like him or not. I do, however, appreciate his music.'

Chris's mouth is hanging open. I take my gaze to the

mountains shooting past, satisfied that I have given a sufficiently social answer and the conversation is closed.

'Aren't you going to ask me what music I like?'

So we are doing this. I clench my jaw. 'Why?'

'Because that's what people do.'

I face him and try very hard to make an effort. 'Christopher, what sort of music do you like?'

'It's Chris. Just Chris.' He smiles and for some reason I think of Goofy in the Disney movies my brother used to put on for me the year Papa died. 'Grunge,' he says. 'Nirvana, that kind of thing, you know, Kurt Cobain.'

He looks at me. Is he awaiting a response? 'Okay,' I decide to say.

It must satisfy him, possibly, because he keeps talking. 'And don't tell anyone, but I rather like Taylor Swift.'

'Do you know her?'

'What?'

He says *what* a lot.

'No.' He laughs, eyes flitting between me and the road. 'No. I mean, I like her music. You know, *Red*, *Twenty-Two*, *Shake It Off*. You've…you've heard of them, the songs, right?'

'No.'

'What? You must be, like, the only person on the planet who hasn't heard of her. What, you don't even know *Shake It Off*?'

'No.' I can feel my irritation rising and start to tap my foot when Chris does something unexpected and strange: he sings.

'This is *Shake It Off*,' he says, in between relaying to me what I assume is the musical song he refers to. I watch him closely. He appears to be enjoying himself, I think, smiling, his head shaking and bobbing so much that I am surprised he can keep track of the road at all.

'Your singing and movement is endangering the car and therefore us,' I say.

He ceases singing and I think that is the end of it, but he simply continues to talk. A vague tiredness at the effort required of me in order to cope with the interaction starts to form in the base of my body and work its way to my head.

'See,' he says now, shifting down a gear as we swerve round a sharp bend that ascends us further up the mountain and into the looming clouds. 'What I love about Taylor is that she's a country singer at heart. I love a bit of country. I mean sure—' another gear drop as we rise '—I like grunge and stuff, but country?' He whistles. 'That's where it's at. Like, it gets to your heart and soul, you know?'

I don't—at all—but, unsure why, I reply yes.

'My mama loved country.' He trails off and, for a moment, I think I can see tears in his eyes. I think of my own mama back in Madrid and wonder if she is safe.

Chris drives for twenty perhaps thirty seconds more and we sit in silence. For me, it helps. The exhaustion that was before bubbling from having to converse is subsiding slightly now and the headache at the front of my forehead is slowly fading away. I keep the window down and let the air fan my face, all the while keeping my eyes directed not just to the front of the car, but also to the back so if anyone is following us, I will know.

'I told you I was from Idaho,' Chris suddenly says after he negotiates a sharp left bend.

I don't reply. Initially, I am unsure what reaction he expects me to give, but then, after a second, he talks on and I begin to realise, with relief, that when Chris chats, he doesn't always expect a response.

'Ma and Pa are from Idaho, too. Pa still lives there. Remarried.' He shakes his head. 'That's why I got into computers, you know? I hated his new wife. I was young and they had a new baby, and so—' he swallows, pushes back a stray hair '—I threw myself into the tech world and *voilà*!' He smiles. 'You got yours truly: a word class hacker.'

His knuckles are white on the steering wheel and when I observe him in more detail, I see his cheeks are streaked with rogue tears that leave dirty tracks on his sun-washed skin, and his hair slaps on his skull with sweat that trickles down his temples at anarchic angles

'What is your mother's name?' I ask.

'Huh?' He turns the car to the right. 'It's... It *was* Janet.'

'Janet. The name Janet is the feminine form of John. It means *God has been gracious*.'

'Okay...'

'You father's name—what is that?'

'What?'

'You said *what* again.'

'Oh, right, yeah, sorry. It's...' He clears his throat. 'Jack. My pa's name is Jack.'

'The meaning of the name Jack originates from Jakin, which is a medieval diminutive of the name John. In the middle ages, it was a slang name that meant *man*. Jack is considered now an American baby name. Do you have siblings?'

'Hey?

'Do you have siblings?'

'Er, yeah. Sister...'

'Name?'

He lets out a small trickle of a laugh. 'Sarah. Her name's Sarah.'

'Sarah means *princess*. In the bible, she was the wife of Abraham. What are your hobbies?'

He laughs again. 'What is this? An interview?'

'Yes.'

The laugh drops. 'Oh. Oh, right.'

'I like you,' I say. 'I am interviewing you to see if we are compatible.'

'Compatible?' There is a curve in the road up ahead that creates a blind spot in the rear-view mirror.

I look to Chris. 'Compatible. Yes. That is what I said.'

'I know, I know, but...' He shrugs. 'Okay. You want to know my hobbies? I like computer games. Dungeons and Dragons. That's my hobby. As well as hacking.'

'And listening to Taylor Swift.'

He laughs out loud now. Shards of spit from his mouth pepper the window, but there are tears in his eyes.

I become concerned. 'You are crying. Are you sad? Have I upset you?'

'Wh-No. No, you're just...' He sighs, slaps back into his seat. 'You're just so funny.'

'I am?'

He nods. 'With a capital *F*.'

We sit in silence and I am suddenly very aware of the heat from his body. It is warm, hot like coals on a fire and I begin to wonder if I have said the right thing, if I have talked as I should. If I have been adequately friendly.

'Okay,' Chris says after several seconds have passed, 'since you got to interview me, how about you?' He shifts to face me. 'I like you, so what can you tell me about you? You got family?'

'Yes. Everyone does.'

'Brothers? Sisters?'

I pause. 'I have a brother.'

'That's cool.'

'Cool.' I try the word out as if it were a hat or a new jacket. 'Yes. Cool.'

The road behind us goes straight, restoring my view of the rear road where dark clouds bulge with rain.

'And are you close, you and your brother?' he asks.

'Close?'

'You know, do you love each other?'

'He loves me very much,' I say. I stop, not wanting to continue, unsure what to say, then remember Balthus's advice to me and so I carry on.

'When my papa died I was ten. My brother's name is Ramon, which means *protector*. He looked after me after the death of my papa.'

'Your papa was…he was nice?'

'Yes,' I say. 'He was nice. And when I was eight and I wet my pants in my bedroom because I wouldn't stop writing about composers and medical procedures, Papa cleaned me up and hid all the dirty linen from my mama and the housekeeper. My brother Ramon often had to do the same for me. Sometimes, because the girls at school wouldn't talk to me, my brother used to put on Disney movies and dress up as Mickey Mouse. I used to get depressed—at least twice a month—because no one would talk to me and because I couldn't understand how to talk to them. Sometimes I would forget moments of time entirely. I recorded two hundred episodes of complete memory lapse between the ages of eleven and twenty-one alone.' I stop, satisfied that Chris now has information to process, facts for his interview of friendship.

But Chris just stares at me. Not just glances, but stares straight out, eyes not on the road at all, but fixed on me as if he were blinking into a pool or a lake.

'I want you to stop looking at me now,' I say, suddenly nervous. 'Please.'

'Huh? What? Oh, yes, of course. Sorry. Sorry.'

We take another blind bend and the car swerves, and I slide in the seat. I dart upwards, check the mirrors. 'What was that?'

'Nothing. Just a rock on the road. I think.' He scratches his scalp. 'Sorry, I should have been watching, but you...'

As he trails off, I crane my head backwards and scan the tracks behind. The rock is there, the one Chris mentioned, about sixty centimetres in diameter, but there is something else too. 'Slow down.'

'What? Why?'

There is a black van and it's getting nearer. Adrenaline shoots straight through me, head to toe. I slip back into my seat. 'Someone is following us.'

Chris leans in to the rear-view mirror. 'Where?'

'Is there another route to where we're travelling?'

'Shit. Yes. No. I think so.'

I glance behind us. The van is approaching faster now. 'Quick. Do you know another route?'

'What? Fuck. Yes, yes.' He jerks the steering wheel to the left and we veer down a side road, dirt flying through the air like shrapnel.

He slams his foot on the gas pedal and the car screeches away. The van starts to disappear, slow at first then faster until it is barely there at all. My fingers grip the seat as the air whips in through the open windows sending Chris's hair flapping in the wind.

I allow my shoulders to soften a little. 'This road will take us to Balthus still, yes?'

'Yes. Yes.' He gulps and when he grips the wheel, the veins in his forearms bulge. 'Jesus, that was scary.' Sweat steams from his brow. 'Who in the hell are you?'

'I told you. I am Dr Maria Martinez. I know the governor—'

'Okay! Please. It's just that I'm not used to this and you are so calm and…' There is a loud crack. 'Fuck!'

A small hole has appeared in the rear windscreen and I jerk my head towards it.

Chris has been shot.

Chapter 17

Montserrat mountain road, nr. Barcelona.
25 hours and 45 minutes to confinement

'Oh, God. It hurts, it hurts. It fucking hurts!'

I check the mirror. There are no vehicles in the background, there are no other cars on the road and, even though I scour the viewpoint for any sign of the black vehicle, there is still no evidence of it anywhere.

Chris cries out. I whip round to him now and crane my head to get a view of his injury. He is bleeding from his right shoulder.

'Stop the car.'

'What? No.' His hand slips from the wheel and we slide across the road. The car skids, twirling round and round and at first I think we will stop, Chris screaming, but then, on the final turn, the vehicle veers to the right and the car lurches forward and the entire bonnet nose dives forward and we skid to a halt.

'Oh, Jesus!'

I ignore Chris and peer over through the windscreen and stop dead.

The entire car is dipping forward and below it is a sharp dip of more than one thousand metres into the valley below.

'Fuck!' Chris shouts. 'Fuck!'

'Shouting will not help,' I say. I inch my torso forwards, instinctively checking for the angle and pivot point of the car as it rests on the road's edge, while outside starlings flit and fly and goats watch from a hilltop ahead.

'What are you doing?' His voice is high, screeching.

I turn to him. 'We are currently stuck on what is—' I glance through the window to confirm my suspicion '—a metal barrier. That is the only thing preventing us from falling down the mountain.'

'What? Oh, fucking great.'

'You said *what* again, and no, this is not fucking great. This is a difficult situation. So, I want you to lean forwards.'

'What? Are you crazy?'

'No. I am not. I simply have Asperger's. Lean forward.'

Rocks trickle past the car and topple by the tyres, clattering down the mountainside and into the valley far below.

Chris begins to hyperventilate.

'You are panicking,' I say. 'You need to inhale big, deep breaths.'

His eyes go wide at me, but he does it, he starts to gulp at a steadier rate.

'Good. Now—' I look at the barrier; it is stable but buckled '—I am going to count to three. On three I want you to lean forwards then, when I say so, I want you to lean back in your seat as hard as you can.' I look at him. 'Do you understand?'

He nods, breathing hard. Satisfied he comprehends what is required of him, I unbuckle my belt and begin to clamber over my seat and into the back of the car. It lurches. A loud crack echoes in the air and by the side rubble and dust tumble over into the sky.

'Shit,' Chris says. 'Shit, shit, shit!'

I make it into the back and slide round so I am facing forwards. My heart rockets but I feel calm and in control, training from the past kicking in now to the present. I check the front screen—the bonnet is teetering now, the barrier bent outwards by a few more degrees, causing the trajectory of the car to shift.

'We're going to fall!'

'Negative,' I say. 'By initial calculation, we will not fall immediately. If we remain as we are it will be one, perhaps two minutes before we completely slide over the mountain.'

'Oh holy crap!'

I scan every corner of the car and do my final sums. It can work—but only if Chris complies. 'I am going to count now—are you ready?'

He nods. 'Uh-huh. Mmmmm.'

I glance to his arm. It is bleeding rather a lot, red staining his T-shirt and the cloth of the car seat. I look forward. The sun strains up from behind black clouds, a weak orange glow spotlighting our crisis.

'I am going to count now.'

He nods and grits his teeth.

'One.'

The car lurches. Chris swears.

'Two.' A bird of prey sweeps in the sky, passing a long shadow over us.

'Three! Lean back!'

Chris cries out, slamming himself as hard as he can into his seat, the force of it juddering the vehicle. As he does, I throw the whole weight of my body into the very rear crease of the car where the back screen sits cracked and broken, ramming my arms and hips and legs into the area so every single ounce of me is weighted in one point.

The car begins to rock.

'Do…do I stay back?' Chris yells.

'Yes. Remain where you are putting on as much pressure as you can.'

'Okay!'

The car keeps moving. I glance outwards to the side and see the barrier begin to bend more, collapsing slightly outwards.

'Is it working?'

I shove my shoulder into the corner. 'Yes. Stay in the seat.'

Manoeuvring my elbow now, I start to sway, to rock my body in the small space. At first, nothing really moves, the entire metal casing of the vehicle suspended, creaking and groaning as it seesaws between the wide open air beyond and the road below. I do the calculation in my head—if we remain like this, we will begin to tip back over the edge, but we need momentum.

'I want you to lean forward again then back once more.'

'What?'

'You said what again—'

'I know what I said!'

I go quiet at Chris's raised voice, the sound ringing in my brain and mixing with the creaking and clattering of the car.

'I…I'm sorry,' he says, exhaling. 'I… Sorry. I'm just…I'm just scared.'

I look up at him and press my lips together. 'I don't like it when people shout at me.'

'I'm sorry. Just…just tell me what to do. You want me to lean forwards again, right?'

'Yes,' I say after a second, regaining my composure. 'I need you to do exactly as we did before so the car will tip back to the road.'

He gulps. 'Got it.'

I look forwards. 'One. Two.' The car swings a little. 'Three!'

Slam! This time it works. Chris's back rams into the seat and my body and arms are raised a little higher than last time as, between us, we topple the car backwards, tipping, swaying until there is an almighty slam as the boot and back wheels hit the road.

'Whooo!' Chris smiles for the first time. 'Fuck!'

'Put the car in gear,' I say, 'manoeuvre it round, back to the road.'

'Okay!'

He does as I ask, gear in place as his hands grip the wheel now and, holding it hard, spins it through his fingers round and round until, gradually, the car veers to the left then right and, finally, to a safe position on the road.

'Holy fucking Jesus!'

I clamber back over the seat and slam myself down, immediately checking that my rucksack and notebook and belongings are safe.

'Stop the car,' I say.

'Roger that.'

'Who is Roger?'

This time he slams on the brakes and we come to an abrupt halt, our bodies flying forwards then smashing back.

'Jesus, that was close,' Chris says, exhaling hard and heavy. He wipes his forehead. 'I mean, fuck. I could see right over the edge and, God my arm is killing me and—' I undo my seatbelt '—the road was like, there one minute, gone the next. Shit, is that van we saw anywhere near? I mean—'

I climb onto Chris

'Hey! What the fuck are you doing?'

I straddle him and, ripping off his sleeve, check his wound. 'I am a doctor. You have been shot. I can help you.'

He mutters something, but my focus is fixed on his arm. I expect, from his reaction, from his previous cries of pain, to see a deep, serious wound, but it is simply grazed, the outer skin layer peppered with glass shrapnel with no bullet entry at all. I let my shoulders relax a little and exhale. 'You've not been shot. Your outer epidermis is grazed.'

'Huh?' He looks to his arm.

I immediately drop to the floor, search for the bullet, finding it lodged in the footwell by Chris's trainer.

'Hey!' he says.

I pick up the bullet and, clambering back over him, drag out my notebook and check my data. I locate the make of the bullet in three seconds, holding it in the air into the fading sunshine as I understand completely what I am looking at: it is Project ammunition. I have used it before, I just do not know when or where.

Chris leans over. 'Hey—your drawing is the same as the bullet. How the fuck is that possible?'

I slap my notebook shut and, pocketing the bullet, I slip

over a protesting Chris, open his car door and jump to the ground. I am immediately hit by the heavy, rain-threatened air. It is warm on my skin, a soothing silk after the rough chaos, the wet, pungent aroma of vegetation from the mountains hitting my nose, calming me, for some reason, and, even though I know I shouldn't, that we could be followed again, I allow my body a rest for three seconds against the bonnet of the dusty car as I close my eyes, images of the Project, of Dr Andersson and my ransacked villa with SIM cards and iron bars whipping through my mind. In the distance, in the earthly, majestic presence of the Montserrat mountain, wild goats snort and mew, bats click and squeal, geckos squawk and claw. Life, carrying on, oblivious.

I reach into the car and start to pull Chris out. 'I will drive.'

'Hey! Maria, what are you doing?'

I pause. This is the first time he has used my name since we met. 'I am helping you. You are injured. I will drive.'

'Yeah, but, you don't have to drag me. I can get myself out.'

I step back, uncertain at what to do. He is injured, he can't drive, I can. It is logical, simple, so why did he push me away?

'You are hurt,' I say after a moment. 'I am...I am trying to help.'

He blows out air. 'Yeah, well,' he says, dusting himself down, 'dragging me out of the damn car without actually saying a word to me isn't my idea of helping. You're supposed to ask first.'

'Oh.' I remain very still, unsure what to do. Think. Patricia told me, in prison, that people like to hear the word please. Could that work now? I make myself look at Chris. 'Christopher—' I pause. 'Chris. Please would you vacate the driver's seat so I can drive? I would be a better driver than you at this current moment given your minor injury and mild shock from our near death fall. Plus, I am faster.'

At first, I do not believe he will move, so solid is his body in the seat. But then he does the Goofy stare and smile combination again, frowns and tuts, muttering, 'For fuck sake,' under his breath, and he jumps down from the car.

I slip into the driver's seat as Chris takes the opposite side, go to switch on the ignition then pause, the keys left dangling mid-air. 'I have trouble conversing with people.'

He looks at me. 'You don't say.' His hair slips into his eyes and I can feel the gentle warmth of him, hear the one-two rhythm of his breath.

'So,' he says after a moment, 'it's just, you know, a shrapnel wound in my shoulder?'

'Correct. The wound requires cleaning, but it is not serious.'

'And you can drive fast?'

'Of course.'

'Good.' He slips on his seatbelt. 'Because I think the van that was following us is back.'

I jerk my eyes to the mirror. There is a black vehicle approaching at reasonable speed on the horizon. Slamming my foot flat on the gas pedal, I spin the car round and pull away fast.

The deep serrated mountain range around us remains unmoved, watching.

Chapter 18

Undisclosed confinement location—present day

When I awake, all I see is darkness.

Slowly, the room sways into focus and as I blink, the bulb above my head swings from the ceiling. I smack my lips together and feel a dry, crumbling sediment around the edges of them, saliva crackled from the effects of the drugs. At first woozy, I forget where I am and then, coming to a little, remember my situation and sit up with a start.

'Ramon?'

'You were out for a while.'

I squint to see my brother, the light above casting a pale, sallow glow on his skin. He is sitting on a crate one and a half metres in front of me. His legs are crossed and his arms are folded, and by his side sits a navy blue box with gold edging that, when the yellow stream passes over it, glows in the dark. I look behind him. The steps to the exit stretch out in the shadows.

'Untie me,' I croak.

He bends in then crouches forward. I immediately recoil.

'Hey, hey, it's okay, it's okay.' He holds up a hand, in it a plastic bottle. 'I just have some water.'

I stay lodged backwards as gradually my sight drifts downwards. In his hand I can just see the outline of a clear plastic bottle and cup. He takes the cup, unscrews the bottle cap and, tipping his head to the left, pours some liquid and raises it to my lips. 'Drink—you'll feel better.'

I let Ramon put the cup to my lips and I sip. The liquid is cooling and I begin to gulp it down, water dribbling out of the corners of my mouth, down past my chin and onto my chest as the coolness of it all calms me where the drugs have raised my temperature.

The cup drained, Ramon moves back, drags the crate nearer to where I am and, reaching to his side, switches on a torch. A shaft of bright, white light instantly beams into the room, but my eyes are unused to it and I blink over and over, desperate to lift my hand to shield my eyes.

'Do you feel better now?'

'The light is too much for me,' I manage to say.

'Oh, of course. I forgot—sorry.'

He angles the torch to the left, uncrosses his legs and shifts in his seat. The rope on my wrists digs into me and there is a sickness in my stomach as the stench of mould takes hold.

'You were talking in your sleep,' he says.

'I was not asleep. I was being drugged.'

He goes quiet. After a while, he says, 'Do you remember how you used to run to me when you had a bad dream?'

'Yes.'

'Papa used to help you.'

'Ramon,' I say, 'have the Project said they will hurt you if you don't sit with me like this? Have they said they will hurt you if you take the needle out of my arm?'

'What?' He drops his foot to the floor.

'The Project hurt people. They could hurt you. They could hurt Mama.'

'M, I don't know what you are talking about, but stop. No one is going to hurt Mama.' He leans forward. 'Especially not you. Not if I have anything to do with it.'

There's a ripple of confusion and something else: fear. 'What do you mean?'

He shakes his head. 'Drop it.'

'Drop what?'

'This. Here.' He exhales. 'All of it. Just stop.'

'Stop what?'

'All of it!' His voice ricochets in my head as Ramon rounds on me now and gets so close to my face that I can barely intake a breath without breathing in his own exhaled carbon dioxide.

'I love you, M, I do, but Jesus!' He steps back now and I gasp out a breath, gulping hard as my chest feels as if it will burst from the pressure, but before I can really inhale again, Ramon is back, tears streaking down his face.

'I'm sorry,' he says. 'M, I didn't mean to shout, it's just that...' He trails off. 'I am so worried about you. This—' he gestures to the room '—this is the only answer.'

'This...' I pause, my throat scratchy, the fear in my gut one ball of lead now. 'This is not the answer, Ramon. They are lying to you. The Project lie. They—'

'Ssshh. Do you know this song?' And then, out of the blue,

he begins to sing. '*At the gate of heaven little shoes they are selling...*'

A crackle of worry prickles all over me now as I realise what my brother is singing: it is the lullaby Papa used to sing to me when he was alive, the same lullaby I used to hear in my nightmares when I would wake up in a sweat after dreaming about the Project.

'*For the little bare-footed angels there dwelling...*'

My pulse starts to hammer into me and I raise my head and see my brother has closed his eyes, one hand rested on his chest, the other on the blue box beside him.

'*Slumber my baby, slumber my baby, slumber my baby, arru, arru.*'

He ceases singing and keeps his eyes shut. I am shaking. I dart my eyes around the room, seeing the door bolted and shut with a small metal touch-pad box, and feel my entire body ripple and crack as I watch my brother hum now into the black air a song that, aside from me, only Papa and Black Eyes knew.

'How do you know that song?' I say, forcing the words out from my brain to my mouth.

But he does not answer, instead hums into the air.

'Ramon, how do you know that song?'

He holds up one hand, palm side out and, opening his eyes so the liquid brown of them flashes in the white light of the torch that beams up in front of him, he ceases humming and places one hand on the box beside him and opens the lid.

'I know it from your journal.'

Montserrat mountain road, nr. Barcelona.
25 hours and 33 minutes to confinement

I concentrate on the road. It is long, winding and, to the side trees stoop, buckled by the edge, half-crumbled buildings lying unwanted and forgotten in the dirt. Three minutes and thirteen seconds have passed and the van is still there, cruising at a normal pace behind us.

'Do you think they are actually following us?' Chris says.

I look, check. 'I cannot say with certainty.'

'So, let me get this right, this Project has been around for years and you only found out about it with Balthus when you were in prison?'

Chris has been questioning me about the Project and I have found myself telling him some of what I know. I do not know why, exactly. Perhaps, despite myself, I trust him. Knowing Balthus recommends him, for me, is an essential reassurance, but it is more than that—I like him, this Chris, and it makes me feel as if I can talk to him, that feeling, that odd emotion of what? Of pleasure? Happiness? It's not something I am used to.

Chris falls quiet and clutches his shoulder and, when he loosens his grip, blood oozes between his fingers. I reach over, press his hand into the wound then glance into the rear mirror. The van is further in the distance now, moving at the same pace as we do, and no more. I calculate the time ratio in my head: the vehicle has slowed down.

'It would be optimum to create a diversion now,' I say, eyes still on the rear road.

'Really?' Chris turns, looks out the back mirror. 'They are still following, but shouldn't we just keep driving?'

'Negative. It is too risky.'

Ahead, there is a sign for a town two kilometres to the east. 'That place,' I say, pointing. 'Is it in the direction we need to go?'

Chris creaks forward. 'Yes. I think so.'

'You either know or you do not know.'

'All right. Jesus.' A pause. 'Yes, it's in the direction we need to go.'

I shoot one more glance to the rear then, flipping the car round, screech off towards the town. Chris's phone bleeps.

'Text,' he says, 'from Balthus. He's there now, waiting for us.'

Two minutes later, I park the car down a dark lane and peer out of the window. The town is quiet and in the distance is a solitary branch breezing through a deserted alleyway. A warren of small dust roads, has allowed me to drive and backtrack on myself so that, when I check, the black van is nowhere to be seen. I pull on the handbrake and scan the area, instinctively calculating in my head ratios and trajectories and routes of easy escape, but the place is empty. There are no people in view, instead just sand-coloured, shuttered buildings, baskets of scorched beige grass rolling in the breeze, crumpled empty Coke cans and, upon first count, sixty-seven discarded cigarette butts. There is one by the front of the car and on it I can see an imprint of red lipstick around the circumference, and I find myself wondering who would have smoked it, where they were headed. I imagine a party, perhaps, with friends, all of them laughing as they swayed, arms interlocked along the road, happy, chatting, years of friendship behind and ahead of them. I've seen people do this. From afar.

I unbuckle my belt and kick open the door. 'We need to go.'

'Where?'

I walk seven paces and analyse the area. Neon lights blink on a building seventy metres ahead, and I have to shield my eyes as my brain registers and logs every single bright flash. I point to it. 'What is that?'

Chris, clutching his arm, walks over. 'Hey? Oh, some sort of inn or club, I guess.'

My hand stays propped on my brow. 'If we head towards this club place, it could provide essential cover. It could help us slip out to another exit so we can locate another car perhaps, but there is a problem.'

'What?'

'Do you have any headphones in your car?'

'What?'

'Headphones. They are items placed in or over the ears, often used to listen to—'

'No, no, I know what they are, just wondering why you need them.'

I look over to the neon lights, to the club, glance to the lipstick-smeared cigarette butt. 'I have trouble with very loud noises, especially when they happen all at once,' I say after a moment.

Chris smiles and it reaches his eyes, the smile, creases fanning, but it isn't the goofy smile. This one is different, more downturned. 'I have some headphones in the trunk,' he says and goes to the car.

I watch him for a second and then my sight locks back onto the lipstick stain on the road.

'Oh, shit.'

My head snaps up, expecting Chris's swearing to indicate his wound to be worse, but instead he is staring down the road into the distance. I follow his eye line.

The van. It is back.

'We have to go,' I say. 'Now.'

This time, Chris does not protest. He jumps out of the car, throws me my rucksack and the headphones, and we start to run.

A gunshot sounds. Then another, the sound hammering a hole in my head.

'This way,' I yell, pointing to the neon lights, both of us ducking.

One more gunshot cracks into the air. This time it flies past my head, clipping my ear and pain stings my skin, blood trickling down my neck.

'You okay?' Chris asks, but I do not reply. We negotiate a warren of rubbish bins, their height giving us good cover, and we reach the neon sign in under twenty seconds, stopping, panting for breath. A rat the size of my fist scurries past my feet.

I press my fingers to my ear and feel warm, sticky blood, but no bullet, just a nicked surface wound. Another shot shatters the air.

'What do we do?' Chris yells.

I look at the flashing neon sign, at the scrawled black paint of the club façade, a faint hum of music pumping from inside. It's going to be too loud for me, almost impossible, but it will provide cover, will scramble the trail of anyone following us. I grip the headphones tight and slide them into my ears.

'We are going inside.'

As we move, the rat halts, stands on its hind legs then, slapping all fours to the ground, it runs away beneath the bowels of the building.

Chapter 19

The club, once we are inside, is heaving with a sea of people
and it does not stop moving. The heat from the bodies is high
and I sweat and stand near the entrance door and find that
my feet won't work. The ear buds are rammed into my ears,
but even then the music, the deep rhythm of it penetrates my
drums and every time the beat bass hits, it vibrates through
the floor and shakes in my legs and bones.

My breathing becomes short. I try to focus, to fix my concentration on something, anything –my hands, the sensation
of the buds in my ears—but I can feel myself slipping away,
zoning out to deal with the chaos in my mind.

'Whoa,' Chris says, 'cool. They're playing Nirvana,
Lithium.' He stops. 'Hey? Hey, are you okay?'

But I cannot answer. Lights are flashing now in all different
primary colours of blue, green and red, creating secondary
beams of orange, purple, yellow and pink. There is intense
flashing of neon lights and I instantly zone out, incapable
now of making myself focus on anything, and Chris, when I

watch him, is speaking and I try to concentrate on what he is saying but my whole body and my entire head feel infiltrated and assaulted by the noise and the people and the bassline music so much that I struggle to determine the different sounds Chris's words make.

'Pull me away,' I shout to him.

He cups a hand to his ear. 'What?'

'I said pull me away. Pull me to the other side of this club, now.' I swallow. 'Please.'

He hesitates, a frown spreading on his forehead and then, finally, he grabs my arms and though I flinch at the touch, he drags me across the throng of people through the dance floor.

It is awful. Crowds of heads and bodies and arms dance and gather all around me without, it seems, any specific direction as to where they are going. It is all random, the movements of the people, the shouting and laughing and screeching setting off all the time around me like fireworks and, as Chris pulls me along, someone bumps into me, then another and another, and each time it makes me jump and I look to them, unsure as to why they would be touching me, the shock of the sensation temporarily forcing me to lose any flicker of focus I may have. And then I move again and I say to myself, *Get across the room. Get to the exit. Get away from the people firing guns*. I say it over and over, fixate on the verbal process, hoping it will be my thread line out, but the music beat is heavy and I lose the trace of my thought. Desperate as we move, jostled, I start reciting mathematical theory to give my mind even a tiny bit of order and numerical control until, finally, we reach the far exit where a metal bar shoots across and where the noise just slightly dissipates.

Chris comes to my side. 'Are you okay? You're murmuring.'

I try to focus and watch his lips move. The ear buds are still in and I take one out and try to slow down.

'I have never been to a club,' I say, gulping.

'I…right, right.' He pauses, glances round the room then looks back to me. 'Breathe, yeah? Do what you told me to do back when I was shot and breathe.'

I do as he says, feel the tightness in my chest lighten a little as the music in the club changes to a slower beat.

'Awesome!' Chris says, grinning. 'Taylor Swift! This one's called *Begin Again*. You like it? It's different from her other ones, cos this one's about hope, you know, not breaking up and stuff, and…'

Chris talks on as I blink and look round and see that, mercifully, the neon lights have faded to be replaced by lower, orange yellow glows that fall in soft puddles on the floor as couples now, men and women, women and women, men and men, they all stand two by two, their arms locked around one another's hips, swaying to the slow tune, to the chorus and words and gently sung melody, and I get a feeling, a sensation in my stomach of a knot, a knot that leaves a hole behind it that I want to fill but I don't know how.

Chris stops talking about Taylor Swift and tugs at my arm. I flinch and he pulls away.

'Why do people find this kind of environment gratifying?'

He shrugs. 'I dunno, it's…it's fun I guess.'

I look round. Fun. I consider the word. 'Fun,' I say, turning now to Chris.

He smiles. 'Yeah.' He pauses, makes eye contact and I force

my eyes to do the same, not allowing them to look down as they automatically tend to do, but instead direct them at Chris's face, then look away, then back again, trying to mirror what he is doing without it ending up in me staring at him for too long.

'Are…you all right?' he says as I am trying to copy what he does.

'What?'

'You said *what* again.' He grins and shrugs his shoulders. 'See? Fun.'

Ahead of us there is an exit and as Taylor Swift continues to sing, I shuffle past Chris, stop and observe the door. For a second, I switch from the door and watch from the muffled cocoon of the headphones the swell of arms and legs entangled on the dance floor, the smiles plastered to drenched twenty-something-year-old faces. And I think: Is this what it looks like, fun? Is this what I have missed?

Chris catches up.

'We are going out this way,' I tell him, pointing to the door that, from what I can deduce, should take medium force to prise open.

'This one? Isn't it wired?'

'Negative. There is no alarm or trigger, so therefore no alert can be generated, therefore keeping our cover safe.'

'What?'

I point to the door. 'We have to go through the exit.'

Chris leans in. 'What? Did you say you want me to open it?'

'No, I can do—'

'I'll do it. Don't you worry.' Stepping in front of me, he pulls at the handle, but nothing budges. Moving back, he smears sweat from his brow, and, sizing up the exit, he then proceeds to slam his body into the door, his torso lighting up an orange slow-dance glow as he travels forward. Yet, still the door remains shut.

'Ow.' Chris rubs his arm. 'Fuck.'

'It won't open,' he shouts as I barge past him. 'We need another way out.'

The music has increased in volume and I can feel myself beginning to zone out again. I have to get out of here.

'Move.'

Chris frowns. 'What?'

But a neon light flashes, just one, and, with the crowd ahead laughing now, shouting, the cacophony of voices rising, I don't want to spend a second longer in here. Taking a run up, I ram myself into the door, so hard, so desperate to escape that the exit, when I smash into it, flies open on the first go and I spill out into the fresh air, coughing as I catch my breath.

Chris runs out behind me, slamming the door shut. 'Fuck, you're strong!'

I catch my breath, relieved to be outside in the quiet, the music from the club now a low hum of beat that hits my feet on the floor but nothing else. Spitting out the stale air of the club to the road, I lift my head and immediately begin to scan the alleyway. It is dimly lit under the umbrella of dark clouds and weak sunshine, and when I breathe in I get old cigarette smoke, bitumen and distant damp vegetation.

I check the time. 'We need transport.'

'Oh. Right. Yeah.'

Turning to the right, I start to scour the road and spot a lone red car, small, Spanish-made, box-shape and sturdy. I stride over to it and find myself wondering who left it here. A young university student, perhaps, or a local waitress working the summer in Barcelona who's now on a trip home to see her boyfriend, catching up with old school friends, maybe. I find myself contemplating what that must be like, to be free to move without hiding, how nice that must be.

Chris catches up and as he looks around, I am already examining the vehicle. I have never, to my knowledge, broken into a car before, but it could be possible that I have done so whilst with the Project, whilst influenced by drugs or by something or someone. I think through what I need to do, and so deep in thought am I that, at first, I don't hear the click. It sounds again, and I jump, alert, but when I scan the car, I get a surprise: Chris is in the passenger seat.

'How did you break in?'

'I didn't,' he smiles, all teeth. 'The door was open. And look.' He holds out a palm. 'The keys were in the glove box.'

'Oh. Okay.'

'So let's hit the road, yeah? Go get Balthus. Don't want to run into, you know, those guns again.'

'Yes.' I glance up and down the road and check that all is clear. 'Yes. Where are we going? Our final destination—I do not know it as I thought it best I did not in case we were captured.'

'Huh? Oh, right. We're going to the monastery, to Montserrat Monastery. It's straight on—just take a left at the top then just keep following the road on up. It's only five or so minutes away.'

Slipping into the driver's seat, I take the keys, watch the mirrors and start the engine. I throw a sideways glance at

Chris. He is checking his shoulder wound and wincing and as I watch him, a strange thing happens: I smile.

He looks straight at me. I whip my head forwards, my features arranging themselves back into a frown.

'Um, Maria?'

'What?' I say, eyes ahead, not daring to look, adrenaline rushing into my bloodstream.

'You've still got my headphones on.'

'Oh.' I look down at myself. The wire is swinging in front of my abdomen, the bottom if it gathering in a circle in my lap.

Feeling my cheeks flush, I slip off the headphones, hand them to Chris and, wiping sweat from my face, kick in the clutch and start to drive away. Even though my eyes are focused on the road, I sense Chris staring at me then he leans his head back and closes his eyes.

In the mirror I see his face, see his chest rise and fall. I drive counting each breath and find the way it moves in time with my own gives me a strange sense of comfort.

Chapter 20

Ramon opens the lid of the blue box by his side and extracts something that I realise with a gasp is my journal from my childhood and teenage years. The cover is hard and black, the word *Journal* embossed in gold lettering on the front, and when Ramon handles it, his fingers sliding over the once-shiny casing, his lips touch two initials that sit tucked in the bottom right corner of the front page.

'Initial *M.M*,' Ramon says now, his eyes on the journal then rising, slowly, to me. 'It's in Papa's writing.'

I feel suddenly unsafe, vulnerable, but I cannot pinpoint why. I shift in the seat, the rope on my wrists and ankles digging into my skin so I can feel it against my bone. 'How did you get my journal?'

His hand glides over the cream pages as he opens the book and, when he glances upwards, his eyes are damp. 'It was at Mama's house.'

I blink in the semi-dark, thinking. He is right: I stored my journal along with others at Mama's before I left for England

and my secondment in the London hospital. So why can I recall that and not the events in the run-up to my arrival here?

I look over to Ramon where he sits now on the crate and try to understand what is happening. The torch he has brought shines bright over to the far wall and I want to look round, study what sits behind me, but, each time I move my neck, a sharp pain shoots from my shoulder right down to the base of my spine, and my muscles cry out to be relieved of the stress position that has been continuing now for a long time.

Beside me, the timer ticks. I track it, focusing on the ordered sound of it, getting some small relief from it, from the odd routine in the chaos the predictability of it provides. If I can determine the space between each dose of the drug I am being administered, I can perhaps determine what drug it is, but it will be hard. Many medicines are given at similarly consecutive doses, and the only hope I have is diagnosing which drug I believe the Project may have used.

Which drug my brother may have used.

'So,' Ramon says now, 'let's look through your journal.'

Panic flies up. 'No.'

He pauses, looks up. 'M, it's okay.' He turns to a page and lets his finger trace the words that I see, in the weak light, are mine, scribbled years ago when I tracked my thoughts every day, when I was trying to forge a record of what was happening to me, even though I could not fully remember it all. I start to get hot. I start to run through scenarios of possible negative outcomes and eventualities in my head as I imagine what events could happen if anyone reads my private thoughts. There is such a thing as too much information. That's why I don't like to look into people's eyes.

'Let's see,' Ramon says now, 'if this journal of yours will help you.' He breathes out. 'If it will help us all understand a little bit more about you.'

'Ramon, no.'

But, instead of halting, he turns one more page and as his fingers move, the timer beside me ticks and ahead a spider scurries along the soot-stone floor and disappears into a hole that the darkness swallows up in one, single bite.

Montserrat mountain, nr. Barcelona.
25 hours and 20 minutes to confinement

The clouds are swollen and black, the sun struggling to push past as we drive up the mountain to reach the abbey.

The car we have taken is old and the tyres splashy and so each time I take a turn on a bend in the road, we jostle inside the vehicle and I have to make myself focus on what we are doing, where we are going in order to stay calm.

I have not detected the black van since we began the last leg of our journey. Chris now checks the road, his head hanging out of the seemingly permanently rolled down window and as I watch him, I worry that, because we have stolen a car, we will be jailed.

'We must return the car,' I say, taking a left then a right as the route chicanes up to the mountain top.

Chris drags his head back into the car. 'What did you say?'

I repeat my sentence and he rakes his fingers through his hair where the wind has shaken it up.

'You're worried aren't you?'

I do not reply, but instead grip the steering wheel, not

wanting to contemplate prison and jail and ever being caught again.

'Look,' Chris says now, 'think of it as...borrowing. We are simply borrowing the car and we will return it. Okay?'

I think about this. 'Okay.'

The sun bursts out suddenly casting rays of struggling light onto the car bonnet, shrivelled petals of burnt orange scattering onto the trees by the roadside, onto the rocks and the old buildings and onto the birds that swing together in packs of pendulums across the marble sky.

I wind down the window and a breeze drifts in. The air is chilled with thick, damp moss and I shiver. As I do, Chris looks over to me but says nothing, and I find myself thinking that I am glad he can cope with my silence. Outside, bats click in the clouds, the ink-swirled sky streaked with their flying shadows and as we drive upwards near our final destination now, the serrated edges of the Montserrat mountain dominate the skyline, sharp, unforgiving blades slicing into the sky.

The breeze picks up to a wind, and goose pimples pop up all over my skin. 'I am cold.'

'I saw a blanket on the back seat,' he says. 'You want that?'

'Yes,' I say, then hesitate. 'Please.'

Chris secures the blanket on my lap as I continue to drive. I concentrate. The touch of his fingers on my legs, the smell of him is distracting, his odd, sugary baking mixture sweat blending with the damp, pungent vegetation of the outside air. Chris's hair flops to his eyes. I fight back the urge to brush it away.

When we arrive at Montserrat Monastery, the scalp of the sun peeks out from behind an army of dark clouds, throwing a deep pink glow over the terrain as if it had been dipped in a vat of candy,while behind us, the dust from the road sparkles a phosphoresce of light and colour that dances in the wind and swirls ropes of deep orange in the sky.

I release my foot a little on the gas and the vehicle slows.

'So,' Chris says, craning his head at the view, 'd'you know this area?'

I scan my data banks. 'Our destination is Santa Maria de Montserrat—it is a Benedictine abbey,' I say. 'The mountain it sits on is 1,236 metres above the valley. The monastery is forty-five kilometres from Barcelona and was founded in 1025 AD.'

From the corner of my eye, I see Chris's stare. 'You're like a human Google.'

'I am not.'

He smiles. 'Google.'

I steal a glance.

Pulling the steering wheel round, I inch the car forwards by a corner, edging through a small chicane until, curving the final bend, we see it: Montserrat Monastery. It rises into the horizon, looming ahead into view, an ancient, colossal, religious sanctuary of sand-coloured stone blocks and arches so high that even the bloated rain clouds behind cannot barge past.

I drive forward, staying slow, searching for a suitable place to park. 'Balthus said to meet here, yes?'

'Yeah, yeah,' Chris says nodding then, frowning, leans forward. 'Hang on a minute, is that..?'

I follow Chris's eye line and shriek. I slam on the brakes, slide the car against the abbey wall and, flinging open the car door, run out.

'Hey!' Chris shouts. 'Wait!'

But I ignore Chris's shout and instead sprint across the wide-open courtyard, stumbling as I run, scraping the heels of my palms against a low wall, the fabric of my jeans chaffing my skin, but I don't care because she is here. Balthus connected with her and brought her, and now she is safe.

I screech to a halt. There, just two metres from me now standing next to Balthus, is my friend. Relief, joy, happiness all rush up inside my head, the emotions coming fast, all at once and the only way I can let it out, the only way I can process it is to whoop and clap over and over, unable to stop the feelings from leaking, neurologically ill-equipped to know how to keep a lid on it all.

'Patricia!'

'Doc!' Patricia runs over. 'I thought I'd never see you again.'

The smile on my face is so wide, my cheeks ache. 'You are here! Are you safe? Why did you come?' My words tumble out so fast that my head starts to spin and I have to really concentrate on my breathing to slow down.

'You okay? You good? Doc, I couldn't stay away. I was so worried about you, and Balthus got in touch after everything that happened in London. He said Dr Andersson was after you.'

'The Project have not found you?'

'No.' She smiles. 'They've not been in touch at all.'

I keep my eyes wide open, not wanting to close them, scared that if I do, she may, like a magician's assistant, disappear and I will be without her again, without my guide. She looks the same as I remember her, the same long limbs, same giraffe neck, same skin the colour of milk with tattoos on her arms of a blackbird and the Virgin Mary, and when I sniff the air her familiar scent of warm baths, soft towels and talcum powder drifts back to me.

'You are not in prison,' I say.

'No.' Her shaven head glistens under the sun. 'They put me on parole.'

'Parole,' I say, trying out the word as if it were the first time. I sniff her again, the smell of her skin giving me an instant comfort I haven't felt in six months or more.

She raises her hand to mine and slowly, I do the same. They rise, our arms, inch after inch until, finally, our fingers fan out—one, two, three, four, five—and touch, our way of communicating, my safety net. We stand there smiling as I inhale her scent some more and I think of a tiny bird flying in the sky, and in my heart and head I feel elation, sheer elation. We remain like that, the two of us connected until, gradually I turn, vaguely aware of two other bodies close by.

'Erm, hello? Maria?' Someone clears their throat. My hand hovers in the air, touching my friend's, not wanting the moment to pass.

'Maria?'

I reluctantly drop my hand and turn and this time speak. 'Balthus.' I peer at him, inspecting his face and torso. 'You look a lot older.'

'And hello to you, too.' He smiles a wide smile with eye creases and I count an extra wrinkle on each side. It looks like Balthus, but now there are deeper blue circles under his eyes, and on his head a dark slick of oiled hair sits speckled now with growing grey sides, his skin as brown as an almond. His once taut, wide frame seems smaller now somehow, shrunken, but still large, and yet somehow he seems weaker, more fragile.

'These past few months have been hard, haven't they?' he says, the smile still affixed to his features.

'Yes,' I say.

'I miss Harry.'

'I miss him, too,' I find myself saying, wanting to say more, needing to, but not knowing how. The dusty courtyard breezes between us and a strange lump forms in my throat.

Balthus coughs then inhales. 'So, were you followed?'

Chris steps forward. 'Yes.'

Balthus's eyes go wide and he throws open his arms and laughs. 'Chris!'

Chris smiles and, stepping forward, greets Balthus with wide, open arms. The two men hug, slapping each other's backs, and I watch, curious at the exchange.

'I'm so glad you're okay,' Balthus says, pulling back. 'You got a nice tan there.'

'Ha, yeah. More than you, grandad.'

'Hey! Who are you calling grandad?' Balthus says, lightly punching Chris in the stomach, to which Chris actually appears to laugh. 'I've tanned pretty good thanks.'

I watch the exchange, not fully understanding it. Are they fighting? 'Are you angry with each other?'

Chris swivels round. 'What?'

I turn to Patricia for some reassurance then realise she does not know Chris, so I try to be social and do what I have seen others do and introduce him to her.

'Patricia, this is Chris. He is a hacker and has been convicted for such crimes. The USA government wanted to extradite him. He has a goofy smile, he likes Taylor Swift and he says *what* a lot.'

There. I step back, satisfied I have contributed to regular social conversation.

Chris stares at me and then shakes his head, bends forward and holds out a hand to Patricia. 'Hi. I'm Chris.'

She takes his hand, shakes it. 'Hiya. Patricia.'

I watch them—I should try to mirror their actions. So, I step forward towards Chris, hold out my hand and, taking hold of his, shake it. 'Hi.'

He smiles. 'Um, hi.' He nods his head. 'You…you do know we know each other already, right?'

I keep shaking. 'Of course.'

'Right.'

Patricia leans in. 'Er, Doc, you can stop shaking his hand now.'

'Oh.' I drop it and step back.

Balthus moves towards us. 'Thanks for helping us out, Chris. Maria, what happened when you were followed? Was it the Project or MI5?'

I inform him of everything that has happened to Chris and me since his villa in the village, and Balthus's eyes go wide.

'We'd best get inside then and out of sight in that case. The Abbot is an old family friend. He's agreed to let us stay here.' Balthus searches behind him. 'Ah, there he is.'

A figure looms into view ahead by the gaping mouth of the monastery, body cloaked in a thick dark fabric that flaps in the wind, as, on the ground beneath, a dust storm snaps at our feet.

'Do you think this is a good idea, staying here?' Chris says, frowning at the apparition ahead.

I look to him. 'Throughout history, the monastery has been regarded as a sanctuary for dissidents and political refugees—which is probably why Balthus has chosen it for us to hide in—and during the dictatorship of Franco, when many people hid in the abbey, over twenty monks were executed.'

'Oh.'

'Well, come on then,' Balthus urges. 'We can't be seen out here.'

We start to move but then Chris stops. 'Oh, wait.' He points to the stolen car. 'The keys,' he says to me, 'are they in the ignition?'

'Yes.'

He smiles. 'Then we have just borrowed it and now—' he runs over to the vehicle and, in the dust on the bonnet, writes something with his index finger '—we are returning it as politely as we can.'

I cock my head to the left and look as Chris stands back and walks over to us from the car. There on the bonnet in its sandstone vehicle dust is one word: Thanks.

Chris rejoins the group, delivers me an eye-creased smile and I find myself smiling back. Balthus, then checking we are all set, tells us to follow him forward. As I walk, securing my rucksack to my shoulder, I glance to Chris then to the ground ahead and notice that the circles of sand that before swirled in the breeze have now fallen still and all that moves where the wind once was is one lone cicada crawling in the dust as, above us, the clouds finally burst and the rain begins to fall.

Chapter 21

Ramon has my journal in his lap and while he holds it, the timer by my side ticks. I am nervous. I don't know how long it is until the next drug dose and even though I try to gain some control and trace the time that passes, it is hard because the air is thick and dark and my mind is distracted not only by all that is in this room, but by my journal and the fact that someone else is reading it.

'You have some days missing,' Ramon says, looking up from the page.

I do not reply. For me, it is too hard. Ramon is my brother but there is an alarm in my head that is telling me that to speak to him too much is dangerous, and yet that voice—I do not understand it. Days, the recording of their events, are missing from my journal because I was taken by the Project and given Versed when they were done, but if Ramon is being coerced by them, how can it be safe to talk to him?

'Papa loved the fact that you taught yourself the piano,' he says suddenly. He must be reading my notes written when I was thirteen, fourteen and those few years beyond when I played piano to hide from my feelings, from the confusion of death and life and growing up amid a world that made no sense.

'How did you do that?' Ramon says now. 'You just played the piano and you didn't even have lessons. I used to sneak in and listen to you when you didn't know I was there because you didn't like people to watch you. My friends used to laugh about you, call you weird. I hit one of them—did you know that?'

I shake my head, eyes down. Tick, tick, tick goes the timer.

'He called you weird, so I punched him there—' he points to his left cheek '—right on the bone…'

Ramon now says something else but I am distracted. The piano, the thought of it sparks something in me, sparks a recent memory and I try to place it, but the rope on my wrists digs into my skin and the timer rings loud in my head colliding, the two of them, to blast any focus I can gain far away.

'He loved you, Papa did,' Ramon continues. 'He loved the way you knew all the composers' names, all the details of their life. I did too—I still do. Who's that composer you liked the most?' He shakes his head then clicks his fingers. I flinch at the sharp sound. 'Erik Satie—that's it.'

I lift my head as a thought springs up. Erik Satie. Erik Satie… I say the composer's name in my head as, somewhere in my memory, in my short-term recollection, something begins to shift, to move in iceberg fashion from hidden moorings to float into view as, slowly, I begin to remember.

Erik Satie. The composer whose classical talent I admire. The composer whose musical piece, *Gymnopédie No 1*, Dr

Andersson played in her office when I was in Goldmouth prison in London during my murder conviction.

Ramon sighs. 'I play his pieces sometimes now, did you know that? Did you know I play piano now, too?'

But I barely hear him, because shards of images are beginning to come back to me as, bit by bit, the cloak slips down from my memory block and, for the first time since I awoke in this room, I remember an element of the events that led to here, to now.

I remember Dr Andersson being at my villa.

I remember killing her. I remember Chris, recall going to Chris's house and reciting his name, just like I recited the name, as I did when I was young, of Erik Satie. I remember being followed by a black van. I remember Balthus on my cell, remember his smile and his laughter when he saw me at the abbey, and, most of all, I remember seeing Patricia by his side, happy and safe, my hands clapping in the evening sun.

'M, are you okay?'

I jump at Ramon's voice and look at myself. My nails are digging into the wood on the chair, scratching into the groove of it as my brain registers the emotions of happiness and sadness and fear all at the same time.

'Take it easy, M.'

I think I nod at him, at my brother—I am unsure—but what I do know is that my mind is beginning to wake up. I have recalled some events, which means if I have remembered those, I may remember more, and what can trigger it is… I look up. It is my journal, it is the pages of my mind that sit now in my brother's lap which can awaken the events and facts hidden deep in my brain, locked away through the drug in my arm, events and facts that I need to know to help me get out of here. To help us both get out of here.

'Can you read more?' I say now.

'Really?' Ramon smiles. 'Of course!' He flicks the page. 'See, I told you it would help.'

'Yes,' I say, trying to keep my mind alight. 'It is helping.'

He begins to read aloud and I listen and I focus and as he speaks the words I wrote more than a decade ago, I will my mind to start recalling every single thing it ever can.

Monastery of Santa Maria de Montserrat, nr. Barcelona.
25 hours and 13 minutes to confinement

I am sitting by a long wooden table in a room that glows orange. We are in the bowels of the monastery. The walls are sand in colour and the air is chilled with a scent of incense, and when I look at the lamps on the wall, I count eight on the left and ten on the right. Inside each bulb is a flicker and even though it is not a flame, it resembles one and I cannot help but watch it, the movement and flow combined with the soft light hypnotising me into a semi-tranced state. I yawn. It has been a long time since I last slept and when I roll my shoulders, they feel tight and solid and ready to drop.

Chris works on a laptop in the corner of the room where he sits on a chair made of wood and red leather, and near him resides Balthus who is sipping water and watching Chris. Patricia is to my right, her hands in star shapes on the table so that each time I glance around, I catch sight of them, catch sight of her presence, and given the new room and space and scent of incense to process, it makes me feel calmer. We have told her now, Patricia, everything that has happened up until this point—the villa, what I found on the SIM card, the flashbacks I had, all of it. Chris, too, listened to the information and the entire time he did so, he looked at me and I felt a heat rise to my cheeks which spread to my feet and stomach.

The Abbot enters now and sets down water and wine at the table, and behind him a monk in brown hessian cloth carries a metal tray of bread and grapes. We eat and, for a while, no one speaks. Exhaustion appears to have taken over and as I lift my hands, I feel weary, aches and pains shooting through me, my brain firing, recording every murmur and bite and grind of the teeth made in the room, and each time the incense smell reaches my nose, my brain threatens to tip into overload mode.

Patricia leans in and moves her hand on the table towards mine. 'Doc, are you okay? You look pale.'

I spread my fingers towards hers and let them touch. The sensation sends tingles up my arm, rippling towards my shoulders and chest. I take a bite of bread and breathe a little easier.

'So,' she says, 'you're really going to try and find this Project facility you had the flashback about?'

'Yes.' I sip some wine, but not too much. Alcohol scrambles my ability to focus.

'Do you think it's a good idea?'

'Yes. They had a dossier on you all. They want to find you all. It has to end.'

She inhales. 'And this other file, the one from your flashback you recall from when you were at the Project—the woman in that said it had details on it that could damage the Project, but you don't know which facility it was at?'

'That is correct.'

She chews her lip. 'So, the SIM card Dr Andersson had didn't have anything on it to find this place?'

'It had a grid reference for Switzerland.'

'The one in Geneva—could that be where the facility is, do you think?'

I watch Chris tapping on the computer and talking to Balthus. 'Perhaps. We need to verify.'

'Doc, I'm not going to lie—if you go to the facility, if you try and find this file this woman from your flashback mentioned, you won't be safe.'

I pick up my water glass. 'I have never been safe. I was not even safe in prison.'

'Okay. True.' She pauses. 'So, it's a case of finding the file, finding out who else is involved, is that right?'

'Balthus says there could be others.'

She nods. 'The other subject numbers.'

'Yes. The Project will not stop. MI5 will not stop. They will not stop going after me and you and Mama and Ramon.'

'And so you have to end it.'

I break some bread in two. 'Yes.'

She sits for a moment and sips some wine. She takes a napkin from the plate and, scrunching it up, wipes her face. 'Doc, it's important you know that—' she glances to Chris and Balthus '—you're not on your own now. We can help you with this, yeah?'

The lamps drift gentle brushstrokes of orange and yellow across the room, and I look now at Chris. He hasn't stopped working on the laptop since we arrived and I don't know what he is doing.

'Do you like him, this Chris bloke?'

Patricia's question takes me by surprise. 'Why?'

She throws him a gaze. 'He's nice. Seems to be into you. Have you chatted to him?'

'I have asked him some questions enquiring into his family and work particulars, yes. But he has been in prison a lot. I am unsure I can trust him.'

'Doc, *you've* been in prison.'

Feeling anxious, I fiddle with my bread, begin ripping off tiny crumbs.

'Look, Doc, I know this stuff is hard for you to process, but listen. You've got so much to offer. You're smart, funny—'

'That is what Chris said.' I lay the crumbs in neat rows of ten. 'He said I was funny.'

'Well, he's right!' She lets out a long breath. 'If you want something to happen with him, you know, if you like him and want a, well, a relationship with him, say—'

'Sex.'

'Okay, um, sure.' She bows her head. 'Sex,' she whispers. 'But that, may I point out, is just one small part of it, then you need to give him a little longer, you need to allow yourself more time for you to get to know him and for him to get to know you. Firing off a line of interview questions is not going to do it.'

'Oh. Okay.' I fiddle with the bread crumbs I have formed into a neat line as my head tries to make sense of what Patricia means. 'Do you mean chit chat?'

'Yeah. You know, things that will help you get to know each other.'

'But I have already interviewed him.'

'I know, but...' She sighs. 'You just, well, keep talking to each other.'

I look down. It is all very confusing, not to mention tiring. Then I get an idea. 'Can I issue him a questionnaire and that would suffice?'

'Um, no.'

'Oh.'

I look over at Chris. He is whispering to Balthus now, his hair flopping into his eyes, and yet he doesn't move it out of the way, and I fight the urge to stride over and do it for him.

'Maria,' Balthus says, 'can you come over here?'

'Why?'

He shoots a glance to Chris. 'We've…we've found something.'

Chapter 22

I scrape back the chair and walk over to the corner and as I do, my hand brushes into the neat lines of crumbs, scattering them randomly across the wood.

I reach Chris and when I stop, Patricia is right behind me. 'What have you found?'

'Well,' Chris says, raking a hand through his hair, 'you know you had me hack into that website with that SIM card and the eye came up, and the documents flashed across the screen?'

Balthus looks at me. 'What documents?'

I tell him. He shakes his head. 'Oh, Jesus.'

'Well, I found a code,' Chris says.

'How?'

'Okay, so, I took the SIM.'

'When?'

'From your rucksack as you were walking into the monastery.'

'That is stealing.'

'Well, no, borrowing—and to help you, see?' He points to the screen. 'Here.'

I look. A series of numbers and letters and black and white symbols stretch like tickertape across the screen. 'How did you access this?'

'I set up a rock-solid proxy, bypassed the firewall and released a hack programme I wrote in—' he shoots a glance to Balthus then leans in to me '—in prison,' he whispers, then raises his volume again. 'The files I found have the same stuff on them as the ones we found back at my place—the 1973 Black September reference, your, what is it, subject number, the 375 thing? But see here?' I squint. 'There's more detail right there. It's that age click thing, it's going down like before, counting down the time, but, well, does that mean anything to you?'

He points to the screen and I look to where his finger lies. There is a series of numbers and one special one hidden among it: 115.

'It's the same number we saw back at my place, right?' Chris says.

It has to be Raven. 'Yes.'

'Thought so. Thing is—' he breathes out '—I think it's connected to something beneath it, to another layer of data and if we could just—'

Balthus steps forward. 'No. No, no, no, no. Guys, leave this.'

'Hey?' Chris says. 'But we're getting somewhere here.'

I look at Balthus and hesitate. I trust him, but this information—it could make a difference. 'This data may lead us to the Project facility. It was you who encouraged me to find it. You who said I should find the file Raven talked about and then, if I did that, we could—'

'End it all. Yes, yes I remember.' He billows out a breath.

'They threatened my family,' I say to him. 'They threatened you all.'

Balthus sighs and rubs his chin. 'Do you think it's a code to crack that will uncover something else, this data you think lies beneath?' he says to Chris after a moment.

I stride to my rucksack, pull out my notebook and return. I flick the pages.

'Doc,' Patricia says, 'what are you doing?'

'I am searching for an algorithm.' My eyes scan fast and after three seconds, I find it. There. At the bottom of the page under some sketches of an intricate iron bridge I dreamt about is the algorithm I need, one I flashbacked to in prison. I show it to Chris. 'This can help. Can you feed it in?'

He whistles. 'Jeez, that's some code.' He begins typing in the data. I instruct him as to what it means, but he seems to know already, his brain working fast and it surprises me the level of intelligence he displays. He listens well, responding to my points and I am surprised at how rapidly he works. I smell the air, his skin—I like the scent of his sweat.

'I don't think it's going to work,' he says after one minute of trying.

I analyse the data. Something is missing. A single number, a solitary dash, dot. I flick again through the notebook, page after page of codes and decryptions and strange sketches.

'Jesus, what is all that?' he says, catching sight of my notebook pages.

'They are fragments of dreams I recall that mirror, I believe, events from being conditioned by the Project.'

'Oh.' He shifts in his seat. 'Right.' He looks at me, his breathing slow, measured, his eyes on my arms then on my neck and lips.

'Try this code,' I say. Seven pages in is a small encryption code I dreamt of during the first traumatic week in prison. I point to it.

Chris peers in. 'Okay, yeah, that's cool. There is another idea, though.'

'Do this first.'

'Okay. No worries.' He types, fast, efficient, but still it does not work.

I step back and stamp my foot.

'Y'okay, Doc? Take it easy.'

'Maria,' Balthus says, 'we can't keep at this forever. We have to leave soon. The Abbot has a car ready for us.'

'Wait!' We look at Chris. He is grinning from ear to ear.

'The code worked?' I say.

'No.'

'Oh.'

'See, what I was trying to tell you is that the age thing, you know, the clicking countdown age odd thing we found?'

'Yes.'

'Well—you're gonna love this, right—I changed the last two numbers on it through a small hole in the encryption programme used to set it up and then I was able to go through a different system, and, well—' he points to the screen '—*voilà*! Information uncovered.'

'Holy Jesus,' Balthus says.

I look at what Chris is now pointing to and cannot believe what I am seeing. There are multiple times, dates and locations, all of them listed throughout the 1980s and 90s, leading up to now, to the present day.

'You see that thing at the bottom?' Chris says.

'Yes.'

'You can decrypt that code fast, right? I mean, right now? Like I can?'

'Yes.'

Patricia leans in. 'What does it say?'

Chris looks to her. 'It says test child. What is the test child?'

A shiver ripples down my spine. 'The test child is me.'

'What? You're this test child chick they're talking about? Have you seen all this they have on you? It's like, full surveillance.'

'Bloody hell,' Balthus says, 'they have everything.'

I read it all, photograph it to my memory, but find myself shaking slightly as I do. Because the file contains extensive details about me and as I scan it, my heart starts to race. There are details on my handlers, on my test dates with the Project, flights I took with my mother from Madrid as a teenager, my trip on the train to Barcelona when I was twenty, surveillance notes, conditioning documents. They all collide in my head and when I sniff, the incense in the air fills my nostrils and then my head, and I feel my mind on the verge of zoning out to cope with it all.

'Doc, are you all right?'

I turn to her but keep my eyes down at her shoulders. 'They have all the details on my movements recorded.'

Patricia spans out her fingers as Balthus scans the information and looks to Chris. 'Is this proxy you set up safe?'

'As houses.'

'Maria,' Balthus says to me now, 'I know this is hard, but can you see any link on here that may indicate which facility that woman was at, the one you remembered?'

I make myself look and focus. There are dates and places, but nothing that, when I correlate all the facts between my head and the screen, connect together to formulate an answer. 'There is nothing about Switzerland here.'

Chris shakes his head. 'I searched for that link, too, but you're right—no correlation. But,' he says, 'look here. If you click on this part of the age countdown, just there—' the cursor hovers over a tiny black dot in the far right corner of the yellow box with my age in '—there's another page hidden beneath it, hard to access, but I managed it.'

'How?'

He shrugs. 'Just used the last segment of your algorithm and adapted it.'

I look at him. 'Oh.'

He grins. 'You're welcome.'

I read the next level of files and, as I do, further facts on my living arrangements are documented. I catch my breath and my fingers shake a little because what I am reading is effectively a map of my life. Each person and place has been categorised and when I cross-reference it all, some elements are hazy due to the Project's drug programme, but essentially, the data is correct down to the last second.

'They have been monitoring every step of my movements.' There is a tiny tremble in my voice.

I read again and arrive at a file towards the end. The font on this one is smaller, but just about readable and, leaning in past Chris's scent, I squint.

'Hey, look at that,' Chris says. 'There's a portion down here that's blacked out in, like, little strips.'

Balthus bends in. 'Can you get to what's underneath?'

He shrugs. 'It's tricky.'

I grab my notebook, open it at page seventy-two and thrust it in front of him. 'Use this code.'

'Whoa! You know how to do this?'

Somewhere in the monastery, monks begin singing a hymn and their voices drift into the room and it distracts me. 'Can you type it in?'

'Right, yeah, sure.' He blinks at me, just nodding for a few seconds and nothing else. 'You're pretty neat.' He stares at me and it makes me uneasy.

'The code,' I say.

'Oh. Yeah.'

Even though Chris's fingers fly fast, the code takes some time to input, but, after thirty-seven seconds, the screen begins to change.

'Whoa,' Chris says, 'it's working. You're freakin' genius.'

The black strips on the end of the document first turn to grey then, pixellating, begin to fade entirely then stall. Chris taps two more keys, then stops, a small gasp escaping his lips.

'What?' Balthus looks at him, at me. 'Maria, what?'

'The black strips have gone.' I look at the screen, at the tiny words revealed, and read them over and over again. 'No,' I say. 'No, no, no!' I stand, a chair to my left toppling to the side and clattering to the grey stone floor.

'Doc, what?'

Balthus presses his face to the screen, frantically reading then, stumbling back, slaps his hand to his mouth. 'Oh my God.'

'What?' Patricia says.

Chris frowns, drags his chair to the laptop. 'Okay, so this reads initials A and V. And there's a name, a contact for the Project programme: Alarico Villanueva.' He swivels round. 'Who's he?'

'Their contact,' Balthus says, his face pale. 'He…he is the contact who's been…' He wipes his face. 'Who must have been liaising with the Project to ensure Maria was always accessible…'

'Huh? But who is the guy?'

Patricia looks from Chris over to me. 'It's Maria's dad.'

Chapter 23

Monastery of Santa Maria de Montserrat, nr. Barcelona.
24 hours and 51 minutes to confinement

I look at the computer and the information on the screen and it all collides in my head. I step back, wander, I think, to the left, but when I do, I stumble and the bread from the board on the table topples and falls, scattering crumbs and grapes all over the floor.

I drop down and begin scraping it all up, my head concerned at the random disorder it has created. Everything is chaotic. The food thrown everywhere, I pick up every fallen piece of bread and place it back on the table in neat, ordered lines, my fingers taking each grape too, and setting them in rows, shifting each one that moves so it stays where I need it to.

Patricia comes to my side. 'Doc? Doc, breathe.'

'How could Alarico be their contact?' Balthus is saying. He is pacing the room, head shaking. 'It doesn't...it doesn't make any sense.'

It is all too much. I close my eyes, count up in fives, recite some quantum theory, try to remember happy times with Papa, the creases by his eyes, the way he would give me firm, strong hugs because I couldn't bear light ones, but when I open my eyes, there is a lump in my throat and my fingers begin to grab whatever they can on the table—plates, glasses, napkins—and rearrange them into neat, set squares. I reach into my rucksack and pull out the torn photo of the two of us from my villa.

'Doc?'

I look up to Patricia. Her hand is held out with five slim, familiar fingers. I blink at it. I watch her arms and her chest and the way her long neck bends, each movement of it pressed to my memory.

'Papa gave me to the Project,' I say. I trace a finger over the rip in the picture of us.

'The document could be false,' she says, 'have you thought about that?'

I hesitate, confused. 'It is a Project file.'

'Yeah, and the sodding Project could have planted the data deliberately. Think about it—it could be absolutely anything.'

But the mixture of the data and Papa's name and the confusion and the smells in the room and even the feel of the denim fabric on my legs all start to overload my mind, and I begin to moan and rock a little to let off the steam of the chaos I feel inside.

'What's she doing?' Chris says.

I sense everyone staring at me, but there is nothing I can do to stop it now. Like an avalanche, it has exploded.

'She's stimming,' Patricia says to Chris, then looks back to me. 'It's all been too much for her.'

'Can she hear you?'

But Patricia ignores Chris and speaks just to me. 'Hold up your hand, Doc.'

I raise my eyes. Patricia's fingers are spread out in front of her and I blink at them, briefly glancing to the blurred faces of Balthus and Chris.

'Is she going to be okay?' Chris whispers to Balthus.

'Doc?' Patricia says, her voice soft, low. 'Doc, your hand.'

I watch her. I keep my sight fixed on my friend and, slowly, my body starts to settle and my humming becomes less then ceases entirely as I focus on Patricia, on her hand, her fingers, her talcum powder scent.

'He was my papa,' I say. 'He worked for the Project.'

Patricia tilts her head. 'We'll work it all out, okay?'

I look at her, her soft cheeks, wide eyes as, gradually, my hand rises until our fingertips touch and my breathing begins to slow.

'Er, guys?' Chris steps into view. 'There's someone here.'

The Abbot stands in the doorway where the room snakes out into a dimly lit corridor. He wears black robes that skim the floor in a triangle shape, and around his neck hangs a single silver chain with a thick cross on the end of it.

Balthus turns to him. 'Father, what is it?'

'We have visitors.'

The Abbot holds out a phone and on it is a photograph. I pull myself up a little now as, ahead, Balthus strides over to the monk, stares at the digital image and shakes his head. 'I don't know them.' He turns. 'Maria, I know things are difficult for you right now, but do you recognise these two?'

He approaches me, crouches down and holds out the cell. 'Have you seen them before?'

My eyes are blurred from zoning out and at first it is hard to see, but, after two seconds, something in my brain kicks in and memories start to function and connect. I rise a little and take the phone from Balthus. The initial face I do not recognise, but the second... Mahogany hair, skin the colour of buttermilk, black jeans painted to her legs, a worn leather jacket. A memory slips into my mind. The counselling sessions after my acquittal, the woman who brought coffee, the one who the Project therapist, officer—Kurt—said was his girlfriend.

Balthus steps forward. 'They are with the Project, aren't they?'

'Yes.'

He looks to Chris. 'Copy those files. We have to leave. Now.'

'This way,' the Abbot says. He turns, sweeps to the left and as he does, his feet seem to hover over the floor as if they weren't touching the stone at all.

We gather our belongings and rush out of the room, shoving past the wooden doorway, plunging into ribbons of walkways, my head switched to a focus I was not sure before I could achieve. Staying close to each other, we criss-cross left then right, bright lights flickering against walls that are arranged in exposed, raw slabs of stonework splayed out under effigies of Jesus Christ and Mary. Everything hits my senses at once. The lights, smells, sounds, thoughts of Papa with the Project. I document all of it. It is almost too much to handle, but I focus on Patricia, on the heads of Chris and Balthus and the ordered robes of the Abbot and I move on.

We turn a corner. Our feet are running now, all in time, but, on a polished tile Chris slips and he topples into a cemented recess, air billowing out of him as his chest hits the wall. I hesitate. The others have not noticed and are racing ahead.

'You go,' Chris says. 'I'll catch up.' He moves to stand but winces, his palm slapping to his injured shoulder.

Unsure what to do, I glance once more to the corridor and catch sight of Patricia's head. They are nearly out of sight. I look back to Chris. We are supposed to be running, leaving—that is the plan, the routine—but the laptop is with Chris and he has a lot of knowledge and…and he helped me.

I drop to the floor. Hooking my arms underneath his shoulders, I heave up his body but he is heavy and the corridor warm, and sweat seeps through the fabric of my T-shirt and jacket, and even though it is cotton, the fabric irritates my skin and makes the whole thing difficult to deal with. But I keep going. Chris locks eyes with me for one second and, for some reason, I find myself unable to look away.

'They must have found you through me,' he says. 'Those people on the phone image—they must have tracked you through my laptop.'

'Negative.' I hoist him upright and tug on his arm. 'The higher probability is that they found me through following Balthus or Patricia.'

Propping up Chris on one elbow, we begin to move again, but progress is slow, the two of us inching along until I can barely hear the others ahead at all, and sweat now forms two dark pools under my arms as the thought that they are here, the Project, somewhere near, makes my breathing short and sharp.

After a few seconds, Chris manages to jog again alongside me as we finally reach a wide arch at the end of the tunnel that stretches out towards the exit beyond. Balthus and Patricia are there, catching their breath as the Abbot ahead unlocks a bolt on a cast-iron door to the right and gestures to Balthus, who goes to talk to the Abbot in hushed tones.

'They've arranged a car,' Balthus says to us now, walking over, his voice dropped, a single light beam illuminating every line on his face, 'out towards the rear side of this section. We can get to it, but—'

'We cannot go as one group,' I say.

Patricia turns to me. 'Doc, we have to stay together. We can't let the Project get you on your own.'

'I won't come,' Chris says. 'They could have tracked you all through my laptop.'

I turn to him. 'It was not your laptop they traced.'

Patricia glances between the two of us.

'It is time for you to leave,' the Abbot whispers.

'Chris,' Balthus says, 'you're coming with us. End of discussion. Okay?'

He nods. 'Okay.' He then reaches into his pocket and gives something to me. A USB stick. 'You should have this. It's got it on all the documents we found just now.'

Unsure why he is helping me, I take the memory stick.

'If we get split up at all and you need to contact me, I wrote down my secure email and cell.' He gives me a scrawl of paper. 'The geolocation's off, so they can't find me. Use Text Secure or Signal to contact me—you can send encrypted messages via those.'

I read his details, memorise them, then rip the paper up into tiny confetti pieces.

'What, you don't want it?'

'No. I memorised it.'

'Oh.' He opens his mouth as if to announce something, but instead simply blinks at me and says, 'Oh,' again.

'Doc?' Patricia says. 'Let's go.'

'My surname's Johnson, by the way,' Chris says, as he goes to move. 'You know, cos you like names, so I figured, well, you could know all of mine.'

'Johnson,' I say. 'It is a patronym of the name John, which means *son of John*. It is a surname of English origin, yet also an American name meaning *Jehovah has been gracious*.'

He smiles. 'Yep, that's right, Google.'

Balthus steps forward. 'Okay. It's time to go.'

The door ahead is open wide, rain from the broken clouds pouring in, and the Abbot is gesturing us over and we start to run.

'Please hurry,' the Abbot whispers as we reach him. 'There are people at the door. We cannot hold them off for much longer. You must go.'

Reaching into my rucksack, I hand out no-contract cell phones. 'These are non-traceable and all preset with each other's numbers to remain in touch should we get separated.' Every one takes them silently and I am about to explain at speed how encrypted text messaging works when there is a series of shouts in the far distance and a loud, deafening crack.

'Holy shit,' Chris says, eyes wide, 'was that a gunshot?'

'This way,' the Abbot now gestures. 'Quick!'

The shots ring loud in my head now as we are plunged into a shower of lights towards the exit where the car engine growls up ahead. We all run, no words spoken, just a rapid rhythm of breath, the escape vehicle forty metres away, and we are near now but I trip slightly and tumble fall, and when I look down I see my shoelace is undone.

'Come on!' Patricia whispers, her arm waving me over.

A shot of annoyance and fear whip through me simultaneously. I can't leave it undone, the lace, loose, out of place like this, but if I stop and fix it, it will waste us time. Shots ring out again from somewhere in the monastery and I flinch and try to focus. I calculate the bullets' distance from us using the echoes and vibration movements that bounce off the cavernous stonework, and determine that the people shooting are two, perhaps three hundred metres away. I look at Patricia then to my lace.

'Take this!' I throw my rucksack to my friend.

'What? Doc—' It hits her and she stumbles back a little like a backstop catching the ball in a baseball match.

'It has the USB stick in it,' I say. I drop to my knees.

'Hurry!' Balthus urges up ahead.

My fingers work quickly on my lace, but something bothers me, a small chink somewhere, a thin sound that vibrates from outside, but I cannot determine its location. I inch upwards. The lights around me are bright and the noises loud and I am sweating from my arms, from my neck, my cheeks, but that is not it, that is not the problem.

A loud crack rips into the air.

We all drop to the ground.

'They're shooting again,' Batlhus yells. 'They're shooting! Everyone run. Quick. Maria!'

How did they get here so fast? We sprint across the court-yard. It is hard to hide, the bulbs floodlighting across the ground, blinding our line of sight, bouncing off the sheen of the polished stone walls that line this section. Shapes and shadows fly left and right as we sprint across the expanse of ground, cold air slapping our faces, my lace only loosely tied, and I am acutely aware that I am behind the group. There are two vehicles I see now and we run past the first car, and I am unsure why until, as we pass it, I see the two rear tyres have been shot and deflated.

Up ahead, the Abbot ushers us to another door at the rear, this one huge, almost three metres in height, wood thick as a tree trunk. It booms open into a secondary vast cave-like space beyond and I can see it, the space, and I spy the glint of what must the metallic bonnet of another car behind, a four-by-four vehicle, and I am not yet there, but then a thought enters my head and I stop. I cease running and stand alone, chest heaving as I watch my friends run on.

Balthus halts. 'Maria, what are you doing? Come on!'

The Abbot is just ahead, Chris near him, Balthus by Patricia, my rucksack on her shoulder, USB stick in the front pocket, when another shot sounds, the noise hammering in my head, but I ignore it, clench my teeth.

'The Project are here,' I say, my voice raised above the noise.

'I know,' Balthus yells. 'So move.'

'No.'

'Doc,' Patricia shouts, 'what are you doing?'

I glance to where the gunshots fire then turn back to my friends. 'The facility from my flashback was a Project one. Raven pointed me to a file, one that can give me answers.'

'Maria, no,' Balthus says, 'it's too dangerous.'

'I have to go.' The volume is getting louder now and dust

whips up in tornados in the air, spiralling my senses. 'The only way I can get to the file is to be there. Is to be inside the Project.'

Wind and rogue rain slice now across our faces, and Chris's hair flicks into his eyes and cheeks as he brushes it out of the way.

'You know my email, my details,' Chris shouts. There is another gunshot, this time closer and he ducks then wobbles to a stand. 'When you are in there, find a phone, get to computer, set up a proxy and contact me, okay? I'll see what I can dig up in the meantime, see what ice I can hack.'

'Ice,' Balthus mumbles. 'Ice… Ice!' he shouts. 'Maria, I remember now!'

'What?'

More bullets crack into the air. We all duck.

'Remember when you were at the villa and you told me about your flashback with the woman you named Raven?'

'Yes. Of course.'

'I said it triggered a memory in me, but I couldn't quite figure out what. Well, I remember now, when Chris said ice. Ines, your mother, when you were in Goldmouth she phoned me and she was babbling. She was ill, it was when she was taken into hospital after visiting you, do you remember? And she was talking on and on about a place called the Ice Room.'

I force my ears to work over the din. 'Did she say where it was?'

'No, but she said that if you wanted to keep secrets then you had to go to the Ice Room and that…and that the room had a computer in there that wasn't connected to a server. I don't know, it may be nothing.'

Mama. She thought she was taking me to a help centre, not

the Project. Maybe she overheard something and, when she was ill with the cancer and worried about me being in prison, she repeated it to Balthus, to my papa's old university friend.

The Abbot now, his black cloak flapping by his feet, urges them to move, the shots so close that they feel only metres away.

'Doc,' Patricia shouts, 'be safe.' And she raises her hand and I go to do the same when there is a loud crack and a searing, hot pain shoots through me. I fall, screaming out as a fire rips into my body as, ahead, I see two sets of boots halt in front me and my brain goes into overdrive. Have I been shot? But I know how that feels, a bullet, the explosion of gunpowder in my body, wet, cold, sickening, but this is different. It must be a dart, a dart loaded with something.

'Doc!' Patricia yells.

My friend! Not my friend. 'Run!' I shout. 'Patricia, run!' Except, I am not shouting, am unable to, because my mouth has become numb, spit drooling from the edges of my lips, my body and legs paralysed. I try to gain some sight, a visual, but all I see are shadows that sway separately at first then, as the sedative from the dart takes hold, the shadows blend together until they forge one large veil of black.

Chapter 24

My brother reads from my journal and I listen very hard. The timer by my side ticks and he will not tell me how long I have until the drugs speed into my system again. I do not move. The rope in the semi-darkness cuts into my wrists and ankles now, but as he talks more, as he reads out the words that sit on the pages of my mind, I start to recall fragments of events that have happened until now.

He pauses talking and, reaching into the box beside him, unhooks the lid and pulls out two bags of popcorn and one silver fork. He replaces the lid in one move, careful so my journal remains on his lap, then holds the popcorn bags and fork in the air and smiles.

'You still like this stuff, right? And look! I remembered you used to like eating popcorn with a fork so your fingers wouldn't touch your mouth.'

In the oppressive gloom, I can just about see that the popcorn packets are red and yellow, and on the edge and top and bottom are faux-gold strips that tail the brand name writing which reads *ButterPop*. The light bulb above swings over the packets as Ramon shifts his crate forward now, the torch he was holding now placed flat on the dirt floor so it shines outwards in a funnel of straw yellow.

I blink. The light is bright and my eyes are becoming so accustomed now to the dark that when the bulb shines, my lids flap until they stream fluid.

'Have some food,' Ramon says, 'and I'll continue reading, okay?'

I nod and, following his instructions, open my mouth. He spears three pieces of toffee popcorn with the fork then slots the fork into my mouth, and the snack immediately melts. It tastes good. I cannot recall the last time I ate and when he next pulls out a plastic bottle of water, I gulp the liquid down so fast that some of it spurts back up and Ramon has to come behind me and tap me on the back to dislodge any rogue droplets to ensure I can breathe. While helping me, he knocks the medical stand and the drug bag swings, causing the needle in my arm to pull at my vein, stinging me with a sharp pain that pierces all the way through to the nub of my elbow.

'Gosh, M, I'm sorry. Are you okay?' he says now, coming back round to the front.

My eyes land on my journal where he placed it on the lid of the box so he could move. I ignore the needle. I have to keep him reciting my diary entries. 'Can you read some more?'

He smiles, and to my surprise, I see eye creases fan out on the corners of his face.

I am recalling more and more details now of events past and I don't want to stop. The urge to ask Ramon again what the Project has asked him to do is strong, as too is the desire to demand that he unties me, takes out the timer and needle, but if I do that, I worry that he will shout and won't read anything else out and then I would be stuck, unable to get out of wherever I am. I remember now what happened in the courtyard of the monastery. I recall the gunshots and shouts and how I was knocked out, and I know that I deliberately let myself be taken by the Project, but I need to recollect what happened after that. I need to unfreeze something that will give me a clue, a clue that will ultimately convince Ramon that I should not be kept in here or perhaps show me what to do or tell me that help is on the way.

Ramon is reading a section on the Project where Black Eyes was testing me to see if I felt pain. When he arrives at the part where I was stubbed with a cigarette, he stops. I look at him; there are tears in his eyes.

'M, why did you write this?'

'I wrote it because it happened.'

He wipes his face dry with a cotton handkerchief. 'Why didn't you tell me?'

'Because I thought you would not believe me.'

He frowns. 'What? You mean this is real? When you said it happened, I thought you meant in your head. I thought this was just a nightmare or a bad dream you had recorded.'

'No. It is real.'

He slams shut the book and I jump. The sound echoes in my ears, making it hard to focus amid the dark and the confusion, but if he doesn't read the journal where will that leave me?

'You know there is a difference between stories and reality, don't you, M?'

'Yes.'

'Then why do you insist on making things up?'

I don't know what to say, am unsure how to act. I have told him it is all true and real and he has read the details in my own writing, but is it that he is now so used to, as the world is, being fed lies that he cannot distinguish any more between truth and deceit, between fact and fiction?

'I liked reading to you when we were little,' he says after a moment. 'It made me feel as if I was looking after you.'

I study his smile and try to mirror it to make him feel comfortable and continue with my journal. 'Yes. Me too.'

He sighs. 'Papa used to read to me, after you went to bed.'

Papa...

'He'd read the classics to me, you know, Dickens, a bit of Shakespeare. It says in your journal here Papa would read *Hamlet* to you. I never knew that.'

Papa...

'M? Are you listening?'

I look up with a start. I am sweating, dribbles of it trickling down my temples and when I shift in my seat, the shirt on my back sticks to my skin.

'Papa read *Hamlet* to me, yes,' I say, but I am not fully focused on the words, instead am fixating on the memory it has dislodged in my brain, a memory of finding something, some information Chris uncovered.

'Ramon, are there date entries in my journal?'

He looks to the pages. 'Yes, mostly. There are some omissions, but, yes, there are dates, why?'

I look at the gold embossment on my journal, think of Papa and what Ramon said about him and, slowly, like a train arriving at a station, the recent memory comes: Chris found out that Papa was possibly a Project contact, that he was the liaison. It rushes in fast now, the short-term recollection, but Patricia said that the data could be unreliable. Could my journal help? The drugs I have been given here have scrambled my photographic databanks, but my journal could reboot them, help me remember. If the dates in it correlate, if Papa could not have been with me on the journal entries where I was at the Project, could that give him an alibi? Could it mean he is innocent or at the very least not connected to the Project in that way?

'M, are you okay? Your eyes have zoned out a bit.'

I jerk my head straight. I have to figure this out, but the timer ticks to my side. 'I...I want to hear more from my journal, that is what I was thinking about. I believe it is helping me.'

'Helping you feel better?'

'Helping me feel better,' I say, mirroring his words, 'yes, but, I think, not having the timer on would help me concentrate on my journal more when you read to me. That would help me greatly. You know I cannot deal with too many noises.'

He sits and says nothing, and for a moment I think he is going to be able to see into my head and know what I am really thinking, but then, without warning, he stands.

'M, that's really great news. Yes, of course I can pause the timer. That's why I am here. I am here for you because I love you. Talking is good.' He walks to the medical stand. 'Talking is really good.'

And as he presses a small orange button on the side of the timer face, the ticking stops and the drug stays only in the bag, and in front of me Ramon sits and picks up my journal and begins to tell me all the dates that are documented inside.

Deep cover Project facility.
18 hours and 49 minutes to confinement

I wake up to see that I am lying in a metal bed with my body covered in a cornflower-blue hospital gown that hangs loose on my limbs. Dulled, medium-glare stimulus lights line the ceiling and when I look to the corners of the bed, instead of sharp angles I see rounded corners and a white sheet made of soft, handwoven cotton.

I crane my neck to see some more then wince in pain and flop back. I track back through events. The dart, the monastery, the two people from the Project. I look around, recognise the white of the walls, the blank, empty space, and I know that I am here. I have made it.

I am back in a Project facility—I just don't know which one yet.

I dart my eyes downwards and scan myself. There are no straps on my arms, no ropes on my legs and when I try to sit up, nothing moves, as if I have been frozen, my muscles temporarily suspended or paralysed. A mild panic begins to rise until I think back to the dart and I remember the sedative, and I calm down. It will wear off soon.

The thought of Papa swims into my head, the information Chris found, and when I contemplate it, I find it hard to cope with the idea that he was involved with the Project, but people lie, even people you believe you can trust. Somehow I need to find out at what facility the flashback was and see if it matches the one I am at now.

I open my eyes and exhale. Unable to move my head and neck fully until the sedative wears off, I take to flicking my eyes around the room to analyse my surroundings in more detail. White non-climb paint is daubed on every side of the room and at the entrance is a grey door made of metal with a secure air lock mechanism. To my side sits a standard issue medical cabinet containing one drawer and a shelf with no contents, and next to it teeters a small stack of fluffed, white towels. When I scan for light I see there is no external window, instead just the low-stimulus lights on the ceiling above and a prison-like glass panel on the back internal partition.

I begin to calculate the distance from the bed to the door, when there is a sound, a high-pitched beep. I jump. The beep fades and is followed by something else I did not expect to hear: music, old-style music from the 1930s. It warbles, quiet at first then louder, more distinct with a tinny, crackled, effect that echoes in the air as if it's being played on an old gramophone. When the first segment launches, trumpets dribble out a tune and there is a wail of a woman's voice linked with jagged jazz notes that slip in and out.

Confused, I shiver, goosebumps springing out all over my body as my eyes take in the corner of a speaker that sits bolted towards the ceiling to my left. The music lurches on and though it is not loud, not booming in my head, the sound still grates my ears, makes the hairs on my arms stand, pricking my flesh with hundreds of tiny warning shocks. It bothers me. I try to trace the jazz notes, gain some order from it so I can think and focus, and am so wrapped up in it that I don't hear the air lock hiss at the entrance sound and see the door slide open into the room.

'You can move, you know. You just have to force it.'

The voice startles me and I look up and freeze.

'Hello again, Maria.' He steps forward. 'You took a little while to find this time.'

'Get back!'

But he moves again so I try to roll off the bed, but my limbs are still weak, and he stalks towards me, the man with the mask from my nightmares and my flashbacks, the man with the Scottish accent. Dr Carr.

Black Eyes.

'Where am I?'

Black Eyes walks to my right side, drags out a chair and sits. I press myself backwards into the bed, muscles firing to work now as I feel the cold metal of the bedstead on my skin. I knew, when I let them capture me, that I would see him again, but nothing could prepare me for the horror of seeing the man in the flesh that for the last six months I have seen only in my nightmares.

'You gave us quite the run around, didn't you? Oh, but it is so nice to see you again. You look tired, Maria.' His skin is pale and rigid, and on his face pockmarks form craters around his chin and on his cheeks, and his mouth, when he speaks, reveals the tombstone teeth that stalk the corridors of my dreams.

'Where am I?' I repeat.

He crosses one leg over the other. 'You are at our Project Facility in Hamburg.'

Hamburg. My heart races, adrenaline shooting out. Something about the city clicks and vaguely connects, but what and how? The sedative is still making my cognitive thought fuzzy and when I attempt to think it through, I keep arriving at a halt, the music colliding to blur my brain. I talk, focus on buying some time until I function correctly. 'Your facility is in Scotland, it is not in Germany.'

'Our Scottish facility, Maria—Subject 375—is merely the one we would take you to when you were younger. We are an international programme. We have more than a single facility.'

'Why have you brought me here?' My eyes flip to the door, the exit, escape.

He follows my gaze. 'There's no need to run.' He picks up a tiny black remote control with three buttons and points it at the ceiling speaker. The music dies and the room slips into a loud silence.

'You can't get out,' Black Eyes says now, returning his focus to me. 'Not yet anyway. And besides, I've missed seeing you. I'm just sorry we've had to get you over to me—us—in this way.'

'Why do you want me?'

He smiles, but nothing happens to the skin around his eyes, no eye wrinkles or creases. I observe him. Without his white mask, I can see his entire face. His lips are thin in a kind of washed-out pale, dishcloth type of pink, and on his left cheek is a two-centimetre scar. His ears, when I track them, are large elephant affairs that seem to flap when he moves, and on his skull are weeds of black hair, his wiry body attired from his chicken neck down in a white robe over green surgical trousers and tunic.

There is a plastic file in his hand and he opens it. He consults a document then looks up and when he does, a shiver ripples down my limbs, as I realise with anticipation that my muscles are thawing now, some feeling returning and my mind is beginning to gradually function.

'Black September,' he announces, 'do you know of it?'

My brain hits alert. Black September: the organisation Chris found data on at his villa. I stay very still while I think, while I try to determine what he is aiming to do.

'Why are you asking me this?'

'You wanted to know why you are here—I am simply trying to explain.' He tilts his head and as he does, it reminds me of the gargoyles chiselled into the stone on Mama's apartment building in Madrid. 'Black September was a terrorist organisation,' he says. 'I believe you discovered one of our documents referring to them.'

A small stab of panic hits my chest. 'The eye on the computer, it was—'

'Me, yes. Well, not actually me, but an image downloaded.' He smiles and I see his murky teeth. 'I thought you would appreciate the…intelligence of it, let's say. Some may not. But, well, I know you well, my dear.' He sighs. 'Oh it really is so good to see you. I get lonely here, you know. Things have… well, they've changed. Time moves on.'

My panic rises. Patricia. She has my rucksack with the USB stick containing the downloaded files from the computer in Chris's house.

'Anyway, Black September,' he says now, 'carried out murders and bombings at the Munich Olympics in 1972. There was also an attack on an electrical installation in Hamburg.' He pauses, scans my face like a laser, then recommences. 'In response to those events, and others, professionally trained counter-terrorism groups were created. Two of these groups were called GSG9 and GIGN. Another was called Project Callidus. Every organisation has a—' he flurries a hand in the air '—a code name, if you will. Ours is Callidus. Project Callidus.'

'Callidus,' I say, on autopilot, unable to stop myself. 'It is a Latin word which means astute, clever or cunning.

Black Eyes nods. 'Good. Good.'

I think now, brain beginning to turn a little faster as some semblance of normal function returns in tiny parts. The classified documents I discovered in Balthus's prison office said the Project began in the 1970s, and the ones from Chris's house correlate with the year 1973. Does this mean Black Eyes is telling me the truth? An unease swells in my stomach and I tap my fingers and clench my teeth as he continues talking.

'Of course, unlike the other groups, no one knows about us.' He looks at my rhythmic finger. 'I see your original little Asperger's traits are still there.' He tilts his head. 'No matter. You have been without our chaperoning for a little longer than we'd have liked. It is to be expected.' He shuts his file then looks up. 'So, I have been informed that you killed an MI5 officer this week. You knew her as Dr Andersson, correct?'

I don't reply, a fear taking over me now. 'How did you know that?'

'Oh, Maria,' he sighs. 'We have known each other for so long now, so when will you realise, hmmm, that I—we—we know everything.' He leans in and I smell his garlic and tobacco stench, and I almost gag.

'Everything,' he whispers.

Chapter 25

Black Eyes moves back from me and sits on his chair. He folds his legs one over the other and delivers me a wide stare. 'We want you back into the Project fold, Maria. Back to your surrogate family.'

His statement takes me by such surprise that a screech slips from my lips. 'No.'

'Yes.'

'Why?'

He regards me for a moment. 'You, Maria, are the one the conditioning programme has worked on. You must know this—you have seen the classified files. Did you think we'd spend all the money we have on training you and what? Just give you up, just like that?' He shakes his head. 'I don't think so. People can only hide for so long.' He pauses. 'My own daughter used to like to hide. Peek-a-boo. Isn't that what they call it?'

Something fires in me. I jump at it. 'You said I am the only one the conditioning has worked on, which implies you have tested on others. Who else have you used the programme training on?'

He smiles. 'A good question.' He shifts in his seat and his surgical scrubs rise up showing mud-brown socks on white, wiry ankles.

He sighs and, without saying a word, scrapes his chair nearer towards me so that when I look to him, I can see the pockmarks on his face so clearly, my brain can count each and every one.

'I want you to know something, Maria.'

My arms press flat and hard into the mattress. 'I said, who else have you used the programme training on?'

He narrows his eyes. 'You think we are the bad guys, is that right?' I open my mouth to speak, but he wags a finger. 'No, no. No need to answer. I know your response.' He leans back a little in the chair. I barely breathe. 'But what you may not be aware of is that we are also known as Cranes. It's a…nickname, if you will.' He waves a hand. 'Oh, I know, nicknames are childish, and I doubt, given your non-typical neurological patterns, they are something you deal in, but this one, well, we are affectionate towards it. You, naturally, know of the country of Japan, yes?'

I do not respond, instead calculate how long it would take me to jump to the exit from the edge of the bed.

'I want you to answer, Maria.' He sits forward. 'Now.'

'I know Japan.'

'Good.' He rests back again and I feel my jaw tremble. 'Now, after World War Two, in Japan, a crane came to symbolise hope and peace. A young girl—her name was Sadako Sasaki—she contracted leukemia due to the atomic bombings. She knew she was dying, so she took to making thousands of origami cranes.' He tilts his head. 'She died aged twelve, and the world held her up as a figurehead for the innocent victims of the war.'

'Why are you telling me this?'

He inhales. 'The cranes Sadako made symbolised peace, Maria. Peace. We, too, stand for peace.' He pauses. 'Cranes— our nickname—it means peace because that's what Project Callidus represents, that's what we are about, what we fight for: peace. The National Security Agency scandal was just a red herring that threw us off track.'

'The NSA were carrying out unauthorised surveillance on non-political citzens.'

'What? And you have a problem with that?' He leans in. 'Let me tell you something: the work we do saves lives, Maria, lives. Does everyone really think they are protected online?' He tuts. 'This is the real world. Terrorists. Cyber hack hits, all of them threatening our infrastructures, our economies—our way of life. We do what *we* do to protect our security and freedom of speech.'

'For the greater good,' I find myself saying.

His lips tilt upwards. 'Ah, you remember our training mantra.'

I ease my back into the bedstead and feel the metal screws of the steel frame dig into my skin. 'The Project is not a peaceful organisation.'

He bolts out of his chair. It is so fast, so unexpected that, at first, I think I am imagining it, but then his face is in front of mine, pressed almost into my nose, his rough skin on my cheeks and his hot breath on me, sending my brain into spirals of chaos. It makes me gag. It makes my stomach want to convulse and my throat want to vomit, yet I do not move. The file. I need to know where the flashback was located so I can get to Raven's file.

'Peace!' he spits. 'We represent peace, Subject 375. You are a member of Callidus and you will not forget that. Will not! Do you understand?'

'Y-yes.'

He remains there for two more heat-filled seconds then finally peels his face away and returns to his seat. I exhale, hyperventilate, desperate to wipe his stench from my skin, wipe away his slimy spit and breath, but I know that if I do so, it will alert him to the fact that the sedative has worn off and I can move. My hospital gown hangs in a tent over my legs and when I glance to my knees, I see they are rattling.

'I am sorry I have to be so sharp with you at times, Maria, but I cannot stress to you enough the importance of what we do.' He leans in. 'You are shaking. You must be cold. Here.' He drapes the end of my gown over the goose bumps on my legs and I go so ridged with fear, my bones feel as if they could snap in two.

'So,' Black Eyes says sitting back, 'we know you were online, hacking.' He smiles, a slit, a sharp spike. 'What did you find?'

'I found surveillance data.'

'On whom?'

I pause. Do I tell him? 'On me.'

'On you and your father.' He consults his file. 'An Alarico Martinez, correct?'

My teeth clench at the sound of Papa's name. 'Yes.'

'And the information you accessed detailed this man as a contact, yes?'

I don't answer, can't.

'Answer me.'

Do it. Buy time. 'Yes,' I force myself to say. I close my lips as I feel my legs and arms returning to me, the sensation of it flowing in and as it does, in my head I can feel my brain finally firing, drug free.

Black Eyes crosses his legs and delivers me a stare. For a moment, I don't know what is happening or what to believe. I want to ask Dr Carr about Papa, but I am scared to, because what, when I ask if Papa was the Project's liaison, will I do if I am informed it is true?

The lights in the room cast out a soft glow. They pulsate into the air and fill it with a sun-kissed colour, and when I look at the walls, at the whiteness of them, they seem cream now in the light, and the familiarity of it all calms me somehow and enables me to think.

'Let me tell you, something, Maria,' Black Eyes says now, his boney face protruding outwards, 'something you should have been told a very long time ago.'

I don't move. I keep my limbs still and try to focus on why I am here and what I need to do.

'You understand,' he says now, 'what it means to be Basque, yes?'

I press my lips together, unsure why he is asking me this. My mouth is dry and the air is tepid, and I can feel my head rush with nerves and adrenaline.

'I asked you a question.'

'I know what it means. Yes.'

'Of course, you do,' he says. 'So tell me, Maria: what do you think I have to tell you?'

'I cannot read your mind, therefore I am unable to give you an answer.'

'Come, on,' Black Eyes says. 'We trained you better than this. You are intelligent, you have an exceptionally high IQ. You tell me what you have deduced from the information you found.'

'My father was helping you,' I say.

'So that is your conclusion. Hmmm.' Black Eyes tilts back his head and looks down at me through creased lids. 'It's interesting to see you notice everything, yet you have not noticed what is right under your nose.' He pauses. 'Fascinating. Peek-a-boo this certainly seems to be.'

His eyes flutter briefly shut and I quickly look to the exit and see the shadow of a person outside.

'Blood,' he says now, eyes opening, 'is the key here, you see. Your blood, its origins, is, well, let's say it is special to us.'

A vague fear begins to surface upwards. 'Why would my blood be special?' I speak slowly, carefully, as if speaking the words too fast would trip me over and I'd never be able to get up again.

He unclips a pen from his jacket and tips it like a spirit level, lowering it forward towards the file that sits, now, fanned open on his lap. 'You are blood type A, yes?'

I nod.

'Aloud!' he shouts.

I jump. Every hair on my body shoots upright, rigid. 'Yes.'

His shoulders soften. 'Thank you. My apologies. And you are Rhesus negative?' He provides me with one, sharp stare.

'Yes,' I hear my voice reply. 'I am RhD negative.'

Dread begins to creep through me as my brain fires, neurons charging. *Blood*, it whispers. *Blood. Blood. Blood...*

'You recruited me for my blood type,' I say, quietly, almost to myself.

He angles his head to the left. 'Very good.'

'Why?'

He taps the nib of the fountain pen on the file. 'Only fifteen percent of Europeans are Rhesus negative, fifteen percent, but you see we have discovered over the decades, that these Rhesus negative types make excellent test sources.' He pauses. 'In Basque natives, did you know, the number of Rhesus negative types is an unusual thirty-five percent, and they all tend to be blood types O or A. Perfect subject material.'

My brain connects and links. 'Why are you telling me this? I am not Basque.'

He regards me for a moment. 'You like patterns, yes?'

I hesitate. 'Yes.'

'We discovered the quality of Basque blood via DNA patterns, helixes. That was how the real core of the Project took off.'

'The Project used only Basque subjects to test on,' I say, repulsed at my words, at my conclusion.

'Precisely, because their blood is perfect for use in our conditioning programme, yes, and, of course, with a thirty-five percent ratio, there have been so many of them at our... disposal,' he says. His pen hovers in mid-air by his side. 'Once we made this discovery, from then on we used only pure-Basque subjects, ideally with some Asperger's, with an autism link, like you. Their blood—your blood and your brain—they are really fascinating.' He pauses. 'Do you understand what I am saying now?'

But I can't speak. My mind is moving fast now, but I want it to stop, want it to halt the course it's hurtling towards at a trajectory so rapid, it will smash everything I recognise into tiny, unrecognisable pieces.

'Maria—Subject 375—do you understand?'

And even though I do understand, my lips say, 'No.'

Black Eyes stays still. He remains in his seat and regards me for a second until, inhaling, he removes the file from his lap and taking his fountain pen from his pocket, he unclips the lid, walks over to me and leans in.

'Then let,' he says, grabbing my arm, 'me enlighten you.'

Fear floods me. He holds his fountain pen above me and plunges it down, his talon fingers pinching my upper arm, locking it down as he starts scratching green ink into my skin.

'No!'

He scratches deeper into me. 'This has to be so, my dear. I know, I know. Ssssh, there, there. It hurts me to do this, it truly does, but it must be done. It must.'

The sound of my own screaming vibrates around the room until I pass out in pain.

Chapter 26

I come to. Black Eyes watches me then replaces the lid on his pen, sits down on the metal chair and crosses his legs. I raise my right arm, my hands and limbs, head trembling, as inch by inch I pull my shoulder round towards my face and view what he has done.

A shriek escapes my lips.

'Rather like your very own custom-made tattoo, hmm? I loved tattoos when I was young. Of course, my father wouldn't allow it.' He studies me. 'I see the sedative has worn off. Good, good.'

The lights glow in the room. With my fingers shaking, I touch my skin and wince as the tips touch the ink from Black Eyes' fountain pen and I see with horror what is now permanently etched into me.

The words: *I am Basque.*

I throw up. I lurch to the side of the bed, haul my head over it and vomit on the floor, drips of food hanging from my mouth and spritzing up my nostrils. Black Eyes frowns. He slides a beige handkerchief from his pocket, flaps it out whole then, bending forward, dabs his shoes clean.

'Can't bear the smell of vomit. Are you better now?'

'Why did you do this?' I croak as I pull myself up and peer again at my arm. The skin around the scrawl is red and raw where the pen nib has torn into it, my body bleeding green ink with my blood.

'Sometimes, people need the truth just a little bit closer to, well—' he gestures to my arm '—home. We call it shock treatment—it's very effective. This way, you will always know who you are.'

'I know who I am.'

'Really? Do you *really*, Maria?'

His voice is soft and low and when I look at him, tiny creases fan from his eyes, and I don't understand. Is he feeling kindness towards me? Raven said I could find out who I really am if I locate the file—what did she mean? Pain throbbing through me, I blink again at my bicep, trying to piece it all together. 'I cannot be Basque.'

'Maria, my dear, you'd be surprised what we really can be if we look hard enough. And yes, you are Basque.'

I don't know how long I sit there. I stare at my arm, ten seconds, twenty seconds. I lose track of time as the words on my arm blur into one and my brain switches off at the overload of it all—at the smells and the sounds and the ink in my arm and even the whiteness of the walls that stare soullessly back at me. I know what it means, biologically, for me to be Basque, but how?

'The only way in which I can be Basque is if there is Basque lineage in my father's and/or mother's family,' I say after a while.

'Finally,' he says, slapping down his hand to his lap, 'a probing thought. But,' he says, glancing at his watch, 'I have to leave you. Momentarily, you understand.'

He rises, clutches his file, inserts his glasses to his top pocket and turns to leave. But my concentration does not focus on that, because something has slipped from his lap and dropped to a pillow of towels that are stacked just to the right of his chair. I dart my sight straight to Black Eyes. I do not want him to notice what I have seen.

'Tests, Maria,' he says now, striding to the door, his fingers resting on the handle. 'We need to carry out some tests on you, small ones, just to ensure you are ready for service. Ready to work for us once more, for Cranes.' He smiles and my skin shivers. 'For peace. It's lovely to have you back in the fold.'

Withdrawing the remote control from his pocket, he directs it to the speaker. The 1930s melody creeps once more into the room and I wince, the woman's voice warbling again, as Black Eyes dwells on me for three seconds, and my arm by my side screams in pain. I don't like him looking at me. I divert my sight, keep my eyes low and quietly count the seconds in time to the melody until he leaves. Finally, on sixteen, he intakes a sharp breath, turns and exits the room.

I keep counting. My sight fixed on the closed door, I wait and count five more seconds and when on six the shadow of the guarding officer outside disappears, I make my move.

First, I scan the room for obvious cameras. There are none that can be detected on initial search, no manufactured spiders on the wall, no unusual pictures or points. Yes, they could still be recording me, but the probability is that this is a secure area, a room where people can carry out whatever procedures they need to do—such as tattooing ink messages into someone's arm—and do it completely undetected and unwatched.

I turn, drop my feet to the cold tiled floor, slipping off the bed. I am unsteady at first, wobbling, almost falling into the chair, but, after a few seconds, I become steady, finding my feet, instructing my limbs to move, and when I do manage to step forward, I peer down and see what I spotted only a minute or so ago. There, on the towels: the fountain pen. Black Eyes' fountain pen.

I glance to the words tattooed into my arm then, looking back to the pen and taking in a breath, I twist the pen nib loose and tear it from the base flute.

It snaps out with ease. I hold the nib in my palm and, slapping back my matted hair, I close my fist around it and replace the lid back on the pen, and start to gently return the outer case to its original position on the towels, the entire time trying to push aside the music that lurches in and out of my ears.

And then the door sounds.

It is light at first, the noise, but there is an unmistakable click followed by silence.

I move fast. Plunging the lid on the pen so it appears as normal, I drop it to the towels, adjust it to its original position, fly across the room and, shooting a look to the door, clamber to the bed. I swing my legs up and over it, pulling my knees to my chest, the nib locked in my palm. My heart pummels my ribs as I try to recreate the position I was in when Black Eyes left. As I do it, as I draw my knees to my chest, clamp my arms around my legs, I realise something. The nib. It can't stay in my palm or they will find it when they inevitably search me either here or at the next place. My eyes fly left and right, hunting for a safe hiding space when the door begins to open.

Panic. The 1930s woman warbles, the nib pricks my skin and the door creaks further into the room. A chill sweeps into the air as the cold from the corridor beyond wafts by, leaving me no time to move, and so I do the only thing I can: I slip the nib into my scalp, hidden under my hair. The point pierces my skin, but I cannot shift it.

Because, right now, the door is wide open.

Black Eyes enters, abruptly halts then strides to the far side of the bed and, pausing to stare at me, he looks down at the towels. My heart hammers. I try to act like me, as I normally would, keep my eyes set downwards, no contact made and when his hand brushes the mattress near my leg, I make sure I flinch.

'Maria, remember to breathe,' he says, the lines wrinkling out from his eyes again. 'We're all on the same side here. I'm not going to hurt you.'

He resumes looking toward the towels, and the music warbles on. My scalp stings from where the nib lies sliced into it and, every other second, I can feel a tiny trickle of blood weeping from the wound. I try not to move. Will he see it? Will he spot what I have done? The writing on my arm sends a sudden stab of pain up to my shoulder, biting and hot, and even though it hurts, I don't react in case the nib dislodges and I give the whole game away.

Finally, Black Eyes picks up his pen and turns. I press my lips together hard, hoping he does not unclip the lid and find the pen empty, knowing that somehow, here, if they know what I plan to do, I may never get out and then the file I need may as well not exist at all.

Black Eyes cradles the pen in his palm and I watch it and hold my breath. He exhales, and the tobacco from his lungs filters to my nostrils, sending my stomach into a spin.

'So, Maria, the tests are to begin soon,' he says now. 'Someone on the team will take you to where you need to go.'

'Where?' The pen nib jabs me.

'Just somewhere in the facility. It is routine.' He pauses, smiles. I shiver. 'Routine. I know you like that word, yes?'

'Yes.'

The door slides open and an intelligence officer enters. He wears black combats, a white tee, grey sweater and black sneakers. He is one metre and seventy-two centimetres tall and his chest is as wide as an American football player's, and when he stands in the doorway, he fills the space so much that the cold air from the corridor behind him stops blowing forth. He looks strong. My nerves start to spike.

Black Eyes nods to him and stands to one side. 'Please take subject number 375 to the conditioning area.' He directs one more look at me and without uttering another word, he strides out of the room and out of view.

Panic floods me.

The intelligence officer walks fully into the room now. I dart my eyes to the exit. 'Stay back,' I say, but he ignores me and keeps moving forwards, each step robotic, his skin in this controlled light glistening with a sheen of gloss.

'Stay back,' I repeat, yet still he comes. I iron myself into the bed and try to think quick. The nib hidden in my hair starts to make the blood from my scalp flow faster and I shout at the officer, try one more time to stop him approaching, but still he comes. He halts by my side and arranges his face into a frown.

'Subject 375, you are to come with me for tests.'

His voice is beige, no accent detectable, no dance to his words and when he lifts his arms, his biceps move beneath his sweater. Blood crawls down my neck.

The 1930s music plays on as the man begins to crane his body closer towards me and as he does his eyes scan every fold and curve of my body. It makes me squirm. I shove myself back along the bed as much as I can, but as I do, my gown rides up on my legs, exposing my flesh, and I am shocked to realise that beneath the gown I am naked.

'You must come with me.'

'No.' Alarms scream in my head and I smell the faint odour of metal from my own haemoglobin.

The officer glances to my leg then, without warning, he flicks out a hand and runs his index finger down my thigh.

I immediately recoil. 'Get off me!'

But he simply drops his hand, slices a smile across his face, then steps forward.

I bolt off the bed, firing myself to the corner of the room, but the officer strides over, blocking nearly all the light. 'There are no cameras in here.'

'Go away.'

'You have to come with me.'

'No.'

'Yes.'

'No!' I yell, heart smacking me, pulse scorching my arteries. 'No!'

And then, without warning, he lunges. He juts out his arm

and strikes, but I am ready. I roll to the side, my shoulder smacking into the wall as to the left, the man jerks his torso round and runs at me, forcing me to heave my whole body in the opposite direction. But even then, he is on me, the heat of his frame pressing down on my chest like a vice, squeezing the oxygen from my lungs. I start to choke. I smack my fist hard into his back, desperate for air, but he grabs my arms, straddling me, pinning me down so none of my limbs can move or fight.

He spits to the side. 'They said you were strong.'

'Get. Off. Me.'

'I think we'll need the cuffs for you.'

He reaches one hand backwards towards his inside jacket pocket, and without thinking, without stopping to risk-assess the situation, I take my chance.

Chapter 27

Fast, with my free arm that the officer has released, I tear the fountain pen nib out of my skull, pain ripping into my skin, and, with one breath, drive the point as hard as I can into the Project officer's cheek.

Blood spurts everywhere. His eyes dilate and on his forehead, a frown fixes then falls as his mouth drops open into a silent scream. I take my chance. I force my torso upward, heaving my shoulders towards his huge frame, as the officer now slaps a hand to his cheek and begins to sway.

My body slips free. I roll to the side, crashing my head into the leg of the bed, a thump of nausea booting me in the stomach, but I haul myself up, not wanting to be marooned or vulnerable. The man now writhes on the floor, moaning, his body temporarily immobile, but it doesn't last for long and, within three seconds, he drops his hand from his blood-streaked cheek and runs at me.

This time I dart to the right, smashing into the metal cabinet, the drawer spilling out and clattering to the floor. The man jumps on me, wrenching my arm to the left, sending a searing pain ripping down my body as if the entire limb is being torn off, but the pen nib manages to stay in my hand and, straining to move then forcing a strong push, my fingers fly round and I gash the man's wrist with the sharp tip.

He yelps, recoils back and I jump up. Slamming by the bed, the man staggers at first then, spinning round, yells at me and begins swinging out punches. One smacks me on the right cheek, splintering my entire face. My legs wobble, feet splay out and I think I am going to fall, believe I will topple when the man flies at me again, hands raised coming but he doesn't see my foot sticking out and trips clean over it.

His whole body falls like a tree to the ground, and although I am frantic and scared, I don't give the feelings room to surface and instead move fast out of the way as he timbers down the side of the bed, smacking his skull on the corner of the bedside cabinet, knocking himself unconscious.

My chest heaves, relief and sweat flooding me as I gulp in huge breaths, the 1930s music still playing above my head. I pull myself up, legs wobbling, and take in the sight of the man now. As I do, I glance at my own body. The gown is ripped and my body exposed, but no matter how much I urgently want to cover up, someone will notice we are missing very soon from where we are supposed to be, which means they could be here soon. I have to get out.

I go straight to the door and pause. I need to think through for a moment what my plan is. Balthus mentioned an Ice Room, one Mama told him about with a non-server-linked computer, a description that could possibly match that of

Raven, and if I can find that here then contact Chris, I may have a chance at locating the files I need. The woman sings her 1930s melody and I take a moment to think, start to formulate a plan when a hand grips my ankle. I shriek, look down.

'Fucking bitch!'

The officer. Gripping my ankle like a vice, he drags me, hard and fast across the room, toppling me instantly. Blind-sided, my hands fly out, clawing onto the bed, my fingers digging into the pillow, tearing it off the sheets as I tumble forward. Levering his torso vertical, the officer tries to get up now, lurching, driving his whole body strength at me, and I know that if I don't act now, if I don't do something significant, drastic, he will win, take me, transport me to a room of sedatives and conditioning and tests against my will and it will never end, this Project, their hold on me. Its cycle will never stop.

The man forces himself upwards once more, shouting now, in danger of alerting help, and this time, I do not hesitate. Something kicks in inside me, an instinct and whether I have been trained to react in such a way or it is my natural, primal survival response, in a split second I make my decision.

I grab the legs of the metal cabinet, jerking it into the air and with one muscle-wrenching swipe, I bring it down hard on the side of his head. He falls. He slides to the ground and instead of running away, I clamber straight on top of him this time, pinning him down with my legs and knees, and swipe the pillow from the floor that has been thrown off the bed. Clutching the edges of the pillow, I hold my arms locked tight and, eyes narrowed, half-horrified at what I am about to do, yet frighteningly focused, I drive the pillow down onto the man's face, wedge my knee on top of it and hold it there. His fists smash into my thighs. They hammer at the pillow and at my legs and at the floor, his nails digging into the cotton, into me, but my head stays fixed and when he squirms and thrashes, I press down harder and harder.

And I don't let go.

Above, the 1930s music still plays.

Undisclosed confinement location—present day

'Would you like some more popcorn?'

I reply yes and allow Ramon to feed me. Things are calm. My brother has been talking for a while now, over ten minutes in the semi-darkness, and every time he looks at me he smiles a smile that spreads creases across his face and it makes me wonder again why he is here.

Ramon has given me dates. He has given times and events and minute-by-minute breakdowns as he reads my thoughts aloud from my journal. Each time he does, I hope that something will trigger a link to an alibi for Papa, but nothing has yet arisen.

I am, though, recalling more and more, as my brother reads, of what has happened in the run-up to me being here. It has been hard to contemplate, being in that room at the Project, my naked body, the gown, the officer on top of me and the pillow on his face, but even the difficulty of it has been surpassed by the elation I feel that my short-term memory is returning.

Ramon shifts the journal from his lap and sets the torch to the side to give me one more piece of popcorn from the prongs of the fork, and, as he moves forward, his hand brushes my shoulder.

'Ow.'

'Sorry, M.'

He has brushed the fabric against my skin, irritating it more than it should. 'It itches,' I say.

'Where?'

'On the top of my arm.'

'Hang on.' The fork still in his fingers, he sets down the popcorn bag, moves forward, pulls up my sleeve to scratch my skin then gasps. 'Maria, what the hell is this?'

I crane my head to see then stop. There on the top of my arm are the red, sore, etched-on words that Black Eyes scratched into my skin. It comes back to me then instantly. The fountain pen, Black Eyes holding me down and breathing all over me, the Basque blood detail, the family tree lineage.

'M, what have you done to yourself?'

'I did not do it. Black Eyes did. He is from the Project.'

Ramon drops my T-shirt, steps back and shakes his head. His voice drops. 'Don't lie to me.'

'I am not lying. This is what they did.'

He looks again towards my arm. 'I mean, I knew you needed help, knew you got confused, lied, but self-harming? I mean, why would you carve *I am Basque* into your arm?'

'It is not self-harm, it is…' I stop, taken by a connection that is sparking in my head.

'Before the popcorn,' I say, 'you were reading an extract from my journal where Papa had a meeting with a man from

his office in a café in the Plaza Mayor. You read how I sat on
the next table eating ice cream with the yellow sauce and red
sauce on separate sides.'

'Maria, I don't think that, given your arm, we should be—'

'This helps me.'

He stops. I keep going, hoping it works. 'Please,' I say now,
fast, eager. 'I need help.'

The light above swings in a buttered glow that smears
across the room and for one small second, it makes the air
seem as if the sun itself were here. Ramon rubs his chin and
taps his foot and then, finally, picks up my journal and opens
it. 'What page?'

I feel relief and try to remain calm. 'Page thirty-five.'

He turns the page and reads my words and it jolts something. That day when I went for the ice cream—I remember
it so well because Papa, unlike Mama, allowed me to have
my sauces served separately because Papa knew I couldn't
cope with red and yellow being mixed together back then,
or even side by side. And I remember that now and recall
it because, the next day…the next day I was taken to the
autism facility by Mama, and Papa wasn't there. But did I
write it down?

'What is the next entry?'

'Wait.' Ramon flicks the page, states the date. 'It says
something about a white room and a computer and a load of
weird tests.' He looks up, a deep frown fixed to his brow. 'M,
what on earth would you write all this for? Is it some kind
of dream?'

But I barely listen, because all I want to do right now is
jump and whoop and clap my hands because even though the

memory in my journal would have been hazy and distorted by Project drugs, it gives me the answer I need: Papa could not have been the Project's contact. The date Ramon gave me kick-starts in my head a domino effect, dates toppling one into the other as I recall the times and days and even the weather on the occasions I went to the Project under the pretense of visiting the autism facility.

Papa did not take me to a single one.

So if he wasn't the contact, why were his initials on the file we found? It must have been ploy, a cyber trail the Project wanted me to follow. That's how they found me—it makes perfect, logical sense now. They knew Dr Andersson had been to my villa, knew I could kill her, take her SIM as I am trained to do, and so they planted false data in there somehow, via their covert asset in MI5, and that plant must have had a virus on it that—when the false Papa contact details were accessed and read, as they knew I would read them—it would instantly trigger a geolocation tracker for them to find me right there and then at the monastery.

'Maria?'

I jerk my head up. Ramon is staring at me, the frown on his head even deeper now.

'You have a huge smile on your face,' he says. 'Does it help, reliving the memories of Papa?'

'Yes.'

'Good.' He beams.

'Because it means that Papa wasn't in contact with the Project. And the Project are corrupt. They hurt people. They scratched words into my arm with a green ink fountain pen and they use people only for their blood type.

Did you know we have Basque lineage somewhere in our family?'

His grin drops and he slams the book shut. 'Jesus, M, stop it.'

'Stop what?'

'Talking about the Project like it's some awful, evil thing!'

He stops, chest heaving. I watch him and slowly, dread and fear rise up inside me all at once, as I connect together what his words signify.

'What do you mean, Ramon?' I say, barely daring to ask. 'How do you know the Project?'

He catches his breath. He wipes spit from his chin and levels me with a gaze. 'You talk about the Project as if they are bad.'

'They are bad. They do bad things and they have done bad things to me. They have made me do bad things, too.'

'No.'

'Yes.'

'No, no, no!' He starts pacing, knocking the light as he goes sending the bulb swinging into the air so the room swims in and out of light and darkness.

I begin to worry. This is not the routine way in which my brother normally acts and when he eventually stops, his eyes are downturned and his face sweats.

'They said you would say this about them,' he says after a moment.

'Who?'

He shakes his head. 'The Project do not do bad things. They are there to help you.'

I keep steady and force myself to ask the next question. 'How do you know this, Ramon?'

He raises his head now and looks to me. 'Because I asked them to help me with you,' he says, then lifts his head high, jutting out his chin and chest. 'Because I contacted them. Never Papa. It was me.'

Chapter 28

I let go of the pillow and throw it to the floor. The officer does not move.

I drop to my knees and, reaching my fingers forward, check for his pulse. There is nothing, no heartbeat, no pump of blood in his veins and when I watch him and wait, expecting to feel the surge of horror and shame I felt when I killed Dr Andersson, I instead feel nothing, not a shred of upset, not a flicker of doubt. I observe his corpse and tell myself that I have done the right thing. *Prepare, wait, engage.* The phrase circles my head.

I stagger to stand, wincing at the bruises that have sprung up all over me, drop my hands to my sides and glance to the speaker where the music still flows. I have to move. Soon—very soon—whoever is expecting me to arrive for tests will question where I am, will wonder where the officer in the sweater is, and, when he does not show up, they will come looking for us.

I observe my scratched, naked body, with its ripped gown

hanging from me and think. I have to get out, but I can't run dressed like this, unprepared. I look back to the man, to the clothes he wears, to his pockets, and, wiping my mouth with the back of my hand, I hobble over to the corpse and start to first pat it down for anything that may be of use. From the large combat pocket on the left leg, I extract an item and, holding it out in my palm I see an old floppy computer disk. This is odd—these have not been used for over a decade, so why does this man have one?

I search the rest of his clothes. Pulling out four more items, I examine them at speed and count a swipe card, a cell phone, an opened packet of gum and a tiny black and silver car fob. I turn the fob in my hand, clocking the make of the vehicle, then, setting the items to the floor, I scramble across the tiles and, with fumbling fingers, begin to rip the clothes from the dead body and put them onto my own.

Slipping the sweater over my head, the clothes baggy but adequate, I scoop the stolen items back up from the floor and thrust them into the combat pockets, tightening the belt as much as it will go. I count to five, turn to the door, expecting a lock to unpick or a code to crack, but it is open, simple. I glance to the officer—he must have thought I'd be easy to handle.

The 1930s music plays as I peer now out into the corner. The area is clear. The walls, like in the room, are white and along the crease where the floor sits is a black strip that runs as far as the eye can see. There are no windows but instead sequenced strips of clear Perspex in sections, pieces that, like the bed in the room, have rounded rather than angled edges, and when I track above me I see the lights that run the course of the ceiling have a low-stimulus glow as each area of the corridor moves along in clearly defined, compartmentalised segments.

Scanning one more time for any officers, I clasp the sweater around my abdomen, tiptoe through the door, thinking of the cell phone. I can use it. I can use the dead officer's cell to contact Chris via secure text so he knows my location. I pad forwards and go as steady as I can with bruised limbs and a beaten face, my eyes scanning every inch of space, and even though there are no cameras at first glance, no hidden recording devices, I tread along the walkway, slow and silent, stopping at short, defined intervals to check for any unwanted sounds.

I turn a corner and immediately hit a problem: an officer is standing nearby talking on a phone. I dart behind a pillar and peer out, heart slamming against my chest as I watch him and think. The best plan right now is to wait—the officer may be finished with his call shortly, meaning he will vacate the area and I can move, but as I observe him and scan the area, something on his shirt catches my attention. There are regular buttons on the shirt, a soft cotton fabric, yet what makes me go very still is what is printed in black just below the right-hand shoulder. It is the letter H followed by a three-digit number.

My mind instantly goes to the flashback. When I entered the room in that memory where Raven was, there was an officer present with the same lettering and number font as this officer here now. I risk another look to check in case I am mistaken, but I am not. The two are the same. Black Eyes said this facility is in Hamburg, so is that what the H on the shirt simply signifies? Hamburg? And if so, does that mean that the image I recalled where the woman told me about the room and the files, is here? I look again at the walls and the lights and curves and try to conjure any memory I have of being here, of walking here, and there are some hazy, smudged thoughts, but nothing I can hold tightly onto.

An idea strikes. Slipping the stolen cell from my pocket and scanning the area before I start, I unclip the SIM from the cell and check for bugs. Satisfied there are none, I return the SIM, switch on the phone and, bypassing the pin code through a fast hack, I go into the device, enable text encryption and, peering around the corner and seeing the officer is still there, I message Chris.

With Project. Injured but ok. In Hamburg. Can u trace my location. Looking for file…

I hit send and almost immediately a reply pings back.

Hiya! Was worried. Your cell has GPS. Project can track it. Am disabling Project tracking so only I can track u then u r safe. Doing it now…Patricia says: five fingers (??)

Patricia, her hand sign to me. I clutch the cell and the nerves I feel pass a little easier at the thought of knowing my friend is there for me and that she, for now, is safe. I wait, anxious for the next reply. I cannot tap my foot or the officer ahead will hear, so instead I clench my teeth and count. On five, Chris finally replies.

Done. Got you. Your location is 7 km outside Hamburg near

disused factory. I can track u to a walkway in building flagging up as a pharmaceutical company. Balthus says: be careful. I say: what ;-)

What. I find myself, for some reason, amid the chaos and anxiety, smiling just a little at Chris's word. I text back.

Tell Balthus: officer here with same letter (H) & number font as in flashback with Raven. Think this could be the facility with the file. Do u concur?

Five seconds later, a reply returns.

Balthus here. Yes. Agree. Sounds the same facility. Be careful. Stay in touch. Chris ready to help.

I clutch the cell, breathing much easier now when ahead the officer finally finishes his call and strides away from the corridor leaving the place empty. The lights glow, casting soft yellow lines to the white walls and when I scan the area, the Perspex shimmers and the rounded edges of the plastic gain a small, gentle glint. I am about to pad through the walkway when a message comes in from Chris, and I slip back behind the pillar for cover and read it.

Balthus said file & computer from flashback may be in ICE room. I have an idea how to locate it.

I try to ascertain how he could do this, but when I come up blank, I text back.

How? Not possible.

Process of elimination, Google he texts back immediately. Do most Project facility rooms, from your memories, have server computers & internet enabled?

Fast, unsure where he is going with this, I think through what I recall.

Yes. 98% probability of server connection/internet. What plan?

Chris: Hacking into their system now via geolocation on your cell...Wait...

I tap my foot and feel nerves rise inside me. The longer I wait out here, the greater chance I risk of being found. After four seconds, Chris replies and I allow myself to breathe out.

OK. Process of elimination. There are only two rooms without server/connection internet that aren't store cupboards. One of them could be the ICE room you need.

I stare at the phone a little shocked. How did he do that so quickly? But before I can think it through, another text comes in and this time it links to a live map tracker of the internal infrastructure of the Project building.

I type straight away.

Is this secure??

100%. The red dots indicate the two rooms for you to try. Can u find them? Side note: located two cameras in the area and switched them to static image so you safe ☺

I look up. He's right. There are two tiny black dots in the corner of the corridor where the ceiling meets the wall, barely visible and when I squint my eyes, I can see two microscopic lenses with a glass sheen. I exhale, wipe a bead of sweat from my brow and, counting to three to stay calm, I look back to the cell phone map from Chris. The rooms are not far away and when I calculate the time it will take to reach the first room, I realise it is only twenty seconds in the corridor to the right. I look up. The area is clear.

Will go to nearest room now.

As I send this, holding the cell phone out so I can watch my movements on the map on the screen, I begin to sprint along the walkway, my feet padding along the tiles.

I reach the first room in twenty seconds as forecasted and stopping, scan the corridor to ensure I am alone. When all seems safe, I text Chris with my status and observe the door that now stands in front of me. It is silver. It stands at 204 centimetres height and when I touch it, it feels cold where the stainless steel sticks to my skin. Hinges roll on the outside of the frame and when I look to the handle, I see a scanner entry system pad with an infrared light under the shaft of metal that lies on the top. The red light shines, signalling that the door is locked, the room barred. I take out the swipe card from the dead officer, look at it then look to the door and to the scanner and see instantly that the two will match, meaning the door will open. But that is not what grabs my attention, what makes me now realise that what I am standing in front of is the room from my flashback, the one Raven was in, the one Mama must have overheard someone talking about and told Balthus of when she was ill.

I look up, scan for any officers and, when I am sure there are none present, I text Chris fast.

Located ICE room

He replies instantly.

What? You certain? How can you tell?

I lift my eyes to the door, to a brushed metal panel with black writing that sits in the top left-hand corner. The panel reads: Isolated Computer Environment.

ICE.

I hold up the cell, click a picture of the panel and, sending it to Chris, text, Track me, then, swipe card in my hand, I steady my fingers and go to open up the ICE room door.

Chapter 29

Deep cover Project facility.
17 hours and 52 minutes to confinement

My fingers pinch the swipe card and are about to glide it under the scanner when a text flashes up on the phone from Chris that says STOP!!

I whip my hand away and read the next message, anxious now that someone will come very soon and find me.

Do not enter ICE room yet. Have detected a sensor on the door that alerts a central control room if activated. Will disable alarm now

I look at the words and think. Disabling the alarm will enable me to enter the ICE room without the sensor triggering, but there is a huge problem with Chris's suggestion. Palms sweating now, I text back fast, not sure if I will be in time to stop him.

URGENT: Do not disable alarm. Control will detect if alarm disabled. Will flag on system. You must instead bypass system and switch sensor to a permanent 'no alert mode.' This will not arouse suspicion

I stop and wait. My heart beats hard against my chest and when I look to the area beyond, the lights on the ceiling flicker and the walls shimmer in frost-bitten white, and in the air a clinical, detergent smell drifts in and out. After five seconds, Chris finally replies.

OK. Good spot. Hacking into control centre system now. Hard. Will be as quick as can :-0

I look at the symbols he has put on the end of the message. I don't know what they mean and it bothers me. My foot begins to tap. I am exposed here in the corridor and even though the cameras have been deactivated and the cell phone cannot be traced by the Project, I am still vulnerable. I wait. My eyes scan the door, checking again the panel where the description of the ICE room lies, the words appearing etched on, thick black, rigid and straight. I risk touching the door and find it is smooth, and when my index finger runs down the centre, a streak of cold comes up so fast and unexpectedly that I have to snap my hand away to stop it from draining of blood entirely.

I check the cell. Chris has not replied and it is now hard to contain the anxiety inside me, so I focus on my breathing and clench my teeth to contain what panic I can and not alert the Project to my position. My fingers hover, about to text a request for an immediate update on progress when there is a sound. I freeze. Boots in the far distance at, on initial calculation, one hundred metres away, the distinct slap of their rubber soles on tiles indicating two, perhaps three people. And they are coming towards this area at reasonable speed. I quickly text Chris.

Urgent I text. Officers approaching. Require update now

I jerk my head up and scan the corridor. They are closer, perhaps fifty metres away, no more, the sound becoming louder and louder in my ears and my head, and when I stop, voices whisper out, drifting up through the corridor. I look again at the phone, but still there is no message.

'Where is she?' I hear a voice say somewhere ahead, words clipped and neat.

They are only thirty metres from me now. I could enter the ICE room and take a chance on not triggering the alarm, but this is the Project and all areas have a high probability of being monitored and checked, and if, upon entering, something alerts them, they will find me. Twenty metres now. I swallow, scan the left side of the corridor. Here, the warrens seem to disappear as if they were going down a hole, the air darker, the lights lower and the glow so muted, the colour appears to be lilac and purple rather than orange. I could run that way. I could sprint right now and take a chance at finding a route through, contacting Chris so he could track me on his laptop remotely and help me escape. I think. Fifteen metres now, round a corner somewhere the boots sound.

The cell vibrates. I nearly jump at the sensation of it in my hand and, fingers slick with sweat, I read.

Done. Go in room NOW

The voices are ten metres away. Keeping my nerves as steady as I can, fast, I swipe the entry card under the sensor and, twisting the handle as softly as I can, slip through the door, and as I click it carefully shut, three pairs of boots stomp past outside and walk straight on by.

Undisclosed confinement location—present day

Ramon ceases pacing and rolls his head. I don't know what to do. The light in the room has weakened and the bulb above us hangs limp in the air from the ceiling where droplets of moisture now gather and fall.

'Why did you contact the Project?'

My brother inhales. It is long and drawn in, sending his eyes up into his brow so all I can see in the dimness of the room is the pale white of his eyes.

'You needed help.'

Worry and confusion collide in my head. How can Ramon believe the Project could help me? The thought scares me because, in all the time I have known about the Project and the hold they have over me, I never imagined that hold would extend to my brother. The fear that grips me now is more than I have ever felt. It rips into me, tearing open so wide what I held true, that reality is barely recognisable any more, because it's not just me they are poisoning—my entire family is infected now, too, and it is all so painful to contemplate that my brain is unable to process the emotions of it. I begin to lightly bang my head on the back of the chair.

'The Project are dangerous,' I say. 'They cannot help me.'

'They are doctors. M, stop banging your head—you'll hurt yourself.'

'They perform tests on me. They will hurt you.' The thought makes me bang my head a little harder.

'No, they won't, and tests can help you.' He shifts forward. 'M, please stop.'

'No.'

'Yes.' He tuts. 'See, M, this is what I don't understand. You've been seeing the Project for years—why won't you just accept that all along they have been there to help you?'

I halt hitting my head. His words, my brother's words. *Seeing the Project for years.* A cold shiver runs down me as I connect it all, as, one by one it all slots into place like a puzzle, the files, the ones Chris hacked into at the monastery upturning the false information about the contact being papa when all along, it wasn't papa at all, just like Ramon said. 'How do you know I have been seeing the Project for years?'

He remains quiet.

'I said how do you know I have been seeing the Project for years?'

'You know.'

'I want you to say it.'

He closes his eyes. 'Because I'm their contact.'

Blood rushes up to my head. I instantly thrust myself forward, rattling my arms and legs to break free. 'Let me out.'

'M…'

'You sent me to the Project! You were the contact, not Papa. You let them test on me! How long have you been with them?'

'M, calm down.'

'How long have you been in touch with them?'

He shifts from foot to foot. 'Several years.'

'How many?' He is thirty-six years old. Two decades of contact would take him to starting at sixteen.

'M, stop!' His voice rises and I slap back into the chair at the sounds, and when I look at my hands they are red and bulging where my fingers and nails dig into the wood.

'Maybe it's ten years? More?' he says. 'I got the information on the Project from Mama.'

And then, when he utters that, it all makes sense. The Project being able to find me. MI5 discovering my villa, the handlers, the file Chris located at the abbey with all the surveillance data on me, my locations, actions, full day-by-day whereabouts right down to the last second. 'You accessed the details Mama believes are for an Autism Centre and you have contacted the Project, and the Project have turned you. They have convinced you they are helping me and are now using my own brother to conspire against me.'

'Maria, that's not true.'

'They are dangerous,' I say, urgent now. 'You can't trust them. Ramon, whatever they have told you, you cannot believe them.'

'He said you'd say that.'

I stop at his words. 'Who said I would say that?'

The light swings once then twice above his head. 'Dr Carr.'

'Dr...Dr Carr.' I say the words as if in a trance and when I blink, the room feels as if it is swaying and yet everything remains still and frozen and set in stone and time. Ramon does not move. He hangs his fingers by his side and, tipping his head to the left, observes me as I now frown and drop my chin, my mind inside grappling with the weight of what is real and raw and utterly urgent.

'M? M, say something. You're worrying me.'

I lift my head. 'You know Black Eyes.'

'Black who?'

'Black Eyes is Dr Carr. Which facility are we at?'

'What? What do you mean facility?'

I look at the room again. The walls I recall from my dreams are white, but here there is no light and the walls are black and soot-filled, so what does that mean? What location can that be?

'If Dr Carr has been contacted,' I say now at speed, 'or if Project officers are on their way, we have to get out of here. They could arrive soon.' I try to pull myself up and out, but the rope drags me back and pins me to the chair. Breathless, I look round. The crate is upturned, my journal sits on it, open on a page where Ramon left it. 'We have to get away from them. We are all in danger. Mama, is, too. It says so in my journal what they can do. It details everything the Project has done to me that I can remember.'

He sighs. 'M, Mama is fine.'

'How do you know Mama is fine? Have you seen her? We could be anywhere now. The Project has facilities in places I still do not know of. We are not safe.'

'M,' he says, his voice low and hushed, 'Mama is fine because…because she is here.'

Mama at the Project? Panic bolts up like lava. 'No! Mama is not well. If the Project has Mama it means none of us are safe now. You must understand this. Mama has cancer—this will endanger her health.'

He shakes his head and rubs the bridge of his nose with his fingers. 'M, please stop.'

'We have to get out!'

He lifts his eyes now to mine. The air is stagnant. One whip of oxygen skins the edges of the walls and floor, and when I look to my journal I see scrawled writing, notes, maths equations and sketched drawings. The fork from the popcorn lies next to the open pages and when the light bulb swings, glints of metal prongs catch the ripples of air as, before me, Ramon bends down, shuts my journal and picks it up, knocking the fork to the floor in front of me. He slides the journal under his arm and, pausing to press his fingers into the cover, he takes one step to the side where the timer and the medical stand sit.

'What are you doing?' I ask. 'It is vital we get to Mama.'

'M, Mama is safe.'

'How can you be certain? The Project has her.'

'You have to stop talking about the Project like this, M. They do not have her.'

'You said she is here. The Project are dangerous,' I say, regardless. 'And if the Project do not harm her, MI5 could take her in order to get to me and kill me, just as they tried to in my villa.'

'What? Kill you? What the…?' He wipes a palm across his mouth and for three seconds, does not speak. 'They won't get to Mama just as much as no one is going to kill you. MI5? Jesus, M. You've always done this ever since we were kids. Exaggerating, saying you've been taken by people, writing down weird made up stories about doctors and white masks and needles. You just wanted to be a doctor, that's all, so you could make people better, give you a sense of control over life's events after Papa died. It had nothing to do with the Project. You've got to stop making things up, blaming other people.' He stops. 'I love you,' he says after a moment, his voice soft, low. 'I really, really do, but you always make it about you, always. I exist too. All Papa ever saw was you.'

'That is physiologically untrue. Papa was not blind, therefore he could see you in the same ratio as he could see me.'

He opens his mouth to speak but then shuts it, huffing out a great sigh of breath. 'That's not…that's not what I meant.'

'How do you know the Project will not get to Mama and hurt her?' I say, fast, my mind calculating now every eventuality of how Mama could be located and used by either the Project or MI5. 'You cannot be one hundred percent certain.'

'Yes, I can,' he says, 'because a) the Project is not who you say they are and b) Mama is not with the bloody Project because Mama is upstairs in her house in Madrid!'

The whole room stands still. All of it, everything. Ramon's words hit my brain and, at first, they just hover there, suspended in mid-air, levitating in my mind.

'Are we in…Mama's city house?'

'Yes.'

I keep my eyes down, not daring to look up in case they give away the fear and bewilderment I now feel. The Project has facilities in several locations, but all along, this has not been one of them.

'We are in Madrid,' I say aloud after a moment, sounding the phrase out. I try to think through my movements before this room, and small flashes of memories whip by of an airport and people and noise and scaling a tall building.

'Which part of Mama's house are we in?' My voice shakes.

'The basement.'

I compute the information and force myself to scan the room. The dark walls, the damp and the droplets and the suffocating air that swings on a pendulum between hot and cold. As a child I would come to Mama's Madrid place many times when she was working on a case in the capital, but I was never allowed into the basement. I was only permitted as far as Papa's study in the room before the top-level entrance to the basement steps below. 'You kept me in Mama's house for the Project. Why?'

He pauses. 'Because I was worried about you. You disappeared after prison and you came here through the window, M, the bloody window, and it scared the shit out of us. I mean, what the hell? So I contacted them. I contacted them about you to see if they could help calm you down.'

He flicks something on the timer now and a rush of liquid floods the still air. I jerk my head to the right. 'What are you doing?'

Ramon turns one more switch then, securing my journal under his arm, steps into full view. His hair has slid to his eyes in the heat and under his arms are two circles of damp.

'Turn off the timer, Ramon.'

'They will be coming soon,' he says now.

I bolt forward. 'No. Ramon, no.'

But he simply sighs and shakes his head. 'M, it's the right thing to do, it really is. You're out of control. The things you say—' he gestures to my journal '—the things you write. M, you need help. I love you, you are my little sister—and you need help. The Project are there for you. Yes, their recommended methods are a little…unorthodox, but they're on your side, at the end of the day.' He exhales. There are tears in his eyes. 'We all are.'

I thrash forward again. 'Ramon, no. Do not give me any more drugs. Ramon, it makes me forget! This is what they do. Do not believe them! Do not tell them anything more about me!' Mama is upstairs. Ramon is with the Project. She is in danger.

'No, M. They said the medicine would do you good, keep you under control until they could get here and help us with you.'

I throw my body forward. 'Ramon, do not leave me here!' And as I say the words, as I smack my body towards my brother with all my energy, snapshots of images begin flooding back to me, click, click, click, one after the other like a camera as my short-term memory finally starts to expose itself in full. I see the Project and a room and the man on top of me and the ICE room that Chris helped me break into undetected. I see it all, finally, recall every single part, right up until I arrived here.

My brother ascends the steps, opens the door and turns. 'It's okay, M. It's for the greater good.'

He leaves, the sound of the door, as it closes, vibrating through the room and into the darkness of my ears and head.

The timer by my side ticks.

Chapter 30

I slam my back against the wall and, catching my breath, recite the name and birthplaces of Mozart, Debussy and Wagner to calm me down. I listen out for any officers coming this way. After counting ten seconds, and when all seems clear, I grip the cell phone tight, pad forwards and observe the area.

The ICE room is six metres by six metres with no windows or soft furniture, and on the walls is a light pattern of leaves that appear as if they have been stencilled on with a grey lead pencil. It is cold. A small fog of my breath billows into the air and I pull the dead man's sweater tight over my chest and hook the combats up to my stomach so they don't slip down my hips. The lights in this room, as outside, are low-stimulus, casting small shadows of my frame across the side of the walls and when I move my arms, they rise slowly across the dimensions of the space making it seem as if my body is bigger than it is.

Over to the right sits a computer. I walk to it now and slowly, I peer down. It seems to be linked, from first glance, to a modem in the corner on a shelf-size table that juts out like an ice sculpture and dominates the room. I remain as I am and keep my eyes set on it. Could this be it? Could this be the computer Raven informed me of?

I text Chris to update my status then take two steps towards the computer, but something is not right. I bend forward and realise what is unusual about it. Old. The computer is old, not a modern laptop or a flat screen update, but a bulbous, cumbersome machine, a small, fat dinosaur of a device with a modem that sits by the potbellied screen where two green lights flash, switched on, ready to be used.

The cell phone vibrates, making me jump a little. I compose myself and read.

Creating a secure line now to speak on. Ready in three. Two. One. OK. You can call me now if safe.

I call Chris's cell and Balthus picks up.

'Oh, Maria, thank God you're okay. Where are you?'

I tell him, my eyes on the computer.

'Does it look like the one the woman in your memory described?'

'It is possible.'

'Doc?'

Patricia. When I hear her voice I instantly smile. 'Are you safe?' I ask.

'What, me? Doc, I'm fine. I'm more worried about you. Are you hurt?'

I touch the bruises now appearing on my wrist where the officer held me down, and glance to the phrase etched in ink by Black Eyes on the flesh of my upper arm. 'I am hurt but not a concerning amount. I am in the ICE room.'

'Okay. Okay, good, good. I'm going to pass you on to Chris, okay? But Doc, be careful. We're all here, yeah? You're not on your own.'

I breathe in and let her words sit in my head and stay there.

Chris comes on the line now. 'Hey, Google, so what can you see?'

'My name is not Google.'

'I know.'

I look to the room and describe the computer as I have seen it so far.

'Sounds like a standalone one, all right. Way old, too. Have you switched it on?'

'It is on standby.' I lean in. 'Pressing the button now. There is an old hard drive station to the right.' I wait, one second, two, until, finally, a fan inside splutters to life and the screen flashes green once, dies, then reappears with an operating page.

To the side is a chair made of grey plastic with black rubber soles. I pull it out, no sound made on the floor and, keeping the cell to my ear so no one passing by will hear any extra voices, I continue to Chris.

'The screen is fully functional now.'

'Cool. Anything on there yet?'

It first appears flat and empty, but then, as the screen flickers and moves, an icon, a red and blue icon with a yellow bar like a vulture's beak, appears. I describe it to Chris.

'Whoa,' he says. 'Really?'

'Yes.'

'Do you know how to access it then bypass the code?'

I think to my notebook, remember all the images photographed in my head of the data and numbers in there. 'I can access the first level and then jump to the second.'

'Nice. If there are more levels after that, I can help. Oh wait—Patricia says five fingers again. What the hell is that?'

I think of Patricia's hands held up to mine and, listening out for any external sounds, I roll back the shirt sleeves and get to work. The first task is to concentrate on the computer and locate the yellow symbol on the screen that matches the one from my memory of my notebook and coding. Almost instantly, a series of numbers flash up, but then: nothing. The screen plummets into black and my eyes tear across the glass, searching for something that is not there. I try to think fast. What have I done? Has clicking on the icon crashed the system? Do they know I am here and have alerted Black Eyes?

I tell Chris what has happened, unsure if he can help but aware that if I waste any more time, I could be found.

'Okay, hang on,' he says, and I hear some rustling and then he's back. 'Sorry. Packet of chips. Okay, so you should see a blue square, top left hand corner. You see it?'

I look. He is right. There is a tiny blue square in the edge of the screen no more than one millimetre in diameter and when I squint at each corner, I see they are curved and round and soft at the edges. 'It is pulsating,' I say.

'It is? Ah, okay. Don't touch that then—it's a trap. Kind of. Okay, now look at the yellow part of the icon instead and hover the cursor over it. I'm trying to access their system now at the same time, so I'll be a sec.'

There is a clash of sound from outside. I don't move, instead wait and listen. It sounds like metal being toppled somehow somewhere, but it is difficult in this room where my breath blows, to determine the exact location. After five seconds, the sound passes and the air returns to quiet. I swallow, look to the screen and carry on.

The cursor, when it hovers over the yellow of the icon, does, as Chris said it would, shimmer. I lean in and study it. There are pixels as it moves, black, tiny pinprick dots that flash in and out, and when I sit back, they seem to disappear.

'Hey, Google, you still there?'

I ignore Chris's name for me and instead describe the structure of the yellow icon.

'Oh, awesome. Okay. I want you to click on it now and, if I've got my sums right, we should be able to get in.'

'How can you be certain?'

'I can't, but it's the best shot we've got, right?'

I hesitate. Mathematical certainty is what I prefer to deal in. It is more reliable than people, more black and white, no grey areas, no hidden meanings, but if Chris is not completely certain, how can I trust him?

'Google, have you done it yet?'

'I am unsure about this route of progress.'

'Why? Because it's not a definitive model?'

I watch the cursor blink at me. 'Yes.'

Chris lets out a breath. 'Look, the way I see it is that life is a series of choices and you can't always predict the outcomes. Even as a mathematician, that's impossible. You deal in numbers, right?'

'Yes.'

'Well even numbers are not straightforward, despite the fact they're infinite. I mean, look at the twin prime conjecture.'

I sit up, surprised that he knows of this complex theory. 'That is the conjecture that there are an infinite number of twin primes.'

'Exactly. Someone in 2004 proved it was true and then the paper was retracted because a load of errors were found in it and so they were all back to the start. So you see, nothing's certain, even when you think it is. So, the only answer has to be, well, to carry on anyway, best you can.'

I think about Chris's words, his theory and idea. Could it be so? Could I even try to live a life where the colour grey was an unknown quantity I could cope with?

Inhaling a large breath, I count to four then take the cursor and click on the yellow logo, and tell Chris. Together, we wait. After three seconds, slowly, an image unfolds on the screen and I watch as one pixel, two, then tens upon tens shower down the screen.

'Are the pixels still coming?' Chris says.

My eyes track every single one. 'Yes.' But then something changes. 'It has become clear now.'

'Whoa. Okay, can you see anything? Any different colour or another logo of some sort?'

I lean in. 'There is a file icon with two dark, black ovals in the far right corner and a name.'

'A name?' It is Balthus now, his voice quick and loud. 'Who?'

I lock the cell between my ear and my shoulder, and look at the screen. The image of Raven sways in my mind, the flashback, the visual of my fingers compiling a report on a computer with dates and details and confidential operational data.

'The name is the author of the report.' My breath momentarily halts. 'It is me. Dr Maria Martinez. And the report concerns two subject numbers.'

'Which ones?'

I stare at the screen, almost too fearful to read them aloud, because it means that the flashback was true—I compiled this report.

'Subject numbers 115 and 375,' I say after a while.

Raven.

And me.

Chapter 31

Deep cover Project facility.
17 hours and 35 minutes to confinement

'This is the file,' I say. My hands are shaking and when I look at the screen, it seems blurred and hazy. I scrunch my eyes shut then open and try to gain some focus, but it is hard. This woman has haunted my dreams for a whole year and now here I am and the answers she told me existed may actually be real.

'Patricia,' I say, the cell still wedged on my shoulder.

'Doc, you okay?'

I swallow and blink at the file. 'You will remain near to the phone, yes?'

'Of course, Doc. Of course. Just breathe, okay?'

I inhale, long and deep, and when I look to the lights, I feel grateful they are low and not bright and glaring. I take a moment to think. The ink on my arm from Black Eyes feels raw and painful, and so I count to ten and imagine slumbering lines of lavender plants, fragrant orange groves fat with fruit, olive trees swaying in a warm evening breeze and the fire pit in the small stone courtyard of my Salamancan villa sparking a roasting fire.

Exhaling hard and heavy, I open my eyes.

'Shall we do this?' Chris says.

I set my back straight. 'Yes.'

'Okay, Google. Tell me what you see.'

I start scanning. I follow the curve of each letter on my name first, each digit and line. 'It is clear the file is encrypted.'

'How d'you know?'

'It is steeped in a code that, on first sight, I do not recognise.'

'Can you try a basic decryption, see if that works?'

Straight away, my fingers begin to glide across the keyboard. They begin accessing the next level underneath the file via the subject numbers on the screen, but the second level comes to a halt, and no matter what I do to enter it, it throws back my access request every time.

'To penetrate the file requires a passcode, similar to others I have cracked,' I say now to Chris, listening out for sounds outside and careful to keep my voice low, 'but this document seems harder and most likely requires a password pattern I may not be able to decipher or an algorithm I do not identify with.'

I pause, exhale and listen for any signs of intruders. When I'm sure all is clear, I squash down my anxiety levels, and think.

'Patterns,' Chris says. 'Accessing the next level could all be a matter of patterns.'

My brain joins in. 'Find the pattern and we gain access.'

'Yep.'

Moving fast, I backtrack on myself, review the numbers that have flashed up in my head and track the patterns that arise and match them to the decryption required to access the file, but nothing penetrates it, no answer, no code, as if my brain has hit pause.

'Anything?'

'No.'

'Okay. Let me see what I can do.'

A pain shoots down my wrists and I wince. Lowering my arms, I look at the skin. Bruises are beginning to emerge in even stronger colours now, blues and yellow and purples smeared like paint across my skin, and the pain of it mixes with the sting of the fountain pen scar on my muscle sending a crackle of spikes into my bones. An anger surges inside me at the thought of what Black Eyes did to me as I stare at the screen, at the empty password bar, the word *black* swarming around my head, thicker, faster, like a plague of locusts, darkening my mind. *Black, black, black...* And as I think of this word, a memory begins to float upwards in my brain, but this time, unlike the others, the recollection doesn't hurtle me back in time with a jolt, but instead takes my hand and slowly leads me to see what was always there locked in my head. It is me at a computer, just as I was in my flashback at the villa, but this time, unlike before, I can see the screen that is in front of me, the one where I was working on the file. There is a pen to my left side and a piece of paper with my notes, and in front of me is a red file with the word *Confidential* printed on it. I see my face, no lines or wrinkles, look to the screen as it asks me for a password and there is a name on the file. My name. And two subject numbers...

'Maria? Maria?'

Balthus's voice comes into my ear from the cell and I come round with a start and sit bolt upright.

'Maria,' Balthus says, 'what is happening?'

I blink my eyes into focus. 'I know the password.'

'What?' Chis says. 'How? Did you crack the code?'

'No,' I say, pulling in the chair now. 'I wrote the code.' I pause. 'I wrote the password.'

'You remembered?' Balthus says. 'You remembered what was on the screen from your flashback?'

'Yes.' My fingers hover over the keyboard.

'What was it?'

I begin typing it into the passcode bar. 'Black Eyes.'

Confinement location—present day

The timer ticks loud and the clock device turns. I crane my head as hard as I can to see it. It is dark, which is good, the lack of light allowing my brain to remain relatively steady and functional. I think. If I let the drug flow now, I will be drowsy and incoherent, and Ramon could return with the Project in tow and I would be unable to defend myself or protect Mama.

The light above swings, one second, two, illuminating the floor for a fraction of time and I watch it and try to move my head forward, when I spot, in the weak shaft of yellow, the item Ramon knocked to the floor earlier.

The fork.

A plan forms immediately and I concentrate on the fork and don't let it out of my sight. It is silver and pronged with four tines. Its handle is slick and elegant, and when I observe it,

I attempt to calculate the distance it lies from my feet, but it is hard—the light flickers and the blackness looms, and each time I reach a close figure, the bulb sways away again and I find I have to guess.

I glance to my feet. They are bare, no socks or shoes, and I am about to flex my toes to check I have enough feeling in them when a bang sounds from somewhere and I freeze. Is Ramon coming back? When all falls quiet, I allow myself to exhale and resume analysing the utensil in the light that now dribbles in and allows me to see. If my calculations are correct, I should be able to reach the fork even though my legs are now tied at the knees to the chair. I pause for a moment. It is a lot to process. Ramon being with the Project, the fact that we are at Mama's house—my brain's automatic reaction is to struggle with it and it is exhausting but I force myself to deal with the problem immediately in front of me and deal with the fallout after.

Checking the door one more time and listening for any suspect sounds, I start.

I use my left foot first. My toes wriggle as, bit by bit, I push out my calf as far as it will go. My foot is approximately five centimetres from the handle to the left of its side, but it is not near enough, and so I have to scuttle my leg as far as it will go until, eventually I feel the cold metal of the utensil.

I count, keep steady and continue. My toes crawl like spiders towards the fork and find I have to grip the handle to get the utensil in my grasp, but it is difficult. No matter how hard I try, no matter how furious I stretch my leg forward, it does not work and the fork remains stranded on the floor.

I flop back to the seat, exhausted, the energy required just to move my toes wearing me out entirely, a vision of Ramon swimming into my head mixed with a thought of how he could hurt Mama. I close my eyes briefly, counting five seconds of rest, turning my feet in circles to get some circulation to them when something slips a little. My eyes fly open. I jerk my head down and look and see that the rope around my knees appears different to the one around my wrists. While they are tied tight, the rope hard, coarse, the tether around my legs is softer, smooth, less like wire and more like wool.

I think I can slip it off.

With a new surge of hope, I start to push and push against the rope on my legs and, gradually, it begins to come loose. I stop, catch my breath, check for any sounds of Ramon returning. When all is clear, I blow a stray hair away with an upturned lip, then recommence, my eyes blinking in the darkness of the basement. This time it is easier. My legs are fuelled by the memories from the sedative, from the stark recollection of what I now know, from the facts, the details, the data—I remember it all now, every part of my journey here. There is a purpose for me to escape, there is a reason.

One tug, two. The rope starts to move, slowly at first then quicker, rapid until I can feel it, but then the needle unexpectedly, digs in, and the pain is sharp, stabbing me hard, but I daren't cry out. I press my lips together. The stinging passes. Finally, the rope slips to the floor and my ankles are free.

I exhale hard, exhausted. My legs throb and my bones ache, and when I move, sweat tickles down my face, dripping into my eyes. I rattle my head, try to rid as much of it as I can, and refocus, glancing now to where the fork lies only centimetres from my feet. My legs untethered, I can try again at reaching it, at pulling it towards me, but it is difficult to see in the growing darkness. I squint, blink over and over, but the light is poor, washed out, and so I drop my foot, weary, slamming it to the ground then stop. There. The fork, beneath my toes.

Steadying my rapid shallow breathing, I spread out my toes in a star shape, grit my teeth and, straining my feet as far as they will go, link them in a claw around the fork.

It works. I keep going, steady, slow, creeping it up, the metal dangling from my toes, mindful of the needle as, beside me, the timer ticks. The fork reaches my knees now and I pause, unsure what to do next. My wrists are tied and the needle is in my arm, and by my waist my hips are straining as my legs jut out at a ninety-degree angle.

I think fast. The only method by which to do this will be to keep hoisting my leg upwards, toes gripping the fork as tight as possible, and so that is what I do. I lift the fork higher until I can almost touch it with my left hand, the fork teetering now by my fingers, the only sound in the room my breathing and the tick of the timer, as my hand becomes closer now to the metal, so near and—

I drop the fork.

I watch, eyes wide, as the utensil clatters to the floor, tinkling by my right foot, clapping to the ground as if I had never picked it up at all. I want to cry out, scream at the frustration, yell, holler.

But I do none of that. Instead, I swallow, blow back the sweat that swarms my face and I thrust my leg outwards and repeat everything I did before and this time, after two minutes of agony, it works. My legs lift the fork high enough to reach my hand and from there I use it to unhook the tethers on my wrists and remaining leg.

The rope slides off. My wrists ache and I rub them, elated at the tiny victory I have just scored, but the happiness is short-lived because a loud click sounds followed by a now familiar whoosh. I whip my head round. The drip, the seda- tive—it is activating.

Panic surfaces hard and fast, and, reaching my fingers to the crease in my arm, no time left, I draw in a large breath and, gritting my teeth, my sights set on getting out of here, I rip the needle clean out of my vein and throw it to the floor.

Chapter 32

As soon as I press the enter key on the password access box, a torrent of information crashes onto the screen.

'What can you see?' Chris asks.

'Data,' I say. 'Reams of data.'

I barely breathe as, in front of my eyes, information flies left and right, small icons that represent hundreds upon hundreds of documents popping up and filling the screen. The assault of it is hard on my senses, but I press on, eager to find out what it is, see if this really is the file that will give me what I need to end it all.

Once the documents slow down, I am able to zoom in on one at a time and read at speed, photographing every part in my head.

'Maria,' Balthus says now. 'Have you found anything yet?'

'Yes. The files are full of names.' I peer forwards. 'They are…Basque names.' I glance to the fountain pen tattoo on my arm.

'Anything else?'

Slightly concerned, I read on. 'There are what appear to be details of people, of other human beings listed here.'

'Others,' Balthus says. 'Maria, could they be other subject numbers like you?'

'Perhaps, although there is no definitive connection and…' I stop. There at the top of the file is my name and subject number next to the file creator section. I was the author of the report.

'It is me,' I say, almost to myself as I realise exactly what I am staring at.

'What do you mean?'

'In my flashback, Raven said the information was linked to a file I created.' I grind my teeth together, anxious now as I start to connect the small dots. 'This is the file.'

'Doc?' Patricia says now coming on the line. 'Doc, it's going to be okay. Keep reading, yeah? Then you'll get to the end of all this once and for all.'

I listen to her words and force my eyes and brain to carry on. 'My number…my number sits alongside the word *Basque* and near it are other surnames.' I read some of them aloud. 'Balthus, your parents are from the Basque country—do you recognise any of the names?'

But he does not answer and I begin to worry that the line has failed completely, when he finally speaks. 'Yes,' he says, clearing his throat. 'Yes, they are…they are Basque.'

'Doc,' Patricia says, 'does that mean you are Basque somehow, too? Your flashback—the woman—said the file would tell you who you are.'

I glance to my arm, to the phrase in my skin and I tell them about Black Eyes, about his explanation of the Project's complex use of people with Basque blood—and his tattoo work on my arm.

'Jesus Christ,' Balthus gasps. 'Maria, I am—' he pauses, coughs '—I am so, so sorry.'

I touch my shoulder and feel the rough grooves of the green ink on my red raw skin. 'How is Papa connected in all this? If I am Basque blood then he must be too.'

'Or your mam,' Patricia says. 'Could she be Basque?'

'Er, Maria?' Chris says now, cutting through my thought. 'I'm detecting some movement on a sensor device I've hacked into further up the system. You're gonna have to get through this file faster.'

The air runs cold and I tug the sweater tight around me, bite down on my lip and focus. Fragments of names roll up again, and at first there are just a few, but then it flips, the file, into something else, into what appears to be a new document, but what is strange is that each name disappears replaced, instead, by a number, and each number is linked to its own genealogy map. I relay the information aloud to the cell then hesitate as, before me the entire screen begins to fill with data and family lineage, until, at the bottom of the page I see a line that makes me go cold.

'There are 2,113 subject numbers,' I say, my fingers trembling as they hover over the keyboard. 'Balthus, the others in the conditioning programme do exist.'

'Dear God. They've been doing this for years and getting away with it. Jesus.'

I read more of the file. 'This gives extensive detail on their origins, what tests have been performed and how the subject has reacted to it all. This is key information we can use to halt the entire Project, and...' I stop. The document, as I move it, seems to now scroll across to the right and as it does, one word emerges, the same word over and over sitting alongside each subject number as my eyes frantically scan it all and a visceral fright takes hold.

'Deceased,' I say, swallowing, even though my mouth is dry.

'What?' Balthus says. 'Who is deceased?'

I look again to be sure, but there is no doubt. 'Against 2,005 of the subject numbers, the document states they are deceased. They died in the middle of being conditioned.' I look down, confused, concerned. I played a part in this. I helped file this document of dead people with extinguished lives and existences, and I don't even remember.

'Doc, oh my goodness.' Patricia's low lilt sifts through my worry. 'Breathe, okay? Breathe.'

I do. I breathe and try to stay calm and read on and see more data that details what Raven said there would be: pages and pages of confidential information on not only who the Project have tested on, but who they have killed on operations, what targets have been eliminated, details and illegal surveillance of regular citizens, of covert terrorism operations in Iran, Germany, France, Afghanistan, Belgium and many, many other countries.

I tell Patricia what I can see. 'How can this be for the greater good?' I say, eyes swimming a little.

'I don't know, Doc. I don't know. But we'll get them, okay? With all this information now, we can get them.'

And as her voice lilts in my head, I see it there, two pages in. 'My subject number is listed.'

'What does it say?'

I wipe the sweat from my head and make my eyes take in what my head does not want to see. 'It lists…' I stop, feel my body rock a little as I struggle to process it all. 'It lists the people I have killed. It says I am the test child and that I am the only one who has completed the full training programme without…without dying.' I stop, scared now at what it all really means. 'Others have died,' I say after a moment, 'but I am alive.'

'Doc, Doc, it's okay. You won't be one of them—you won't die.'

'That is not based on fact though. Your thought is being led by emotions.' My mind is gripped by a feeling of horror and shame, but when I read a census of what appears to be ten people I have eliminated through operations, I cannot feel upset. I cannot recall any of what I did and instead, work through the names and try to spot any clues. I see lists of cyber ops I have been involved in at various ages, look at data containing the training I have completed and against all of it, against every one is my age at the time, all culminating in the same countdown device Chris and I discovered on the computer at his house in Montserrat. But what is it counting down to?

'Balthus, she was right,' I say.

'Maria?'

'Raven said this file would tell me who I am.' I look at the numbers and facts on what I have done. 'This is who I am.'

'No,' Patricia says, 'it's not who you are, Doc. You never knew what you were doing.'

I want to believe Patricia's words, but something inside me is not convinced. I look at the data. The Project have made all this happen, here in Hamburg and in places elsewhere, these deaths and crimes and no one in the world but us seems to know about it.

'Is Chris there?' I say.

His voice pops up. 'Yep.'

'I want you to access the files on here. There is a modem.'

'Already on it. I can duplicate what I see by bypassing the system. I'm still getting some movement on the sensor somewhere in the facility, but I don't think it's too near you. I'll get this done then you can shut it down and get the hell out of there.'

The temperature of the room drops a few degrees more and my limbs begin to shake as I realise I have been sitting ramrod straight for the entire time. I set down the cell for a second, roll my head and, stretching my arms, pick up the phone again when Chris's voice crackles in fast and urgent.

'Whoa. Whoa, Maria? I'm getting something odd here. It's linking up to something.'

My pulse quickens. 'What is it?'

'I don't know…it should be appearing on your screen now. It looks like some kind of…Wait—is that a list of drugs?'

Nothing comes up at first on the screen, but then, after three seconds, a report emerges. It has a black border and on the main body, the page is yellow. 'This is an eyes-only document.'

'Holy shit.'

I scan the classified file and see details on drugs, on the names of specific medcines, ones that I know and have seen, as a doctor, before. 'These are cancer drugs.'

'I'm reading the same document now,' Chris says. 'Is that what they have been doing all along, d'you reckon? Testing cancer drugs on people?'

I examine the data further and see that each drug is linked to a test subject number, and as my fingers hover above the keyboard a frightening realisation of what I am looking at hits me. 'Have they tested these drugs on…on me?'

'Oh, fuck,' Chris says.

My eyes check the information again, almost in a haze, a bubble. It does not add up. 'Why would there be a need to test cancer drugs in this way? Is that why I have been ill in the past, because of these trials?'

'Think back to the times when you've been sick,' Chris says, 'try to link the symptoms to the drugs on the screen.'

I think, but there are no direct correlations to any illness I can recall within the date parameters on this file. 'If these drugs are trial phase only, then their effects would not be documented and no one outside the Project would ever be aware of the consequences.'

'Look at the final part of the document,' Chris says. 'It's got information on specific amounts of money in different denominations and they're linked directly to a cancer drug, and by each amount of money is a date and time.'

He's right. Leaning in, I look at the dates and see that they span three decades. 'The dates spread back into the 1970s.' I steady my hands and track the dates forward, when something changes and a feeling of dread floods me. 'In 1979, the amounts rise substantially and there is a location, a place. A place I know.'

'Madrid.'

Facts slam into me, hard, forging connections as I talk fast now, thinking aloud, my brain overriding emotions with data to help me cope.

'Three decades ago Black September began terrorist activities and the Project was created. These dates stretch back to that time. The cancer drug details spread back to that time also, as do the money transactions, many in Madrid.' The conclusion screeches in and knocks me sideways. 'Was Papa a part of this?'

'Maria?' It is Balthus. 'You can't tell from this who is involved. Alarico might have had nothing to do with it.'

'The correlations are clear and linked.'

'Yes, but what if it's not linked to the cancer drugs? Which means Alarico is not connected at all. The dates don't match. He was in court a lot at the times this file states. I remember because we used to talk a lot then. He was never ill, either. There's one person who has been ill, though.'

'Er, sorry to interrupt,' Chris says, 'but you've got some people approaching. They're reasonably far away, but it's hard to tell—best not risk it.'

I look to the screen. 'There is one more file unopened. Can you access it?'

'Copy that. I'll download it now.'

'Doc,' Patricia says, 'you've got what you've come for and Chris can help crack open anything else that was on there so we have the full data. But right now, you have to get out, okay?'

'Yes.'

I stand, pick up the cell and, with Chris finished his download, go to leave.

An alarm siren sounds and begins to shriek through the air.

Chapter 33

The alarm tears through the air, ripping it apart. I crouch down, one hand covering my head, the cell to my ear, my brain desperate to escape the auditory assault.

'On the plans, there's a main exit at the end of the corridor fifty metres to your left,' Chris says fast over the siren. 'The sensor is hacked and set up for you to leave. When you get out, aim for Hamburg station. I'll get a contact I know to drop you off a fake passport and cash in a locker there so you can travel onwards. I'll text the details.'

'Maria, go!' shouts Balthus. 'Go!'

I run to the door, stop and listen. The low lights help me to think and I can hear voices shouting, but because the alarm is so loud, it is hard to determine their distance from me. The siren bursts in quick, sharp shocks, and slapping one hand to my ear, inch by inch, I click the door open.

I peer into the corridor. There is a white walkway straight to my right and when I look both ways, it is clear. No intelligence officers, no sign of Black Eyes. I place my hand on the ice wall outside and, checking one more time in both directions, I sprint down the corridor towards what I hope is the exit, and after exactly fifty metres, I find a corner and I stop to assess the situation.

Drawing in long deep breaths, I scan the area, locate the exit Chris identified then go to calculate a second contingency option, when voices shout out ahead. Heart racing, I sprint straight to the initial exit then halt, scan it fast and realise with a deep pit of dread that I have nothing to make it through—no key, no access code, no way to contact Chris without alerting whoever is near. The alarm wails on.

I move. With the sound of shoes echoing on tiles, I turn and run, breath heavy, pulse spiking. I push against each and every door I see, but they are all sealed shut and surrounded by a black plastic mesh that is soft and sticky to the touch. Panic peaking, I race forwards and reach a red double door and brake, the rubber soles of the dead man's sneakers screeching on the floor. I glance to the right of the exit. There is an access key pad by the handle, but it is unusual: there are no buttons to press, no code to crack and I crouch a little, peer at it until I know what I am looking at: a fingerprint access scanner, one that will require approved users only.

A single shout rips from my right. I duck. I drop to the floor, crawling along to where the wall tucks in to the side and jerk my eyes left and right. The lights have an ever softer glow here and I know I need to hide, to move fast now, but all I spot at speed is a crevice one metre to my left and a gap that opens up all the way to the ceiling, like a chasm between two sheets of ice. The footsteps stomp closer. I glance to the exit scanner one more time, but there is no time to make it back over there, so I sprint to the chasm gap and squeeze myself into it.

My chest compresses, the oxygen wheezing out as the ice walls lock me in, but despite the sharp pain, despite the immediate discomfort, I cannot move. Because to my right are two armed intelligence officers.

I hold my breath as they scour the area. I count, one second, two, three, four. On five, I hear them turn and walk away, and I breathe out.

I peel my body out from the crevice and sprint back over to the exit and examine the access sensor. There are prints there, sweat residues from the skin of previous users leaving marks on the scanner. I think. If I could replicate the prints, if there was something to stick on to the glass then I could get out. Sweat pouring off me, the combat trousers I wear start to slide down and I pull them up when I feel something in my pocket that makes me stop: the chewing gum packet.

A vague memory floats into my head of Raven. She is working on an operation and smiling and saying, 'The Americans like their gum.' But she is not using it to chew. Instead, she is turning to a code pad and pressing the gum into the sensor.

The memory rolls away like a tide going back out to sea, and I intake a breath, short and sharp. The woman, her veil, the scent of mint gum mixed with spice and turmeric drifts away. I look up.

I know what to do.

Moving fast, I now throw my hand into the cargo pocket and, feeling for the sharp edge, pull it out. The floppy disk from the dead officer. The floppy disk with the sticky tape on the sides.

Steadying my fingers, I peel the tape and it comes away within a second. Crouching down, I survey the corridor and, as certain as I can be that all's clear, I hover the tape over the scanner and, using the torch on the cell, allow my eyes to track the small, flat screen, locating the best unsmudged and whole fingerprint I can find.

Pinching the sticky tape between my thumb and forefinger, I place the strip over the middle section of the scanner where the print sits, pressing it firmly into the glass then pause. The gum, what did she do with the gum? An image of a smile spreading like silk comes to me, of fingers working diligently, elegantly, gliding in air. I catch my breath as I realise I liked her, this woman, whoever she was, as if she was good to me, kind.

I swallow, slot the image back away and, slipping my fingers to my pocket, rip out the stolen packet of gum. Not giving myself time to doubt my plan, I pop a piece in my mouth and chew. The gum soft, I squeeze it dry on the roof of my mouth and, clamping it between my teeth, peel off the tape from the screen and extract the gum from my mouth. Sweat runs past my brow now. Lowering the gum, I hold it onto the tape and keep it in place, counting fifteen seconds, eyes searching the area for officers the entire time. Done, I carefully unwrap the chewing gum from the tape and allow myself one small smile.

Because there, in front of me, is a print. An authorized fingerprint.

The alarm still shrilling, I put all my energy into shutting the sound out and I turn the gum right side down and press the fingerprint gently into the scanner, using it as a substitute person. I wait and hold my breath.

A buzzer sounds. I feel a wash of relief as the door clicks open and a whoosh of cold air hits my face, followed by a beam of sunshine streaming onto my cheeks. There is more shouting and, from the far left direction, people are running this way.

Chest tight, throat dry, I drag open the door and, not looking back, not daring to check how far away any intelligence officers may be, I click the exit silently shut and run towards a distant car park deck in the early morning Hamburg sun as back in the Project facility, the siren wails on.

Confinement location—present day

The needle is out. I stumble to my knees and gulp in large breaths. My arms and legs are throbbing, muscles weak from the ropes and when I raise my head, my neck aches so much that my shoulders seize up almost entirely, nearly cramping, and blood drips from the crease of my arm to my wrist and fingers.

I stagger to a stand and observe what I can of the room. Blackness, two crates, padded walls. I feel dirty. I feel unwashed and smelly and when I run a hand through my hair, strands of it stick in clumps to my skin. Not wanting to remain in here a moment longer and fearful of what may happen next with Ramon, I spin round and go to escape to the door when my attention is taken by what is on the far wall where the light stream dribbles. Curious, I hobble over and halt. It is a cross of Jesus Christ. I rub my eyes, a weariness rippling across them, crouch down and look. The light is weak here, but even through the blackness I can see that, this close to the cross, something is not right where the wall runs by. I wipe my fingers free of sweat and, in the absence of full sight, let my sense of touch do the exploring.

There, to the left of the cross sits a stretch of padded wall the same as I had seen towards the door in front of the chair where I was strapped. I feel my way along it and stop. A corner of the leather fabric is curling at one edge and when the light above swings over, I notice something under it, some writing. Kneeling down fast, I pinch the edge of the leather and pull it. It rips away. It comes free in my hand to reveal numbers scratched onto the bare brick wall underneath, numbers 31, 100, 75, 13, 21 and 26, each with specific places of birth in the Basque country and what seems to be a set of calendar years: 1976, 1985, 1989, 2001, 2009, 2010, none of which relate or have a specific pattern. And even though I am tired and hungry, I look at them and remember the ICE room in Hamburg and call up the picture of the numbers and places and instantly know that they all correlate somehow, that what I am seeing here, the numbers at least all match to what I saw on the file, on the file Raven directed me to.

For a moment, I do not move as my brain attempts to compute it all. Have these been scratched on by others like me? Other subject numbers? And if so, how? Does that mean Ramon has been keeping them down here for the Project like he has with me? But how do the calendar years relate to my brother? Some of them stretch back to when Ramon was very young and therefore way before he could ever be involved as a contact for the Project. I study them again, trying to make sense of it all.

As my head drops down, my eyes catch sight of the cross

where it sticks out at the bottom. A cross. A religious symbol that represents not life or caring for others or doing good, but killing and hurting and retaliation. At the top of the wall where the padding is pulled and the subject number etchings lie, the cross is flat, but at the bottom, I can see now something sticking out from underneath the wood where the feet of Christ sit.

I kneel down and begin to pull at it. At first it does not move, and so, listening out for any signal of Ramon or the Project, I reach over, grab the medical stand from the drug and the timer and, angling it at forty-five degrees, I use it as a hook and smash it down hard.

The cross comes away in one go and when I pick it up from the floor a photograph drops out. Curious, nervous, I unfold it, as there in my hands is a photograph of a mother and her newborn baby, and in the top right hand corner where the faded colour of the image bleeds into the card, is a name and a year:

Maria. 1980.

Chapter 34

Floodlights hit my face as I duck and sprint the one hundred metres by the hidden crevice of the building. My arm stings and bruises ache, but I keep moving.

Another alarm shrieks from the internal left flank and, through my periphery, I see officers dispersing, prowling in the shadows that link from the area at the back to the series of outbuildings to the left. In my pocket is the car fob from the dead officer and I intend to use it, but there are no cars immediately near here and the parking deck is sixty metres ahead. A figure scuttles somewhere beyond and I drop to my knees. My legs wobble with exhaustion and my feet prickle with pain from the shoes that rub where they are too big.

I carry out rapid reconnaissance. There is an additional building further to the right. The roof is blue and the walls are green, and on the door to the side black skulls are imprinted onto yellow beaks where a shadow creeps into the right. I count to three, crouch down and run.

Reaching the far car deck, I slap my back against the wall. It is warm, almost hot to the touch, but I remain rooted to where I am, watching everything, trying to blink the brightness away, stay steady, hidden. There are two officers there now in the spot where I was stood just five seconds ago, which means, at this angle, if I run now, they will see me.

I stay put. The shapes ahead move and I refocus and track them, waiting until my trajectory is in line with the officers', and when a blind spot is created, I keep my nerves steady and creep along the edge of the green-walled building, reaching the entrance of the car deck in four seconds. I glance up. There are no guards on obvious watch, no surveillance cameras pointing my way, instead three silhouettes shift towards the left side of the building where I came from. I calculate their angles. They are facing outwards, which means, right now, they cannot detect me. For the moment.

I slip into the entrance of the parking deck and halt. At least one hundred cars stare back at me, my brain clocking every single one to my internal inventory. I immediately start pressing the fob, but no lights flash, no indicators tick. Feeling a shiver, I pull the sweater a little tighter and walk further in, uploading all the registration plates to my memory, counting every single make and model until I reach one car. A Volvo. Four-by-four. I look at the fob; the symbol, the make and mark match. Clicking the button, I hold my breath. The lights flash. The car is open.

Glancing around me, I fling open the door, switch on the engine and pause. Whichever way I go, there will be a gate, a guard, a gun. I sit there for two seconds thinking, pulling at the thread of cotton that dangles from the T-shirt, when I feel a corner dig into my leg from the trouser pocket: the swipe card.

Not wasting any time, I whip it out, look at it. Could this

work? But there is no way. Our faces are different shapes and our builds conflict between small and large. I get out the cell and call Chris.

'Hey, Google, you okay?'

'I need you to access the data base to help me get out of the facility.'

'No problem. You got an ID number?'

I look at the swipe card and read it out.

'Doc.' Patricia's voice feeds in. 'Stay safe. Balthus is here, too.'

I cling to her voice, then wait for Chris, tapping my foot. I need to go.

'Okay, you're done. Get to Hamburg station. I've texted you the locker with what you need—clothes, cash, cell—then from there you can catch a flight out. We're gonna scramble our route.'

The thought of enduring a train ride, a flight with crowds of people—I push it for the moment to one side.

'Maria,' Balthus says. 'Get to Madrid. We're headed there now to catch a train to Lisbon and then an evening flight to London so we can do something with these files.'

A shadow floats up ahead. 'I have to go.'

I slip the cell in my pocket and, taking extra precautions, I look round the car and, bending over to the glove compartment I slap my hand in and find what I need: a baseball cap.

I slip on the cap but then almost rip it off because it smells of the dead officer, of his smoke and metal and stale beer. Gulping hard, I count to three, recite the birthdate and place of Mozart, then, trying desperately to ignore the stench, I pull the car out and drive towards the main exit.

Up ahead, the metal, monitored gates are over 25 metres tall. In the corner where the wiring reflects like a mirror in the lights, surveillance cameras teeter on barbed wire that spikes the top edge. I drive up, pull the cap down as much as I can bear and, adrenaline shooting through me, and reach the scanner. Slow, steady, I reach out, the stolen card in my hand and, holding my breath, swipe. One second, two pass as I wait until, on three, the gates finally swing open and I drive out, careful not to go too fast and so arouse suspicion until I am far enough away to be gone.

I breathe out. The air, when the window is down, keeps me alert, and when I swallow I can taste flowers and metal and a mix of mint gum. Forcing myself to keep the sunglasses firmly in place, I set my eyes forward and focus solely on driving the car away from the Project towards the road ahead, my mind set on the documents we have found and revealing every last single source of it all to the world.

Confinement location—present day

I look at the worn image of the woman and baby, and my fingers shake. 1980 is the year that I was born. The photograph I am staring at, if the writing in the corner of the photo is correct, is of me as a baby, but I do not recognise the woman in whose arms I am being held.

Confused, I trace the pattern of the baby blanket as if it will give me a clue or provide me with some much needed order. The only noise in the room the sound of my shallow breath, I smooth the snapshot down with my palm and blow away the residue dust that sits in a film on the front. My body trembles a little from the aftershock of the drugs and a chill chatters down my limbs, bones, feet, making my hands and arms jitter.

I bring the photo close to my face in the weak light and examine the image as best I can. The woman has long, black, bushy hair that hangs in curled wire across her shoulders down to her stomach, and on her slim tanned legs rests a long, billowing skirt with a delicate crocheted flower pattern that flows at her bare feet. She is about twenty-two years old. She wears a loose cotton brown vest and underneath is the outline of her heavy, loose breasts. I squint, angle the light—she doesn't look like Mama when she was younger, but I cannot be certain. There is an arm to her right in the photo, just out of shot, and when I narrow my eyes and my head leans in as far as it can go, I see the arm belongs to a man—black hairs, tanned skin.

Turning it in my hands, I flip the picture to the back and stop. Words. Words are etched in a pencilled scrawl on the underside of the image. Feeling a bolt of uncertainty now inside me at what I am looking at, I inspect the scrawl, rubbing the writing with my forefinger, the soft padding of my skin swirling in tiny circles on the rough paper. At first, with the light dim and the darkness almost too overpowering, it is difficult to decipher what anything says and so I shift closer to the bulb, almost upon it as I thrust the photograph upwards as, slow and steady, the words illuminate.

Isabella Bidarte.

It is a name, a Basque name. Something inside me stirs. What? A memory? A dream? I think of all the Basque names blacked out on the file in the ICE room at the Project. Is this woman one of them? Another subject number? I run the name through my brain: *Bidarte*. I track the meaning. *Bide* means *way*. *Arte* means *between*. *Between the ways*.

I place the picture on my palm. *Isabella*. It is from the name Isabel, a variation on Elizabeth, which means devoted to God. There are letters scratched further towards the middle, but it is lighter here as if it has been written in the softest, most buttery pencil and, when I peer at it, eyes straining, slowly, I manage to make out the words. *Weisshorn Psychiatric Hospital, Geneva. Switzerland*. A hospital in Switzerland. And then one more line with two key dates next to her name. *Born: May 1968. Died: June 1989 (?)*. But it is what is next to it that makes me almost drop the image, because there on the flip side of the photograph is a grid reference number.

The same grid reference number as the one I found on Dr Andersson's cell phone.

I lean back, cortisol levels peaking as I think it through, and, for some reason, raise my fingers to my arm where the ink tattoo from Black Eyes sits. 'I am Basque,' I say aloud, the sound of my own voice seeming strange, odd in the lonely silence of the room. I hold up the photograph. *Isabella Bidarte*—a Basque name. Am I looking at a woman who was involved in the Project? Who perhaps knew Mama or Papa when I was a baby? And this hospital—is that where she met them? I think, connect the dots but keep hitting a wall, not recalling a time when Papa or Mama mentioned a trip to Switzerland.

I begin to analyse who the woman is and why she has hold of me and how it is all connected to Geneva, when there is a sound, a clatter, then silence. I freeze. Ramon.

I spin round to the wall where the cross once stood and

thrusting the photograph in my trouser pocket, I get to the medical stand and haul it back up, then, pulling it hard, I wrench the main shaft free from the base.

Logical, mechanical, I move quick now towards the steps, ready for Ramon, and I think I am done when I spot something on the floor: the cross. There is a sound of a ring tone— Depeche Mode's *Enjoy the Silence*, and it gets nearer, louder with every second that passes. My eyes surge round the room. Ramon will be here soon and I have to be ready, because this time I am getting out. I need to get to Mama and get to Patricia and Chris and Balthus, and all I can do right now is hope they have some idea now of where I am.

My pulse juggernauts in my wrist as, with the ring tone closer, I count to three and, taking a chance, I run to the wall and grab the cross and, looking down in my hand, slip off something into my palm. It is the nail, the nail from the foot of the cross.

There is a low buzzing sound followed by a creak of the door. One second, two. With no time left, I grip my fingers around the nail, drop it into my back pocket and, rushing to the steps, with the metal stand gripped in my hands, I stand by the door and wait for my brother to enter.

Chapter 35

Balthus stays on the phone to me the whole time I get through the airport. I reach the Madrid terminal and try to breathe.

'Are you okay?' Balthus says, the cell pinned to my ear.

'No,' I say and carry on. I take out my passport and check my appearance in a walkway mirror between an escalator and a shop. My hair is now copper to match the passport photograph from Chris and when I blink, my eyes are green from temporary contact lenses that match the dark make-up on my skin. The sneakers are still on my feet from the train journey I took from Hamburg to Paris before my flight to Madrid, but on my body now I wear a loose khaki shirt and white vest with close fitted combats on my legs, rolled up at the ankles. A seasoned traveller look, Chris said in the note that he left for me in the Hamburg locker. I do not know what that means.

I can smell multiple scents as I walk towards the nothing to declare zone. Coffee, toast, bacon, burgers, flowers, pollen, beer, salmon. It hits me in a tsunami all at once and combines with the sounds and the crowds and the streaming lines of people, some of them brushing past me as they walk, making me wince, making me want to curl up and run away.

'Just keep walking straight on,' Balthus says. 'I know airports are hard for you. We'll get you through this.'

I want to thank him but am rendered mute by the whole assault of the journey. I hate it. I pull my baseball cap down and walk through customs where it is busy and loud. There is a small grey rucksack on my back and when people criss-cross the walkways, different sounds, smells, fluorescent lights, all blink at me all at once sweeping my mind up in chaos and fragmenting my sense of self. I think of Papa and how he used to be with me in these situations, always calm, always guiding me through.

'Are you still there?' I ask Balthus.

'Yes,' he replies, pausing. 'Always.'

His chocolate voice, the pebbled boom of it gives me a bit of comfort and I find, as the minutes pass, that I am able to continue forward and get through the airport and the noise and the chaos and the people upon people that scurry by without obvious cause, and I make it to outside without melting down.

'I am out,' I say now to Balthus as I exit the terminal and step ito liquid sun that spills down from the sky and bathes the tarmac and the cars and the heads of the people that pass with a soft sheen of silent sunshine. Outside, I instantly breathe easier, the excess of the noise muted slightly, allowing me to continue at medium comfort level. The whole time I scan every inch, crevice and corridor for any signs that I am being followed.

'You did it. Great. Catch a taxi,' Balthus says on the cell. 'We'll meet you on the corner of the old post office by the market in Madrid at the agreed time.' My heart drops—markets are good cover, but they mean more crowds and noise.

I check my watch and, slipping into a cab, feel a wash of relief as the taxi pulls away in an air conditioned bubble that mutes the sound and calms my head.

'Thank you, Balthus,' I find myself saying.

'You're welcome, Maria. You are so, so welcome.'

One hour later, I arrive at El Rastro market and very nearly do not get out of the car. People mill everywhere, great crowds of them gathering in packs on the streets and the market stalls and the bars and restaurants that run along the roads and pavements and terraces beyond. I step out of the cab, pay the driver and am hit by the multiple smells that fire at me all at once. Chorizo sizzling, chocolate churros frying, fresh lemonade, calamari, petrol, exhaust fumes, the wet feet stench of Serrano ham hanging from hooks under canvas canopies in the shade of the sun.

I duck my head down and scurry to the meeting point by the old post office. The noise is overwhelming. Bodies stand everywhere, chattering, shouting, shopping, all wandering, it seems to me, with no clear sense of destination, stopping then walking then stopping again with no apparent set pattern that I can define, and it scrambles my mind, as it did at the airport, into chaos. The only way I can cope with it is to set a clear goal in my mind—get to a clearing free of crowds and wait.

By the time Patricia and Balthus and Chris arrive, I am standing in a corner hiding behind a cheap pair of sunglasses trying to keep as much away from anyone as I can so they will not touch me.

'Doc!'

I prop my hand to my brow and see Patricia bound towards me followed by Chris and Balthus.

As soon as Patricia reaches me, she holds out her fingers and smiles. I reach up my hand to hers, so relieved to see her I could flop forward and never get up, but then someone brushes near me and it makes me jump.

'Doc, are you okay?'

'People are in my space. I know they are not being rude, but I do not like it. Why did we meet here?'

Chris comes over, a lopsided straw hat on his head and a white T-shirt that reads *Nerds Rule*. 'We're here to give us some cover.' He grins and I see his stubble has grown. 'Hello, Google.'

'That is not my name. And nerds do not rule.'

'I know. Geeks do.' He winks.

'Maria, oh thank God.' Balthus rushes over, sweat trickling down his cheeks as he takes out a white handkerchief from a grey linen shirt and dabs his face. He smiles and his eye creases fan out. 'I cannot tell you how relieved I am that you're okay.'

I look at them all. They are safe, my friends are safe, but I don't know how to express the feeling it gives me, of happiness, of contentment. 'Statistically,' I say, 'only one of us had a chance of dying. The fact that we are all here is a leap over probability.'

Chris nods. 'Right. Yep, just what I was thinking.' He grins like Goofy and I ignore him.

The crowd ten metres ahead begins to swell and the noise levels rise. My shoulders, in response, scrunch up, my head ducking down at the sudden audio assault, and so, on Patricia's suggestion, we move to a quieter area where an empty canopy sits over bare wooden slats that once housed oranges and lemons. We stand under the canvas for shade, spritzed with a gentle citrus scent, and, as we rest, Chris takes out his laptop.

My body, as I lean against the stall, suddenly feels exhausted, my mind shattered from the chaos and noise of the train and flight and now the Sunday market. I look to Patricia and to Balthus and only at the sight of them, do I allow myself to rest a little and let my shoulders soften.

'Ok, so,' Chris says. 'I managed to make it into that file.'

'Ah yes,' Balthus says. 'We have everything now to hit the Project where it hurts.'

I lean forward and look now to where Chris attaches a device to the laptop then, opening it, boots it up. The screen comes to life fast.

'Here you go,' he chirps, fifteen seconds later. 'The file, this one that was left, unlike the others had a name.'

Feeling oddly nervous, I move in and, brushing back a strand of hair from my wig, I peer at the screen. Instantly it is clear that the file is about her. Raven. The woman from my hazy memories.

Because there next to what must be her photograph, the one I recall from my flashback of her caramel skin, pool-brown eyes, black hijab, is her name, is finally the woman's name that, when I tried to recall it, was blocked out in black.

'Sadeqa,' I say to myself, reading the name that sits at the top of the confidential document, a document compiled by me. 'It is an Arabic name that means truthful, true.'

'Um, you okay?' Chris says.

'Doc…?'

But I don't reply, because what I am reading, what I am seeing for the first time is the answer to what I have been seeking since my trial, since the moment I recalled the vague whisper of a memory in court and then again at my villa. Her face, her pooled eyes, her black breezing veil. We worked together. It says that here, now, in black and white and no grey. We worked together on a covert operation and I went undercover.

'She was an asset, trading information from a new terrorist cell that was surviving,' I say, fast, reading. 'It was growing through cyber network links, via encrypted message codes that even the NSA, the CIA or MI5 could not crack.'

'I know, right?' Chris says. 'That's some pretty deep stuff you were involved in.'

I scan the file then look up, a sick feeling in my stomach. 'She knew all about the NSA, this woman. It is all here. She knew who they were, what they did. And she could hack.'

'Doc, talk more slowly.'

I read it all now, my eyes racing across the screen, pressing it all to my memory banks. 'Sadeqa had a high IQ, could get into the CIA's system and they did not like it, the organisations, the Project, the governments. She was a danger, and they wanted her dead. And they assigned me to do it. She said they would make me kill her. But before I did, they made me use her as an asset, get as much intelligence data out of her as possible.'

I pause, swallow a little as I read the next section, because what is there, what I now witness in black and white, smacks me hard in the chest. I sway a little, toppling slightly into Chris.

'Whoa, steady.'

'What does it say, Doc?'

A lone, solitary tear escapes because the answer, finally, is clear.

'I killed her,' I say, a quiet whisper amidst the drum beat of the market. 'I killed Raven. I killed Sadeqa.'

'What?'

Patricia scans the file as my sight swims a little and my brain struggles to process the facts and detail.

'You didn't kill her,' Patricia says now.

'I did.'

'But Doc, you didn't, not knowingly.'

'What if there was a part of me that really knew? What if, deep down, it is who I am?' I look at the stall and trace my finger in the wood, finding refuge in the ordered pattern of the swirls and grooves. 'She said the file would tell me who I really am, and it has.'

'But, Maria,' Balthus says now, 'the file has told us what the Project has really done, the atrocities of how they have tested on thousands and blanked out their identities. They took you for tests against your will.'

'We can use this stuff, you know,' Chris says. 'We can email it to the government and show them what's happening right under their noses. We have the definitive files.'

'That's what we should do,' Balthus says. He ruffles his shirt, billowing the creased linen fabric in the heat so cool air flows. Somewhere in the distance, a chicken squawks. 'There's a flight out of Lisbon to London tonight. We're all going to catch that and I'll get this file to Harriet.'

'Balthus's ex-wife, Harriet, is the UK Home Secretary,' Patricia says to Chris.

'No,' I say.

'She actually is,' Chris says.

I stand up. 'No, I can't go to Lisbon.'

'Maria,' Balthus says, 'we have to stay together.'

But I shake my head. 'I have killed people. I killed this woman called Sadeqa and the Project know everything I have done. MI5 know everything I have done. The only person in that loop who doesn't know everything I've done is me. I thought this file would prove I haven't killed but I have.' I pause as the sentence sinks in and a strange wave of sadness passes over me, casting a cloud over any sun that may ever shine. 'Being the person I am puts people in danger.'

'Doc, no.'

'Yes. That is what I needed to know, that is why I had to see this file, the Sadeqa file. You three are in danger near me. And because of me and what I have done, my mama and brother are not safe either. Now I know I have killed, now I know I have eliminated major assets, I am a target, my friends and family are a target. That is what I needed to know, and now I do know, I have to go and see them. I have to make certain they are not in danger from the Project, even if that means hiding them away.'

'What? Doc, no,' Patricia says. 'You have to stay with us now. It's not safe. The Project could be watching.'

I turn to Chris. 'Keep the files and make copies. When I

return from seeing Mama, we will need it. Can you help me with her security?'

'Sure.'

'Maria, please, no.' Balthus says. 'It's dangerous.'

'I need to know they are safe. I...' I stop, throat dry, a strange feeling of unease inside me. I look at them, at my friends, at Chris who I barely know but feel as if I want to know more, at Patricia who means the world to me, who calms me, at Balthus, my father's old friend who I feel an unusual bond with, a bond I have missed for so many years. They want to help me, these people, and I fight it, sometimes, because I don't know how to handle it.

We stand there, the four of us, amidst the humming and the market rumble and the chorizo and the chickens, we stand there and we think and we contemplate what comes next.

'I have to go to Madrid,' I say after a moment, looking up. 'I have to see if my family are okay.'

Patricia lets out a deep sigh. 'I know.'

'We'll be close,' Chris says. 'If we get at all concerned, we can be there.'

'Yeah,' Patricia says. 'We'll follow you over, stay near.'

She steps forward and spreads out her fingers. I inhale her talcum powder scent, not wanting to leave her again, wishing the feeling of calm and safety she gives me would last forever.

Balthus steps forward. 'Maria, do you really think this is necessary?'

'I have to see them,' I say after a moment, quiet, eyes downturned, suddenly tired. 'I can't keep running and hiding and leave my family open to danger, not now, not when I know what I know.'

He smiles, eyes creasing, and nods, and a lump scratches my throat.

'Hey, who's that?' Patricia says.

We prop our hands on our brows and, squinting in the sun, look. There is a woman and a man, each of them dressed in black and they are scanning the distant crowd. On their wrists are heavy grey watches and as they look ahead, their sight stays fixed and locked. We are out of view where we stand, cloaked by the cover of the canopy and the narrow tin roof that juts from the wall next to an old fruit shop.

'Do you think they're from the Project?' Balthus says.

'I don't know,' Chris replies, 'but, Maria, I think you shouldn't stay to find out.'

I watch the two figures as they levitate among the crowd. Their boots are black and leather, their movements methodical and robotic, and on immediate glance, they appear out of place among the floating summer fabrics of the Sunday market shoppers.

I look to Patricia. 'Stay out of the way, don't let them see you.'

She nods and, for the last time, I hold my fingers to hers and feel her warm, soft cotton pads of fingertips, as, from my periphery, I see the figures moving in. My heart charges up and my pulse spikes.

'Maria,' Balthus whispers, 'go. Contact us when you get to Ines's. Stay in touch.'

I glance to them all, take a photograph of them with my eyes, try to recall every scar, pimple, curve, wrinkle, smile, crease.

'Oh, shit,' Chris says.

I turn. The black boots are approaching faster now. I spin back to my friends, give them one last look and, thrusting my cell deep into my pocket, I run to the wall, leap on a bin, and catapult myself over to the other side.

Chapter 36

I reach the edge of Mama's apartment building in the centre of the city out of breath.

The early evening sun is sighing down onto the pavements, the cars on the roads having a siesta on the street. I slip behind a tree so I can see clearly across the road and check if I have been followed. The building Mama lives in when she is in the city shines with bright, white marble, and, when I scan the vicinity, I spot two figures sitting on a park bench across from the main entrance, one reading a newspaper, the other in running gear, doing up her laces. Neither looks to each other, but it is clear they are watching, two intelligence officers from either MI5 or the Project waiting for me to show up. And while that concerns me, what worries me more, what makes me tense and eager to get into the building, is that if the Project are here, what have they done to my family?

Pulling my cap down low, I stride forward along the road to a department store building made of cream-coloured stone that soaks up all the yellow of the sun, and slip into a hidden side street. The light plummets here as if in a cave and I stop, scan the area, sight adjusting. I take out my cell, text Chris my status and look around. To my left there is a set of external steps that snake up the building, zigzagging to the roof. As I turn to face where my mother's apartment building would be, my brain automatically calculates the length and trajectory of the scale of the high wall. I think it through. If I can get up the steps that snake towards the top, I can sprint to the roof of Mama's apartment then enter in through her balcony doors without being seen by the Project or MI5 below. It is tight, a risk, but no matter which way I turn it, I cannot see another viable route. A siren wails from the road beyond, making me jump and, not giving myself time to contemplate my options any longer, I slap a stray sweat bead from my face and scramble up.

After one hundred and seven steps, I reach the top, my thighs burning. Catching my breath, I can instantly see that the height gives me a clear view of this area of Madrid. I can see the cars circling the gardens beyond and below, spot people the size of small beetles secreting themselves along the walkways, and as I observe it, all of the noise and activity continues, and yet here it is relatively quiet and calm. I inhale. I am grateful for small mercies.

I start to move, sight set on Mama's building, and am going so fast that I don't spy a metal bar that juts out on the route my feet take. I trip up instantly, flying through the air and tumbling over, smacking my head onto the ledge, and, for a moment, I almost go over the side. I gasp and drag myself back, as blood trickles down my brow. I stop and wait. The airport, the market, the chaos of earlier still rattles in my head and so I think of Patricia and of Balthus, think of what they would tell me to do right now, and I find myself breathing easier, counting to ten, wiping my face and starting over. I move forward five, perhaps six steps next when I glance down and immediately halt. There is a drop. It bridges between the two buildings and is sheer, like a rock face, almost, of marble and window ledges that poke out at ninety-degree angles. Fast, I calculate the size of the gap and therefore the speed I need to run up then jump. If I am to clear the edge, I have to have a long sprint.

I count to three, think of Patricia and, swallowing hard, I run.

I fly off the edge. My legs scramble in the air as my arms reach out, heart slamming against my chest so hard that it feels as if it will explode out as my arms now spin round in a failed flap. Wind whips through my hair, cold and slicing, and when I look down, I can see the drop by the apartment roof. It rushes in closer, closer, closer…until I land with a thud, rolling to the side, knocking my shoulder hard into a long steel pipe. I come to a stop. Everything aches. My shoulder, my legs, my arms and my knees. I drag my body up, take stock and, assessing no major injuries, steady my hands, wipe the sweat from my cheeks and carry on. I have cuts on my face, and a sharp pain in my collar bone that makes me wince, but other than that, I am fine, and now I stride straight to the ledge and look down. The balcony is just below, Mama's apartment stretching over three floors.

I go left foot first now. Inching along a ledge of stone that juts out from the level below the roof, I grip on as hard as I can but it is more difficult than I anticipated, my fingers struggling to hold on. But, bit by bit, and against my judgment, it starts to work and, eventually, the balcony comes into view. Iron railings, ornate fixtures. Gilded. Guarded.

I take one step more, two and—

I trip. I topple backwards and my cell phone slips from my pocket and, unable to stop it, I watch the phone tumble in the air, spinning to the ground below. It smashes to the pavement. I watch it for a second as my whole body drags myself upwards, sideways, anyways, my abdomen crunching inwards, until, finally, breathless, I do it. My body swings itself over and my feet land back on the flat stone and to safety.

Taking one last look at my lost broken cell below, not knowing how I can contact my friends, I gulp in oxygen and get ready for the next part.

Counting to ten, I ease myself up now to the higher ledge. This one is thicker, wider, leading to Mama's private window, and I make quick progress, not glancing down once, not taking my eyes off the balcony ahead. In fifty-two seconds, I make it. Carefully as I can, I swing my legs over the corner of the wrought-iron barrier and parachute my feet to the floor. And within ten seconds, I am on Mama's balcony.

Slapping hair and sweat from my eyes, I get my bearings and silently look around. The French doors to Mama's apartment are yawning open, heavy, patterned curtains swinging in a lukewarm breeze and from this angle, I can see the room is empty. When I move next, it is slow, measured. I enter Mama's house, tiptoeing looking for where Mama may be, anxious to check she is okay, that she is safe, and just as I call out for them, for Mama and Ramon, something smashes into my head, so fast and hard that it knocks me out entirely and sends the rooms swimming to nothing but a tiny black dot.

And some time after, I wake up with a jolt. The room is dark, damp. I cannot see properly. I have been caught, that much I know, but I am unsure by whom. The Project? MI5? Someone else?

I don't know how I got here.

I don't know how I am going to escape.

Chapter 37

Ramon opens the door of the basement, light flooding in, and I charge at him.

Before he can move away, before my brother can register what is happening, I smash the metal stand across his shoulders and, locking my arms around his neck, kick out his shins. His legs buckle instantly.

I yank Ramon's head to the side, fast, sharp. 'You are going to take me out of here. Now.'

'What are you doing?' Ramon says, choking.

I drag him towards the exit. 'I am getting out of here.'

'Stop it, M! Stop!' His legs are kicking forwards, his heels slipping as if on ice. I tighten my grip around his torso and shove him forward with my knee.

'Move.'

We reach the stairs and Ramon tries to thrust his arms out, but my grasp is so strong, the fuel of my intention, of my determination so forceful, that my muscles clamp to him like a vice. He staggers up the steps, lopsided in my clench, feet half flapping along the stone and he trips a little, and I wobble, hands loosening slightly. For a second, I feel Ramon's arms push outwards, but, sharp, I regain my footing and haul him to the door.

'Unlock it.'

Snot trails from his nose. 'M, don't do this.'

I squeeze tighter. He winces. 'I said unlock it.'

His hand falls to the side, slipping into his pocket.

I jerk my head, immediately on alert. 'What are you doing?'

'The key,' he says, spit dribbling from his mouth. 'The key is…it is in my pocket.'

'There is a touch pad.'

'I know…I know… It uses both systems.'

I thrust my hand into his trouser pocket.

'Why…why are you doing this?' Ramon yells out, yet I barely hear him, the only focus I now have being getting out of here, on ending what is happening, my whole short-term memory now of how I got here, of all the data I uncovered from the Project, from the Sadeqa file, all fresh in my mind.

'You are with the Project,' I say. 'You have been helping them for years and somehow implicated Papa in it all, even though he had nothing to do with it.'

'What? No! M, this is crazy. Stop and think about what you're saying. The Project…they help you.'

My fingers touch the key and I wrench it out like guts from a fish. Pulling Ramon with me, I drive the key into the lock and turn it.

'You're hurting me,' Ramon says.

But I ignore him, because there is one more obstacle now: an access code. I scan it, brain fast, tracking every curve.

Key pads get smudged when they are overused, but it can be hard to define if the code is changed. Keys three and seven are almost obsolete.

'The access pad—the first two numbers are three and seven. What are the remaining two digits?'

'M, please…'

I squeeze his skin tighter. He chokes. 'Nine and…five.'

Not wasting a second of time, worried the Project or MI5 have got to Mama upstairs, rapid now, I punch in the numbers and click. The door unlocks.

Heart firing on maximum, I complete the final and third step and haul across the three iron bolts that guard the entrance.

A creak slices into the silence as, before my eyes, the door groans open and stairs emerge, biblical, like Jacob's ladder in the Book of Genesis. The steps are stone and painted with a black, sleek gloss, and the walls are adorned with slate grey paint that sits matt against the glare of the gloss. When I look at it, the colour instantly dulls the air, making it dark and cold, and, as I drag Ramon forward, I realise that I have never been here before, in this part of Mama's town house; she never allowed it.

'Where does this lead to? Papa's study?'

'M, you can't… Please, just stop.'

'You are with the Project. It has to end.'

'Do you even know what the Project is? M, I think you—'

But I ignore him and, gripping his head in the crevice of my arm, I haul my brother up towards the stairs and, together, we ascend the steps.

We halt next to another door. It is white and constructed of metal. There is no lock or alarm system and so, eager not to waste time and knowing Balthus, Chris and Patricia will be concerned now as to my whereabouts, I tighten my arms around Ramon's neck. 'How long have you had me down here for?'

'What?' He splutters saliva all over the wall.

'How long have you kept me in the basement for?'

'Twenty-three…hours.'

Nearly a whole day. 'How many others have you held down there?'

'Huh? What? No one.'

'Do not lie. I have seen the other subject numbers etched on the wall. I have found a photograph.'

'I…I don't know what you're talking about. M, please.'

Ignoring his pleas, I push him through. 'You first.'

But Ramon does not move, instead he digs himself in, heels acting as brakes on the ground. I shove him hard, poking my elbow into his back. 'Move, now.'

Yet, he still stays. 'You won't be able to get out.' Spit pools on the corner of his mouth. 'The Project is set on helping you, M.' He coughs. 'Let them help you.'

'The Project do not want to help me. They want to help themselves. They want to help governments and presidents and generals to win wars that they themselves have created. They all lie. Everyone lies. No one is allowed to be themselves. No one allowed to simply live in harmony.'

'What are you talking about?'

I lock my focus on the white door ahead, set on opening it, on getting out, but at the angle we stand, Ramon's body fills the entire frame and his shoulders, torso, arms are the same width as the door is wide. There is only one option: I have to get him to do it.

'Open the door,' I say.

'No.' His heels dig in further now as my arms begin to tire, my hands sweating, the stairwell warm, damp. 'M, I care for you. Please, let me go. Stop this. You're only…you're only hurting yourself.'

'What did the Project make you do?'

'What?'

'What did the Project instruct you to do? How were you trained?'

He splutters. 'M, this is insane. The Project didn't train me to do anything. They just gave me advice on how to help you. M, you came into the house via the balcony shouting out for us. That's not right. You're not well.'

'You knew about the subject numbers on the wall.'

He shakes his head. 'No. The pencil marks were…'

He stops, seems to stare into space.

My brain begins to connect. 'The pencil marks were what?'

His body drops, limp and wilting. When he speaks again, his voice is low, scratched. 'I found them a long time ago.'

'When?'

He swallows. 'I found them one day when I snuck down there when Mama said I couldn't. I used to play down there without her knowing, then for a long time, when Papa was away for a long time on trial, it was all locked up and I couldn't get in, and…and when I returned the padding was there covering the pencil up until you found it just now… Please, M, let me go.'

I consider what he says, unsure what to think. Mama was in charge of the basement? 'Move.'

'What? M, please. I'm telling you the truth!'

'How much time do I have until the Project arrive?'

'Erm, erm…three, maybe four hours?'

I think. That means one hour at the most.

'We need to sort this out,' Ramon says. 'M, let me help. I'm not moving.'

I look at him. 'Yes, you are.' And I kick him hard in the calf.

He immediately buckles, his legs folding as he cries out in pain. I jab my fingers straight into his throat, my training activating, winding him so he stumbles back, unblocking the exit.

I move quick now, sharp, bolting for the door, but, before I can roll out of the way, Ramon flies at me. It is so quick, so unexpected that at first I do not dive. My fingers jut out and I manage to grip the door handle, but Ramon hooks my legs and the metal slips from my grasp. I feel a twinge, the sharp snap of a punch, and then a bigger hit as Ramon drives his fist into my back. I crumble forward, pain spiking down my spine, stumbling, the confined space giving me no room to swing round, to lever my hands into a combative position.

I form two fists as I focus on my body, my mind, on what I have been trained to do. Ramon dances near me, yet this time, as he thrusts a punch towards my head, I duck, dropping to my knees. He trips over my body, his entire frame teetering there for a moment, suspended in motion above the drop below to the bottom of the stairs, as if the pause button has been pressed on a television recording.

His eyes go wide. 'M! Help!'

I go to move then, for some reason, I stop and watch him and for a moment find myself contemplating letting him fall, thinking that if he died, it would give me an advantage to get away because he is the Project and the Project are not good. And then I shake my head. This is my brother, he wants to… he wants to help me. He loves me. What am I thinking?

I thrust out my arm to catch him. 'Ramon, grab onto me.' But his mouth shrieks open in silence, his whole body suddenly sinking backwards.

I lurch forwards, grasping for him. 'Ramon!'

He falls. He topples backwards and his head smacks on the stone steps as he plunges to the bottom, coming to a halt in a slump, his body thudding in a crumpled heap in the darkness.

'Ramon!'

I don't move, chest gasping for air, eyes locked on the shrouded shadow of my brother's broken body at the foot of the stairs. What have I done? What have I done? The need to check on him, to ensure he is alive is almost too overwhelming to resist, but I stop myself, because what if he grabs me, hurts me, keeps me here for the Project to come?

I look to my brother, heart pounding, then look to the door, to the hot, white metal, silver handle. Without turning, without allowing myself one more glance down, I swallow and, pressing down hard on the handle, I slam open the door into Mama's apartment.

Chapter 38

I stumble into a side room, out of breath. I slam the door shut behind me and, slapping my back to the wall, try to steady myself as the image of Ramon in a broken ball on the basement floor stalks my head.

I left him there, my own brother, most probably with internal bleeding. A small moan escapes my lips. I cannot bear to think about what I have done and yet knowing at the same time that my brother was with the Project and with him as part of them, none of us were safe.

Pulling myself up, I smear the snot and sweat from my face and peer now at the room before me. It is small and, as my eyes adjust, I see a lamp glowing in the corner that casts carved out shadows across the length of the area. There is a feeling of familiarity, of déjà-vu here that I cannot place.

I brush my fingers along the wall, along the items that stand in the dimly lit darkness. A mahogany cabinet containing wine glasses stands to my right and by it rests one dark wooden side table with a silver tray and coffee pot on top. I look at it, gaze at its curve in the buttered lamplight and get a stab of something, a memory that comes in a wave and crashes into my head. I have been here before. Is it what I thought it may be? I spin round, assess as much as I can, my skull becoming dizzy as the picture emerges, switching on as I remember. I am young, ten, no more, my limbs skinny and bony. I am with Papa and it is the week before he died. I see him. He takes the silver coffee pot and pours coffee into a cup, holding it out to me.

'Here you go, my little bright spark.'

I take the cup, my thin, small fingers angling into the hot handle.

'Careful now,' Papa says. Then he smiles, soft at the edges. 'Your white cup, my baby. I know you can't drink out of anything else.'

I have a surge of gratitude towards him, but I am in my emotional cage and I don't know how to express how I feel.

Papa sets down the coffee pot now and I watch him. 'Papa,' I say, voice a small bird's, 'don't go down there to the basement without me. Let me come this time.'

He turns, eyes drooped, no smile or creases. He crouches down to me and takes my arms in his hands—the only person I will allow to touch me. 'I can't let you come with me, sweetheart.'

'Why?'

He sighs, heavy, long. 'There are things there that…' He pauses then smiles, wide with creases this time. 'You run along upstairs now to Mama.'

'No.'

'Maria, please.' And he stands, walks away and opens the door into the room I am never allowed into.

The image blows away and my eyelids flicker as I look now to the room in the present day and try to grasp onto the vision. To my surprise, tears streak my face and I lift my fingers to wipe them away. I turn to the wall, skim my hand along it and locate on the far section a small white switch. I flick it on so a low but steady light beams down from the bulb above, as I understand now where I am, my sight taking in the now clearer view and I register where I am.

Papa's study.

Could Ramon have kept anything connected to the Project in here? I trace my palms along every piece of furniture, along every wall and curve, as if each one contains memories of him, of Papa. My feet feel the plush woollen carpet fibres beneath my soles as the thick strands ooze between my toes. I drop to my knees, inhale the scent of the carpet, the familiar comfort of rubber and musk and lavender, just as it was when I was ten and Papa was still with me. I lie there, unmoving, sniffing and breathing, rocking a little and for a moment, for a sweet split second, I pretend that none of this ever happened at all, not Papa dying, not the Project being founded, not Mama ill or Ramon betraying me—none of it. I inhale the fibres and the scent and the whole room entire one more time, then, standing, I lock my sight on Papa's desk in the corner and, walking over to it, open it up.

The desk is just as it was from my memory. It is flat and rectangular and the mahogany it is fabricated from contains light scuffs marks on the rounded edges. There is a wooden chair with a curved backrest and a leather seat and when I smell it, it reminds me of Papa and the cigars he used to smoke.

Pulling the chair out of the way, careful not to knock the wood, I lean in and scan the bureau. There are six small drawers on top of the desk, built in, three each side. I slide open every one, quietly, soft, nothing there, just empty wooden shells, and the wistful scent of sandalwood, but what catches my attention the most is the long drawer that stretches across the middle. It is shallow and when I open it and click on a low lamp that sits on a side cabinet next to a vase of fake lilies, I start to get a better look.

The drawer still appears empty, until I run my hand on its belly and feel something bumpy underneath. It is a switch. Pausing, checking for any sounds, for any movement from Ramon or the arrival of the Project, I steady my hand and flip the switch. There is a soft click, like a small puff of air, and something drops to my palm. It doesn't feel like a gun or an alarm, but instead seems crisp, starched, like paper.

I move rapidly, silently now as, heart racing, I pull out the item, carefully placing it on the desktop, find myself staring at documents, detailed technical documents. I peer in and, opening the top copy, I read the name that sits on the middle of the page: *Garcia Building Company S.L.* I turn the paper. The next few pages are simply construction notes and calculations for a building project Mama must have commissioned, because her name and signature are at the foot of each page. Not wanting to waste any time, I am about to close the report, search for other information that may be in the bureau that Ramon may have secretly stored, when a number catches my eye. The date on the file: 1976.

Mildly wary, I flip all the way to the end of the file, check the address of the property the building plans relate to and see that it matches here—it matches this address where I stand now: Mama's Madrid house. A strange feeling begins to form in my stomach, a knot, a knoll, as, slowly, I reopen the document and look more closely at the pages.

The technical drawings, at first, detail an extension to the rear of the property, but then, further in, it switches to the basement. I pause, an unease rising, as, cautiously, I read on, the light on the bureau casting a biblical orange glow over my hands and the paper in front of them. There are measurements, calculations, numbers, all in great, accurate detail, all appearing normal, natural, yet, when I analyse them more, they are anything but.

Because, what I am looking at now are complex plans to widen and strengthen the wall in the basement to create a soundproof room. My pulse quickening, I read further on and learn that later, in 2001 and then in 2010, both the walls and the window in the cellar were replaced and reinforced using some of the most expensive materials available, with one specific item detailed to be included in refurbishment: padded walls. The installation of them was carried out in 2009 with the originals installed in...in 1985.

They are all the same calendar years that were scratched onto the brickwork by the subject numbers in the basement. The same calendar years and subject numbers that correlated with the data found on the file in the ICE room in Hamburg.

I grip the table tight and read on as, on the last page, towards the bottom where the builder has signed on behalf of his company, there is another name, another signature on the contract agreeing for the work to be carried out.

And it is not Papa's. It is not Ramon's name or the Project's or anyone else's.

It is Ines. Ines Villanueva.

My mother.

'Hello, Maria, dear.'

My eyes dart up.

Mama is standing in the doorway.

Chapter 39

Apartment buildings, Central Madrid.
Present Day

My mother leans on the door frame, her wrists gilded with jewellery and her limbs draped in Chanel. She smells of jasmine and orange and caramel dipped in cream, and by her left is a shiny wooden walking stick. I don't move. She raises a bony hand and touches her scalp, her hair sitting in clumps on her head, tiny islands of frayed follicles fuzzing in small, balled patches.

She tucks up the heel of her palm to the base of her skull and delivers me a thin smile. 'My dear, if I knew you were coming I would have put on my wig.'

I am alarmed at her appearance. Thin, translucent, a pencil drawing of her former self. The cancer must have taken hold. I don't know what to think. I am so glad she is safe, and yet something is holding me back from any elation, but I cannot place it.

'Mama,' I say, my hand on the file I have just seen. 'You look ill.'

'Always direct,' she sighs and glances to the documents

on the bureau. 'So you found them. Ah, my clever, clever girl. Come,' she beckons me with a finger, 'I have things to tell you.'

I look to the files, confusion turning to fear. 'What is happening?'

She gestures forward, out towards the twinkling ceilings of the apartment beyond. 'Let us go to somewhere…cosier, my dear. I need to sit.'

She looks at me, waiting, eyes pierced and brown with no creases at the sides, and I am paralysed. This is my mama, yet I feel not myself when she is near me, instead doubtful, withdrawn, and this has always, when I think of it, been so, but I do not know why, her fingernails clacking on the wood of the door frame, her pointed chin held high, her gaze rippling over me, over my attire and my face and my hair.

'My dearest,' she says now, 'you do look a fright. Come.' She leans on her walking stick. 'Come.'

I am led to the drawing room adorned with soft, yellow light and embers glowing from a fire that sits at the centre of the room. I instantly recall it straight from my childhood. The fireplace is embroidered with gold leaf, and at the edge of the wall locked cabinets rich in mahogany stand to attention. To their side are ornate, vast window frames that line up from outside, graced with sumptuous, rich woollen drapes that sweep the floor around them. There are bookcases, decanters, crystal-cut chandeliers, thick piled rugs, all of them dripping with the hushed flutter of money. Of wealth and power.

My mother lowers herself into a high-backed chair, the brown of the leather overpowering her pale, milk skin. Her tan, once bronzed and rich, is now gone and her glorious, crowning hair has disappeared. She is a whisper of her former self.

'Maria, my dear, would you like some water?'

I shake my head, not daring to speak, completely paralysed by seeing Mama as my brain connects the dots with what I have found in the drawer and the logical conclusions I have made. She pours a glass of water from a decanter on a table to her side, and, letting out a mew of a sigh, takes a sip.

'Did you know Ramon was holding me here?' I say.

'Pardon, my dear?'

'He held me in the basement for twenty-three hours. I was tied up and drugged. He said he was keeping me there because he was helping me.' I stop, realise I am shaking. 'Did you know I was in the basement?'

Mama's knuckles go white where they grip the glass, but she does not say anything. Instead, she dabs her cheek with one hand then sets the glass back down to the table. 'Yes,' she says eventually. 'I knew.'

Her answer blindsides me. I stumble a little to the side. 'Why?' I say after I have regained my footing.

'Oh, Maria,' my mother says, 'do you not remember?'

'I… You…' I halt, suddenly realising that I don't know what she means.

'You came to us through the balcony of all places.' Her voice is soft, a warm blanket of words. 'You were…erratic. Upset. My dearest, we didn't know what to do. You were, well, a little out of control. I gave the number of the Project to Ramon and he called them.'

I go quiet as inside, my brain begins to fire and connect,

but seeing Mama shakes me, makes me nervous 'Mama, do you know what the Project is?'

'Well, yes, they've helped you for a long while, my dear. They are the clinic people I used to take you to when you were little.'

'So, Ramon is the contact now for the Project?'

'He is. They are there to help, aren't they? I haven't dealt with them for a while—it's all Ramon now. That's their name—the Project.'

I go dizzy, not sure what to do think. Nothing is making sense. Ramon knew about the Project, that's what he said, but now Mama is saying she knows them, too, but that she thinks they are someone else—something else—my old Asperger's clinic she used to believe she was taking me to. I have to tell her the truth.

'Mama,' I say now, sweat springing up in patches on my chest and palms, making myself speak even though just looking at Mama makes me doubt my own mind, 'the Project is a covert conditioning programme. It is part of the UK intelligence services operation and has been ongoing for three decades. It is not an Asperger's clinic, as you thought it was.'

She lifts her hand to her mouth. 'Oh my goodness. Maria, this…this sounds so far-fetched. Are you sure?'

'Yes. How did they contact you originally, Mama, when I was young?'

She hesitates, touches her neck with fingers frail as twigs. 'Well, my dear, you had…troubles. The Project said they could help you. I took you to the doctor's appointments, they were quite groundbreaking, I was told, it was just for your

Asperger's, really, for when you had...issues. We travelled a lot with you because of it—they had facilities all over the world. Father Reznik—do you remember him? He helped enormously when Papa was away on...business.'

'Mama,' I start to say, but it is hard to speak, the uncertainty hitting me, Father Reznik's name spoken aloud destabilszing me. 'It was not simply a doctor's appointment or a visit to the priest,' I say. 'I was being tested on. Father Reznik was a handler for the Project. For MI5.'

'What?' She laughs, a crumpled laugh like a scrunched up piece of paper, and it tears me inside that laugh, rips my confidence in one swipe. 'Oh my dearest, surely not. I used to take you there! Well, no wonder Ramon was concerned about you and...and...'

I begin to worry, start to think, as she laughs at me, that perhaps I have made a huge mistake when her shoulders visibly drop. She shakes her head, neck scrawny, flesh stretched, worn.

'Mama?'

'I'm sorry, I can't keep up this pretence,' she says after a second, her voice barely a whisper. I remain rooted to the spot, unsure. The lights glow and the fire crackles. 'Ramon—he drugged you, my baby.' A small sob slips out. 'He took you down into that cellar, saying you needed help.' She shoots a hand to her mouth. 'Oh my goodness, was he not telling me the truth? Should you not have been in the basement? I told him I didn't like it one bit, but he said the Project insisted, said it was some new, radical treatment.'

She lifts her gaze now, eyes moist and I don't know what to say or think as I hear her speak. 'Oh, I was so worried.

Ramon was acting crazy. I was scared. I didn't know what to do. I knew he had you in the cellar and he was becoming increasingly erratic. I didn't know this Project was really what you are saying they are. If it is true, then dear Lord, forgive me.' She pauses, dabs a cheek. 'Your brother's been...different recently. Distracted, preoccupied. I thought it was simply work, the busy legal circuit, but then he started talking about this Project more and more—even mentioned Balthus, yes, I believe he mentioned Balthus. Oh my—is he involved, too?'

My fingers scratch into my leg for control as my mind tries to connect what Mama is saying, but it doesn't make sense because, mostly, I don't want to believe it. Because if Ramon was in contact with Balthus about the Project, then Balthus is their contact, too, all along he was their contact.

The smells in the air now collide in my senses with the glitter of gold and the confusion of the words spoken, and I struggle to get some order over it. There is a loud crack. My head jerks to the left; Mama jumps.

'What was that?' she says, hand on her chest.

There is a rattling sound, sharp, piercing like a rod of metal being thrust down hard on the ground, then, nothing. Silence. My whole body is on red alert. The Project—are they coming?

Mama stays in her seat as I lean to the door and listen. There is a tap, then another, soft first, then louder until it is nearer, closer, outside.

'Maria, my dear, I am worried. Please see what that is.'

Uncertain, I take seven steps to the door, stop and listen. There is a rustling outside, a scrape and then, without warning, the door slams open sending me flying backwards landing in a heap on the floor. My brother stands there looking like a walking corpse, blood smeared on his skull and cheeks and on the front of his neck, and his hair is soaked and matted where he must have hit the stone steps.

'Ramon!' my mother shrieks.

I dart back and at first, I think my brother is going to run at me, to throw himself at me for leaving him for dead on the stairs, but instead, he turns and, staring straight at my mother, flies head on towards her.

'You liar!' he yells. 'You fucking liar!'

Chapter 40

Apartment buildings, Central Madrid.
Present Day

Ramon lunges at my mother, toppling her cane to the floor, the metal clanking on the air vent, sending a sharp snap vibrating through the air.

'You liar!' he shouts, trying to drag her now up out of her chair, onto the floor.

I run, grab him by the shoulders, tear him away, his body hot and heavy. His fists fly out, teeth gnarl, but then Mama begins to cough, splutter, and Ramon suddenly deflates, dropping in front of me like a stone, hauling in great gulps of oxygen.

I slap back my hair. 'Why did you attack Mama?'

He doesn't look at me, instead he locks his sight on our mother as she clutches her throat now, gasping for breath. I run over, help Mama to her seat, her wisps of charred hair pointing out like palms trees from her patchy scalp. She tries to smooth them back, but they spring up, swaying.

Ramon stands, stumbles a little then slaps a hand out to a cabinet to his right and pulls himself up. 'Mama's a liar,' he says, blood seeping from his lip. He spits it to the floor. Flecks of red pepper the rug, and Mama's eyes go wide.

'Ramon! Manners.'

He laughs, low, steady, a growl, a feral moan. I step back. I do not understand what is happening.

'You manipulated me to do what I did,' my brother says to Mama now, 'and it's me you call the liar? I heard you, I heard everything you said to Maria just now.'

Mama looks from him to me then back again. 'My son, I don't know what you're talking about.' Her voice is low, hushed. 'What did you do to your own sister?'

'What did *I* do?' He paces. 'What did *you* do? It was you who told me to put Maria down there in the cellar. You who told me all about this Project thing. You said it would help her, you convinced me! So I did it, I did what you asked. But I found out, Mama. These Project people of yours—they have DNA. Oh yeah—I did some digging and found out.' He turns to me. 'M, you have a photo, don't you? I found it, too, but I didn't know what to do about it.'

My hand, without thinking, reaches into my back pocket and pulls out the picture from the cross. I look at my name and year of birth scratched into the corner.

'I found some information on you,' Ramon says to me, 'something on some documents the Project sent to Mama's email and I read it thinking it was just a standard advice report on you, M, but it wasn't—it was a DNA report. M,' his shoulders drop, 'you're adopted.' He exhales. 'You're not my sister. And she—' he points to Mama now '—has lied about who you are and what she does all along.'

Adopted. The floor feels as if it is slipping out from under me. I stagger back, eyes down, unable to make contact or see in their eyes what they see of me. 'Mama, is…is what Ramon says correct?'

She looks now to where I hold the photograph in my fingers then she exhales. 'I said I had something to tell you.' She nods to the image. 'That is it.'

I stare at the photograph and I think I begin to shake, but I am unsure. I look at Ramon. 'You are not with the Project?'

He shakes his head. 'No, not the one you describe and definitely not in the way Mama described. M, she set you up. She set us both up. I thought it was a specialist doctor's clinic, that's all. That's what Mama told me. M, I meant it down there when I said I loved you.' Tears streak his face now, past his cheeks, falling from the tip of his chin. 'I didn't mean to hurt you, I'm so sorry.'

'Ramon!' Mama says. 'Enough tears. Real men don't cry.'

'Like hell they do! Tell her!' Ramon yells, rounding on her, and I wince at his volume, at the chaos that is setting in. 'Tell Maria about the knee-deep shit you've got our whole lives into!'

Mama does not move. Her hair sways and her skin is pale and translucent even in the glow of the embers. She picks at a cotton fibre on the corner of the chair then sighs and, tilting her head, talks.

'Maria, my sweet, you are not…' She searches the air. 'You are not our biological child.'

The words drive a knife right through me and when I fall back, Ramon catches me. 'I am not Papa's daughter,' I say to him. 'I am not your sister…'

'Oh, M.'

The room swirls and it feels as if my whole world has been snatched away from me. Papa. He was everything to me and that fact throbs now in my head and I can't stand it. I can't stand the sadness that forces its way through me, clashing with the smells in the room, with the colours and the sound of the traffic outside and even with the messy wisps of Mama's hair.

I blink past tears that flow unbidden now down my cheeks and past my chin, and a surge of anger and despair rises up and I slam my feet into the carpet and scream. 'Tell me!' I yell to Mama. 'Tell me now how this happened! Tell me what you did!'

Mama sniffs and dabs her nose. When she eventually speaks, her voice is low and measured.

'Balthazar came to me,' she says, 'It was in 1979. He was engaged to be married to Harriet, his now government wife, but, well, he had a wandering eye—as men do—met some young girl named Isabella when he was visiting his parents in San Sebastian. She got pregnant and Balthus panicked. He was on a political career trajectory, his wife, of course, even more so—she is currently making a fine British Home Secretary. So, a rogue pregnancy would not do. I…helped out. I took Maria off his hands. Alarico, well, we had you, Ramon, and we loved you, but your Papa was desperate for a daughter, so when you came along, Maria, well, he was delighted. He could help out an old friend and gain a child.' She holds her head up high and, inhaling, narrows her eyes to me. 'My dear Maria, Balthazar—Balthus—my dear—he is your biological father. And the woman in the photograph, she is your real mother.'

'No.'

'M? M, it's okay.'

But I push him away. 'No, no, no.' There is a set of irons and fire fork in the grate all in disarray and I stagger to them now, drop to me knees and begin to set the fire items out in neat orders, first by size then by weight, then by grades of black shades, anything to feel order to stop my thoughts and being from becoming utterly fragmented. Order after order after order.

I stop, fingers black from the dust and look at the photograph in my hand but when I do, it all blurs into one and all I can think of is the fact that Papa is not my papa. Not my real, biological papa. Balthus is. I stamp my foot, unable to contain the confusion and upset. Why did he never tell me? All that time we were in Goldmouth and he never said a thing.

I round on Mama. 'You lied to me. You lied to me! You all lied to me!' I point to the woman in the picture. 'Tell me again her name.'

'Isabella,' she says. 'Isabella Bidarte.'

The name on the reverse of the photograph. Isabella Bidarte. Mama is telling the truth. The truth.

I wipe spit from my mouth, tears from my cheeks. 'Where is she from? Is she alive?'

'The Basque country. Like…Balthazar. And, well, I think she died, my dear.'

Dead, like Papa—dead. I fall back. The Basque blood data, the information Black Eyes told me on why Basque blood was so important to the conditioning programme. It all dazes me, disorients me and, as if my mind is operating on its own, I raise my shirt sleeve, inch by inch until my arm is exposed to the fountain pen tattoo. *I am Basque.* I am Basque not because Papa has Basque roots, but because I am not in his blood line at all.

As my fountain pen tattoo is fully visible, I hear Mama gasp. As she does, bile shoots up my throat and I swallow it back, throwing out my hand and finding Ramon's hand to steady myself.

'You made me feel like I was not myself. You never went near me, never attempted to hold me like…' I stop, wanting to say 'like Papa did,' but finding now that those words can no longer come out and have still the same meaning. 'Who let the Project have me? Was it Balthus and…and this Isabella?'

Mama regards me for two seconds then emits a small lemon-scented sigh. 'My dear girl, I have been ill with cancer for a long time. Longer than you think.' She pauses, wheezes in a sharp breath. 'I was at Cambridge University when MI5 were recruiting people, bright, intelligent people.' She shrugs. 'It wasn't something I wanted to get involved with, but I made contacts. Valuable contacts. I knew about a trial Project they were developing after the atrocities of 1973 and Black September. It was just after that I began to get ill, after the cancer was diagnosed, and my contact at the Project told me about experimental cancer drugs they were developing. The drugs were a miracle, but weren't licensed. Nothing else was working for me, so when they offered me the medicine, with conditions, I did what anyone would do: I took the chance. They were looking for Basque people for the programme and I had you, so it was a straight exchange.'

'You gave them Maria,' Ramon says, 'to test on in exchange for medicine.'

I stand still. I cannot move.

'My boy,' Mama says, 'I only did what anyone would do. The Project had not really had a child before entering the programme, so it really was a very exciting opportunity for everyone. And, the programme directors thought it best if the child was, day to day, brought up in a normal, natural environment. They suspected Maria could develop Asperger's—Isabella was on the spectrum, dear—and so I kindly offered to keep Maria, house her in a normal developmental environment so they could put her on the programme and help her...achieve her potential.'

The shock is so much I can barely speak, 'Did...did Papa know about this?'

'Oh no. Alarico didn't know.'

'And what about Balthus and...Isabella?'

She pops in a breath. 'Ah, no. He didn't know. May have complicated things, what with him being engaged then married to a government official.'

Ramon shakes his head. 'You selfish bitch.'

She waves a hand. 'Don't be so naïve, my dear. I had a career. I had a life. And the drugs worked. It is self-preservation. This is called life.'

'And what about Maria's life?'

'My boy, I had cancer. I wanted to keep my life.'

I do not move, because now, in my mind, I can see him. Black Eyes. Dr Carr. His explanation of Project Callidus being called Cranes. Black September, the secret government files I discovered in Hamburg about the drugs—the cancer drugs. It all links now, explodes in my head like one big bang.

'It was you,' I say, almost to myself, barely recognising my own voice. 'I saw the classified files about the cancer medicine. There were dates tracking back three whole decades, right into the 1970s, with cash amounts linked to each one. In 1979, the money amounts rose substantially, the cash wired to Madrid. The Project began when you gave me to them.'

'The Project began, young lady, when Balthus and Isabella gave you up because they didn't want you!'

'1979?' Ramon says. 'M, that was the year before you were born. You took cash in exchange for looking after Maria?'

'So they paid me to keep you. Sue me.' She sits back, twirls a bony finger on the edge of the glass.

I force my eyes to rise up now, make myself look Mama in the eye. 'Why are you telling me all this now?'

But she doesn't reply.

'Tell her!' Ramon shouts.

Mama takes the glass, has one sip then lowers it. 'When Maria was acquitted she then hid. No one could find her, which meant the Project could not get to her…'

'And if they don't have her, you don't get your drugs.' Ramon shakes his head. 'This is fucked up. You lied and got me to keep my own sister in a basement so you could get your medicine? You want to sacrifice Maria so you can be well enough to run to be the fucking Prime Minister of Spain.'

'I want to sacrifice Maria so I can live!' she yells. She stays still, glaring at Ramon, her blouse low on her shoulder from when she bolted up and flecks of spit in the corner of her mouth. She sits back, takes a breath and then smooths down her skirt and dabs her lips.

'Jesus Christ,' Ramon says now. 'Jesus fucking Christ.'

I swallow, breathe hard, every part of me wanting to run now, desperately needing to rock and moan as the emotions force their way into me. Nothing I knew to be true now is. The family I thought I had does not exist, and without knowing where we are from, without having that foundation a solid family provides, how can we truly grow to be the people we were meant to be?

'You...you knew why I was in prison,' I say after a moment. 'You knew, all along, that I didn't murder the priest. You knew...you knew the Project set me up. You knew because you were working for them, letting them use me right from the start. You told Balthus about the ICE Room.'

'Ah, yes. That was a mistake. Had been pumped too full of morphine that day. There was a time, you see, when I used to confide in Balthus about everything.'

'Except the Project,' Ramon says.

Mama remains still then, slowly, she tips her head. 'The Project are doing great things, Maria. *You* are doing great things.'

'No. No...' Memories flood in, a torrent of them, rushing forward in quick succession. 'You took me to the Project's facilities,' I say. 'The flashbacks I had with you at my bedside while Dr Carr tested on me. Black Eyes...' My voice trails off as the memories slash into me, one after another. My mother standing as Black Eyes cut into me to see if I could feel pain. 'I was only a child,' I say now. 'I was only a child.'

'Mama, how could you do all this?' Ramon says, but she ignores him, her focus totally on me.

'Dr Carr said that you would be helping people, my dear, that you were so intelligent, so unique that only good could come out of what they were doing with you.'

'For the greater good,' I say now and, turning from her

begin to rock as inside me a tsunami of emotions rages. 'My handlers—did you help to arrange them? Father Reznik, my university professor, my hospital bosses? Did you know they were all working undercover for the Project? Was Balthus involved?'

Mama angles her head back so her eyes look down on me. 'I knew about your handlers,' she says. 'Balthus wasn't involved.' A small sigh slips out. 'I helped arrange the handlers' positions, of course, helped ensure they would have access to you. It was for your own good—' She dabs her cheeks. 'You needed to be monitored so they knew the tests and the conditioning they were carrying out on you were safe, controlled. And it helped—look how well you've done! You're so sharp, so intelligent, my little angel.'

'This is all fucked up.' Ramon shakes his head. 'This is all utterly fucked up.'

Chapter 41

Apartment buildings, Central Madrid.
Present Day

I stand by the fireplace now and rearrange the ornaments one way then the other, then the other, putting them in order, in a set pattern. Ramon stands near me, looking at Mama, her arms and legs arranged in the armchair in an elegant bag of bones.

'You've called them, haven't you?' he says. 'The Project.'

She sighs. 'They may be on their way, yes. The cancer is taking hold now, my dear. I need help.'

Ramon paces three steps then stops. 'You told Maria that it was me who had the room soundproofed—I heard you. But that paperwork Maria found—it was all you. Why?' he says. 'Why did you get all the work done?'

She looks away over to the window and watches the curtain billow in and out. 'I would…look after people sometimes for the Project.'

'Subject numbers,' I say, now, finding my voice, my heart racing. 'There are numbers etched to the wall. I have seen them. The years correlate with your documentation in the bureau. They have your signature.'

'Why did you install the padding and the reinforced walls?' Ramon says.

She shrugs. 'They would be loud, the subjects sometimes before the Project collected them. For many, the drugs they were given didn't quite work as planned. There were...complications. We had to keep them safe from themselves, you understand.'

Ramon stares at her. 'And you didn't want anyone to hear. You didn't want Papa to hear.' He drops his head. 'Oh my God.'

She smiles. 'What is it, dear?'

'He found out, didn't he?'

I put the ornament in my hand down and listen. A fear, a dark, heavy fear begins to build in the base of my throat. It mixes with the pungent jasmine and orange blossom scent that seeps from Mama's skin, and, as Ramon stares at Mama, I find myself slowly walking to her and, before I can fully understand what I am doing, I thrust the photograph of Isabella with me in front of her. 'Who put this in the cellar?'

She frowns, shakes her head, finally glancing to the picture. 'I, I don't know, my dear.'

'Yes, you do,' Ramon says. 'Tell her.'

'No, I don't—'

A huge surge of anger and loss and sheer overwhelming sadness engulfs me and before I can stop myself, before I really know what I am doing, I slam my hand forward and grip Mama's throat. 'I said. Tell. Me.'

'Al...Alarico,' she finally croaks. 'Alarico put it there.' I release her neck and she rubs it, eyes wide, pressing her back into the chair.

I force myself to ask the next question, to make myself say it. 'Why did Papa put this picture in the cellar all those years ago?'

Ramon stands tall as we both look to our mother now, waiting. She shifts a little in her seat, tries to cough then stops, chest sinking backwards.

'I put him in there,' she says after a moment.

'You did what?' Ramon says.

She looks up now, eyes narrow, a strange smile sliced into her mouth, as ahead, the glow of the lamps and the embers cast dark shadows across her face. 'I put him there; he gave me no choice.'

My mind fires, connections fuse. 'You got the room sound-proofed and you put him in there and he hid this photograph.'

Ramon jerks his head. 'Why did Papa hide the photo, Mama? Why did he feel he had to do that?'

Mama coughs, levels my brother with a stare. 'Ramon, my boy, you don't understand.'

'Try me.'

'He didn't realise—' she coughs '—he didn't realise what he had stumbled onto,' she says finally. Ramon and I go still. 'Alarico,' she continues, 'he discovered some documents I had about your conditioning, Maria, about the tests I took you for. Well, as you can imagine, it was all highly confidential back then, very hush hush.'

'Jesus Christ…'

'And, well, one day he found some conditioning documents and, well the Project directors advised me to keep Alarico down there for a while until they could decide how to handle the information leak. We made it look like…like a robbery.'

Ramon drops his head. 'Except Papa knew it was you, didn't he? He'd figured it out by then. That's why he hid the photo there. He'd found out about it all, thought he could hide it, come back for it and expose it all.'

'You have to understand, my dear, I loved him so much.'

'But what did they do to him, Mama?' Ramon says.

'My boy...'

He punches his fist into the wall. 'Tell us!'

'My children, please! I did it for you, you must understand that. I had no choice. I was ill, I *am* ill. They are not giving me the drugs any more until I give them to you, my dear Maria. I only have three months left to live without the medicine.' Then she stops, sighs. 'My dear, he loved you so much, your papa, Alarico.'

'What did they do to him?' I find myself saying, but it doesn't feel like me, as if I am detached somehow from my own body.

Mama pulls herself up to a stand, her whole body shaking, and takes two tiny steps forward.

'What did they do to Papa?' I say again.

'They killed him,' Ramon says.

I turn to my brother, confused. 'How do you know?'

He glances to Mama then he gazes back to me. 'Because I did it, M.' He stops, smears his damp face with his sleeve. 'I think I killed Papa.'

I stare at my brother now, not understanding what he means. 'You could not have killed Papa, he died in a car accident.'

Ramon glances to Mama and back to me. 'She asked me to do something to his car.'

My head starts to spin. 'Do what? Do what to his car?'

'My dear boy,' Mama says now, hobbling nearer, knuckles bulbous on the handle of her stick and I think of the witch in the Hansel and Gretel fable Papa used to read to me. 'Please don't...'

But Ramon wipes his eyes and keeps his gaze on me. 'It was in the morning. I...I remember it as if it were yesterday. Father Reznik had been teaching me how to fix up cars.' He shakes his head and smears snot from his nose. 'Father Reznik was your handler for this fucked-up Project, but I didn't know, and there he was, teaching me how to fix a car, or so I thought.' He spins round to Mama and steps back. She is closer now, so close Ramon can almost touch her.

'Ramon, my dear, do not say any more.'

'Why?' he says, spit flying from his mouth. 'Scared I'll say something you don't want anyone to hear?'

She takes one more step forward. 'Stop. Please, my son.'

But Ramon just smiles and, gritting his teeth, leans in to mama so his face is almost touching hers. 'Fuck. You.'

Stepping back, he twists to face me. 'The morning of Papa's death, Mama asked me to fix something on his car.'

Cogs begin to spin in my head, but I don't want them to, don't want to face the reality of what Ramon is beginning to say...

'She asked me if Father Reznik had taught me what she needed me to do on the car and he had, the week before. I was excited—I was getting to fix Papa's Jaguar all by myself.'

'Ramon. Son. Stop.'

But he continues, fast. 'I got the wrench...I...I remember now. I had to dislodge something underneath the car first, get all the way under it, then Mama showed me the bonnet and asked me to disconnect something. I...I remember at the time thinking it was odd, but it was Mama, and she was telling me to do something Father Reznik had taught me, a priest.' He looks straight at Mama now. 'Except he wasn't a fucking priest was he?'

'He was working with the Project,' I say, to myself, in a bubble of shock.

'Children,' Mama says, eyes slicing us both, 'I think you are getting too excitable, inventing stories that...that don't exist.'

'Bullshit!' Ramon snaps. 'I did what I did to Papa's car and that morning, on the way to work, he crashed. The car—the car that I altered, that *you* told me to fix—veered off the road and he died.' Ramon sniffs. 'Papa died. And you made me do it, for what?' He searches her eyes. 'Because he found something out that uncovered it all—your drugs, your illegal payments, didn't he?' Ramon laughs now, head nodding. 'He found out what you were doing with my sister and he confronted you.'

'Ramon, you will stop this at once and—'

'Don't you dare!' His hands swing in two fists by his side. 'Don't you dare tell me to stop. I have seen you—manipulating, plotting. But I loved you, made excuses for you, protected you because that's what families are supposed to do, except you don't, do you?'

The door to the side swings back a little, half closing. Mama shuffles forward.

'Son, calm down. We can work this out.' She reaches out a frail hand. Ramon smacks it away.

'You lied about me to Maria,' he says, tears flowing down his cheeks. 'You implied it was all my idea to put her down there. I am your son! Your own son, and yet you would do that to me, despite everything—everything—I have done for you, for what? Power? Money?'

Exhaustion washes over me, confusion, fear—every emotion I feel courses through my bloodstream. But there is something in my mind, something clear, present. Dangerous. 'Ramon—the Project. When you contacted them, when did they say they would arrive?'

He turns to me. 'Oh God.'

'When, Ramon?'

He stops, checks his watch. 'Shit, in about an hour now, maybe even less.'

I swallow, slapping back the panic. 'We have to go.'

'No.' Mama has picked up her cane and has locked it across the frame of the door. 'You cannot go—and anyway, I have contacted them, too. They need you, Maria, my dear. You are one of them now—the Project is good for you.'

'Rubbish,' Ramon says. 'You just want your drugs so you can rule the fucking world in parliament. It's nothing to do with what's good for Maria, and everything to do with what's good for you. That's all politics ever fucking is—everyone in it for themselves. You even got me, your own son—a child—to rig a car so your own husband would be killed. What wouldn't you do, Mother, hmm, to get what you want? Where the fuck is it all going to stop? The whole world is not about you!'

The cane still blocks the door. 'You cannot keep us here,' I say. 'We are going to leave.'

Mama holds out her weak arm, frail fingers gripping the cane still in front of the door. 'I can't, my dear. I cannot let you go. I am so ill.'

Ramon lunges at Mother. He does it so quick, slips his

fingers round Mama's bone china throat so fast, that I don't have time to stop him, to shout for him to step back.

'Be ill, you bitch,' he spits. 'And when we get out, I'm going to tell everyone about this. I'm going to go to the press, to the government, to your precious cronies on the political circuit and tell them what a lying, selfish, conniving old bitch you really are.'

He drops his hand and Mama gasps for breath, cane clattering to the floor, her hands rubbing her neck.

Ramon turns to me. 'You ready to go?'

I glance once to Mama, a coldness forming inside me as I look at her, as I feel the vast enormity of what she has done to me, to my brother, to Balthus. To Papa. 'I am ready,' I say, and rush to the door, when there is a crack, a loud snap that vibrates in my head that sends shock waves down my entire body.

'Ramon?' My eyes go wide as, ahead of me, Ramon slumps against the wall, hands clutching his chest. Between his fingers, blood oozes, pumping out at an alarming speed.

'No!'

I run to him, dropping to my knees, desperately trying to stem the blood loss, but there is so much of it, I can't see his chest properly.

'Step away from Ramon, Maria, dear.'

I twist my head round. Mama stands holding a gun. And it is pointed at me.

'Why did you shoot him?' Frantic, I fly my head to my brother as he goes into shock, his body convulsing, his eyes wide. I press down on his wound with the heels of my hands, take his pulse, but nothing makes any difference. His body is going cold, his heart rate is slowing fast.

'Maria, dear, I said come away from your brother.' The gun is pointed at me. I glance to the door; it is open. I see Ramon's eyes fall to it, too, his body weak now, heart failing, and then, silently, his fingers find mine, squeezing them. I look at him now, my brother. I thought he was with the Project, assumed he was lying to me just like everyone else, but it was him that was being lied to. He was just doing what he thought would help me because he loves me.

'Move now, my dear,' Mama says. 'You can't help him.'

I glance to the door and Ramon squeezes my fingers one more time then lets go, hands falling like feathers to the floor.

Slowly, I rise, eyes on the door the entire time as, behind me, Mama still points the gun.

'That's it,' she says. 'Good girl. You know it's the right thing to do, to stay. It's who you are. You can't run from that.'

I breathe in, get ready and, glancing one more time to Ramon, to my brother dying on the floor, I bolt for the exit.

Chapter 42

Apartment buildings, Central Madrid.
Present Day

A gunshot rings out now as I sprint down through the hallway, past the vast line of gilded mirrors and art deco paintings. The entrance hall is up ahead, the main door, the exit. I hear Mama scream as, more shots sounding, she moves, faster than I expected her to, out of the drawing room.

I dash through the door to my left, to the lounge, hoping to find a new route out, but the windows are locked and there is no additional exit. My heart slams against my rib cage as I dart out, back into the hallway then stop dead. My mother is standing at the foot of the stairs, hair clumped to her head in wisps, gun pointed, arms shaking.

'You can't leave, Maria dear.'

I look down the barrel then back to Mama. 'You killed Ramon, you made him do something to Papa's car.'

'I didn't know what would happen.'

'I don't believe you.'

She sighs. 'My darling, I can understand that. I can. But right now, I don't have time for this conversation, because I need you to go into that room and stay there until the Project come. What will everyone think if you keep making this racket, hmmm? So, please,' she says, levelling the gun at me, a slip of a smile on her lips, 'be a dear and pop in the lounge, hmmm?'

'No.'

Her smile drops. She angles the gun towards my leg. 'I don't want to kill you, my dear—naturally. But I will shoot you so you cannot run. So, please, co-operate for Mama, yes? I'm really very tired.'

I stay still, not a muscle moving, every nerve ending in my body on fire. 'You are not my mama.'

There is a knock on the front door.

We both freeze. Mama frowns, tilts her head. I twist, whip my eyes to the frosted pane of glass that is cut into the wooden frame. Shadows, three shadows loom large.

'The Project,' Mama says. She waves the gun at me. 'Well, what are you waiting for, my dearest? Open it.'

The weapon is directed right at me and, no matter what trajectory calculations I do in my head, no matter how many times I try to formulate a fresh plan, nothing really sticks, because I am trapped. The Project is here, Ramon is dead and Mama has a gun to my head.

The knock sounds again, louder this time. I take one step, two, sweat waterboarding down my back, my body spent and beat, mind washed away. I reach the front door and rest my palm on the handle. Mama waves the gun, mouths, 'Open it,' and I turn. Drawing in a large breath, I pull back the lock and swing open the heavy, black door.

'Doc! Thank God you are okay.'

My mouth hangs open as I peer at the people in front of me now, shocked, relieved, desperate, because they are not the Project or MI5.

Balthus, Chris and Patricia are here.

'Oh, Maria!' Balthus says, 'thank goodness you are okay! And Ines—I was worried.' He falters. 'W–what is—?'

Mama points the weapon at him. 'All of you, in the lounge. Now.'

'What? Ines?'

Patricia looks at me, eyes wide.

Mama moves towards us, looks to Patricia and Chris, 'And whoever you two are, go into the lounge. Now.'

We enter the lounge, Mama behind us as she shuts the door, switches on a ceiling chandelier and the room rotates in a twinkling kaleidoscope of light. I glance to Balthus and feel the bile return to my throat.

We halt by the empty fireplace. 'Mama is with the Project,' I say.

'Ines?' Balthus says, mouth dropping open, 'what on earth?"

Mama shuts the door, leans her back on her chair and smiles. 'Balthus, dear, you of all people should not be surprised that someone has had to do what was necessary to survive.'

Balthus frowns. 'Ines, I…I don't know what you mean.'

She laughs, the gun still suspended mid-air. 'Maria knows.'

'I don't understand what you mean.'

I glance to Patricia, to Chris. They lower their eyes, shaking slightly

My hand slides to my pocket and mama raises her gun to me. 'What are you doing?'

Almost in a trance, I take out the photograph and spread it out in my palm.

Balthus gasps, his shoulder shaking, as I pinch the edge of the picture between my fingers and hold it out to him. 'Isabella,' he says, his voice barely audible.

Tears well in his eyes as he looks at the photograph now that I hold in front of him unable to speak the words of sorrow and loss and confusion that I feel, locked in my emotional cage.

Tears slide down his face. 'Maria, I'm so sorry.'

'Oh, deary me,' Mama says. 'Balthus, you have got yourself into a pickle, haven't you?'

Balthus raises his head, eyes narrowed at Mama. 'Ines, I asked you for help. You agreed to take Maria in when Isabella couldn't look after her. And are you saying you gave Maria to the Project? You bitch, you fucking heartless bitch.' He wipes his eyes, jaw locked, cheeks flushed.

Chris throws his eyes to me and mouths, 'Are you okay?' but before I respond, the lights flicker and the air turns to a chill as Mama holds the gun out at us.

'Maria,' Balthus says, tears streaming down his face now, unchecked, unbidden. 'I didn't mean for you to find out this way. I was young and stupid. I…' He drops his head into his hands, his shoulders shuddering.

Mama tuts. 'What, that's it? No explanation?' She sighs.

'I didn't know about the Project,' Balthus says to me now. 'Maria, when I saw you were in trouble—the conviction, the murder—I had to try and help you. You were—are—my daughter. I spoke to…I spoke to Harriet and she secured you a place at Goldmouth.'

I blink back tears that I didn't know were there as inside my head, everything seems to be happening at once. 'Does she...' I stop, swallow. 'Does your wife know that I am your daughter?'

'No,' he whispers. He raises his eyes to mine. 'Maria, that first time I saw you in prison on the day you arrived, I couldn't stop staring at you—you were so beautiful.'

I blink over and over, confused, sad, angry, happy—all of it. All the feelings at once and no way to express them. 'You... you have been...' I stop, struggling to find the words amidst the confusion and the chaos. 'You have been a friend to me. And...and I do not have many of those.' My finger starts to tap my thigh.

Patricia looks at me. She shuffles a tiny amount, barely noticeable, nearer to me, when Mama suddenly lets out a large sigh.

'So, not that this hasn't been touching,' she says, 'but I think we've all said enough for one day. The Project will be here soon. They know how to deal with Maria.'

'Deal with her?' Balthus snaps, stepping forward. 'Deal with her? She's not a piece of fucking machinery, Ines, a fucking robot for you to discard for your own means.'

Mama stares at Balthus then, smiling, says, 'Oh really? You dumped her just to save your own career. You dumped her mother in some freak Swiss nut house to die, and it's me you get cross with? Well, it's good your precious daughter sounds like a robot most of the time, my dear Balthus, isn't it? Because she's perfect for the Project. She always has been and she always will.'

'You bitch!' Balthus says. 'You fucking bitch!' He launches

himself at her, pounding his fist into her fragile face. 'She was my daughter! She was my beautiful baby daughter! And you gave her to those fucking butchers!'

'Balthus, stop!' Chris shouts.

Chris tries to drag Balthus away, but Balthus is too quick, darting at Mama, toppling her to the ground. She slams against the floor, smacking her head into the carpet, crying out, but Balthus springs up, and Chris goes again to grab him out of the way, all of us shouting at Balthus to calm down, the noise like a hammer in my head, when there is a loud blast. We all freeze as before us, almost in slow motion, Balthus slumps to the floor.

Mama stands, gun held out in shaking hands.

Blood pools from Balthus's skull and immediately I drop to my knees, rip open his shirt and begin CPR, pressing my palms into his rib cage. I pinch his nose, breathe into his mouth, my own tears mixing into his spilt blood until I cannot tell one apart from the other.

'Come on!' I shout, sitting back up, recommencing the cardio pulmonary resuscitation. I repeat the procedure over and over again, oblivious to everyone around me, tears streaking my cheeks, chin, blood in stripes on my arms and legs and hands. One minute passes, two, three.

'Doc,' Patricia says after four minutes. 'Doc, he's gone.'

My eyes lift to hers, sweat streaming down my face, blood specks littering my arms.

'He's gone, Doc.'

I pause the compressions, my lungs heaving, and look at Balthus's lifeless body. Everything becomes a blur, a wash of colour and darkness merging into one deep, cavernous hole as, slowly, I stagger up, wobbling, Patricia, Chris steadying me. 'Balthus was my friend,' I cry. 'He was my friend.'

I look at all the blood, blink at it as it pools on the wooden floor, seeping between the slats to nowhere. I smear the snot and tears from my face and touch my arm, feeling faint bumps of the words that Black Eyes scratched onto me: *I am Basque.* Balthus, his blood, his DNA. My papa. Ramon. My brother who loved me.

All the thoughts colliding in my head at once, I spin round, blinded by a sadness so strong, so powerful that I barely know what to do. I take in Mama's frame. She leans against the chair now, her bony body jutting out at angles that won't protract.

'You killed him,' I say, now, my hand slipping into my pocket, feeling for what I need. 'You killed Balthus, you killed Ramon. And you killed Papa.'

'Doc? Doc, take a breath.'

Mama takes a step back. 'Maria, dear, let us talk. Balthus would have only messed the whole thing up anyway. You are better off without him—he gave you up, abandoned you, hmm? There is a solution here, sweetheart. You have to look at the bigger picture, at what can be achieved through the Project—peace, global harmony. It's all for the greater good. I can't let you run. And if you do,' she points the gun at Patricia and Chris, 'I will be forced, I'm afraid, to shoot your friends. Needs must.' She levels the gun directly at them.

I run at her. Without thinking, I jump on Mama, shielding my friends from the gun, clawing at her wisps of hair, but she cries out, shoots, misses, and I charge at her again, yelling, 'You don't hurt my friends!'

I topple down, panic as she aims now at Patricia. Fumbling

for what was in my hand, I dive, and ducking a bullet, I run at Mama and, raising my arm high in the air, I drive what is in my fingers down on her neck, every single emotion coming out through me as I do. It hits her jugular vein, blood spurting out and she starts to gurgle and her hands scratch for her neck.

Mama slumps to the floor, so much blood around her that it is difficult to separate it from the colour of her skin.

Patricia catches me as I stagger, lurching, Chris near her side.

'She would have killed you both,' I say to them. 'She killed Ramon because he was going to go to the press about her. She killed Balthus—she would have killed you both.' I look at Balthus's broken body, at Mama's bleeding corpse. 'I'm sorry,' I sob and start to rock. 'I'm so sorry.'

I collapse and Patricia kneels down, gripping me tight in her arms, rocking me back and forth. 'Ssssh. Ssssh.'

Chris falls down to kneel beside us, grasps my hand and uncurls my fingers, something falls out, dropping to the floor, sharp, splattered with Mama's blood.

The item from my pocket that I drove into my mother's neck.

The nail. The nail from the foot of the cross where the photograph lay.

Chapter 43

Madrid Barajas Airport, Spain.
Present Day

We sit in a dark corner of the airport as far away from the noise and the passengers and the smells as we can possibly be.

None of us speak. The television in a nearby café delivers a steady chatter of news as each of us cradles scalding hot take-out coffee in our hands. We heap in sugar and sip. The liquid burns my mouth but I barely notice, a numbness spreading tentacles over me with the pain of what we witnessed just hours ago at Mama's house—at what I did. At what she did.

We have cleaned ourselves up, but still I feel shaky. The images of Ramon, Balthus and Mama swirl in my mind in a red-tinted whirlpool, and, when I think of Balthus's face, I see his black hair, his white teeth and I find myself thinking about the way he would check on me, often without me realising, so he could be reassured I was okay. He is gone, but I don't know how I feel, because Papa will always be my father, and yet Balthus was connected to me. He was my friend.

'Doc,' says Patricia. 'You okay?'

I look down—her fingers are in a star shape. I touch mine

to hers and breathe out, and, without saying anything, I feel a connection that a year ago, I could have never imagined I would have ever had with anyone.

Chris is working on his laptop. He has secured us flight tickets in different names to Zurich, hiding out at a place he knows through his hacking contacts, having arranged passports for us all and cash that will last us until we need to get small jobs in a faraway place where we can easily go unnoticed. Chris has dyed his hair bright blond. He wears a smart navy suit with a white shirt and around his neck slips a golden yellow tie. Patricia wears a brown wavy wig, black trousers, cream blouse and matching black jacket, while I have a new long blonde mane with an emerald green skirt suit, all of us dressed in smart clothes, hoping to pass as co-workers simply travelling through Europe on business. Chris has said that now he's on MI5 and the Project watch list, he may as well take his chances hiding out with us.

'Hey,' he says now, 'isn't that your mom's house?'

We glance up as, on the screen above, the news anchor reads a breaking bulletin.

'…a triple homicide was reported in the Spanish capital of Madrid in what is being cited as a cartel crime. Spanish lawyer and member of parliament, Ines Villanueva, her lawyer son Ramon Martinez and a British prison chief, Balthus Ochoa, have all been implicated in what sources are saying is a decade-long fraud ring stretching into millions of dollars and includes the trade of illegal medical drugs. The bodies of the three were found at Villanueva's central Madrid house this afternoon. Villanueva, who was hotly tipped to become the next leader of the right wing and prime minister-in-waiting…'

'Fuck,' Chris says. 'They've covered it all up.'

'They are lying.' I spin round to Patricia. 'Why are they lying? Balthus was not involved in any cartel.'

'The Project must have got to the scene, rewired the story. And in the meantime, this Project bollocks continues to exist and there's nothing we can do about it.'

'Oh, I don't know about that.' Chris sits forward, scratching his chin.

I turn to him. 'What do you mean?'

'Well, I still have a copy of all those files, right, the ones we—you—hacked in Hamburg and the one I got into at the monastery.' He taps his laptop. 'So, how about we send those files to someone who can blast the living fucking daylights out of the Project's ass?'

I pause. 'Does that mean expose what the Project does?'

'Yep.'

'If we expose the Project,' Patricia says, fast, 'then it all stops. They won't be able to chase Maria and use her, because the public profile of the whole scandal will be so high, just like with Snowden and the NSA Prism files.'

'The trick is,' Chris says, 'knowing who to send the documents to. It has to be someone who can really do something about it. Do you know anyone?'

'Harriet,' I say, immediately. 'Harriet Alexander—the UK Home Secretary.' I pause. 'Balthus's wife.'

'Do you have her email?' Chris asks.

'No.'

He bows. 'Then allow me to hack into the British government system and find out what it is.'

The flight boarding due soon, Chris works fast and hard,

until, hacking straight into their system, he locates the right address, uploads all the encrypted files and prepares the message. He looks to me. 'Okay, so, it's on an anonymous proxy and I've encrypted it to your email, uploaded the files, so all it needs now is a message from you about what's been happening with all this Project shit, and we're good to go.'

Hesitating, glancing to Patricia, I reach forward and, tapping the keyboard, write a detailed message, including all the facts, dates and details I can use to make the communication as authentic and believable as possible. Done, I lean back and exhale.

Chris looks up. 'Ready?'

I nod, thinking of Balthus, Papa, Ramon. A family but not in the normal sense, but then, what is, these days, normal? Has the concept ever really existed? Normal is not necessarily safe. 'Yes,' I say to Chris. 'I am ready.'

We all glance to each other as Chris hovers his index finger over the enter button.

'Wait!' I say. Chris looks to me. 'I did not ask her about Isabella. I did not ask where her grave was, if she knows anything about it.'

'Doc, you know she could be alive.'

'No. We saw the documents from the files. So many died. She would be old now, too. If the Project subjected her to unregulated tests, she has died, also.'

Patricia and Chris throw each other a glance as, leaning to the laptop, I tap into the keyboard my enquiry then step back. I look at the words on the screen, at the finality of them, and want them somehow to make me feel better, to fill the new hole that has gaped open inside me, but no matter how much I stare at them, read the words *gravestone* and *Isabella*, nothing changes, and the empty feeling I have at my loss still sloshes around inside me, untethered and free.

'You all done?' Chris says. I nod. He hits send. 'Then bye bye, Project.'

We all stand staring at the laptop for a moment, and then while Patricia and Chris start to walk over to the departure board, I stop. Something is digging into me through my back pocket. I reach my hand behind me and, slowly, I pull out the item. It is the photograph. It is the picture of Isabella and me, the one hidden by my papa, hidden by him so the truth would always exist. I flip it over and read the name of the hospital in Switzerland.

Patricia comes to my side as I blink at the image in my hands.

'Don't you want to find her?' she says. 'See if she's still alive?'

We look at the photograph together. 'She is dead. Mama said she is dead, and the dates of her life are written down on here.'

'But your mam, Ines, well, Doc, you can't trust what she said, can you?'

My sight swims at the image in my fingers. 'I might go to the grave if Balthus's wife knows of it.'

Patricia sighs. 'I'm sorry for all of this, Doc.'

'Why are you sorry? It is not your fault.'

She smiles at me.

'Your eyes are downturned.'

'I know,' she says, her voice heavy. 'I know.'

Up ahead, Chris calls our names, jabbing a finger at the

flight board. Patricia nods to him then, turning to me, holds out her hand and I hold out mine, and they touch, our fingers, just for three seconds, a wave of calm spreading over me.

'Ready to go?'

I look at the image of Isabella for one last time, at the dates and the details, then, folding the picture in two, slip it back into my pocket.

One step in front of the other, we catch up with Chris, the Zurich flight notice flashing on the screen. Arriving at his side, he hands me his iPod player and ear buds and we walk away, all of us, away from Madrid and away from the Project, until all that remains to prove our existence at all is an email—one email. An email among the millions of miles of fibre optics that span the globe and are tracked every day without our knowledge.

An email that will expose the entire Project and put an end to it all. For the greater good.

Acknowledgements

Thanks to everyone in getting *The Killing Files* out into the world. Thanks to Sally, my Editor, to Cara, Alison and all the team at HQ Harper Collins. Also thanks to Adam, my agent (cheers, A!) and all the stellar PFD team. Big up to the supportive, beautiful book bloggers and Facebookers who make this such fun. And super shout out (once again) to Kelly Duke for reading this novel when, well, it wasn't really one, and to my mum too, for giving it the thumbs up. Hugs to Marg and Brian for being the best friends and neighbours – Bri, you will always be in our hearts. And to Barry and Wendy for being the most amazing parents in law (and gardeners...) But, as ever, my biggest thanks has to go to my beautiful little family – Dave, Abi and Hattie, whom, without, I could never, ever write. DJ – you and me against the world, babe.

And, finally, to you now, holding this book – yep, you – thank you for reading *The Killing Files*! Without you, this book lark simply can't exist. I am mighty, mighty grateful.